LL
– THE ROWLAND SINCLAIR MYSTERIES

'Well-researched and atmospheric, with a brisk pace, colourful

'Glossy, original and appealingly Australian
– *Australian Women's Weekly*

'There are a lot good crime writers in Australia and Gentill is up with the
pack, providing interesting characters, punchy plots, a lively and witty style,
and some sobering reflection on dangerous times in our history'
– *Sydney Morning Herald*

'It takes a talented writer to imbue history with colour and vivacity. It is all
the more impressive when the author creates a compelling narrative'
– *Australian Book Review*

'I must confess I've become rather fond of artist Roland Sinclair and
his bohemian friends who divide their time globetrotting, solving
murder mysteries' – *Herald Sun*

'Containing an intriguing mystery, a unique sense of humour and a range
of historical characters, this is a highly recommended read for lovers of
Australian fiction' – *Canberra Times*

'Again, Gentill has turned her deft touch to weave little-known details of
Australian political intrigue into an engrossing, easy-read mystery novel'
– *Daily Telegraph*

'Gentill has written an absorbing story about a crucial but underwritten
slice of Australian history' – *The Courier Mail*

'Gentill immerses us in an unfamiliar world that quickly becomes one we
willingly reside in' – *Herald Sun*

– *Sydney Morning Herald*

The Rowland Sinclair Mysteries

A DANGEROUS LANGUAGE

SULARI GENTILL

A ROWLAND SINCLAIR MYSTERY

The Crime & Mystery Club
Harpenden
crimeandmysteryclub.co.uk

First Published by Pantera Press

A CIP catalogue record for this book is available from the British Library.

ISBN
978-0-85730-371-4 (print)
978-0-85730-372-1 (ebook)

2 4 6 8 10 9 7 5 3 1

Typeset in Adobe Jenson
by Avocet Typeset, Bideford, Devon, EX39 2BP
Printed and bound in Great Britain by Clays Ltd, Elcograf S.p.A.

For more information about Crime Fiction go to @crimetimeuk

I am not a teacher:

only a fellow traveller of whom you asked the way.

I pointed ahead—ahead of myself as well as you.

George Bernard Shaw

1

PREVIEWS OF
SHOW EXHIBITS

———◆———

Outstanding features of the Motor Show
described by Table Talk's
Motoring Correspondent

CHRYSLER SHOWS AIRFLOW

INTRODUCED to Melbourne by Lanes Motors and with Miss
Judy Price and Mary Guy Smith as official hostesses, Chrysler
for 1934 springs one of the most complete Show surprises by
co-ordinating aeroplane and car design and construction in the
production of a truly amazing car.

Claimed to be two years ahead in design and performance,
the Airflow Chrysler Eight is being featured at the Show in a
way that makes impossible a display of the Morris and M.G.
cars, also marketed by this firm.

The Airflows shown are the model CU Eight—a 33.8 h.p. car
developing 122 h.p., and the larger Imperial Eight, of the same
rating but at 128 h.p. development. Both cars possess a speed
of 90 m.p.h. and a completeness and originality of streamlining
and body-plus-chassis unit engineering that leaves one gasping.

Fundamentally, Chrysler in these cars has set out to remedy
inherent defects in normal cars by new methods. He has built
body and chassis on the plan of a cantilever truss—an amazingly
strong yet light structure—then has dispositioned the weight
and placings of engine, luggage, and passengers in such a way,
relative to the axles, that an ideal of suspension is provided. By
adding an improved springing and new type steering, a car has

been produced in which it is possible to "read, write, and sleep" in comfort on any road at 60 m.p.h.

The astonishing interior carries three passengers with comfort on each seat, the seats in turn being of a new armchair type, wholly isolated from the body walls and made very modern by the provision of chromium-plated arm rests, which incorporate ash trays and match the predominating body motif.

Perfected draftless ventilation and floating power engine mountings, to eliminate the transmission of vibrations to passengers or body, are other comfort features and added control is provided by the novel steering, improved hydraulic braking, coincidental starting, all silent transmission, cam and roller free wheeling and extra large low pressure tyres.

A remarkable innovation, an automatic over drive transmission is optional on the C-U and standard or the Imperial model and reduces engine speed by 30 per cent at speeds above 45 m.p.h.

The aerodynamically streamlined body cannot be described. It must be seen to be appreciated, and for its advantages to be understood.

Table Talk, 24 May 1934

She never knew that she was found by a man leading a footsore bull. She didn't see him tether the beast and clamber down to where she lay, and so she felt no embarrassment for the nakedness of her body where the clothes had been burnt away. It was not the burlap sack covering her face that kept her in darkness. The world would always be dark now. And she would keep the secret of how she came to lie alone in a country ditch.

The 1934 Melbourne International Motor Show was in its final day. Several thousand people had passed through its doors to view the latest in engineering and innovation and marvel at advances in technology.

The great British names of Austin, Vauxhall and Hillman vied for attention with the brash American houses of Studebaker, Pontiac, Oldsmobile and Chevrolet. The Rolls-Royce Phantom II stood with as much decorum and dignity as possible, among the miles of bunting, balloons and roving brass bands. The show sensation was, however, undisputed. Elevated on a rotating stage it seemed to reign over the other displays. Even surrounded by the world's best machines its revolutionary shape caught the eye. Motoring enthusiasts jostled the popular press for the best vantage from which to view the ultramodern lines and avant-garde design of the Chrysler Airflow.

The gentlemen from Sydney stood back from the main crowd, observing the Chrysler exhibit at a distance. They stood shoulder to shoulder: a flamboyantly dressed Bohemian with a Leninist goatee; a solid, sturdy man whose weathered face aged him beyond his thirty-two years; and between them, the tallest of the three, whose immaculately tailored suit was offset by dark hair that refused to stay in place.

"What do you think?" Rowland Sinclair pushed his hair back, trying to ignore an absurd feeling of disloyalty.

His companions showed no such reluctance.

"She might just be the most beautiful thing I've ever seen." Clyde Watson Jones was determined to encourage Rowland to finally bury the 1927 S-Class Mercedes he'd lost in the racing accident that had nearly taken his life. To Clyde's mind it was time Rowland got over his first love and allowed another to take her place.

"I wouldn't go that far," Rowland murmured, distracted for a moment by a thought of Edna. She'd refused to come to Melbourne with them on the grounds that she preferred not to witness "grown men reduced to simpering lovesick boys by shiny machines". Edna was ever direct. He missed her.

"Aesthetically she's a little unusual," Rowland offered as both praise and concession. The automobile was yellow, as the Mercedes had been, but the similarities stopped there. The Chrysler was sleek and low with a chrome grille that cascaded over its curved hood like a waterfall. The rear wheels were encased in fender skirts and the full metal body rested between the wheels rather than upon them. She was like no other car on the road. Rowland thought her a work of art.

"There is no exquisite beauty... without some strangeness in the proportion." Milton Isaacs nudged Rowland companionably.

Rowland smiled. "Poe," he said, acknowledging the author whom Milton had clearly no intention of crediting. Some years before, Milton Isaacs had been introduced to Rowland as a poet, a title he embraced in every way but by actually writing verse. Instead he maintained his erudite literary reputation by randomly quoting the work of the great romantic bards without the tedious formality of attribution.

"She'd cost a small fortune, I expect," Clyde said halfheartedly. What did small fortunes matter to a man who had such a large one? The Sinclairs' holdings had begun as pastoral enterprises but under the astute control of Rowland's elder brother they had become an empire that seemed to Clyde to know no bounds.

"Johnston's getting old," Rowland replied.

Clyde nodded. Johnston, Rowland's chauffeur, had begun in the service of the Sinclairs in the days of horse and carriage. He had come with *Woodlands House*, the Sinclairs' grand home in exclusive Woollahra of which Rowland was now master. Use of the Rolls-Royce which also came with *Woodlands* necessitated the use of Johnston, who took any attempt to use the vehicle without him very personally. It was the nature of Rowland Sinclair that he would buy a new motorcar rather than risk offending his chauffeur.

"Are you going to buy her then, Rowly?"

"Yes. Actually, I already have. I thought we could drive her back up to Sydney."

"Well that's cause for celebration. Good show, comrade!" Milton responded as though Rowland was a new father, clapping his shoulder and shaking his hand in congratulations. "This calls for a drink. Bloody oath, won't Ed be surprised when we pick her up in that jalopy?"

"If she even notices," Rowland said, laughing. Edna was determinedly disinterested in automobiles. Particularly since his accident. They were to meet her train in Albury early the following day then travel together to a house party at the Yackandandah abode of a fellow artist.

"Mr. Sinclair, sir! I trust you're enjoying the show." The gentleman who approached was almost as tall as Rowland. Sporting a luxuriant waxed moustache and top hat, he looked rather like a ringmaster.

Rowland shook his hand. "I am indeed, Mr. Carter." He introduced his companions to the automobile dealer. "I was just informing Mr. Isaacs and Mr. Watson Jones that we will be driving the Airflow back to Sydney."

Carter addressed Milton and Clyde. "Your friend is a man of singular good taste, gentlemen. There are few men in this room who are worthy of a vehicle as fine and progressive as the Chrysler Airflow."

"I don't know, old boy…" Milton airily adopted what he called the inflection of the capitalist establishment. "I rather liked the look of the Rolls-Royce, myself. Mother would approve, I think. Tell me, my good man, has the one on display been spoken for yet?"

Clyde groaned audibly but Carter was already baited. "Not at all, Mr. Isaacs. I had no idea you were looking to… Why don't I personally show you the motorcar? It would be a truly excellent and discerning choice, I assure you."

Clyde and Rowland watched as Carter escorted Milton towards the Rolls-Royce display.

"Poor bloke's salivating," Clyde observed. "Perhaps we should tell him."

Though he so easily adopted the airs and graces of a well-heeled aristocrat, Milton was as penniless as Clyde, a status only belied by their association with Rowland Sinclair, who kept his friends in the same manner to which he was accustomed.

"I wouldn't worry about Carter," Rowland replied. "He's already made at least one very healthy commission today."

"Then perhaps we should leave him to it and go find that drink Milt suggested."

"Capital idea."

The Mitre in Bank Place was a comfortable stroll from the Royal Exhibition Building in which the International Motor Show was being held. En route Rowland and Clyde discussed the engine specifications, shock absorbers and capacity of the Chrysler Airflow. Clyde muttered about oil and valves and pressure. Rowland's Mercedes had not often been welcome in the mechanics' garages of post-war Sydney, and so Clyde had taken to servicing and repairing her himself. At first by necessity, and then because he'd come to see it as one small way in which he could repay his friend's generosity in all things. Naturally he assumed the maintenance of the new Airflow would also fall to him.

Rowland had never expected anything from the beneficiaries of his largesse beyond their company, but it was easier to allow Clyde to tinker with his car if that was what he needed to do.

They found a table by the window of the small gothic drinking house and Rowland signalled the publican. Having already patronised the tavern a number of times in the week they'd been in Melbourne, they were welcomed with the kind of friendly presumption reserved for locals—a pint of beer and a tall glass of gin and tonic duly placed before them. Rowland and Clyde were still removing their coats when they were joined by a contingent of the many artists who frequented the Mitre. The conversation turned to painting—a robust discussion of technique and motif.

Justus Jörgensen sat at their table and invited them once again to join his scheme to found an artistic community. Rowland had known the Victorian artist for years and painted with him on occasion. Earlier that week, he had taken Rowland out to view the acreage he'd purchased in Eltham, outlining his plans for a grand hall constructed of mud brick and stone to be built by his students and fellow artists. Rowland liked Jörgensen but he thought him a little mad.

"Creative communities inspire creative lives, gentlemen." Jörgensen pounded the table, making the glasses jump. Rowland's hand shot out to save his gin. "We will build a lifestyle surrounded by art, break bread each day with men and women who are like us in passion and vision, unfettered by the constraints of middle-class monogamy and social convention."

Clyde laughed. Their lives at *Woodlands* were not far removed from the utopia Jörgensen envisaged. Over the years many artists, writers and actors had lived for a time in the Woollahra mansion. Three had never moved out.

"We're not bricklayers, Jorgie." Rowland downed his drink before the artist decided to pound the table again.

But Jörgensen would not have it. "Affluence stagnates the creative spirit." He pointed at Clyde. "You cannot compare a community of artists, working for a common good with Rowland's domestic arrangements. Middle-class comfort makes for fat commercial artists whose creative life is dictated by the profit-driven, critic-enslaved demands of exhibitionism!"

"Just who are you calling fat?" Clyde demanded.

"You! You are fat! Fat and complacent!"

And so the debate warmed. Jörgensen waxed lyrical and loud, Clyde stood his ground. After all, he exhibited, so did Rowland. The publican, and a number of other patrons at varying degrees of sobriety contributed from time to time, but Rowland refused to be drawn. He liked Justus Jörgensen but the man seemed to take his daily exercise by shouting, and Rowland had learned long ago that anything remotely resembling a defence of the wealth for which he'd done nothing beyond being born, was a fool's errand. Instead, he extracted a notebook from his breast pocket and sketched the battle in the tavern—capturing the movement and urgency of men at philosophical combat, in what he considered a more worthwhile use of the time.

The afternoon was passed, not unpleasantly, in this way. It was dark when Milton Isaacs walked into the fray.

"What are they arguing about?" he asked Rowland, glancing towards Clyde and Jörgensen.

"I'm not sure anymore," Rowland replied.

"Look, Rowly, I just ran into a comrade from Melbourne. There's a meeting tomorrow which I think we should attend."

"We?" While he moved with Communists, Rowland was not a member of the faithful. Milton knew that.

"It's not a Party meeting, old mate. MAWF is gathering to discuss Egon's visit. They have a problem I reckon you could help with. I think we should go."

Rowland frowned. The World Movement Against War and Fascism, while having a natural affinity with the Communist cause, did not belong to the Party. Rowland's experience of German Fascism had seen him join the Australian branch of MAWF, though to date his support had been purely financial. He expected the problem Milton mentioned was also financial in nature. MAWF had invited Egon Kisch—a journalist and speaker of international renown—to speak at its National Congress against War and Fascism in Melbourne.

Rowland knew Kisch personally, indeed, he owed the activist a great debt, and he looked forward to seeing him again.

"Ed's train gets in early tomorrow morning." Rowland glanced at his watch. "She's probably already left for Central."

"We could send word to the station master… let Ed know to take a room at the Albury Terminus and wait for us. She won't mind… she can go to the cinema or shop for a new hat or something."

"Or something, more likely," Rowland said ruefully.

"I really think we should be at this meeting."

Rowland nodded slowly. He trusted Milton's instincts on matters such as this. Though Rowland Sinclair was not a Communist, he and the poet had, at heart, always been on the same side.

"Ed will understand," Milton prodded further.

"Of course. I'll book a call through to the Albury station tonight."

2

WAR AND FASCISM

◆

HENRI BARBUSSE SUMS UP
(TO THE EDITOR)

Sir,— While all capitalist countries are in one stage or another of fascisation; in the process of being led, or of having been led, back to the barbarism of middle ages; while ideas and schemes of a fascist character are being flaunted abroad as Socialistic, e.g., the Roosevelt plan, claimed by the N.S.W. Labor Party Leadership as being synonymous with the "Lang Plan"—as a "socialistic road to prosperity"; while the fascist flame spreads in Australia with the proposed Disloyalty Bill, and a great class conscious movement gathers its forces in active opposition, your readers will be interested in the following from the pen of Henri Barbusse, eminent French writer, and noted leader of the worldwide movement against war.

"It is desirable that we draw up a balance sheet for 1933. Those who have been labouring under illusions, those who have been hoping that things would improve, those who have remained outside of our great worldwide movement, would do well to pause before this balance, and—reflect. The ten months of Hitler's rule has been sufficient to convince everybody of the dangers that fascism brings in its train. His promises of better conditions have proved false one after another. Only the terror has proved real. In January 1933, the eyes of the workers of the whole world were turned upon events in Germany. Everywhere the question was raised: Would the revolutionary unity necessary to smash fascism be at last set up? Tens of thousands of socialist and non-Party workers grouped themselves during that month around the revolutionary front. But they weren't sufficient. To smash fascism more were necessary—the majority of the working class... We are headed again for a new world war..."

The Cessnock Eagle and
South Maitland Recorder, 19 March 1934

The offices of MAWF were conveniently located on Bourke Street near Unity Hall which housed the offices of the Australian Railways Union, the Tramways Union and the Storemen and Packers Union. The premises were utilitarian: the furniture patched and hodgepodge—possibly scrounged from the homes of members. The space was cluttered with boxes and stacks of propaganda leaflets and paraphernalia. There were three desks, two with typewriters and what looked like an old rotary stencil duplicator. The bright colours of the political posters which adorned the walls were muted by what seemed to be a permanent haze of pipe and cigarette smoke. In one section of the office was a large wooden table which bore a history of past campaigns in smears of paint and ink. About this were gathered some of the nation's most eminent writers, poets and journalists—the newly convened Kisch Reception Committee.

Milton facilitated the necessary introductions. Arthur Howells insisted they call him "Bluey" and explained that he, as a member of the MAWF executive, had been tasked with organising the Reception Committee. Among the gathering's intellectual luminaries were novelist Vance Palmer and his wife Nettie, an established literary critic of considerable influence; the internationally lauded writer Katharine Prichard who it seemed had travelled from her home in Western Australia to be present; journalists Gavin Greenlees, Edgar Holt and John Fisher, son of Australia's fifth prime minister; Percy Beckett and Antonio Falcioni who called themselves philosophers; and the artist Max Meldrum whom Rowland had met before.

In this assembly Rowland began to feel a little out of place. Clearly the intention was to receive Egon Kisch with a dazzling show of literary and artistic distinction. While the name of Rowland Sinclair was not entirely obscure, it was more commonly associated with scandal than anything else.

Milton did not seem burdened with any such awkwardness, but perhaps that in itself was the secret to being a poet without ever writing a line of original verse. He chatted easily to Katharine Prichard about socialist realism in literature and advised Vance Palmer on iambic pentameter.

Arthur Howells called the meeting to order, announcing somewhat unnecessarily that Egon Kisch had accepted an invitation to be the keynote speaker at the inaugural National Congress against War and Fascism. There was applause—heartfelt—and excitement.

For some time the discussion focused on how Egon Kisch would be publicised and promoted. John Fisher, who was currently on the staff of the *Melbourne Herald*, was given primary responsibility for press coverage. He accepted the role enthusiastically, vowing to pull whatever journalistic strings were necessary to ensure the Kisch campaign was afforded adequate publicity.

They spoke also of how Kisch would be entertained while he was in the country, to whom he would be introduced, at which venues he would speak and what sights he would be shown.

Through all of this Rowland said very little. He knew nothing about promotion and he didn't really feel in a position to suggest how best to occupy the great man. In fact, he was beginning to wonder why Milton had insisted they attend the meeting. Rowland would happily have written a cheque for the cause without being privy to the deliberations.

It was only after these other matters had been thoroughly discussed that Arthur Howells raised a logistical problem. It appeared that Kisch's ship would not reach port in Melbourne until the twelfth of November, thereby missing the National Congress. "As you can imagine, having the keynote speaker arrive after the congress is something of a difficulty."

Many voices concurred that it was indeed a difficulty.

"We'll simply have to change the date of the congress," Katharine Prichard declared.

"And lose the impact of Armistice Day?" Fisher groaned.

"When does the ship actually reach Fremantle?" Vance Palmer asked.

Howells nodded. He was thinking along similar lines. "If Mr. Kisch disembarks at Fremantle and catches a train, we could get him here on time. It'll be a close-run thing, but possible."

Milton leant over to Rowland and whispered, "Rowly, what if—"

Rowland was ahead of him. "I could fly him," he said.

"Fly him? Whatever do you mean, Comrade Sinclair?" Katharine Prichard spoke over the murmur of voices.

"In an aeroplane. I could fly across to Fremantle, meet his ship, and fly him directly to Melbourne."

"May I enquire what manner of aeroplane you own, Mr. Sinclair?" Nettie Palmer said.

Rowland laughed. "My plane's a Gipsy Moth. But I don't propose to use her—she wouldn't be much faster than the train."

"Then what do you propose, Mr. Sinclair?"

"A twin-engine craft. It won't be as comfortable as the liner but it will be a jolly sight quicker."

"And you have such a craft?"

"I'll get one."

"An aeroplane… we can't expect a man like Egon Kisch to come to Melbourne in an aeroplane!"

"I'm sure he'd prefer it to not arriving in time," Fisher mused. "Under the circumstances, we can't risk him missing the congress. It might also circumvent any visa issues."

"Yes, of course!" Katharine Prichard leant forward enthusiastically. "Collecting Egon from Fremantle will mean he's in the country before the government has a chance to ban him. They'll think they have till he arrives in Melbourne to trump up some charge."

"It's too dangerous," Palmer persisted.

"Rowly was taught to fly by Kingsford Smith," Milton offered by way of assurance. "Egon will be in good hands."

Both Vance and Nettie Palmer raised a number of further objections which were countered at first by Katharine Prichard and then Fisher. Howells joined the case for flying Kisch from Fremantle and, eventually, Rowland Sinclair's offer was accepted.

"Success depends on utmost secrecy," Katharine warned. "No one must suspect Herr Kisch will disembark in Fremantle."

A general murmur of agreement served as a pledge of silence on the matter.

The meeting adjourned to the Swanston Family Hotel where they spent the evening in increasingly high spirits. There was a definite air of celebration—it was an optimistic party. After months of trying to make his countrymen understand the threat of German Fascism, Rowland was hopeful that Egon Kisch would meet with greater success.

Clyde joined them after having spent the afternoon checking over Rowland's new car for himself. His eyes were bright as he described the automobile's performance and for a time he and Rowland were immersed in praise of the Airflow.

"She's built like a battleship, Rowly... an elegant battleship," Clyde said. "I know you miss the Mercedes, mate, but she's a worthy replacement."

"I'm looking forward to seeing what she can do," Rowland admitted.

"We'll have to do that before we pick up Ed," Milton warned. "Ever since the accident she wants you to drive like you're bringing up the rear of an ANZAC parade!"

Rowland grimaced. Edna had become irrationally nervous about his ability to keep a car on the road. In fact, he'd purchased the Airflow with that in mind. He hoped the motorcar's radical safety features—the all-metal body, the shatter-proof windscreens—would allay her fears to some extent.

They drank with the Kisch Reception Committee until the early hours of the next morning before finally taking their leave. The short walk in the bracing cold to their accommodation had a conveniently sobering effect, though it was hardly long enough to mitigate the effects of the evening entirely. Perhaps for this reason Rowland did not wonder overmuch about the message, awaiting him at the reception desk, that a Detective Delaney from the Sydney Criminal Investigation Bureau had telephoned.

———————————————

Rowland was becoming increasingly frustrated. They had intended to leave for Albury first thing that morning but they had been delayed by paperwork, without which Carter could apparently not release the Airflow. It was nearly midday now.

"Did you telephone Delaney?" Milton asked as they waited.

Rowland nodded. "He wasn't there—called away apparently. I wonder what was so important he had to contact me here."

Milton grinned. "The police have spies everywhere, mate. The good detective probably wanted to know what you were doing at the MAWF meeting."

"Possibly." Rowland wasn't sure. Delaney was perfectly aware of the company he kept. It was hardly cause for alarm.

Carter finally emerged to hand him the keys, diverting to engage Milton about the Rolls-Royce in which he'd shown so much interest. "Thank you, Mr. Carter," Rowland said impatiently. "I'm afraid we must be going. Mr. Isaacs will have to put off any purchases until our next visit to Melbourne."

"Oh I see... perhaps I could just..."

"We have your card," Milton said, smoothing his cravat. "As tiresome as it is, I'm afraid Mr. Sinclair is correct. We'll have to make do with the Airflow for now. I must say, Rowly, it's a bit common having to share an automobile, wot!"

Rowland ignored him, sliding behind the wheel and turning over the engine. The Airflow was a great deal quieter than the supercharged Mercedes had been, but there was no denying the power of her eight-cylinder motor.

On the open road outside the central business district, Rowland was able to open her up as he became accustomed to the way the Chrysler responded. A wistful knowledge that he would never drive his beloved Mercedes again gave way to an admiration of the Airflow. He looked forward to introducing her to Edna.

They crossed the border and drove into Albury just before sunset. The Airflow turned heads. People stared and pointed, children ran after the car and grown men surrounded the vehicle as they parked.

"Bloody odd-looking motorcar, Mister," a youth observed as they got out. Emboldened by the first commentator, others offered opinions and asked questions. Some wanted to see the engine and have a demonstration of how the windscreen opened. Still buoyed by the drive and in the throes of newfound love, Rowland and his companions obliged in good humour. And so it was nearly dark by the time they finally walked into the Terminus.

Rowland took rooms for the three of them before enquiring about Miss Edna Higgins.

"We sent a porter to meet the train from Sydney as you instructed, Mr. Sinclair, but Miss Higgins was not on it."

"Oh." Rowland glanced at his friends.

Milton shrugged. "She probably missed the train, Rowly. You know what Ed's like."

"We thought that may be the case and sent a man to meet this morning's train, sir. But Miss Higgins was not on that service either."

"I see." Rowland dragged the hair back from his face. "Might I trouble you to book a call through to Sydney?"

"Certainly, sir."

The hotel manager invited Rowland to use the telephone in his office as *Woodlands House* was raised.

"What gives, Rowly?" Clyde asked when he emerged a few moments later.

Rowland shrugged. "I spoke to Johnston. He says he drove her to the station and watched her board. She should have been on that first train."

"Why would she get off the train before Albury?" Clyde asked.

"Particularly as she expected us to meet her," Milton murmured. They turned back to the manager. "The bloke you sent to meet the first train, is he here?"

The manager nodded, signalling a young man in a porter's uniform. "Eugene! Here!"

"Shall I take your luggage, sir?" Eugene clearly assumed that was the reason for which he'd been summoned.

"No... actually yes, why not?" Rowland noted the manner in which the manager hovered. "We may as well settle in while we try and determine what has happened to Miss Higgins."

The moment they were out of earshot of the manager, they questioned the young man.

"Are you sure Miss Higgins was not on that train?"

"I don't know what she looks like, sir, but I had a sign with her name on it. Nobody came."

"Were you at the station when the train arrived?" Milton asked shrewdly.

An awkward pause before the answer came.

"Just a few minutes after—Mrs. Harty wanted her bags taken up to her room straightaway. She insisted, sir. I ran over to the station straight afterwards."

"Well that's it, Rowly," Clyde said, relieved. "Ed probably took a taxi to another hotel before hookum here arrived. We'll ask at the station."

Rowland agreed. It seemed a likely explanation.

The young porter shifted nervously. "Will you be mentioning…"

"Don't worry, comrade." Milton braced the boy's shoulder. "We're on your side."

Eugene looked confused.

"We don't need to talk to your manager," Rowland assured him.

They had Eugene take their bags up to their suites while they walked the block to the railway station. Being the end of the New South Wales line, it was a busy terminal. The platform was unusually long to accommodate the disembarkation of entire trains as the tracks changed to the wider Victorian gauge. They went straight to the station master's office.

Rowland explained the situation to the assistant station master, a simply enormous man who pressed so heavily on the desk when he stood that Rowland was afraid it would collapse. "Oh yes, Bill passed your message onto me. Told me to make sure that Miss Higgins got it the very moment the train arrived."

"So you spoke to her?"

"Well no… I didn't fancy running around the platform trying to locate one young lady from possibly hundreds. It's a big platform." He tapped his brow. "I used my noggin."

"I'm not sure I follow."

"Miss Higgins' train had already left Central Station when you called and so I telegraphed Junee Station. Had them find Miss

Higgins on the train and give her the message when the train stopped there."

"And are you sure they did that?"

"Absolutely. One hundred percent. The station master at Junee telephoned to confirm that he'd handed the message to Miss Higgins himself."

"Do you recall the exact wording of the message?" Clyde asked.

"Of course. It was not complicated. It stated that Rowland Sinclair was detained and asked her to wait at a hotel."

"A hotel… not the Terminus?"

"It's a hotel, isn't it?"

"Yes, but did the message specify the Terminus?" Rowland's patience was becoming brittle.

"Well no… one doesn't like to favour one business over another…"

Rowland exhaled. "Very well. If Miss Higgins returns please tell her that Rowland Sinclair may be reached at the Terminus."

"Well yes, happy to do that for you," the assistant station master puffed, realising for the first time that they might not be pleased with his last efforts.

"Well this is a bloody cock-up!" Milton said as they walked out of the station. "Ed could be in any hotel in Albury."

"Except the Terminus," Clyde corrected. "We know that she's not at the Terminus."

"We'll have to check all the others," Rowland said. He was beginning to feel a little uneasy. "I wonder why she didn't leave a message at the station to tell us where she was taking a room."

"That does seem odd," Milton agreed. "Ed's not the feather-brained type."

It was by now completely dark, and bitingly cold. Even so, they did not consider leaving locating Edna till morning. They were not yet anxious, but neither were they entirely unconcerned.

By ten o'clock they had checked at every hotel that was open, with no success. One was closed for the night, and another refused to give out any information on guests. They left their names and that of the Terminus at the latter and resolved to call at the former first thing in the morning.

Too late for supper at the restaurant, they went to bed hungry, and now, though they did not speak of it, worried.

3

"MISSING PERSONS"

What would you do if your best friend were reported missing? You will see many vanish in this thrill picture, "The Bureau of Missing Persons," to support "Midshipman Jack" on Wednesday, Thursday and Friday of this week, and you will also see Pat O'Brien and Bette Davis together for the first time.

Cumberland Argus and
Fruitgrowers Advocate, 8 March 1934

Rowland grabbed a tie out of his bag and slung it around his neck while he finished shaving. It was still too early to check the remaining hotels but he hadn't in any case been sleeping. Showering and dressing was at least something to do aside from staring at the ceiling.

Edna's disappearance was probably just a misunderstanding. But still...

He glanced at his watch. Seven o'clock. Perhaps the restaurant would be open for service and they could get on with finding Edna. A quick Windsor knot and he grabbed his hat.

Scanning the restaurant to see that Clyde and Milton had not yet come down, Rowland decided to duck out and check the hotel that was closed the night before. With any luck he would bring Edna back for breakfast.

The manager caught up with him on the stairs. "Mr. Sinclair, I was just coming up to your room. There's a Detective Delaney here to see you, sir."

"Delaney?"

"Yes, he's waiting at reception."

Colin Delaney smiled broadly, extending his hand as Rowland approached. "Hello, Rowly. How are you, old son?"

"What on earth are you doing here, Col?" Rowland shook his hand. "And how the blazes did you know where to find me?"

Delaney tapped the side of his nose. "I am a detective, Rowly." He laughed. "I knew you were coming to Albury, and I figured the Terminus was the only hotel fancy enough for a gentleman of your calibre."

"Are you planning to arrest me?"

"For what?"

"Then why would you come all the way to Albury to find me?"

"I was already in Albury. The Superintendent sent me down to help the local boys with a case... it's why I was trying to get hold of you when you were in Melbourne. Then I remembered Miss Higgins saying she would be meeting you in Albury when I ran into her last week. So I thought I'd just wait for you to get here."

"I see."

"Look, Rowly, there's something I could use your help with. How about we have a chat over breakfast?"

Rowland rubbed his brow. "Can it wait, Col? I'm afraid we seem to have lost Ed."

"What do you mean you've lost her?"

"She came in on the morning train two days ago, and disappeared from the station without leaving a message as to where she was going. We've checked all but two hotels—I'm on my way to do that now."

The colour drained a little from Delaney's face. If Rowland had not himself been so distracted, he might have noticed. "What say I come with you, Rowly?" the detective said. "The presence of a policeman might help."

Rowland accepted gratefully. Delaney could well prove useful at the hotel that was reluctant to give out any information on its guests.

"God help us, what the hell is this?" Delaney murmured as Rowland led him out to the Airflow.

"I bought a new motorcar." Rowland unlocked the door.

Delaney said nothing more about the automobile.

They called at each of the two hotels that hadn't been checked the night before. Neither had any knowledge of a Miss Edna Higgins. Rowland pulled out his notebook and showed both managers a sketch of the sculptress' face. No recognition.

They returned silently to the car. Rowland was frustrated and quite bewildered. Edna was not a child... she would not have wandered off or got lost. She had been on that train... but where was she now?

Delaney waited until they were in the car before he spoke. "You say Miss Higgins arrived two days ago... the thirty-first of August?"

"Yes. At least she should have arrived then."

"She was in a sleeper carriage?"

"Yes."

"So she might have been asleep when the train got in."

"Maybe... but it's the end of the line. She couldn't possibly have missed the stop."

"What does Miss Higgins wear to sleep?"

"What the hell does—"

"Just humour me, Rowly. Do you have any idea what Miss Higgins is in the habit of wearing to bed?"

Rowland sighed. "She wears pyjamas." He omitted that they were usually his pyjamas as the fact seemed misleadingly salacious.

Edna regularly helped herself from the wardrobes of the men with whom she lived. She was particularly fond of Clyde's old shirts and Rowland's pyjamas.

Delaney swore. He put his face in his hands and shook his head, and then he swore again and something about his voice chilled Rowland's blood.

"What?" he demanded.

"Rowly, I was sent down here to help identify a body found in a ditch near Albury. A young woman. She'd been battered and murdered and then doused in fuel and set alight."

Rowland frowned. "Once I locate Ed, I'll be happy to help in any way I can."

Delaney swallowed. "You don't understand, Rowly. She was wearing pyjamas."

"Pyjamas...?" Rowland's hands were on the steering wheel. His knuckles were white. "Bloody hell, Col, you're not suggesting—"

"I don't know, Rowly. Her face was so badly damaged by the fire..."

"Why were you looking for me?"

"I wanted your help... thought you might be able to draw up an idea of what the deceased might have looked like from... what's left... God, I'm sorry, mate. I didn't know Miss Higgins was missing."

"It can't be her. Whoever this poor woman is, she's not Ed."

"No other young woman has been reported missing," Delaney said as gently as he could. "Not one. And this body is the same height and build as Miss Higgins."

Rowland said nothing for a long time. Delaney waited.

"Can I see her?" Rowland asked finally. There was a kind of hollow panic in his voice.

Despite himself, Delaney flinched. "Rowly, are you sure? The body's pretty badly—"

"Yes, I'm sure."

"Perhaps we should let Milt and Clyde know first."

"No."

Delaney didn't argue. He thought briefly about suggesting they go for a drink first. Lord knew he could have used a stiff whisky himself and Rowland would need something to get him through the identification... and afterwards. But already it was clear that any proposal to delay would be refused.

Rowland entered Albury Hospital beside Colin Delaney.

"This way." The detective led the way to the hospital morgue.

The room which housed the body was under police guard. Delaney spoke briefly to the officer. "Mr. Sinclair is here to identify the body."

The door was opened and they were allowed into the room.

She lay on her side on a metal gurney, her knees bent as if she'd been sitting, her feet crossed. One arm sat out, hand on hip. The other arm was crooked about her head. Most of the body had been blackened by the fire. It was hard to tell exactly what colour her hair might have been.

Rowland stepped back, staring. He gasped, for a moment incoherent. His knees felt weak. The artistic eye which had so often followed the lines of Edna's body now fell upon those of the damaged corpse; the petite bone structure, the curves of a figure which had once drawn the gaze of men.

Delaney's hand on his shoulder. "Rowly?"

"Excuse me." Rowland turned and walked out of the room.

Detective Delaney followed, closed the door behind him and waited.

The officer on guard cleared his throat. "Did the gentleman identify her, sir?"

"No... not yet, but I fear he may have recognised her."

Several minutes passed before Rowland returned. He'd loosened his tie, but he was composed.

"Sorry about that, Col. I needed some air."

"Perfectly all right, Rowly. Shall we go back in?"

"I don't need to. It's not Ed."

Delaney's eyes narrowed. "Come on, mate. You didn't even look at her face properly!"

"I didn't need to. I know Ed's body and that's not her."

"Rowly, I know you want to believe..."

"It's not her, Col, the proportions are wrong. Ed's calves are longer, so is her neck. That poor woman had petite hands. Ed's a sculptor... her hands are strong, the nails short." His fingers flexed as he remembered the feeling of Edna's hand in his.

To Delaney, Rowland's reasoning seemed thin and desperate. "The body was damaged by the fire, Rowly."

"That wouldn't change the proportion of the limbs."

"The peculiar position of the legs is probably misleading..."

"I'm an artist, Col," Rowland said sharply. "I know how to account for bloody perspective!"

"Mate..."

"It's not Ed."

Delaney left it. Perhaps Rowland Sinclair just needed time. The detective also found it hard to reconcile the beautiful, spirited sculptress with the cold, contorted body in the morgue, but the correlations were too many—the same height, the same slim build, she was wearing pyjamas, not to mention that Edna Higgins was missing and no other girl had been reported as such.

He accompanied Rowland back to the Terminus. Clyde and Milton met them at the door.

"Bloody hell, Rowly, we were beginning to think you'd vanished too," Clyde growled.

"Sorry, I didn't think I'd be gone all that long," Rowland replied.

"What are you doing here?" Milton shook the detective's hand. "Whatever it is, we all have alibis."

"Rowly, are you all right?" Clyde asked warily. "You look like you've seen a ghost. Where the devil have you been?"

"We'd best find somewhere to have a drink," Delaney suggested.

"We can use my suite," Rowland said, anticipating the conversation to follow. "I'll have drinks sent up. Then we can get back to finding Ed."

The sitting room in Rowland's suite was small but adequate for the purpose. Delaney told them about the young woman's body in the Albury Hospital morgue, and the reasons why he thought it might be Edna Higgins. He tried to be kind because he knew that all the men in the room had loved the sculptress.

Rowland said nothing until Delaney had finished. And then, "It's not Ed."

Delaney looked to Clyde and Milton for help.

"Poor wretch," Clyde murmured.

"Do you have any idea who she is, Col?" Milton asked.

"Yes, I think she is Miss Higgins," Delaney said, exasperated. This was hard enough without everybody denying the obvious.

"Rowly's seen the body, and he says it's not Ed," Clyde replied.

Delaney lowered his voice. "Look, Clyde, the body was in bad shape. Damaged beyond recognition."

Clyde shook his head. "Rowly would recognise Ed."

Delaney cursed. "I'd better get back to the station. I'll call back this evening after you've had a bit of time… Look, I am sorry."

"I'll walk you out," Milton said as he held open the door.

Delaney waited until they were outside the hotel before he tried once more to make Milton see sense. "Look, Milt, Rowly couldn't even bring himself to look at the girl's face. What does that tell you?"

Milton shrugged. "That he didn't need to. Ed's Rowly's model. He's painted her hundreds of times from every angle. He's spent more hours staring at her naked body than he's spent doing anything else in the last few years. I don't care how damaged the body was, if it was Ed, he would have recognised her."

"I think he did recognise her. I think he just can't face it."

"That's where you don't understand Rowly, comrade," Milton replied. "In spite of all our advice, the poor sod loves Ed, really loves her. If he had any notion that the unfortunate woman lying in your morgue was Ed, do you really think that he would walk away and leave her?"

"Grief does strange things to people…"

"Don't let the posh accent and fancy manners fool you, comrade. Rowly's one of the toughest blokes I know. If it was Edna lying on that slab, his grief would be terrible but he wouldn't deny her, he wouldn't hide from it."

"If this woman is some stranger, then why was Rowly so affected by viewing the body?"

"Well by your own account the condition of the body was pretty grim. Aside from that, Ed's missing. And it seems there's some bastard out there murdering women and setting them alight." Milton didn't raise his voice. He spoke calmly, almost casually. "Rowly's not grieving, he's terrified that Ed's in danger, that this could happen to her if you don't stop telling us she's dead and help us find her."

Delaney cupped his hands to light a cigarette. The poet had a point. Rowland Sinclair had proved many times that he was not the kind of man to buckle. The smoke plumed around his head, "Thank God," he said finally.

"What?"

"Believe me when I say I'm glad it's not Miss Higgins. But I'm a policeman, I had to be sure."

"And now you're sure? You believe Rowly?"

"I'll get a description of Miss Higgins out to the local patrols. Maybe someone saw her leaving the station." He paused. "If we don't find her, you or Mr. Watson Jones may have to look at the body."

4

GIRL'S BODY IN CULVERT

GRUESOME MURDER NEAR ALBURY

One of the most gruesome murders in this State for some time was revealed on Saturday when a farmer found the partly burned body of a young woman clad in pyjamas under a culvert on the Howlong-road, about four miles from Albury.

The discovery was made by Thomas Hunter Griffiths, a well-known farmer in the Albury district, who was leading a bull past the culvert, when he noticed something protruding from it. On investigating, he was horrified to find in a sack the body of a good-looking young woman with fair complexion and light brown bobbed hair. Griffiths hurried to his home, from which he telephoned the police. Police were soon on the scene, and they were horrified when they took from the culvert the sack containing the body. They found that the body was clad in white pyjamas with yellow borders, but these had been partly burnt. The lower limbs and the lower part of the abdomen were badly charred, and the police believe that some inflammable substance was poured over the body and set alight in an endeavour to remove all traces of the crime... The spot where the body was found is only a few yards from the main road from Albury to Howlong.

Singleton Argus, 3 September 1934

Three men walked the long platform of Albury Station showing hand-drawn pictures of a beautiful young woman to every railway employee they could find. Perhaps it was difficult to recognise someone from a sketch or perhaps it was the days that had passed, but no one seemed to recall the lady in question.

"Her hair is auburn," Rowland said as he showed the picture to the elderly man in charge of the ticketing booth. "She's about five foot two."

"A bonny lass if ever I saw one... but I didn't, I'm afraid. Sorry, lad."

"Are you sure? She'd have come in on the early train from Sydney."

"I'm sure. Doesn't mean she didn't come in, just that I didn't see her. It can get as busy as Pitt Street here in the mornings."

Rowland thanked the man and stepped away from the booth.

"Oi, mister!" A ragged man in a coat that was more patch than coat motioned him over to the edge of the platform. "You wouldn't be able to spare a smoke, wouldya?" he asked when Rowland came within conversational distance.

"I'm sorry, sir, I don't smoke."

"Oh." Thin shoulders slumped. "I guess I'll have a gander at yer picture anyway. I will."

Rowland introduced himself as he showed him the drawing.

"Pleased, Mr. Sinclair. I be Gus Hancock."

"A pleasure, Mr. Hancock. Have you seen her?"

Hancock nodded vigorously. "I seen her. I did."

"Was she alone? Did you notice where she went?" Rowland asked eagerly.

"I want something first. I do."

Rowland extracted a couple of crisp pound notes from his pocketbook.

"No, I don't want yer money. I don't. Let me have the picture?"

"Why do you want the picture?"

"To remember her by."

Rowland's blood chilled. Remember? What did the man know? "Why do you need to remember her?" he asked.

"She was pretty. I like to remember pretty things. I do. When I were a boy, there was a blossom tree in front of the house. I wish I had a drawing of that."

Rowland handed him the drawing. "Her name is Edna. I'd really like to find her."

"She arrived on the early train." Hancock gazed at the photo. "It were real cold. I was asking for a contribution yer know, I ain't a beggar but if the good people should wish to contribute to my cause… The chief porter told me to clear off. He did. But she give me two shillings and told him not to be a bully. Can yer imagine that? Gawd I laughed." He smiled with the memory. "And then she winked at me, like we was friends. Like we was old friends."

Rowland wanted to cheer. Finally. Headway. "Yes. That's Ed. Was she with anyone?"

"Yes. A fancy fella. I didn't much like the look of him."

"Why?"

Hancock shrugged. "Dunno. Just didn't. Anyways she chuffed off with him, she did."

"How did they leave? Did they walk?"

"No—they got into one of them motorised carriages."

"A motorcar? What kind?"

Hancock shrugged again.

"What colour was it?"

"Green. It were green. It were."

"The man you say was accompanying her—do you know who he is?"

"Naw. Never seen him here before."

Rowland took out his notebook and pencil. "Do you think you could describe him, Mr. Hancock?"

Hancock removed his hat and rubbed his head as if he were massaging his brain in preparation for the task. "His face were long… like a horse…" For the next several minutes Rowland sketched and adjusted until Gus Hancock cried, "That be him!"

The result was a drawing of a young man with fair, curly hair and a narrow face. There was something a little sinister about his features but it was hard to tell if that came through as a result of Hancock's description or Rowland's current state of mind. Even so, the face was familiar.

"Are you sure this is who you saw, Mr. Hancock?" Rowland asked, concerned that he had biased the sketch somehow.

"That's him." Hancock knew no doubt.

Rowland thanked him and made a contribution.

By then Milton and Clyde, having had no luck themselves, had returned. Rowland showed them the sketch. "Are you serious?" Clyde gawked at the drawing.

"Middleton!" Milton cursed. "What's he doing here?"

Bertram Middleton was a journalist by trade and a novelist by aspiration. He had been in ardent pursuit of Edna's affections for some years and so he was known to them all.

"Doesn't he live in Canberra now?" Clyde gave the notebook back to Rowland.

"Last I heard."

"Why would Middleton abduct Ed?" Milton said angrily.

"The chap who recognised Ed was of the opinion she left with him quite voluntarily."

"Without leaving a word for us?" Milton would not have it. "Bloody nonsense."

"Where the hell would he have taken her?" Rowland was aware that they didn't know a great deal about the writer despite the fact that Middleton had courted Edna on and off for years. That was his fault.

He had always borne the sculptress' loves by ignoring them wherever possible, and perhaps Clyde and Milton had followed his lead.

"We'd better let Delaney know." Clyde calmed the conversation with practical action. "This is something at least."

"Just a moment." Rowland caught sight of the platform guard and walked over to him. He showed him the drawing of the man they thought was Middleton. The guard looked at the picture and called over a colleague. They consulted for a while before returning to Rowland.

"Middleton you say? Joe here reckons he may be the gentleman that left his tennis racquet behind. He telephoned the station this morning to see if we had it in our lost property."

"It was left in the gentlemen's rest room," Joe said. "Is he a friend of yours, sir?"

"Yes." Rowland elected not to explain that he wasn't actually interested in Middleton.

"I only ask because if you are calling out to see him, we could give you the tennis racquet to return to him."

"I'd be happy to. Where is he staying?"

The platform guard was more hesitant. "What did you say your name was, sir?"

"Sinclair, Rowland Sinclair." Rowland handed the man his card. "I'm staying at the Terminus."

The card, which listed Rowland's residence as *Woodlands House*, Woollahra, below an embossed Sinclair crest did much to reassure the guard that Rowland wasn't trying to steal the racquet. Middleton, it appeared, had given his details when he called so that return of his property could be arranged. When Rowland finally rejoined his friends, he had a tennis racquet and an address.

Willowview, on the way to Howlong, was set well back from the road and so its grandeur was not visible until the Airflow was well down the elm-lined drive. The colonial mansion was secluded by tall pines. Its location, miles from town and well away from any other house, might have rendered it ominous if there were not more than a dozen vehicles parked on the grassy flat near the entrance stairs.

Rowland brought the Airflow to a stop beside an Armstrong Siddeley and the three of them stepped out. Milton grabbed the tennis racquet from the back seat.

A maid in a traditional black and white uniform answered the door. "Mr. Middleton is with other guests at the tennis courts. If you'll wait here, sir, I'll fetch him."

They waited on the doorstep for fifteen minutes. Still there was no sign of the maid's return.

"Sod this for a joke." Milton rang the bell again.

"She said he was at the tennis courts," Clyde said. "Maybe we should just go round and find him."

"It might be more useful than standing here." Rowland was frustrated. Though he knew that the body in the Albury Hospital morgue was not Edna, the murdered woman made the sculptress' disappearance a terrifying thing.

The tennis courts were not difficult to find once they'd made their way to the grounds behind the house. A long, linen-draped trestle table had been laid with a feast of cakes and lemonade. Servants with trays of cordials moved among guests in tennis attire.

Rowland looked for Middleton, but it was Edna he spotted first. She stood encircled by young men observing the match at play. For a moment Rowland just watched her, too relieved to speak. She turned as if she sensed his gaze. She smiled, the natural enchanting smile that never failed to cause Rowland's breath to catch though he knew it well. She pushed out of the circle and approached them with her arms outstretched.

"Finally… where have you been? Did you forget about me?"

Rowland nearly laughed, the idea was so absurd. He had thought of nothing else.

"What do you mean?" Milton was cross. "We've been looking everywhere for you. We were worried sick and you've been here doing God knows what!"

"That's not true!" Edna embraced each of them in turn regardless of Milton's censure. "We left a message at the station."

"By we you mean you and Middleton?" Rowland asked.

Edna looked at him. "Oh, Rowly, you're not cross too, are you? I ran into Bertie on the train. When I got the telegram that you were delayed, he suggested I go with him. He needed a partner for mixed doubles and he was sure Maggie would have a spare tennis dress… He spoke to the station master to make sure you'd know where to find me."

"Where is Middleton?"

"Right here, old chap!" Bertram Middleton emerged in tennis whites. "You got here, finally! Edna was beginning to think you'd abandoned her entirely. It's a good job I was on hand to rescue the lady."

A slight wrinkle appeared in Edna's forehead. "You did leave a message with the station master, didn't you, Bertie?"

"Of course." He beamed at Rowland. "Don't tell me it wasn't passed on!"

"It was not." Clyde handed him the tennis racquet. "The station master had no knowledge of where Ed went, though he did receive the message regarding your flaming racquet."

"Good Lord, you don't say." Middleton practised a few strokes. "Well, I'll be having words with the station master's superior whoever he is. Clearly the incompetent fool failed to pass on my first message!" He winked at Edna. "Still, all's well that ends well. We've had a smashing time, haven't we, Eddie?"

Rowland resisted a vague urge to punch Middleton. It was a misunderstanding after all—the writer could not possibly know the panic Edna's absence would cause.

"Rowly, we should probably let the police know that Ed's no longer missing." Clyde spoke quietly but Edna overheard.

"The police?" she said incredulously. "You called the police?"

"I say, Sinclair, that's a bit of an overreaction, isn't it? Surely you didn't expect poor Eddie to just wait around for your pleasure?"

"We had no idea where you were, Ed." Rowland ignored Middleton.

"For pity's sake, I'm a grown woman… and you were late." Edna would not tolerate any attempts to constrain or control her. Not even those that were well intentioned.

Middleton added fuel. "Good heavens, Sinclair, not being where you told her to be is hardly a crime. Did you expect to have Ed arrested?"

Edna's eyes flashed. "I hope the police had enough sense to tell you not to be silly."

"Actually the police think you're dead," Milton replied.

"Did I hear someone mention the police? Surely we're not that rowdy!" A sturdy gentleman, physically softened by middle age, joined them.

Middleton introduced the Honourable Thomas Ley, who had apparently served in both the NSW and Federal parliaments. The erstwhile politician was only just returned from England.

"These gentlemen are friends of Miss Higgins who were so concerned by her stepping out with me that they contacted the constabulary to keep her from my clutches," Middleton declared, laughing.

"How very chivalrous." Ley gestured to a servant. "Do grab a lemonade, gentlemen, and allow me to introduce you around."

"We don't wish to impose, Mr. Ley. We only came to find Miss Higgins and return Mr. Middleton's tennis racquet."

"Nonsense, Miss Higgins and Mr. Middleton are playing in the finals this afternoon. It'd be a jolly shame to miss the match."

Middleton piped up. "It would indeed. We're the favourites, you know. Don't be such a wet blanket, Sinclair."

The blue of Rowland's eyes darkened dangerously.

Edna intervened. "Don't be ridiculous, Bertie. It's not Wimbledon." She turned to Rowland, forgetting that she was piqued and declaring her allegiances. "There are any number of ladies who will play in my place if you want to go now. And I don't mind. I want to hear what the three of you have been up to... aside from bothering the police."

Rowland glanced at Milton and Clyde. The former had somehow acquired a drink and a slice of cream sponge. Clyde shrugged; he was uneasy in the soirees of the well to do, but it did seem rude to demand Edna abandon the tournament.

"I'm sure we can wait until you finish the match," Rowland said finally. "But I will need to telephone Delaney to let him know you've been found."

"Why don't I show you to the telephone while Miss Higgins and Mr. Middleton take the court?" Ley offered. He led Rowland into the house.

"Is this your home, Mr. Ley?" Rowland asked.

"Oh no... it belongs to dear friends who are holidaying in New Zealand of all places—they go every year. They very kindly invited Maggie and me to use it from time to time while we were in the country."

"And are you in Australia for long?" Rowland inquired more to make conversation than out of any real curiosity.

"Well that depends. I'm considering standing for office again. If things go well, I may find myself residing in the Antipodes once more."

"I see." They'd reached the library in which the telephone was located.

"Retirement doesn't suit me, I'm afraid. London is well and good but I am a man of the people and there is much to be done here."

"Indeed."

"Politics is a funny game." Ley seemed to be in no hurry to bring the conversation to a close. "Now that Bruce is gone perhaps they'll let bygones be bygones."

"Bruce?"

"Stanley Melbourne... our venerable eighth prime minister. He decided I was not made of the right stuff for the Nationalist Party. Perhaps the United Australia Party will be more welcoming."

Rowland had become well acquainted with Stanley Bruce when he was in London the year before, and Lyons, the current prime minister, just recently. They were undeniably very different men. "Well, best of luck, Mr. Ley."

"Why thank you, my friend." He gestured towards the phone. "Please be my guest. Do let the constabulary know that not only is Miss Higgins no longer missing but she has a deceptive drop shot and a capital serve."

5

POLITICAL FALSE
ALARM

Mr. John Thomas Ley

Since Dick Whittington started the fashion of aspiring to and actually managing to grab the crown of glory, despite the most humble and inauspicious beginning, he has had numerous disciples. One of the long list of "self-made" men of today is Mr. John Thomas Ley, Minister for Justice in the Fuller alleged Government.

Somewhere between ten and twelve years of age—a time when most nippers are concerned with kites, conundrums and copy-book cogitations—John Thomas ventured forth into the hard, cold world to wrest from it a living—and, incidentally, step on the lower rung of the ladder to fame. He found the world even colder than most, for he had to rise before dawn every day to take up his duties on a milk-cart. And, as in the case of the admiral in W.S. Gilbert's "H.M.S. Pinafore," his success in such a mundane business as the transportation of lacteal fluid started him on the way to becoming a ruler. But Mr. John Thomas degenerated into politics. Of the law he knows quite a lot.

The milk-ladler's first great deed as a politician was to spur on proportional representation, by which means he topped the poll in St George. As Ley's politics are not designed to provide the wage-earner with milk or honey, it is a tribute to the vote-milking properties of the new electoral system. Mr. John Thomas Ley's ambition is unbounded. He has hitched his wagon to a star—possibly one of the Milky Way constellation. When defeated by Charlie Hoax for the job as right-hand man to Fuller, and the "king pin" when Fuller gets full of the job, he turned his eyes on the leaderless prohibitionists and sectarians.

The Legislative Council has poured a cold douche on the sectarian serpent, and Brother Hammond has ungratefully scowled on Ley's schemes for removing the whisky-bottle and substituting the milk-jug. Further, at the impending elections there is an immense possibility that all Nationalists, including Minister Ley, will be asked not to minister for the next three years, and this despite an unblemished and milky white sheet bearing a record of Ley's achievements — nothing! His ambition is likely to get a jar that will make it feel like a milk-shake.

Hobby: Seeking votes on the "Ley-by" system, or in other words pandering to the prejudice of sectarians.

Vice: Threatening to resign, but declining.

Truth, 19 October 1924

When Rowland returned, Clyde and Milton had found deckchairs from which to watch Edna and Middleton's final match.

"Lemonade?" Rowland asked, nodding at the drinks they held.

Milton opened his jacket to reveal a flask. "We may have flavoured it with a little something. Ley must be a Temperance Leaguer."

Rowland took the deckchair beside them.

"You all right, Rowly?" Clyde asked.

Rowland glanced at Edna who was warming up on the grass court. There had been a few seconds in the mortuary when he had thought the worst. Before he'd taken in enough detail to realise that the poor wretch on the table was not the sculptress. And many hours since then when he had feared the worst. "Yes. I am now."

"Do you think Middleton left a message at the station, or was it all malarky?" Milton observed the journalist from a distance.

Rowland said nothing. He was aware that he was unlikely to be truly fair to any man who sought Edna's affections. Even so,

Middleton was brasher than he remembered. Perhaps the writer was being more creative in his attempts to keep her attention.

"What did Delaney say?" Clyde noted the angry glint in his friend's dark blue eyes and elected to change the subject lest Rowland decide to deck Middleton.

"He said he'd never been so glad to be wrong."

"Have they found out who that poor girl is?"

Rowland shook his head. "Delaney said something about preserving the body."

"Why?"

"So they can put it on display in the hope someone recognises her."

"Jesus, Mary and Joseph!" Clyde crossed himself. "Where on earth does Delaney expect to display her?"

"I'm not quite sure. He wants me back in Albury so I can make a sketch of what her face might have looked like."

"Really? Are you keen?"

"Not keen. But I'll do it. Hopefully they'll identify her before Delaney needs to turn her into a sideshow." Rowland feared death was not to be the last outrage the unfortunate woman would suffer. She could not be buried until she was given a name.

Aside from the distinct absence of alcohol, Ley's hospitality could not be faulted. Hors d'oeuvres came out at regular intervals and there was lemonade aplenty. Their host was congenial and at pains to ensure they were appropriately introduced.

It was during one of these introductions that Rowland Sinclair and Miss Jemima Fairweather were reacquainted.

"Rowland Sinclair, I know you!" The stylish brunette reached up and kissed him quite passionately, and without any hesitation or warning. Rowland was too startled to resist.

He hadn't seen the lady in nearly fifteen years. But he hadn't forgotten her kiss.

"I was Rowly's first love," she announced to everybody in earshot. "We might have married if we hadn't been children!"

Rowland had been not quite fifteen years of age when American-born Jemima had come to spend the summer with her grandmother in Yass. She'd been a year or two older than him and he had been completely at her mercy. His memory of their association was one of awkward adolescent passions and utter bewilderment. She'd decided he was in love with her and demanded he act accordingly. He'd not been unwilling, but by the end of the summer she was gone. Still, the memory of her was not unpleasant and he was glad to see her again.

Now in her early thirties, Jemima's Boston lilt was much less pronounced. The years had, if anything, made her more attractive. Dressed in the latest tailored style, she was clearly not playing tennis.

"And look at you," she said gazing at Rowland. "Still devastatingly handsome. Those eyes!" She traced her hand along his jawline. "That's changed… you're shaving now I gather."

Rowland laughed. He introduced Clyde and Milton. "Miss Fairweather and I are old friends."

"Friends?" she gasped, clutching her hand to her chest. "Mr. Sinclair was madly in love with me! It was all terribly innocent of course… he was so frightfully shy."

Rowland felt a familiar bewilderment. Jemima had always been something of a whirlwind, sweeping the world helplessly before her. She chatted to Clyde and Milton for a while, making outrageous claims about her past with Rowland Sinclair, daring him to react. He did not. In the end she granted him a private audience and dragged him away to the fernery to ensure he took advantage of it.

Clyde and Milton watched them go, unsure if Rowland needed help. They were not in the practice of defending him from beautiful women, but Jemima Fairweather was unusually forthright.

Jemima laughed as she led him away. "Your chums are worried I'm going to take advantage of you."

"I'm sure that's the last thing they're worried about." Rowland stood back to look at her. "It's grand to see you, again, Jemima. What are you doing here?"

"Maggie Brook and I are old friends. She invited me. Personally, I abhor tennis but she promised me there'd be other entertainments."

"And Miss Brook is…"

"Mrs. Brook. Tommy Ley's mistress." Jemima smiled. "She and Tommy are perfect for each other but of course they're trying to keep a low profile while they're here… on account of Lewie."

"Lewie?"

"Tommy's wife."

"She doesn't know?"

"Of course she does. But there's such a thing as discretion. Tommy is rather keen to gain preselection and stand for parliament again."

"What about Mrs. Brook's husband? Does he know too?"

"He's dead. Tommy was his lawyer." Jemima seized Rowland's hands in hers. "I'm positively sick of talking about Tommy and Maggie. Tell me what you've been up to."

Rowland glanced over his shoulder at the court. "The match has started. Shouldn't we watch?"

Jemima's eyes softened. "There's that shy boy I knew."

"It's not that…" Rowland left it. "What do you want to know?"

She asked him about what he'd been doing since last they'd met, where he'd been, and who he'd loved. Rowland ignored the last question and answered the others as truthfully as he could remember.

"Grandmama mentioned someone had finally shot him," Jemima said when he told her his father had died just a month after they'd parted last. "I wanted to come back and celebrate with you but Grandmama wouldn't hear of me leaving school."

At this Rowland smiled slightly. He'd always found Jemima Fairweather's refusal to censor herself admirably honest. She'd known about Henry Sinclair's disciplinary violence, witnessed it to some extent. She did not pretend to be sorry for Rowland's loss or expect him to be either.

In turn she told him about a failed marriage when she was just twenty-two—"It's Mrs. Roche now, I'm afraid"—and her subsequent travels through Europe. "The Continent is a most delightful place to play, don't you think?"

"What brings you back to Australia, Mrs. Roche?"

"Grandmama's estate. Tommy's sorting it all out for me."

Rowland expressed his condolences. He'd not heard that old Mrs. Fairweather had died, but then, admittedly, it had been some months since he'd last been in Yass and he and Wilfred had not spoken a great deal in that time. The thought reminded him of the current antipathy between him and his brother.

Jemima shook her head. "Grandmama's not dead, Rowly. But she is getting on. The Fairweathers like to be organised."

"Oh. Pleased to hear it."

"Poor Grandmama," Jemima said. "I'm the old dear's greatest regret, you know. They sent me to live with her so she could turn me into a respectable young lady, and all I managed to do was corrupt Yass's favourite son."

"I was never that."

She smoothed his lapel and toyed with the knot in his tie. "I'm assuming you married, Rowly?"

"No."

"Good show!" She punched him on the shoulder. "Not that it would have mattered to me. I'm not that superficial." She pulled on his tie and kissed him deeply. He wasn't as surprised this time. "Tell you what, Rowly, it's about time we became lovers. What do you say?"

"I—"

She laughed. "I wondered if I could still make you blush."

"Good Lord, you're still incorrigible."

"It's why we were so in love. Do you remember?"

"Vaguely."

"You asked me to marry you."

"Jemima, I was fourteen."

"Nearly fifteen. Are you going back on it then? How very ungentlemanly!"

Rowland smiled. He remembered being besotted with Jemima Fairweather. She had been a loud, unexpected blast of fresh air with a strangely alluring American accent. It had probably helped that his father could not have been more appalled.

"Sinclair!" Thomas Ley strode over with a bevy of his male guests. "I say, old chap, is that amorphous yellow lump in the driveway your vehicle?"

Rowland regarded his host coldly. "If you mean the Chrysler Airflow, then yes."

"Well I never!" Ley beamed. "Can you really bounce a brick off the windscreen?"

"I haven't actually tried—"

The gentlemen with Ley spoke up. "What model is that... the eight cylinder?"

"Never seen anything like it!"

"I don't suppose we could peek under the bonnet?"

"Hood." Clyde had left the tennis to join the group of men. "American cars have hoods, not bonnets."

"Well, what say we have a look-see under that hood?"

"Would you mind, Sinclair?" Ley asked. "Not sure when any of us will see an automobile like yours again."

"Shouldn't we be watching the tennis?"

Jemima rolled her eyes.

"They're pretty evenly matched… we have time to duck out," Ley assured him. "How does she run, Sinclair?"

"Pretty smoothly, actually."

"That'd be the shock absorbers," Clyde offered.

There were further questions, progressively more eager. It seemed the gentlemen had become bored with tennis. Now that Rowland knew Edna was safe, his enthusiasm for the Airflow returned. And so, most of the final tennis match was viewed by a somewhat diminished audience as the men gathered about Rowland Sinclair's new motorcar exclaiming at her design and engine capacity and marvelling enviously at the custom installation of a radio set and heater in the thoroughly modern dash.

They rejoined the tennis party in just enough time to see the final game, applauding and cheering with compensatory gusto.

"Your Miss Higgins is certainly in fine form." Jemima Fairweather found him again. "Is she your girl?"

"No."

"That's fortunate. She's clearly mad about Bertie Middleton."

Rowland's brow rose.

"And you can see that Bertie's devoted to her."

Rowland moved his gaze to Middleton. The writer's eye was rarely on the ball. The match was being won by Edna alone. "I expect he is."

Jemima studied Rowland thoughtfully. "Oh, my poor darling boy."

He smiled. "What are you talking about Jemima?"

She took his hand and, beckoning him to lower his head, whispered in his ear. "I've decided that you and I are going to indulge in a passionate and scandalous affair."

"Have you?"

"Yes. It'll do us both good. We can start tonight."

Rowland's face was unreadable. "You can't shock me, Jemima."

"I'm sure I could." Her hand rested inside his jacket on the buttons of his waistcoat.

Rowland laughed. "Sadly we're not staying. We must get on as soon as the tournament concludes."

"Why?"

"We've already imposed on the hospitality of Mr. Ley. None of us was actually invited."

"Poppycock. Tommy promised me that I should not be bored. You'll be helping him keep his word."

"I'm sure you won't be bored."

"I tell you I will." Jemima frowned.

Rowland reached into his pocket and extracted a calling card. "Will you be in Australia long?"

She took it from him. "I've just decided to extend my stay."

"Then there'll be plenty of time for us to catch up properly."

She pouted. "I'm really most put out that you are not more enthusiastic!"

"On the contrary," Rowland said. "I couldn't be more delighted to see you." Jemima had changed little from the wild sixteen-year-old girl who'd scandalised the pastoral society of his hometown at a time when the flappers were products of the sinful city and still largely unknown in rural Yass. Both the memory and the presence of her now called a wry smile to his lips. "Will you come to Sydney?"

She sighed. "Yes, if only to save you from—"

A resounding cheer and applause interrupted her. Miss Edna Higgins and Mr. Bertram Middleton were triumphant. An awards ceremony of sorts followed with Ley making speeches and Mrs. Maggie Brook presenting bouquets and boxes of chocolates to the winners.

"I'll just change and fetch my luggage," Edna said as her friends offered their congratulations. "I won't be long."

Middleton protested. "Eddie, you can't leave before the victory party! Come on, Sinclair, tell her you'll stay to toast the greatest mixed-doubles team since Daphne Akhurst and Gentleman Jack Crawford!"

"Would you like to stay?" Rowland asked Edna quietly.

"No, she wouldn't," Milton said flatly.

Rowland glanced at the poet, surprised. Clearly Milton wished to go.

Edna laughed. "You haven't forgotten we were supposed to be at the Hansens' in Yackandandah yesterday?"

Rowland had forgotten.

"They must think us all terribly rude and inconsiderate." Edna grimaced.

"Yes. We should at least make an appearance," said Milton.

Edna turned to Middleton. "I'm sorry, Bertie, but we really must get on."

"When will I see you again?" The man sounded desperate. Embarrassed, Milton, Clyde and Rowland all turned away. The eventual realisation by Edna's suitors that she was not theirs was often awkward for all concerned. The sculptress did not deceive the men she loved from time to time. But they invariably refused to believe that, as much as she liked the company of men, Edna Higgins was not interested in belonging to one. It seemed that Middleton was, on that matter, being particularly obtuse.

"I'll visit you in Canberra," Edna promised. She pressed a silver chalice into his hands—the Ley Cup. "You keep this to remember me."

"I'll keep it close to my heart until I see you next, my darling."

"That sounds uncomfortable." Edna kissed his cheek. "I'm sure the mantelpiece will be a much better place for it."

6

ALBURY CRIME

Victim's Identity
VITAL TO POLICE SUCCESS

Detectives who are investigating the murder of the woman whose battered and charred body was found under a culvert off Howlong-road near Albury are facing one of the most difficult problems in police history. They believe, however, that once the woman's identity is established they will make rapid progress.

INQUIRIES AT ALBURY

Detective-sergeant Allmond and Detective McDermott have been tireless in their investigations at Albury. They visited Culcairn Show yesterday and made inquiries from showmen and others about young women who travel about the country with troupes for a livelihood. They learnt nothing of value.

AMENDED DESCRIPTION

The police have issued an amended description of the murdered woman and of the clothing and towel found wrapped round the body. She is described as having been between 20 and 30 years of age, 5ft 2in or 5ft 3in in height, of slim to medium build, with blue-grey eyes, plucked eyebrows, and light brown hair, which was darker near the roots and may have been peroxided or bleached. Her fingernails were manicured to a point and bore traces of red tinting. Two teeth in the right lower jaw were missing, and the tooth farthest back in the right lower jaw had been filled with gold.

Sydney Morning Herald, 6 September 1934

They didn't speak of the unidentified body, or the police investigation or the message that wasn't left. Neither did they talk of Bertram Middleton or the tennis party at Myrtleford. Edna, as yet, knew nothing of the murdered girl. Instead they praised Rowland's new motorcar—its speed, its handling, the smoothness of its ride— and discussed the Kisch Reception Committee and the part they would play in Egon Kisch's visit to Australia.

"It's a long way to Fremantle from Sydney, Rowly. Are you sure Doris is up to it?" Edna opened the glove box and peered inside.

Doris, more formally known as the *Rule Britannia*, was Rowland's prized Gipsy Moth.

"I'm certain she isn't. I'm not taking Doris. I'll get hold of a twin-engine plane."

"You're going to buy another aeroplane?"

"I don't think it'll come to that. I'll borrow one if I can."

Having satisfied her curiosity about the glove box, Edna fiddled with the knobs on the radio.

"A little to the left and you might find a signal," Rowland said. "Do you like her?"

Edna ran her hands along the dash. "Yes, I do. She suits you."

Rowland handed the car keys to Clyde when they arrived at the Albury police station. "Why don't you all have a drink somewhere—I don't think this will take long. I'll have Delaney drop me back at the Albury Hotel when I'm done."

Clyde nodded. He knew Rowland was trying to keep Edna apart from this. As far as the sculptress knew, Rowland was filling in paperwork to verify that she was no longer missing.

Delaney met Rowland on the threshold of the station and waved to Edna as the Airflow pulled away.

"Thank you for coming, Rowly. In addition to everything, I can apologise in person. You must think me an incompetent fool."

"It was an easy mistake to make, Col. Ed was missing."

"Still, I'm sorry I didn't take you at your word when you said it wasn't Miss Higgins. I feel like a heel asking for your help after what I put you through."

"I'm happy to help."

Delaney introduced him to Detective Sergeant Allmond who had been despatched from Sydney to take charge of the case. They took him back to the Albury Hospital morgue where the unidentified corpse had been preserved. This time Rowland was more prepared for the state of the body. Steeling himself, he inspected the blackened and damaged face, looking closely for bone structure and definition among the distorted features: the distance between the eyes, the bridge of the nose, anything that might reveal what she once looked like. He made brief notes and sketched the unusual shape of her ears.

It took him less than an hour to complete a preliminary pencil sketch of her face and another of her profile. He handed the drawings to Allmond.

The detective sergeant frowned. "Are you sure?"

"Not at all—it's just my best guess."

"She's not very pretty."

"Not everybody is."

"The newspapers are reporting that she was a beauty."

"Does it matter if she isn't?"

"No, I suppose not."

———————

They found the Hansens of Yackandandah and their guests out by the dam, settled on deckchairs with sketchbooks or standing before field easels. A sturdy young woman with blonde hair in braids sang without accompaniment, and a linen-draped table was laid with an extravagant supper under gauze against the insects. The crowd was theirs, artists and writers and actors.

Hector and Mabel Hansen had, in Sydney, always been just a canvas away from complete destitution. This disposition had seen them living at *Woodlands* from time to time. They'd revelled in their poverty, convinced that it added a certain clarity to their work and a hunger to their love. Regrettably for those things, Mabel had come into an unexpected inheritance, which included the homestead in Yackandandah. They'd moved, started a family, and settled into the more conventional existence they'd once derided. Once a year, in a kind of homage to the lives they once lived, the couple invited their old circle to Yackandandah, to paint and drink and entertain one another in whatever way they saw fit.

The party from *Woodlands House* was welcomed like the return of family, with warmth and laughter, questions and teasing.

"Well, well, if it isn't Lazarus Sinclair!" Hector Hansen called as he walked over to greet them.

Rowland laughed. It had been widely reported in the popular press that Rowland Sinclair of *Woodlands House*, Woollahra, had been killed in the spectacular speedway crash that had destroyed the yellow Mercedes. His housekeeper had been mortified by the well-meaning wreaths sent to the house in condolence.

"The critics have been unkind to you." Hector spoke quietly as he shook Rowland's hand.

"Yes." Rowland's most recent exhibition had ended in violence and been widely derided as an exercise in anti-German propaganda by radical elements.

"You did a brave thing, my friend. Sacrificing one's life is one thing but one's life's work, completely another."

"It was just one exhibition, not my life's work, Hec."

"Perhaps, Rowly, but you will always be remembered as the man who libelled poor Germany in the Communist cause. Your work will always be viewed in that light."

"Sadly, I fear Germany herself will vindicate me."

Hector placed his arm around Rowland and shook off the sombre conversation. "Well, in the meantime we shall celebrate your resurrection!"

"As long as you're not expecting me to provide the wine."

As the sun slipped low in a sky beginning to bruise, a bonfire was built and paper lanterns hung in the trees. There was music and dancing until it became too cold to remain. The gathering then moved back to *Hillend*, a grand if slightly shabby homestead. Mabel Hansen had inherited the property but little else, and consequently the sprawling abode was currently run without staff. As a result, the servants' quarters were available, albeit a little dusty, for the Hansens' guests. Sufficient beds were found and allocated though most remained undisturbed till the early hours of the next morning when passionate conversations about the state of art and mankind gave way to sleep.

Accordingly the house was largely silent until nearly noon the next day. Only Rowland Sinclair awoke in what could still be called morning. As *Hillend's* water supply—a series of poorly maintained rainwater tanks forever springing leaks—was unable to cope with so many guests it was a tradition of necessity that the gentlemen bathe in the stream about a quarter mile from the homestead. Rowland was quite happy to use the waterway, but, excruciatingly aware of the swastika that had been burned into his chest, he was not enamoured with the idea of communal bathing. The brand had not been applied with his consent—far from it—but still, it embarrassed him. Recounting how it came to be there was awkward and, to his mind, humiliating. It was easier to avoid situations in which the scar would be noticed.

Being September, the water was icy to the point of being painful. Rowland bathed and re-dressed as quickly as possible, wondering why the Hansens didn't simply pump to the house from the stream. It would solve the water supply issues and ensure their guests didn't die of hypothermia. Hector had thoughtfully secured a shaving mirror to one of the riparian trees, and basins, Sunlight soap and a methylated spirits burner were stored in the lean-to beside it. Rowland lit the burner to heat water so he could shave. He smiled as he noticed a vase of wildflowers that had been left in the lean-to—Mabel's attempt to make the rustic ablutions more civilised, he supposed.

Now that his blood flow was returning, Rowland found himself quite enjoying the alfresco bathroom. The stream was lined with willows through which the muted light of late morning made its way gently. Though it was nearly eleven o'clock, a wispy fog persisted, casting the world into watercolours. Gurgling birdsong, the distant screech of a flock of black cockatoos disturbed, and the running of the stream—there was a noisy quiet about it all. He poured the warmed water into a basin and unfastened the top button of his shirt before lathering his face.

He was still shaving when he became aware of the feeling that he was not alone. Some instinct told him it was not one of the other guests. Rowland wiped his face but he kept his razor open, studying the mirror for any sign of someone behind him. A crack in the undergrowth and then another.

He turned.

"What the—bloody hell! What are you doing here?"

"A little jumpy, Sinclair?" Arthur Howells eyed the razor in his hand.

"What are you doing creeping up on a man?" Rowland folded the razor into its Bakelite handle. He felt a bit silly now.

"I've been following you since you left the meeting."

"What? Why?"

"Precautions. We know there's a spy in our organisation, we just don't know who. With your background, you understand, you are a definite possibility." Howells took a tin of tobacco and papers from his pocket and proceeded to roll a cigarette. "I must say, when I saw you with the coppers, I thought we'd found our traitor." He lit the cigarette. "Then I saw the papers... poor woman... terrible business."

Rowland turned back to the mirror and knotted the tie which he'd slung round his neck while he shaved.

"Then you call at some fancy joint to play tennis with the Canberra set and I thought, here we go..."

"We were simply collecting Miss Higgins," Rowland said. "Is that why you're here, Bluey? Because you're under the misapprehension I'm a spy of some sort?"

Howells shook his head. "I came to talk to you... you were walking across here as I pulled in. Gotta admit, I thought 'Who's he meeting while everybody is still asleep?' So I followed you... just one last check. Interesting scar you've got on your chest, I must say, Sinclair."

"I can assure you it wasn't self-inflicted."

Howells drew on his cigarette. "Who?"

"The SA, while I was in Germany."

"Why?"

"They didn't like the way I painted."

"So that's a review?"

"They broke my arm and forcibly burned a swastika into my chest with cigarettes," Rowland said, hoping that would be the end of Howells' curiosity. "I met Egon Kisch when I was trying to escape Germany."

Howells dropped his cigarette and crushed it under the ball of his foot. He shrugged. "Fair enough."

Rowland buttoned his waistcoat over his tie and grabbed his jacket from the low hanging branch on which he'd hung it.

Howells took a seat on a fallen trunk, his elbows on his knees, and his hands clasped loosely together. Clearly he had more to say. "Look, Sinclair, our intelligence is that there's a plot afoot to scuttle Kisch's visit."

"A plot?"

"We think that they intend to convince the Commonwealth Government to deny Egon a visa."

"Who's they?"

"To be honest, we're not sure. There are plenty of candidates in the Fascist corner."

"I see."

"I don't suppose you fancy a trip to Canberra, Sinclair?"

Rowland didn't. Indeed he couldn't think of any sane individual who actually fancied a trip to Canberra. There was very little there aside from the seat of parliament. "Just what exactly do you want me to do, Bluey?"

"We were hoping you might be our man in Canberra."

"You want me to spy for the Communist Party?" Rowland's tone made clear what he thought of the proposition.

"No, we know you're not a member. Look, we're a little concerned that the Fascists will do anything to keep Egon out. We just need a man in Canberra to speak for Egon in the right circles."

"I'm not exactly welcome in the right circles anymore."

"You're the best we've got."

"Surely you've got an actual Communist you can send to Canberra."

"We do have a man in Canberra. He's quitting."

"What do you mean quitting?"

"Exactly that. Something's spooked him. He says he'll give us till the end of this month to replace him and then he's done."

For a moment, Rowland paused, and then, slowly, he shook his head. "I'm not a spy, Bluey, and I'm certainly not a Communist."

"This is important, Rowly."

"I know, and I'll do what I can, but I can't—I won't—report to the Communist Party."

Howells regarded him silently for a moment. "Well, can't say fairer than that, I suppose. All right, Rowly, we'll send one of the faithful."

Rowland was mildly surprised albeit relieved that Howells abandoned any further attempts to persuade him. They talked then about motorcars, the Airflow in particular. And in that way they walked amiably back to *Hillend*. A good part of the household was now awake and Arthur Howells was invited to join them for breakfast or whatever a first meal taken after noon was called. He accepted gladly and sat down at the massive table in the homestead's grand dining room to what was a strange buffet of whatever the Hansens' houseguests were capable of cooking at that time, rather than a coherent meal.

His appetite stirred by bathing in the frigid creek, Rowland partook heartily of honey on bread, ham, quince paste and field mushrooms. A tureen of coffee was placed on the table and cups of brew ladled out. As a poet, Howells fitted rather well into the informality of the Bohemian gathering. Indeed, after eating his fill and participating in heated debate on A.D. Hope, he accompanied Hector and the other male guests back to the stream.

Rowland sat on the wide verandah with the women, sketching lazily into his notebook.

"I'm sure Hector imagines he's off to the Roman baths!" Mabel laughed as they watched her husband lead a troop of men with towels across the paddocks. "Poor man seems to believe bathing in freezing water with a dozen men is some kind of virility ritual."

Rowland grimaced.

Edna laughed. "Good Lord! I wonder what they get up to!"

"Let's try not to think about it," Rowland murmured.

Nora Blackwick, a printmaker, picked up the newspaper that Howells had brought with him and gave it a cursory perusal. "They still haven't identified that poor girl."

"What girl?" Edna asked.

"How could you not have heard?" Mabel was shocked. She handed the paper to Edna. "Poor lass was murdered and left in a culvert near Albury. Apparently the body was so horribly damaged—burnt, I understand—it's hard to be sure what she looked like."

Edna glanced at Rowland.

Mary Creswell shuddered. "Simply ghastly, and to think it happened so close by. Mabel, you must be careful."

"Don't be silly, Mary! We're all perfectly safe here." Mabel removed a tabby cat from the wicker settee and sat down.

Edna folded the paper and held her hand out to Rowland. "Shall we go for a stroll, Rowly?"

"If you'd like." He closed his notebook and took her hand.

They stepped out into the once formal garden. The box hedges had not been clipped in some years and the concrete statues looked somehow alive in a garden allowed to run wild. Mabel and Hector had repurposed the rose beds for growing vegetables. At the moment they were mostly fallow but for a few rows of parsnip and broccoli.

"Rowly, I'm so sorry." Edna looked up into his face.

He placed an arm around her shoulders. "It wasn't your fault."

"You really thought that poor girl was me?"

"I feared it might be. Until I saw the body."

"You saw the—oh, Rowly."

"It wasn't that bad." He lied for her sake. "I knew the moment I saw her that she wasn't you."

"That's why you were so cross," she said.

"I wasn't cross with you."

She sighed. "Bertie promised he'd left a message... I'm sure it was just a misunderstanding."

On that, Rowland did not comment. But he did break his usual rule with respect to Edna's loves. "What exactly do you see in Middleton, Ed?"

"I know you find Bertie tiresome, Rowly. But you mustn't judge him by the way he is with you."

"How else am I supposed to find him, Ed?"

"You intimidate him, I think. He's not like that otherwise."

"Why in heaven's name would I intimidate him?"

"Because everything comes so easily to you, darling. Wealth, social graces, connections... Bertie's not a Communist—he values those things. You don't even struggle with your art. You decide to paint something and suddenly it's there... perfect and magnificent."

"You know that's not true."

"Nonetheless, it's how it seems to Bertie. He's been writing the same novel for seven years and I don't think it's anywhere near finished. He's working for *The Canberra Times* reporting on parliament to make ends meet, and it's boring him silly."

"I see." Rowland had never before considered how Edna's loves regarded him. "You still haven't explained what you see in Middleton."

Edna smiled. "Bertie's a writer. He has a rather clever turn of phrase."

"If I'd known you could be won with adjectives..."

She rolled her eyes. "Don't be silly, Rowly. I can't be won."

7

TRAGEDY OF
YOUNG LOVE

Calf love is the easiest thing in the world to laugh at. That it is
less easy to endure was revealed by a boy criminal last week in a
strange letter to the magistrates who tried him. In that document
he described the stages of his downfall from the moment when
he realised that his first love could not be reciprocated.

Happily most boys and girls recover from the shock of their
first love affair without ruining themselves in the process. Yet
no one who has studied the adolescent mind can doubt for a
moment that, as a rule, the struggle is a severe one (writes
John Dean in the London "Daily Mail"). The first love affair
is far more serious, far more anxious, than people who have
grown up are ready to admit. Nor are its dangers made less,
or its burdens lightened, by the attitude commonly adopted
towards the vicinity—those who should be his friends. Almost
invariably they laugh and deride when a word of sympathy is
most eagerly desired and most urgently needed... This does
not mean, of course, that boys and girls are to be encouraged in
sentimentalism. But their feelings, however exaggerated, must
be accepted as genuine for the moment and honoured as such.
They must be taken if not seriously, at least respectfully. If they
feel that their strange emotional experience is being understood
and regarded sympathetically, their own common sense will
come to the rescue...

Kalgoorlie Miner, 11 January 1923

They were several hours into the long drive to Sydney when Milton mentioned the task entrusted to him by the Communist Party of Australia.

"You're going to Canberra?" Edna said.

"Well, Rowly's doing his bit to make sure Egon's visit goes without a hitch—I thought I should too."

"What exactly are you going to be doing?"

"Apparently the Fascists have sworn to stop Egon from speaking. The Party's worried that they might use political channels."

"And how do you plan to stop the Fascists?" Edna asked sceptically.

The poet shrugged. "They don't expect me to stop anything... just to keep them informed. Surveillance. They have a man there already, but he's got to leave before the end of this month."

"Why?"

"I don't know. His wife probably wants him home. Anyway, all I've got to do is relieve him. I'll meet with a few friendly parties, attend a few Party meetings, settle myself in the public gallery when parliament sits again, hang around the corridors eavesdropping, talk to people, drink at the right places... that sort of thing. Canberra's a small place—if they are planning to legislate against Egon it won't be difficult to find out."

Rowland recalled his discussion with Howells at the stream and shook his head as the reason why Howells gave up so easily became clear.

Milton noticed. "What?"

"Won't the New Guard be more likely to kidnap Kisch when he gets into the country? Abduction is more their style."

"Possibly, but it's not the New Guard. Rumour is the latest Fascist army is calling itself the Commonwealth Legion," Milton said. "The government will be wary of them too. The Party's worried that Lyons will feel obliged to legislate to stop Egon if for no other reason than to prevent a Fascist backlash."

Edna addressed more practical considerations. "How long do they want you to remain in Canberra? Where will you stay?"

"Until Egon arrives, I guess. I'm not sure where I'll stay... I was hoping to find a comrade to put me up."

"What about Bertie? He's minding a cottage in Ainslie for a friend... I could come with you if you like."

"Why don't we all go?" Rowland said, in no doubt that it was what Howells had intended all along. "We'll find a hotel. If Middleton is a part of Ley's tennis set, I doubt very much he'll want a Communist Party operative staying with him."

"I think operative might be overstating the case," Milton muttered. He brightened. "But why not—if we all go it might not be so unbearably dull."

It was with a little sadness that Rowland manoeuvred the Chrysler Airflow into the space that had been once occupied by his Mercedes in the converted stables at *Woodlands*. Milton and Clyde had mounted the mangled grille of the wrecked motorcar on the brick wall as a kind of memorial. Rowland had relinquished the Airflow's steering wheel to Clyde between Holbrook and Goulburn, and they had driven through, stopping only to refuel.

It was now ten in the evening but their arrival at *Woodlands* was amply announced by the voluble joy of a one-eared greyhound. The lights came on in the mansion before Rowland could calm his dog, and Mary Brown opened the door in her housecoat.

"Good evening, Mary," Rowland said sheepishly. "I'm so sorry we woke you."

The housekeeper sighed, conveying irritation, vexation and resignation in that single exhalation of breath. "If you'd telephoned, Master Rowly, I might have had some supper ready."

"We don't need supper, Mary. Please go back to bed."

"It'll have to be bread and butter! I can't do anything more!"

"Mary, we really don't..."

But she was already on her way to the kitchen.

They carried in their bags, Rowland taking Edna's up to her room, and though they might all have preferred to retire immediately, they returned to the breakfast room to eat a supper of bread and butter. The housekeeper had, it seemed, also managed to find a plate of cold roast beef, pickled eggs and a round of cheese which she served with a pot of tea and another of coffee. All this regardless of her employer's repeated instructions that she return to her bed. Mary, like many of the older servants in the Sinclairs' employ, still seemed to consider Rowland a child. Even in the house of which he was, for all intents and purposes, master.

It was a subdued meal as they went determinedly about the business of eating so that they could all be allowed to turn in. Rowland reached back to the sideboard to grab the silver tray of letters and messages which had accumulated in their absence. There was a number of telephone messages left by Detective Delaney from the previous week, the cause of which he now knew. A few invitations to dine, but none of the invitations to submit to exhibitions which had once filled his correspondence tray. Doubtless, the establishment was using its power to ensure that Rowland Sinclair was not given the opportunity to pedal his pro-Communist, alarmist views to the Australian public again.

As much as he'd always believed that he was not interested in the public recognition of his work, Rowland was vaguely wounded by the ostracism of the artistic hierarchy.

"Give them a couple more months, Rowly," Edna said quietly as he tossed the letters one by one back onto the tray. "They'll be sick of punishing you by then."

"I suspect it might take a little longer than that." Rowland was irritated that it bothered him.

The last letter had been delivered only that morning. It had been sealed with wax and smelled of eucalyptus. The writing on the envelope was florid. Rowland opened it.

Inside a sprig of gum leaves had been folded into the paper and, as he read, he smiled.

"Who's sending you leaves, Rowly?" Milton asked.

"Jemima... Mrs. Roche."

"From the tennis party?" Edna asked, surprised.

"She and Rowly are old flames," Milton said.

"Really? I don't remember—"

"Older than that. Childhood sweethearts."

"Oh, that's lovely! She's so very beautiful." Edna put down her knife and fork. "Why the leaves?"

Inwardly, Rowland flinched. He really wished Edna would not be quite so enthusiastic about the other women that crossed his path. "There's a gum tree on the Fairweathers' property with our initials carved into its trunk." He continued reading the letter. "Apparently it's still there."

"You carved your initials into a tree." Clyde laughed at the youthful sentimentality of it all.

"Actually, that was Miss Fairweather, as she was then. She's quite handy with a knife. I was just a fellow traveller for the most part."

"What do you mean?" Edna asked.

"Jemima told me what she wanted, and I did it."

"Really? I can't imagine you so easily persuaded."

"Nonsense!" Clyde said. "Rowly's too polite to refuse a lady. How many times has it got him into trouble already?"

Rowland smiled. "I was not quite fifteen. I expect I was too surprised Jemima had actually selected me for the role to put up much of a resistance."

"Young love," Milton sighed. "Tell me, did she break your heart, old mate?"

"Not specifically. We both went back to our respective boarding schools in February. As you know my father died in March of that year and I was shipped off to England. I haven't seen Jemima since."

"Oh, that's so sad." Edna heaped sugar into her tea. "Dragged apart by the most horrible circumstances. Perhaps now…"

Rowland folded the letter back into its envelope. "It was a youthful attachment, Ed, not Romeo and Juliet. But we were good friends. I didn't realise that I'd missed her till I saw her again." He tapped the envelope absently. "She writes that she needs my help."

"With what exactly?"

"She doesn't say… which is so very much like Jemima. She's summoning me."

"Will you go?" Edna kept her eyes on her cup.

"I could duck across to Yass while we're in Canberra, I suppose… Wilfred will probably be expecting me to call in and pay homage at some stage."

Wilfred Sinclair presided over the family's pastoral interests and the family itself from the Sinclairs' main holding near Yass. Personally mortified by Rowland's last exhibition, Wilfred's anger had not yet receded. Exchanges between the Sinclair brothers had been terse and bitter, if not blatantly hostile. As much as he regretted that Wilfred and his wife had been embarrassed, Rowland did believe the reaction disproportionate, and he was becoming fed up with Wilfred's need to repeatedly rebuke him.

Milton grinned. "I'm looking forward to seeing what Wilfred makes of the Airflow."

———————————   ———————————

They were greeted in the morning with ongoing newspaper stories of the young woman's body found in a culvert. The murder was described as either shocking or gruesome, its victim as beautiful. *The Sydney Morning Herald* was calling it the Albury Crime. The *Truth* was calling her the Pyjama Girl. She had not yet been identified.

Edna seemed particularly moved by the story. Perhaps it was because for a time it might have been her. "No one misses her enough to give her name... how very lonely she must be."

Rowland noted that his sketches had been amended a little before publication. The victim was given a fuller head of hair in a fashionable bob, her face made more angular. The body had now been embalmed and would be moved to Sydney in a specially designed coffin. Additional senior policemen had been assigned to the case.

Rowland's mother, who now resided in her own wing of *Woodlands House*, and who had of late acquired a taste for the *Truth's* lurid style, devoured its account of a body mutilated by a hammer. As she read, she made notes in a small notebook.

"What are you doing, Mother?" Rowland asked when he found her thus.

"Good morning, Aubrey dear. I'm making notes to remind myself of the details," she said. "I'm so busy these days it's the only way I know what I'm up to."

"You need to remember the details of this?" Rowland was perplexed. His mother had forgotten him entirely, addressing him only by his late brother's name for years. She'd selectively forgotten a great deal of the past twenty years, including the manner in which her husband had died and the man he was when he was alive. In recent months, she seemed to have also forgotten her own age, convincing herself that she was in her mid-thirties, despite the fact that her eldest son was forty-three. It seemed odd that the details of a murder would be the one thing she thought important enough to write down so she didn't forget.

"Everybody at my club is talking about it and you know I don't like speculation. I want to make sure I have the facts somewhere when I need them."

"I'm not sure the *Truth* shares your fondness for the facts, Mother."

"Oh, you're becoming as stuffy as your brother!" Elisabeth made a note of the colour of the pyjamas in which the young woman's body had been found.

"Mother, I was just speaking with Aunt Mildred. She's about to take the *SS Marella* to Singapore next week. She wonders if you might like to join her." In fact Elisabeth Sinclair had agreed to the trip months before, but the arrangement was one of those things she was predisposed to forget. As the date of departure drew closer, Rowland had taken to broaching the subject more regularly, obtaining her agreement all over again each time. Experience told him that this was the best way to handle any change in his mother's routine.

"I know, she already asked me. I told her I couldn't possibly leave you on your own for three months. Whatever would people think?"

Rowland smiled. His parents had taken a tour of the Continent when he was three, leaving him and his brothers in the care of a nanny and the housekeeper for nearly a year. "I won't be alone, Mother. There's Mr. Isaacs and Mr. Watson Jones not to mention Miss Higgins. And I am a grown man."

"I'm not sure it's becoming for a woman in my position to take a cruise unescorted."

"Aunt Mildred will be there to chaperone you. It couldn't possibly be more proper."

Still Elisabeth was reluctant. "It's not just you, Aubrey. Mr. Isaacs and I are reading 'The Rime of the Ancient Mariner' together. We've only just finished the preludes. I couldn't possibly leave now."

Rowland was aware that his mother was besotted with Milton. The poet, who'd been raised by his own grandmother, had a way with old ladies and was unfailingly kind to Elisabeth. And, of course, Elisabeth believed she was thirty-five.

"To be honest, Mother, Mr. Isaacs, all of us in fact, find we must go to Canberra for a while."

"My Lord! Canberra? Whatever for?"

"Milt has some business there."

Elisabeth leant towards Rowland and whispered, "Poetry?"

Rowland wondered what exactly his mother thought the business of poetry entailed, but he nodded.

"I see." Elisabeth sighed. "Well I suppose I'd better sail to Singapore then. We'll be the first that ever burst into that silent sea."

Rowland kissed his mother's cheek, a little alarmed that she, too, had taken to robbing the romantic poets. "I'll let Aunt Mildred know and make the arrangements."

Milton walked in then, a thick volume of Coleridge's extended rime under his arm.

"Mr. Isaacs." Elisabeth's face lifted. "Aubrey tells me you're going to Canberra!"

"I'm afraid so, Mrs. Sinclair. And I hear you're going cruising."

Elisabeth's smile was coy. "I am sailing for Singapore, Mr. Isaacs."

"Are you indeed? Well, I guess Coleridge has never been more relevant."

In the following week Rowland booked suites at the Hotel Canberra and ensured his mother and her entourage of private nurses would be adequately accommodated on the SS *Marella*. He made several telephone calls and sent telegrams in his search for a suitable craft in which to make the proposed trek to Fremantle. Aviation was an expensive business and so he was reasonably confident of borrowing an aeroplane in return for investment, or sponsorship, or some other form of cash flow. He would use the Gipsy Moth if he could get nothing else.

Since he could not possibly install his greyhound in a hotel, even one in Canberra, he spent many guilty hours with his dog to compensate. Lenin took his master's attention, as he did Rowland's absences, in his stride. *Woodlands House*, with its doting servants and several cats was, after all, a comfortable place to wait.

Finally, Rowland drove out to *Tudor House* near Bowral where his nephew was a boarder so he could take the boy for a ride in the new Airflow. With Lenin in the back seat, Rowland put the motorcar through her paces.

Seven-year-old Ernest Sinclair seemed quite overwhelmed by the Chrysler.

"What do you think, mate? Do you like her?"

"You can't put the top down," Wilfred's eldest son noted disapprovingly. Ernest's small face pulled into one of his father's more severe expressions.

"No... but look, there's a sunroof. You could pop your head through there if you really wanted to feel the breeze." Rowland retracted the roof hatch so Ernest could satisfy himself that indeed one could.

"What's that?" Ernest jumped at the crackling static.

"It's the radio." Rowland showed his nephew how to tune in a station, smiling as he watched the boy thaw and become enthralled.

"You're not going to race this motorcar, are you, Uncle Rowly?" Ernest wound open the windscreen. He had been watching when Rowland's Mercedes flew off the Maroubra Speedway and collided with a light pole. As much as he was his father's son, responsible, well-brought-up Ernest loved his wayward uncle.

"No, Ernie, I don't think I'll be racing again."

"I think that's best."

8

PEACE FORCE

———————◆———————

Special Police At Canberra
TO PATROL CAPITAL
ONLY DOZEN MEN ON DUTY NOW

CANBERRA, Tuesday

Immediate steps are being taken by the Commonwealth Government through the Chiefs of Commonwealth Police, Major Jones, to recruit a special body of Commonwealth peace officers to protect Canberra, in the event of any civil disturbances. Special officers will be appointed under the provisions of the Peace Officers' Act, 1925, which may be invoked by the Government this week. The vulnerability of Canberra at the present time is recognised by the Ministry, as Canberra's police force consists of only about a dozen men who, in the event of serious trouble, would easily be outnumbered. Further, the Federal capital is extremely isolated. While no actual threat of trouble has been made, it is recognised no time should be lost in view of the present state of affairs in seeing the capital is adequately safeguarded. For this reason some hundreds of Canberra residents will be called on to act as volunteers. They will be armed with batons. Major Jones has already begun a canvass for special men and his first approaches have been made to ex-students of the Royal Military College, Duntroon, who were given employment in the Commonwealth public service when Duntroon College closed at Canberra 18 months ago.

TROUBLE NOT CONTEMPLATED

While the possibility of invasion by members of a lawless organisation is not contemplated, strategists nevertheless point out just how easily Canberra could be taken by force, even if only for a few hours. But in that few hours much could be done to create endless confusion and possibly irretrievable damage to valuable records and documents in Government departments, and at Federal Parliament House. It would be possible for an invading force to reach Canberra in five hours by fast motor cars from Sydney and for them to take possession of Parliament House before the alarm could be given. Their exit could be made before Canberra officials were aware of what had taken place. Already the Prime Minister, Mr. Lyons, has taken the precaution of having a police guard at his residence every night, but this is dispensed with during the day.

LIFE THREATENED

It was disclosed that Mr. Lyons has received letters recently threatening his life. One letter, signed by "Gunman", declared that the writer had "shot better_____than you and Bruce. I'll get you too," he added.

Daily Examiner, 11 May 1932

A t *Woodlands House* servants packed trunks and sent them on ahead by rail to avoid overloading the Airflow. Clyde and Rowland also despatched travelling kits of paints and brushes and the various tools of their trade. Edna packed her camera and developing chemicals. If they were to spend the next weeks in the fledging capital, they would need something to keep them occupied besides vague notions of skulduggery. Founded some twenty years earlier, Canberra's population was small and for the most part transient. Though she now housed the Federal Legislature, the city was not much more than an interim Parliament House.

Clyde, who'd always been particularly interested in architecture, looked forward to inspecting Walter Burley Griffin's designed city in the middle of the bush. He hoped the contrast of structure against isolation would provide much potential for the composition of landscapes. For Rowland, a portrait artist, the city also offered subjects. Those who walked the halls of power, and those who built them. Edna was keen to capture both the structures and people on film. Indeed, as much as the decision that they all go to Canberra had been a whim, they were finding themselves increasingly and unexpectedly enthused about the possibilities for their art.

Rowland had received another letter and two telephone calls from Jemima Roche while they were in Sydney, each demanding he come to see her as soon as possible. She would say nothing more about the matter with which she needed his help, but her letter and conversation were so cheerful that Rowland was not particularly concerned by the plea.

"Shouldn't you go now?" Edna asked. "Perhaps she's in danger of some sort."

Rowland laughed. "Jemima screams 'help' if she needs a cup of tea, Ed. I expect she's simply bored in Yass."

"But still…"

"If it was urgent, she'd tell me. She knows I'd come immediately."

They waved Elisabeth Sinclair bon voyage from the dock. By the time the *Marella* set sail, she was excited to go. Milton had brought her the works of William Somerset Maugham, Rudyard Kipling and other former residents of Raffles—where she would spend her time in Singapore—and had somehow ignited a passion for the tropics.

While Rowland did wonder if the cruise was an independence too far, he was comforted by the knowledge that Elisabeth would be accompanied by three nurses and his formidable Aunt Mildred. She would not be alone, uncared for, or misunderstood. And though Elisabeth would probably not remember the details of the trip for long, while she was on it, she would feel as youthful as she believed she was.

The United Australia Party under Lyons was returned to government on the 15th of September 1934, albeit in coalition with Earle Page's Country Party. While the result was not celebrated at *Woodlands House*, it was not unexpected, and they danced and toasted the new term regardless. On the 19th of September the NSW police continued their campaign to establish the identity of the Pyjama Girl by embarking on the massive task of tracing every woman under forty who had not voted in the election.

Woodlands House was left in the sure hands of Mary Brown as its residents headed west of the Great Dividing Range. On the long road to Canberra, Rowland became better acquainted with the various sounds of the Airflow's engine. She did not roar like the supercharged Mercedes but she had her own song.

The Hotel Canberra had been designed to accommodate parliamentarians, the odd visiting dignitary and the most senior public servants. As Canberra became more established, its initial clientele found more permanent accommodation and the hotel was now open to casual guests.

Rowland had booked a suite for Edna and double bedrooms for himself, Clyde, and Milton, each with their own bathroom. Appointed in the style of a First Class hotel, it was, as a base, quite adequate. Luxurious enough, indeed, to quite distress Clyde.

"They're double bedrooms, Rowly. We could share."

"Yes, but I'd rather not." Rowland appreciated Clyde's attempts at thrift on his behalf, but he had no intention of implementing such extreme measures. "Wil tells me our wool clip was excellent this year. I may yet squander my fortune but it will not be with a hotel bill."

Rowland had also taken an additional private sitting room which he'd had cleared of furniture for use as a studio. This too Clyde thought an extravagance.

"It would be an extravagance to spend a month in Canberra doing nothing," Rowland replied firmly. "At least this way we can work."

"Terrific... the not quite idle rich!" Clyde muttered.

Edna laughed and Milton told him to quit being such an old woman. The poet had always been more comfortable with what he called the redistribution of Rowland's wealth.

As parliament was not due to resume for over a week, the Hotel Canberra, indeed the city itself, was relatively quiet. They settled in and set out to explore the capital before dinner, familiarising themselves with her concentric geography. They returned to the hotel feeling as though they'd been for a walk in the country more than in a city centre.

It wasn't till quite late that evening that Milton left his companions to make contact with the man he was relieving.

Rowland tossed him the keys to the Airflow.

Milton tossed them back. "The Chrysler might be a bit noticeable, comrade."

"Yes, of course. Sorry."

"No problems, Rowly." Milton wrapped a deep red scarf around his neck against the plummeting evening temperature. "It's not far. I'm going to take shanks' pony."

"Where are you going?"

"Parliament House."

"Won't it be closed to the public?"

"I expect that will make it easy for him to show me around so I can get my bearings."

In Milton's absence they played cards in the sitting room of Edna's suite. Having no idea how long the meeting would take, they did not think to be concerned about the poet until about eleven o'clock. When he had still not returned at midnight, Rowland and Clyde decided a stroll to Parliament House was in order.

"You stay here, Ed, in case he gets back."

"And if he does, don't let him go looking for us," Clyde murmured as he buttoned his coat. "Or else we could be chasing each other in circles all night."

Parliament House took on a new beauty at night. Her white walls seemed almost luminescent, monolithic. They could see the building from the Hotel Canberra, a white-iced wedding cake lit by lines of streetlights.

It was not till they were much closer that they saw the Federal Police vehicles parked outside the House with their lights directed at the main stairs. The area around the stairs had been cordoned off and constables stood ready to move any passers-by on. A body lay crumpled near the base of the stairs, a man. A pool of dark blood stained the concrete. He had fallen facedown, up the stairs, a red scarf visible under the turned lapel of his overcoat.

Clyde cursed under his breath and he and Rowland tried to get through the cordon.

"Fellas! Over here."

Milton stood with a uniformed policeman.

"What—" Rowland began, relieved to see the poet.

"I was passing by on my evening stroll," Milton emphasised the last two words, "when I spotted this poor chap. I tried to help, realised he was dead, and raised the alarm."

"Are you all right?"

"Me—I'm perfectly well. I'm afraid someone's killed Mr…" He looked hopefully at the policeman with him.

The officer shook his head silently.

"Unfortunately," Milton said, his eyes darting towards the men standing near the body, "nobody's quite sure who's in charge, so I can't leave."

In the light, Rowland noticed the subtle differences in uniform.

"The unfortunate gentleman's demise is being attended by the Commonwealth Investigations Branch, the Commonwealth Police, and something called a Commonwealth Peace Officer." Milton leant over and whispered loudly, "I'm not sure any of them are real coppers."

At this, the officer beside Milton seemed noticeably affronted.

Rowland attempted to clarify the situation. "Can you tell me who's in charge, sir?" he asked the officer.

"That would be me." The man who walked over to claim authority was military in his carriage. He was about fifty, his hair a distinguished grey, parted in the middle and cut close at the sides and back. "Major Harold Jones, Chief of Police. Can I ask your name, sir?"

"Rowland Sinclair, Major Jones. This is Mr. Clyde Watson Jones and I presume you've met Mr. Isaacs."

"What brings you here at this time of night, Mr. Sinclair?"

"Mr. Watson Jones and I were looking for Mr. Isaacs. He'd stepped out for a stroll and hadn't returned."

"Returned to where, Mr. Sinclair?"

"We're staying at the Hotel Canberra."

"Can I ask your business in the capital, Mr. Sinclair?"

"Mr. Watson Jones and I are artists—we plan to paint."

"And Mr. Isaacs?"

"I'm a poet."

"I see." Major Jones looked Milton up and down. "Is there any particular reason you chose to walk here, alone, at this hour, Mr. Isaacs?"

"No, not really." Milton shrugged. "I could see Parliament House from the hotel... I like to walk at night—it clears the mind, puts me in the frame of mind to write. There's something about starlight that unleashes the muse, don't you think?"

Quite admirably, neither Rowland nor Clyde scoffed.

"And you've never met the deceased before?" the major pressed.

"No, sir." There was no deceit in Milton's voice. "I thought the poor bloke was just drunk at first... then I saw the blood."

Major Jones nodded. "Very well. If you'd just give the constable your details, I'll let you gentlemen get on." He turned to the body and then back. "For the moment I'd be grateful if you gentlemen say nothing about this."

"I beg your pardon?"

"It's in the interests of the investigation that the details and indeed the fact of this incident are not made public."

"I'm not sure I understand, Major Jones." Rowland glanced sideways at Clyde and Milton. It seemed an unusual request.

"What about his family?" Milton asked.

"What family?" Jones asked sharply. "Didn't you just state that you did not know the deceased, Mr. Isaacs?"

"I don't... but everybody has a family of some sort."

"The deceased's next-of-kin will be contacted, in due course. We only ask that you say nothing to the newspapers until the relevant facts have been established."

"Yes, of course," Clyde replied for all of them. "We were just passing by."

"Thank you, gentlemen. I'll say goodnight then." He shook their hands in turn. "You'd best get in from the cold."

They said little on the walk home, aware they were being followed. By this, Rowland was not alarmed—a routine verification of their whereabouts he assumed. Despite the hour, they went directly to Edna's suite. The sculptress was much relieved to see them.

"I was just beginning to think I should go after you," she said. "Whatever were you all doing?"

Clyde and Rowland looked to Milton.

Though they were alone in the suite, Milton kept his voice low. As he had told the police, he'd noticed the body as he passed, but he added, "I suspect the poor bloke is Jim Kelly."

"You knew him?" Clyde frowned though he had suspected as much.

"Not really. I was supposed to meet Comrade Kelly outside Parliament House. We were to identify ourselves by wearing red scarves."

It was only then that Rowland noticed Milton was no longer wearing the red scarf he'd put on when he left. The poet pulled it from the large pocket of his overcoat. "I took it off before the police arrived... in case Kelly's killer was still hanging around looking for Communists to murder."

"But why didn't you tell the police who the poor man was?" Edna demanded, horrified.

"They'll find out soon enough... if they didn't know already. I couldn't tell them his name without revealing that I was meeting him and why I was meeting him."

"You lied to the police!" Clyde shook his head in disbelief.

"Depends how you look at it. I don't know for sure that the dead man was Comrade Kelly... it might have just been some unfortunate bloke in a red scarf."

"You really should let them know who he was, Milt," Rowland said quietly, an image of the nameless girl in the Albury morgue flashing upon his inner eye. "He deserves that dignity."

Milton exhaled. "You're right. If they haven't worked it out by tomorrow, I'll tell them, or at least get Bluey Howells to report him missing."

"Had he been shot?" Rowland asked, deciding to leave the veracity of Milton's police statement alone.

Milton closed his eyes. "No, we would all have heard a shot. His throat had been slit—I saw it when I checked to see if he was breathing. The blood was still warm... it was steaming in the cold..." He looked down at his hands, the browning blood on the white cuffs of his shirt. "I tried to help him, but he was dead."

"Oh, Milt, how horrible." Edna took his hand. "Are you all right?"

He embraced her fondly. "I could use a drink."

On that score Clyde obliged from the contents of the drinks cabinet. They could all use something to warm the blood a little.

"So what now?" Rowland asked, loosening his tie.

Milton groaned. "I don't know. Kelly was supposed to brief me and hand over whatever he'd found."

Edna regarded Milton carefully. "You're only here to raise the alarm in case the government attempts to legislate against Mr. Kisch aren't you?"

"Yes, of course."

"And nothing else?"

"You have my word."

"Why would someone kill Mr. Kelly over a visiting speaker?"

"We don't know that it was anything to do with him being a Communist." Rowland stifled a yawn. "It's possible that he was killed for an entirely unrelated reason."

"Or not," Clyde added. "If it was discovered that Kelly was keeping an eye on parliament for the Party, there are many people who would consider execution justified."

"Poor blighter couldn't have been doing much," Milton murmured. "Parliament hasn't sat for a while. God knows how he's kept himself occupied."

"Perhaps we should go home," said Edna. "Milt could be next."

"You're assuming there's no one who wants to kill him in Sydney," Clyde muttered.

"What do you suppose Major Jones' 'say nothing of this' edict was all about?" Milton pondered aloud.

"Blood on the steps of parliament is probably not ideal, especially with the Duke of Gloucester about to visit," Clyde replied.

Rowland yawned. "Surely the newspapers will get hold of it…"

"I didn't see any reporters, did you?"

"No, I didn't." Rowland did wonder why not. Perhaps it was because parliament was not sitting. Or because it was so late.

Edna looked at him and smiled. "We should call it a night," she said. "Rowly's falling asleep."

Clyde stretched. "Not just him. This may all make more sense in the light of morning."

9

SECERT

SECRET

DECIPHER OF A CABLEGRAM FROM SNUFFBOX, LONDON, 13.10.34.

DS/107 OCTOBER 12TH REFERRING TO YOUR TELEGRAM OCTOBER 11TH

Egon Erwin KISCH, Czechoslovak, born Prague, April 29th, 1885, important Communist member International Society Proletarian authors. International speaker for anti-war and anti-Fascist cause. Has specialised in Far Eastern social and political conditions. His landing in the United Kingdom is prohibited. Description - About five feet eight inches, sturdy, thick set build, black hair, straight, parted on the right, black eyebrows and moustache, swarthy, slightly hooked nose, slight frown between eyes, Dutch doll looking face.

Major Harold Jones appraised the four young people sitting in his office with an air of indulgent patience. They were an interesting group to say the least. Sinclair was clearly a man of means, well-dressed and groomed with just enough carelessness to give him a slightly rakish air. The intelligence man noted the smear of green paint on Sinclair's sleeve, and that his dark hair had been combed without the benefit of styling cream to keep it in place. It spoke of confidence as much as indifference. There was a sharp observance in the deep blue of the artist's eyes. Jones knew that his scrutiny was being returned. Sinclair was sizing him up and it was probably not for a painting.

The woman was intriguing. Beautiful—unusually so—she was clearly not intimidated in any way by his official capacity. The files revealed she lived with Sinclair and the other gentlemen in what might have been called a morally questionable artistic commune if it wasn't in Woollahra. The precise nature of her relationship with Sinclair, Isaacs and Watson Jones was the subject of speculation and, as yet, unestablished. According to the officer who had been assigned to their most recent surveillance, they had all gone directly to her suite when they'd returned to the hotel the previous night. It seemed ludicrous, but perhaps this slip of a girl was the cunning mastermind... perhaps the men reported to her.

Watson Jones' person belied the ostentatious double-barrel of his name. He had the weathered face and strong hands of a labourer and was indeed a unionist and a Communist. His accent was quite broad—of rural origin perhaps. He seemed the most uncomfortable.

And then there was Isaacs, in his purple velvet jacket, gold-spotted cravat, and a beret, for pity's sake. A Leninist goatee more than hinted at his politics. The good major shook his head. Isaacs' surveillance file was extensive.

"Mr. Sinclair, suppose you tell me what you and your companions are really doing in Canberra," Jones said, not unpleasantly.

"I believe I've already told you, Major Jones. Clyde and I are painting and Milton is doing whatever it is that poets do."

"And Miss Higgins?"

"I'm a sculptor, Major Jones," Edna answered for herself. "I'm rather interested in the way the capital is being carved out of the countryside. I think I may base a piece on it when I get back home. In the meantime I plan to take photographs from which to work."

Jones seemed impressed. "Photography, you say?" He tapped his forehead trying to shake loose a name. "There's a chap in the Federal Capital Commission you should meet... what's his name... he's been taking snaps of Canberra for the last decade... Mildenhall! That's him. You should have a chat with him."

"I'd be delighted, if he has the time."

"I'll tell him to get in touch."

"Why thank you, Major Jones. That's so very kind of you."

"A pleasure, Miss Higgins. Now, Mr. Isaacs, are you trying to tell me that it is a coincidence that both you and the deceased are members of the same political party?"

Wrong-footed by the abrupt change in subject and tone, Milton faltered briefly. "So you know who the dead man is?"

"Yes—a Mr. James Kelly, previously of St. Kilda, Melbourne. A known Communist... like yourself."

Milton shrugged. "A small coincidence. Mr. Kelly and I possibly have other coincidental matters in common."

"Like the fact that you were both wearing a red scarf last night?"

"I beg your pardon?"

"The peace officer who was first on the scene recalls you were wearing a red scarf."

"It's hardly an unusual fashion choice, Major Jones." Milton had found his step once more. "It was a cold night. I'd warrant most sensible people out were wearing scarves. Some of them, surely, would have been red."

Jones considered him silently for a while. "Can you tell me, Mr. Isaacs, how exactly you plan to spend your time in Canberra?"

"I'm composing a poem in the epic style, Major Jones, using the journey of a new nation as it searches for its political home in a world where the gods of right and left are at war and the winds of change push the ships of government into daunting and uncharted waters."

"And where precisely will you compose this epic poem, Mr. Isaacs?" Jones looked as hard at the poet's friends as he did at Milton himself. Rowland and Clyde maintained faces trained by poker marathons at *Woodlands House*. Edna laughed.

"Have you ever heard of such a dull poem, Major Jones? For pity's sake, forbid him to write it!"

"I'm afraid poetry, whatever the subject, is not a crime, Miss Higgins." Jones smiled faintly.

Milton scowled at Edna. "When the people's elected representatives eventually return to work, I plan to sit in the public gallery of Parliament House and absorb inspiration from democracy at play. Until then I might call on my local member, apprise him of my concerns as a constituent."

Rowland made an attempt to redirect the conversation. "Do you have any idea who killed Mr. Kelly, sir?"

"I'm afraid I'm not at liberty to say, Mr. Sinclair. But we have not made any arrests." Jones stood. "Thank you for your time, gentlemen, Miss Higgins."

And so they were dismissed.

They decided to walk back to the Hotel Canberra, stopping to take tea at the Kingston Tea and Supper Rooms. Milton took a copy of the *Canberra Times* from under his arm and dropped it onto the table.

Clyde unfolded the broadsheet, scanning the front page. Stories of the young woman's body found near Albury still dominated. "Does it say anything about Jim Kelly?" he asked.

"Yes, there's a small article." Milton directed him to the third page. "Says James Kelly died of a wound inflicted by an unknown assailant, in Canberra."

"In Canberra? They weren't more specific?"

"Absolutely no mention of Parliament House."

"This is rather a strange place," Edna said, pouring tea from the china pot that had been delivered to their table.

"What did Bluey Howells say?" Rowland asked, knowing Milton had telephoned him that morning.

"Not much I feel comfortable repeating in front of Ed."

"Does he have any idea who might have…?"

"Bluey believes that Kelly might have stumbled onto something the Fascists wanted to keep under wraps." Milton sweetened his tea with honey.

"What exactly?"

"No idea."

"Do you think it's likely?" Clyde was sceptical. "All poor Kelly was doing was keeping an eye out for an attempt to legislate against Egon's visit. It's not even illegal. Surely no one would kill him for that."

"That's all I'll be doing," Milton said slowly. "We can't be sure that's all Kelly was doing."

"That's true," Rowland conceded. Parliament had not even resumed. Kelly may well have been keeping himself busy with something else for the Party. Something that would get him killed.

"Still," Clyde said, "we're talking about a bunch of Australian polo and tiddlywinks types, not the Brownshirts. Kelly's throat was cut."

"Do you remember when Rowly's uncle was killed by the Fascist Legion?" Edna reached for Rowland's hand—an unspoken apology for raising the tragedy. "They hadn't meant to kill him… someone just went too far. Perhaps that happened here too."

Rowland pressed her hand gently to let her know he was not offended. His beloved uncle had been killed nearly three years before. It was that which had first set Rowland in opposition to the Fascist militias which until then he'd treated as a joke. His perspective had changed a great deal since then.

"It's possible," he allowed. "But it's hard to imagine how one could unintentionally cut a man's throat."

"Perhaps they intended only to rough Mr. Kelly up, to frighten him off," Edna suggested. "But he resisted and in the process—"

"Had he been robbed?" Clyde asked. "Perhaps we're looking for a grand scheme in what was actually a simple slash and grab. I presume things are as tough here for some people as they are anywhere."

Milton shook his head. "He hadn't been robbed. I saw his pocket watch when I was checking to see if he was alive. A thief would have taken it."

"And you heard nothing?" Rowland asked. "Before you found the body?"

"No." Milton stroked the hair on his chin. "I did think I heard something afterwards, when I found the body, but it might just have been that I was rattled. I thought I heard someone curse... but maybe it was me."

"What did you do?"

"I shouted. A guard, I'm not sure if he was private or some kind of police officer, came running from somewhere... I'm not sure where exactly."

"And he telephoned for help?"

"Actually he arrested me."

Rowland put down his cup, surprised. Jones had mentioned nothing about Milton being a suspect let alone arrested. "How—"

"The major and his cronies arrived, ascertained that I didn't have a weapon and I wasn't covered in enough blood to have committed the act. Apparently this chap who arrested me—Constable Smith, I think they called him—had overstepped his authority in any case."

"Did they find a weapon anywhere?"

"No."

Rowland frowned. "Until we know what this is all about, Milt, perhaps you should—"

"Sorry, Rowly," Milton said firmly. "If someone killed Comrade Kelly over this, it's even more important that I try and find out what the ruling class is up to."

Rowland hadn't really expected Milton to respond otherwise. "Fair enough, but we need to watch your back."

"You could at least stop attracting attention to yourself," Clyde muttered.

"What do you mean by that?" Milton demanded.

Clyde pointed to the beret. "You're dressed like a French clown. If nothing else you're embarrassing the Party."

Milton laughed good-naturedly. "Dost thou know who made thee... gave thee clothing of delight."

"Blake," Rowland said. "I believe he was talking about a sheep."

"That figures," Clyde said tersely.

Edna intervened more diplomatically. "Perhaps you should try to look less memorable... more like Rowly... just while you're sitting in the public gallery. Consider it a disguise."

"Less memorable?" Rowland said, affronted.

Edna sighed. Navigating a route between three male egos was occasionally awkward. "You know what I mean." She smiled at him and he forgave her everything.

They walked by way of Parliament House on their way to the hotel, partly because it was the most direct route, and partly because they wanted to look again at the scene of the crime, hoping to ascertain where the assailant may have hidden, if indeed that was who Milton had heard cursing.

To their consternation there was no police cordon. The cement stairs had been scrubbed clean of blood. There was no sign that James Kelly had died between the coats of arms of Britain and the

Commonwealth. Public servants, Parliament House staff and the visiting public walked unknowingly on the place where Kelly had taken his last breath.

"There might easily have been someone behind there," Edna pointed out the low walls that defined a terraced walkway at the top of the steps. "He could have slipped away afterwards."

Rowland scanned the green fields around them. There were few buildings or trees to provide any sort of cover. Parliament House stood starkly in the middle of a planned landscape that was as yet nowhere.

"He might have gone into the House," Clyde suggested.

"Wouldn't it be locked?"

"There'd be ways to get in," Milton said confidently.

They proceeded into Parliament House through to King's Hall. Edna paused before the bronze statue of George V in cape and garters, considering it with a sculptor's eye.

"What do you think?" Rowland asked.

"It's not a bad piece," Edna said thoughtfully. "I'm not sure it works in here though."

Rowland understood. George V seemed more lonely than regal in the middle of the grand space. Perhaps he should have been depicted with Queen Mary to keep him company, or at least sitting with a book. Alone, in full regalia, he seemed a little at a loose end. Rowland patted his majesty's heeled court shoe sympathetically.

To the monarch's left was the green chamber of the House of Representatives, to his right the red Senate. Rowland cast his eyes across the art deco patterns and details echoed in the balustrades and windows, the classical allusions in the plaster work and light poles designed to suggest the Greco-Egyptian ruins. There was a glorious modern symmetry and simplicity about the building that appealed to him.

They fell into a conversation about the lines and features of the building and the artworks within it. They were artists after all, and no matter what they found themselves in the middle of, that was how they looked upon the world.

Distracted by Montford's bas-reliefs on the pillars either side of the lonesome king, they didn't notice the gentlemen who emerged from the Parliamentary Library.

"Rowly?"

Rowland turned.

Two gentlemen of similar ilk: immaculate, conservative, bastions of the establishment, and comfortable in the halls of power.

"Wil... Your Excellency..." Rowland's eyes moved from his brother to Stanley Melbourne Bruce who stood beside him. Bruce had been Australia's eighth prime minister and a minister in the previous Lyons government. Now he was officially Australia's High Commissioner in Britain.

Rowland and his companions had met the Bruces when they were in London the year before. Indeed, they had become particular favourites of Mrs. Ethel Bruce whom they remembered as an ally.

Stanley Bruce and Wilfred Sinclair tipped their hats to Edna and stood in expectant silence for Rowland to explain himself.

Rowland offered Bruce his hand. "Welcome back, Your Excellency. You may remember Miss Higgins, Mr. Isaacs and Mr. Watson Jones."

"Indeed, I do." Bruce shook hands with Clyde and Milton.

"What brings you to the capital?" Rowland asked.

"I was about to ask you the same question," Wilfred said curtly.

"We have a friend who lives here, Mr. Sinclair," Edna said sweetly. "We thought we'd pay him a visit and take in the capital."

Wilfred looked around the hall. "Where is this friend of yours?"

"Oh, he's not here. I'm afraid we haven't got round to visiting Bertie yet. We've been rather distracted by this marvellous building."

"Is Mrs. Bruce with you, Your Excellency?" Rowland asked, ignoring the scepticism in Wilfred's gaze.

"Ethel is at *Oaklea* with Kate," Bruce replied. "This is rather an unofficial visit. She's adamant that she's seen quite enough of Canberra, and she does enjoy the company of the Sinclair children."

Rowland smiled. The Bruces had been the first couple to live in the Lodge, the official residence of the prime minister. He could imagine that Ethel Bruce found the nation's capital a little dull.

"Where are you staying, Rowly?" Wilfred demanded.

"The Hotel Canberra."

"I presume you'll be heading back to Sydney soon."

Rowland was saved from responding by the approach of another gentleman. Tall and long-limbed, he wore a black suit and small round spectacles. He strode rather than walked, with a rhythm that made his long gait almost a march.

It was Bruce who greeted the newcomer. "Blackrod! Can we be of assistance?" Unfailingly civil, he took the time to introduce Robert Broinowski, the Usher of the Blackrod, despite the clear urgency of the civil servant's approach.

Broinowski glanced briefly at Rowland and his companions before speaking. "If I could have a private word, gentlemen."

It was then Rowland caught sight of Major Jones entering the hall with a number of officers in tow.

"What's going on?" Clyde whispered as Bruce and Wilfred stepped away to talk to the Usher of the Blackrod. Both men clearly alarmed by the information to which they were being made privy.

Jones spotted Rowland and his companions. He nodded to Broinowski as he walked past to demand their business at Parliament House on that day.

"No business, Major Jones," Rowland said calmly. "We were just viewing the House."

The chief of police signalled one of his officers. "Would you wait here with Sergeant Cook, please?"

"Why?"

"I would like to speak to you, but there are some matters I must attend to first."

"Are you arresting us?" Milton demanded.

"No, I'm simply requesting your co-operation."

"Yes, of course we'll stay," Edna cut Milton off.

Sergeant Cook ushered his charges through to the Parliamentary Library so they could take seats while they waited. It was a welcome consideration as it was nearly two hours before Major Jones returned. Bruce and Wilfred entered with him and stood in the background, arms folded, and silent.

Rowland rose to his feet. Clyde and Milton followed suit.

"I ask you again," Jones said slowly. "What are you doing in Parliament House today?"

"We wanted to look again at the scene of last night's crime," Milton said defiantly. "Of course we were surprised to find no sign whatsoever that a man had been brutally killed on the steps of Parliament House!"

"What did you expect, Mr. Isaacs? A memorial?"

"We came into the House as tourists, Major Jones, that's all," Rowland said before Milton could explode.

"Where in the House have you been?"

"We didn't get much further than King's Hall. What's going on, Major Jones? Has someone else been killed?"

Jones' eyes narrowed. "Are you expecting someone else to be killed, Mr. Sinclair?"

"Not at all. But I can't imagine the chief of police would be taking such an interest if someone was stealing cutlery from the dining room."

"I understand the four of you were in the town of Albury earlier this month."

"Yes." Rowland wondered uneasily where Jones was going with the question.

"I believe you attended a tennis party at *Willowview* on the Howlong road."

Rowland could see Wilfred's face darkening. "Yes, briefly," he said, watching his brother tense further.

"What is this about, Major Jones?" Edna asked.

Jones studied the four of them. "You will tell me if you intend to leave Canberra."

"Are you seriously telling us not to leave town?" Milton demanded hotly. "Of what exactly are you accusing us?"

"I am simply making a request, Mr. Isaacs."

Wilfred could stay silent no longer. "My brother will be only too happy to let you know when he or his companions leave Canberra, Harold. I'll see to it. You have my word."

"You'll what?" Rowland turned, flaring at his brother's presumption.

Wilfred pulled Rowland aside. "You and I, dear brother, need to have a conversation. But now is not the time and this is certainly not the place!" He glanced at Milton. "I suggest you go back to your hotel before the chief decides to throw that long-haired Bolshevik in prison!"

10

CANBERRA

———————◆———————

IN ITS AUTUMN BEAUTY
SEEN FROM MOUNT AINSLIE

(By Our Scribe)

Messrs. Stuart Williams (architect) and W.H. Pinkstone (Our Scribe) spent last weekend at Canberra, guests of Mr. and Mrs. Fred Parr, formerly of Cootamundra and Stockinbingal. (Mr. Parr was postmaster at Stockinbingal and is now assistant at Canberra; and at times acting postmaster there. It is a very fine office.) The run from Cootamundra to Canberra is a little over a hundred miles—66 to Yass direct, and 37 across from there, and can be comfortably cruised in from 3 ½ to 4 hours…

…We arrived at 4 on Saturday afternoon. Tennis was being played here, there, and everywhere. "We're tennis mad!" was the reply to a query. There were 37 teams in competition that afternoon in connection with the association, in addition to private play. It appears that the Commission will build courts as fast as the clubs apply, at a rental of 6 per cent per annum on the outlay. It pays the authorities, and suits the clubs.

Cootamundra Herald, 11 May 1934

It took Rowland a couple of telephone calls to track down Colin Delaney. The detective had handed over the case of the Pyjama

Girl to his colleagues, and returned to Sydney. Rowland found him eventually and was put through.

Briefly, and without mention of Milton's particular role, he told the detective of Jim Kelly's murder and the strange activity at Parliament House.

"Major Harold Jones?" Delaney asked when Rowland first mentioned the chief of police.

"Yes—do you know him, Colin?"

"Not personally, Rowly, but I do know he wears two hats. He's not simply the Chief of Canberra Police but also Director of the Central Investigation Bureau."

"And what does that mean?"

"Jones runs intelligence. For want of a better term, he's Australia's spy master."

Unseen by Delaney, Rowland grimaced. "I see."

"If he's involved, you can jolly well bet it's more than a simple murder for financial gain," Delaney warned.

"Kelly was a Communist. Would that be why Jones has become involved?"

"I wouldn't have thought that would be enough. Communists aren't unusual. Unless Kelly was involved in some plot to overthrow the government or he was spying for the Russians or something of the sort." Delaney paused. "Clearly there's something going on at Parliament House."

"Parliament hasn't resumed sitting, Col."

"Perhaps it's a security issue. Prince Henry is arriving in the country next month. The powers that be are a little prone to overreact at the moment."

"Thanks, Col, I'll keep that in mind." He asked about the progress of the Albury murder.

"We've still no idea who the poor wretch is." Delaney's tone betrayed his frustration. "There are a few rumours about that the chap who found her is involved, but there's nothing to support that. God knows, Rowly, if we were hanging people for finding bodies, you'd be long dead."

"There is no Communist plot!" Milton was adamant. "A plot against the Communists possibly. After all, it was one of us who was murdered." He paced the sitting room agitated. "I swear, Rowly, Bluey hasn't asked me to do anything illegal—the public gallery is called the public gallery for a reason."

Rowland recalled his conversation with Howells in Yackandandah. "Kelly wanted to be relieved. Howells said he'd been spooked. Do you know why?"

"Not a clue."

"Do you know where he was living? Would he have confided in anyone?"

"He had a room in a boarding house over in Queanbeyan," Milton said, naming the New South Wales town on the Australian Capital Territory's border. "The peace officers have no jurisdiction there and from what I understand it's easier to get a drink."

"Perhaps we should see if anyone at the boarding house knows why he was concerned for his safety."

Clyde looked up and regarded Rowland dubiously. "Because although the peace officers have no jurisdiction, you do?"

"It might be useful to know why Kelly was worried, since Milton's taking over from him," Rowland replied.

Milton sided with Rowland. "For all we know he had gambling debts or something else completely unconnected with the Movement Against War and Fascism."

"I'd feel better if we knew no one was going to cut Milt's throat." Edna emerged from the suite's bedroom in a long-sleeved navy sheath. Her hair was caught into a low knot at the nape of her neck around which she wore a locket set with seed pearls.

Rowland forgot about Kelly and Jones. He knew he was staring, but Edna was accustomed to having that effect on men. She barely noticed now.

"You look pretty, Ed."

"Why thank you, Rowly." She smiled as though no one had ever told her that before. "Bertie wants me to go to dinner with him and some of his friends from the Ainslie Tennis Club." She laughed. "I rather think the Ley Cup has gone to his head."

Rowland said nothing, consciously dragging his eyes away from the sculptress.

"When do you want to go across to Queanbeyan?" Clyde asked. He was becoming resigned to the fact that they were going to involve themselves in the Kelly murder, no matter what he said.

Rowland glanced back at Edna. "What time are you meeting Middleton, Ed?" The journalist did not own a motorcar and, considering that a man had been murdered barely a quarter mile away, Rowland was reluctant to allow the sculptress to catch a bus alone.

"About six o'clock."

"We'll drop you off and pop out to Queanbeyan from there."

Edna frowned. "I'm not sure I like the idea of you three going without me. You always manage to find trouble when you set off on your own."

Milton snorted. "We've never shot anyone."

Rowland flinched, anticipating the quarrel to come. Edna hated being reminded that she'd once shot him, which was probably why Milton took such delight in doing so. It had been an accident, of course, and, ironically, she'd probably saved his life by shooting him. But Edna was very sensitive about the subject.

She responded as he expected, and Milton added fuel to the flame of her indignation because apparently it amused him to do so.

It was possibly because of the raised voices that Rowland didn't hear the first knock or the second. The third resembled pounding more than knocking. Rowland opened the door. He was surprised to see Wilfred only because it had not occurred to him that when his brother had said they needed to have a conversation, he had meant so soon.

"Wil, hello... Do come in."

Wilfred shook his head as Milton called Edna the "surviving member of the Kelly gang" and she threatened to despatch him accordingly. "Perhaps it might be better if you come with me, Rowly," he said, turning on his heel.

"One moment." Rowland ducked back into the suite to retrieve his hat and jacket. "Wil," he said to Clyde's enquiring glance. "I shan't be long."

"Good luck," Clyde said quietly.

Rowland followed Wilfred outside the hotel. "Where's your automobile?" Wilfred asked.

"Just out the back in the car park."

"Good. I'd rather not have this conversation with my driver present. Shall we?"

"Yes, if you wish." Rowland took his brother past gleaming Rolls-Royces, Armstrong Siddeleys, Vauxhalls and Oldsmobiles, stopping finally by the yellow Airflow.

Wilfred stepped back. "This... This is yours?"

"Yes."

"It's American."

"I believe it is."

"For pity's sake, Rowly, how did you get stuck with this hideous jalopy? Did you lose a bet?"

Rowland ignored him, opening the front passenger door. Wilfred got in. Rowland walked around and slipped in behind the wheel. "Where did you want to go?"

"We don't need to go anywhere, I just wanted to have a word in private."

"I see." Rowland presumed that Wilfred expected to shout or else the bar would have done as well for the purpose.

Wilfred didn't waste any time. "What are you doing in Canberra?"

"I've told you—visiting."

"Bunkum! Do not treat me like a fool. A Communist is murdered on the steps of Parliament House, the weapon is delivered to the prime minister, and, in both instances, by some uncanny coincidence, you're there!"

"Wait a moment—the weapon is delivered to the prime minister? I say, is that what was going on today?" Rowland asked.

"Yes."

"What kind of weapon?"

"A razor."

"Well, we were all in King's Hall nowhere near the prime minister's suite—how could any of us have delivered anything to him? Unless Lyons was lurking about King's Hall."

"Don't be daft, Rowly! The weapon was placed in a Lamson tube and delivered onto the prime minister's desk where it was opened by his secretary. She was understandably shaken and alerted Broinowski, the Usher of the Blackrod, who immediately called Jones."

"A Lamson tube? Where did it originate?" Rowland was aware that Parliament House was serviced by a network of copper pipes which used pneumatic pressure to move cylinders of documents around the building. He'd always thought it an ingenious system. If the razor had arrived on the prime minister's desk it must have been sent from somewhere within the building.

"It's hard to tell. There are several routes by which it might have ended up in the prime minister's office." Wilfred pulled off his spectacles and polished them with his handkerchief, before replacing them to look intently at Rowland. "What do you and your Communist hangers-on have to do with it?"

Rowland met his brother's eye, wondering what Wilfred had hoped cleaning his spectacles would help him see. "Absolutely nothing. None of us had ever seen Kelly before Milton found the body. Nor have we been sending murder weapons to the prime minister."

"I want you to go back to Sydney tomorrow."

"I'm afraid I can't, Wil."

"Why not?"

"Major Jones has all but mandated that we are not to leave town."

"And why, if you have no involvement in this, would the chief of police be making such a request?"

"For God's sake, Wil, surely you don't honestly believe I… any of us… would cut a man's throat."

"Kelly was, from what I gather, a Communist. An active fifth columnist."

"Precisely. You'd be far more likely to kill him than any of us."

Wilfred Sinclair wasn't finished. "What were you doing at *Willowview*?"

"*Willowview*? Oh Ley's place. It was a tennis party. We were collecting Miss Higgins. Unfortunately, she and her doubles partner kept winning so we were compelled to wait for the finals."

"So you have no other relationship with anyone at *Willowview*?"

"No… actually yes. Jemima Fairweather was there."

"Fairweather?"

"Old Mrs. Fairweather's granddaughter... you won't remember her. You were in Sydney most of the summer she spent in Yass."

"I do recall Mother mentioning her once or twice. What was she doing there?"

"Ley's undertaking some legal work for her, I believe." Rowland chose not to mention Jemima's relationship with Thomas Ley's mistress.

Wilfred's face was unreadable. "I believe you and Miss Fairweather were quite the item."

Rowland laughed. "We were very young, Wil."

"The Fairweathers are a good family. The property adjoins *Oaklea*... excellent sheltered pastures."

Rowland regarded his brother, amused.

"I presume Father disapproved of her," Wilfred murmured.

"Yes, he considered her a girl of modern taste and easy virtue. Did Father tell you—"

"Didn't say a word. I just know that you're inexplicably drawn to the inappropriate."

Rowland chose not to be offended. There was probably some truth to it. "As I said, Wil, that was a long time ago. I believe Jemima is back in Yass with her grandmother at the moment."

"I'll let Kate know. Perhaps we should invite them both to dine at *Oaklea*."

Rowland's brow rose. He wasn't sure how his respectable, gentle sister-in-law would find Jemima. He used the thaw in the conversation to question his brother. "What's Stanley Bruce doing here?"

"It's an unofficial visit."

"Is there something going on, Wil? What are you doing in Canberra?"

Wilfred sighed. "It's to do with the report of the New States Commission. Nothing you'd be interested in, more's the pity.

There's a lot more to the business of government than your infantile Communist friends would have you believe. It's a bit more complicated than impassioned rhetoric and red flags."

"Leave it, Wil," Rowland warned.

"Rowly, listen to me. Be careful. Do not give me any reason to doubt your loyalty."

"My loyalty? What the devil—"

"Do not give me any reason."

Rowland's voice became hard. "You have no reason. But I am not you, and I answer to my own conscience."

"Regrettably after your last stunt, my faith in your conscience is not what it once was."

Rowland exhaled. This again. "I truly didn't intend to embarrass you, Wil."

"Well you most certainly did, and worse, you humiliated Kate. She personally rang everybody she knew to make sure they came to your exhibition. You used her. I never thought you'd sink to that."

Rowland flinched. He hadn't set out to exploit his sister-in-law, or to hurt her in any way, but he couldn't deny he'd done so. He rubbed his face. "I'm sorry, Wil, it's not what I meant to do," he said for the hundredth time.

"What did you mean to do?" Wilfred demanded. "I can't for the life of me fathom what you could possibly have hoped to achieve with an exhibition of Communist propaganda."

"It wasn't propaganda. It was what I saw in Germany, what I felt."

"Then why did you need to deceive people as to the content of your blasted exhibition?"

"It's the people who turn their faces away whom I wanted to see—"

"Why? Why do you feel the need to inflict your radical politics on decent, patriotic citizens?"

Rowland dropped his head back against the seat. "I admit it, Wil. It was a bad idea and I didn't achieve anything aside from destroying my professional reputation and offending my family. I don't know what more you want me to say!"

"I want you to say you'll never do anything like that again, that you'll never work with the bloody Communists again and you'll not again bring our family's good name into disrepute. I want you to tell me that you'll abandon this ridiculous obsession with Eric Campbell—the man is a spent force! You're the only person in the country who believes he's any kind of threat! I want you to realise that nothing good can be achieved with radical ideas and dangerous language. Most of all I want you to grow up and stop behaving like a petulant brat!" Wilfred slammed his fist on the dash. "I'm sick of having to rescue you, Rowly. You're becoming a perpetual disgrace to the name of Sinclair!"

In the closed quarters of the Airflow the tirade was loud and bitter and it did not miss its mark. Rowland bore it in silence. Then he waited because he was unsure if Wilfred was finished. The silence extended, the air was brittle. "I wasn't working with the Communists, Wil," he said finally. "I'm not a Communist. The dangerous language you speak of is the truth. As for growing up, if you mean that I should forget what I know, deny my friends and join the ruddy Country Party... I'm afraid I can't do that."

Rowland braced himself for a second dressing-down.

Wilfred shook his head. He opened the passenger door and got out.

"Wil... where are you—"

"It doesn't sound as though we have anything more to say to each other." Wilfred closed the door.

11

QUEER COLLECTORS
AND COLLECTIONS

By URBAN L. BROWNE

IN New York one Philatelist murdered another in order to possess himself of a certain rare stamp. The history of rare gems is full of drama and tragedy. The real collector will risk death and disease while on the trail of some rare specimen…

…The collection of toy soldiers is not an occupation only of the nursery, as some may imagine. It is a well-recognised grown-up hobby nowadays, and there is an international association of such collectors, many of them distinguished men, who have some wonderful specimens of historic uniforms among their tin, wooden, and lead soldiers. Dolls are another interesting hobby, and they possess historic value.

Cumberland Argus and
Fruitgrowers Advocate, 8 March 1934

"Rowly?" Edna peered into the Airflow. "What are you doing out here?"

Rowland opened the door and stepped out. The afternoon had cooled sharply into the evening. "Wil wanted a word in private."

"Oh, I see." Edna had observed Wilfred Sinclair's Rolls-Royce drive out over twenty minutes before, but she didn't mention that. Instead she took Rowland's hand. "Was Wilfred very cross?"

"Yes. But that's not unusual." He removed his jacket and wrapped her in it. "It's still too cold of an evening to step out without a coat, Ed."

"What did Wilfred say to you?" she asked, carefully studying his face. As much as they battled, Edna knew Rowland admired his brother deeply. Indeed there was probably no one who could truly wound Rowland as Wilfred could... as he had.

"Nothing I didn't already know." He glanced at his watch. "We'd better fetch Clyde and Milt, not to mention your coat, before we're late."

She reached up and embraced him. "I'm sorry things are so difficult between you and Wilfred. He'll come round."

"I'm not sure he will, Ed."

"Darling, for thirteen years your brother believed you'd shot your father. He stood by you then. Surely this pales by comparison."

Rowland smiled. "Our father was a common enemy. I'm not sure Wil believes we're on the same side anymore."

"Well you are. He'll realise that eventually."

Once they had collected overcoats and the rest of their party, they returned to the Airflow. They spoke no more of Wilfred on the short drive to Ainslie where Bertram Middleton boarded. The writer was a little flustered to open the door to Edna and three gentlemen.

"Don't worry, Middleton, we're not staying," Clyde said. "Just escorting the lady to your threshold."

"We would, however, thank you not to disappear with her again," Milton added.

Middleton stuttered nervously about misunderstandings in a manner that was barely coherent.

"He doesn't seem that clever with words," Rowland whispered in Edna's ear.

She smiled but went to Middleton's defence nevertheless. "Stop bullying Bertie!"

The writer kissed her hand. He spoke with barely contained emotion. "You look exquisite, Eddie, I can barely believe I'll have the privilege of escorting so beautiful a creature."

Rowland cleared his throat. "We'll get on then. When should we come back for you, Ed?"

"No need for that," Middleton said quickly. "I'll see the lady to her digs when we're finished. I give you my word as a gentleman that I'll not leave her side until I return her safely, though parting will be such sweet sorrow."

"Shakespeare!" Milton said. "The man's stealing from Shakespeare. I'm on to you Middleton—you can't just steal poetry..."

Mortified, Middleton was reduced to incoherence again. Edna pushed Milton out of the door. "Stay out of trouble," she warned as she waved them away.

"All right, Rowly, fill us in." Milton rested his elbows on the backrest between Rowland and Clyde as the Airflow's unusual grille was nosed towards Queanbeyan. "What did Wilfred have to say?"

Rowland told them about the murder weapon surreptitiously delivered to Prime Minister Lyons' office via the Lamson tube system.

"'Struth! So it could have been sent from anywhere in the House?" Clyde asked.

"The tube system is pretty extensive," Rowland replied. "I understand there's also a line that goes out to the Government Printing Office in Eastlake."

"And they have no way of establishing exactly where the razor came from?"

"Apparently not. They can't even tell precisely when it was sent."

"Why would any sane murderer send the weapon to the prime minister?"

"Perhaps it was meant as some kind of threat?" Clyde suggested.

"I suppose."

"Is that all Wilfred had to say?" Clyde asked. "You were gone for a month of Sundays."

Rowland smiled. He assumed Edna had been despatched to the Airflow on behalf of all his friends. "Wilfred is still less than pleased with me. He was making sure I understood that."

"The exhibition?"

"Among other things. He's right—"

"Like hell he is!" Milton snapped. "Wilfred doesn't know what he's bloody well talking about."

"The exhibition was not received as well as it could have been," Clyde said more reasonably, "but that doesn't mean—"

"Wilfred told me a long time ago that Eric Campbell and the New Guard were a spent force. He's probably right about that."

Clyde sighed. "Nobody thanks the bloke who prevents disaster from happening, mate."

"The Fascists may not be having parades anymore," said Milton, "but I wouldn't write them off. They're just trying more socially acceptable routes to dictatorship. Campbell is a determined bastard— he may yet find himself in parliament."

"Perhaps." Rowland frowned.

"Rowly, maybe the three of you should head back to Sydney," Milton suggested. "I'm perfectly able to do what I said I would on my own… and while it's occasionally amusing, there's no point upsetting Wilfred if you don't have to."

Rowland glanced back at the poet. "I'm not having second thoughts, Milt. Just preparing myself for what's going to happen when Wil finds out I'm involved with Egon Kisch."

Clyde whistled. He had not thought of that. Despite their divergent ideologies, the Sinclairs were fiercely loyal to one another. This could finally shatter that. "Oh damn."

Even Milton put his enthusiasm for the cause aside for a moment. "Oh bugger, Rowly. I'm sorry—I shouldn't have got you involved. I wasn't thinking about Wilfred. We could find someone else…"

"I volunteered my services," Rowland said firmly. "I don't regret it… just how Wil's going to see my involvement."

"But—"

"If not for Egon I'd probably be rotting in some German prison, or dead. It's important that people have a chance to hear what he has to say." Rowland would not countenance withdrawing to appease Wilfred. "I am very happy to be involved in this."

The wide main street of Queanbeyan was divided by a row of parked vehicles down its centre.

For the gentlemen from Sydney there was a relief in crossing the border into New South Wales. There was a constraint about the national capital, a tidiness and method, which pervaded everything. In contrast, Queanbeyan was a bustling agricultural centre, with buildings old enough to sport rust and peeling paint. It was faded, worn in and, for that reason, somehow more comfortable. Unconsciously, they all let out their breath a little.

The boarding house in which Kelly had lived was, from the street, a less than salubrious establishment. The verandahs had been curtained off with old blankets to create accommodation. The weatherboards had not seen paint in at least a generation and someone had used empty beer bottles to build a pyramid on the lawn.

"It's not quite the Hotel Canberra," Milton muttered.

Rowland parked the Airflow directly outside the old bungalow and they proceeded up the crumbling steps to the front door. It took several knocks to raise a response. A middle-aged woman, attired in a pinafore apron, her hair caught up in a floral scarf, answered the door.

Milton introduced himself and his companions. "We're old mates of Jim Kelly and we happened to be in town. We were hoping to grab him for a beer."

"I think you have the wrong address, there's no Jim Kelly here."

Milton pulled some opened envelopes from his pocket. "Are you sure, Miss?" He looked at the envelope. "He used this address whenever he wrote to me... said he was boarding with a lovely lady who cooked better than his old mum."

The boarding house proprietor hesitated, blushing slightly. "I'm afraid Mr. Kelly's not here anymore."

"Oh." Milton made quite a good fist of looking disappointed. "I was looking forward to catching up with Jim... we were such great mates at school. He didn't say where he was going did he? His mum wanted me to bring back news of him... poor old thing is not enjoying the best of health of late."

The boarding house mistress hesitated. "I'm afraid... oh dear. Perhaps you'd best come in for a moment."

She took them into a large sitting room which was separated from a dining room by a wall of concertinaed panels. Despite the house's external appearance, the parlour was scrupulously clean and tidy. Its walls had been shelved to the ceiling, and displayed upon them were scores, perhaps hundreds, of porcelain dolls, all staring into the centre of the room with glass or painted eyes. A Jacquard-upholstered chaise longue also hosted more than a dozen dolls sitting primly in crinoline dresses around a picnic blanket complete with miniature tea set. Miss Marjorie Curtis, as she told them she was, invited them to take any of the armchairs while she bustled out to make tea.

"I can see why Kelly was spooked," Clyde whispered, sitting stiffly.

Marjorie Curtis returned with a traymobile. She poured tea into a full-sized version of the tea set around which her dolls picnicked, and handed a steaming cup and saucer to each gentleman. Rowland noticed she'd also applied lipstick and removed her headscarf.

Once they all held a cup and a slice of her pound cake, she said, "I'm afraid I have some terrible news for you gentlemen."

"Lovely cake, Miss Curtis," Milton said with his mouth full.

"Thank you, Mr. Isaacs—my grandmother's recipe. I'm afraid Mr. Kelly is dead."

"Dead?" Milton looked shocked and grieved enough for the three of them. Clyde and Rowland let him go. "How?"

"I'm afraid he was murdered, Mr. Isaacs. I don't think the police have found the culprit."

Milton gasped. "But who would want to kill Jim? Everybody loved Jim."

"Well, Mr. Isaacs, I'm afraid he may have got himself in trouble. Would you like another slice of cake?"

"What do you mean trouble, Miss Curtis? I wouldn't say no to more cake... is that orange essence—quite extraordinary!"

"Mixed peel," she said as she cut another slice. "I assumed it was gambling. A lot of my gentlemen get into trouble that way. He asked me to tell anyone looking for him that he didn't live here. It's why I was so unfriendly—I'm not usually like that, Mr. Isaacs."

"Oh we can see that, Miss Curtis. You've been very kind and hospitable. Did anyone come looking for him?"

"Aside from you gentlemen—yes, there were two men. And they called by twice... wouldn't say who they were."

"Did Jim say exactly why he wanted you to tell people he didn't live here?" Milton asked.

"No, but he sure was nervy. I was worried about him to be truthful."

"I'm sure Jim appreciated your concern. Can I ask, are his possessions still here? Perhaps I should take them back to his mum."

Marjorie Curtis bit her lip. "There is a bag but I don't think I'd be comfortable doing that, Mr. Isaacs. As his landlady, I think I should send them on myself."

"Of course." Milton smiled reassuringly. "That's proper. What a fascinating collection you have here, Miss Curtis. My sister collects dolls too... though she has barely two dozen."

"Really? How wonderful. Let me show you my most prized babies."

The next hour was lost to an introduction and explanation of several dolls: their origin, their maker and the manner in which Marjorie Curtis acquired them. Rowland glanced at Clyde who was beginning to look like he was ready to make a run for it. He honestly couldn't blame him. It was really quite an odd way for three grown men to spend an evening. But he assumed there was a purpose behind Milton's show of interest.

Finally, after a dissertation on a particular doll fashioned after Queen Mary, Milton said, "I guess we really should be going. I don't look forward to giving Mrs. Kelly my condolences. It'll break her poor old heart."

"Oh." Marjorie seemed moved. "You know, Mr. Isaacs, perhaps I could give you Mr. Kelly's bag to take back to his mother. It'll save me the expense of the postage."

"Only if you're comfortable with that, Miss Curtis."

"We know each other now. I'm sure it would be all right." She disappeared for a few minutes and returned with a carpetbag, which she handed to Milton. "You tell Mrs. Kelly that I'm so dreadfully sorry, that her son was a gentleman even if he was behind with his board."

"Thank you, Miss Curtis, I will."

Clyde and Rowland stood quickly lest Milton feel moved to talk about dolls again.

"If it's not too intrusive a question, Miss Curtis, just how far behind was Mr. Kelly with his board?" Rowland asked quietly as she showed them out.

"Oh don't you worry about that, Mr. Sinclair," she said blushing. "I shouldn't have mentioned it."

Rowland took five pounds from his pocketbook and pressed it into her hand. "Please do allow me. In Jim's memory."

"It's not necessary."

"I'm sure Jim wouldn't want you to be out of pocket, Miss Curtis."

"It's too much—half that would cover it."

"You've been very kind." He took out his card. "We're staying at the Hotel Canberra. If those men call by again you can reach us there. We might be able to stop them bothering you."

12

THE LIQUOR PROBLEM AT CANBERRA

Successful as it has been in the construction of buildings, the provision of essential services, and the accommodation of the people, the commission has failed to cope with a problem that is perplexing the Territory. This (says a correspondent) is the liquor traffic. The sale of liquor is prohibited, and the commissioners are known to favour the holding of a local option poll to decide whether the prohibition shall continue. Under the present system hundreds of pounds worth of liquor is brought into the Territory every week, some of it from the neighbouring New South Wales town of Queanbeyan, and some of it from farther afield. Queanbeyan is only nine miles from Canberra, and its hotels and picture theatre, but especially the hotels, are the architectural ornaments of the town. To be the licensee of a hotel in Queanbeyan is to be, to use a colloquialism, "on velvet." Since the population of the Federal Territory began to increase rapidly, the earnings of the Queanbeyan hotels have been enormous, and several fine hotels have been erected, and old ones remodelled. There are bars in the Queanbeyan hotels as palatial as any in Melbourne or Sydney.

Monaro Mercury, 17 October 1927

The Royal in Queanbeyan was a fairly new establishment sporting a modern art deco facade rather than the broad verandahs of the older public drinking houses. It was crowded. Despite the fact that the prohibition which operated in Canberra till 1928 had been lifted, the habit of crossing the border to drink had not yet faded. The hotels were full of workers who had become accustomed to saving their thirst for a night out in Queanbeyan. Clyde fought his way to the bar and came back to the small round table they'd commandeered with three froth-topped middies.

"I might need something stronger to get over those blessed dolls," Rowland murmured. "I swear some of them were breathing."

"Sadly, old mate—" Clyde drank deeply—"you're driving. Bloody oath that was peculiar."

Rowland raised his glass to Milton. "I thought you'd lost your mind there for a moment, but you did well, Milt."

The tapestry carpetbag Marjorie Curtis had given them had been stored in the back seat of the Airflow. They would go through the late Jim Kelly's possessions later in the privacy of the hotel suite.

"I felt a bit bad in the end to be honest," Milton admitted. "Poor lonely old thing, sitting in her one nice room talking to china faces."

"It's a wonder that the police hadn't collected Jim Kelly's property themselves," Clyde said thoughtfully.

"The Commonwealth Peace Officers probably have no jurisdiction in Queanbeyan. And New South Wales has its hands full with its own unsolved murders at the moment," said Rowland.

"Who do you suppose the blokes looking for him were?"

"Could be anyone really. Maybe there's a clue in the bag."

"This place is barely a jump from the boarding house," Milton said suddenly. "I'd bet London to a brick that he drank here regularly—to get away from the dolls if nothing else."

"Possibly..." Rowland began but Milton was already standing.

He banged the table with his hand until the pub quietened a little. "Gentlemen," he said loudly. "I ask you all to lift your glasses in the memory of Jim Kelly, a diamond of a man who drowned his sorrows here from time to time." Milton thrust his glass into the air. "To Jim!"

Rowland and Clyde both watched the crowd carefully. Some men toasted with gusto and shouted "Jim" with inebriated fervour. It was hard to know if they actually knew Kelly or were simply caught up in some sense of intemperate solidarity. One or two murmured "Jim Kelly" with contemplative feeling. Some ignored Milton and still others watched him and kept their glasses purposefully lowered. One group in particular seemed offended by the toast. They began to walk over.

"Here we go," Milton said triumphantly.

The group stopped a few feet away and simply stood, drinking and watching.

"What are they doing?" Milton muttered.

"I think they're waiting for us to leave," said Rowland. "I believe this is an invitation to step outside."

"What do you think?"

"There's three of them, it's even odds."

"We'll have to leave eventually," Clyde agreed.

"Just a minute." Rowland reached for his notebook. Quickly he sketched the faces of the three men, who assisted by staring in their direction. When he was satisfied with the likenesses, he closed the book. "We can go now."

They stood, stepped out of the Royal and walked back towards Marjorie Curtis' house where they'd left the Airflow. The men from the pub followed.

Rowland stopped as they reached the side street that led to the boarding house. While they could still hear the crowds and activity in the main street, there were few passers-by and no street lights. As they turned they saw that the three they'd spotted in the Royal had acquired another four to their cause. The odds had turned. "Right, gentlemen, what can we do for you?" Rowland asked calmly.

"What's Kelly to you?"

"A mate," Milton said.

"So you're working with the Commie mongrel?"

"How do you gentlemen know Jim Kelly?" Rowland kept one eye on the men fanning out around them. In the dark he couldn't make out their faces beyond the glow of their cigarettes.

"We're going to tell you what we told him—we're onto you. We're going to stop you."

"Stop us doing what?" Rowland asked. "Perhaps if you tell us what your issue is with Mr. Kelly we could—"

The first punch was thrown. Rowland ducked and swung back. A cigarette went flying as he hit his mark. And so the affray began. Outnumbered, they might have been in real trouble if they hadn't been so close to the main road, if their assailants had not been shouting "Commie bastards" and "red mongrels" as they fought. As it was, the brawl was announced and it seemed Communists had friends in the main street of Queanbeyan, as did the men who took offence to them. Soon it had nothing to do with Rowland Sinclair and his friends. Clyde and Rowland dragged Milton out. It was no longer obvious who was fighting whom, and the police had arrived.

"I think we should go," Clyde gasped.

"Yes, that might be wise." Rowland wiped blood from his lip with the back of his hand.

They broke away from the melee and returned briskly to the Airflow.

As Edna was still out, they used the private sitting room at Hotel Canberra that Rowland had hired for use as a studio to examine the contents of Kelly's bag. Rowland grimaced. In the well-lit room it was clear that none of them had escaped the brawl unscathed. Milton was sporting a rather spectacular black eye, Clyde's chin bore a matching bruise, and Rowland was aware of a stinging graze above his right brow which he vaguely remembered had been gouged by a wristwatch. He rang reception for ice and supper, and they opened the bag.

There was a second suit, a couple of shirts and other items of clothing. "They've been washed and pressed," Milton noted.

"Miss Curtis I expect." Rowland opened a leather satchel that had been under the clothes. He pulled out an open envelope in which had been stored three studio photographs—the kind of glamorous portraits that women sent to their sweethearts.

Rowland laid them out. "Looks like Mr. Kelly was rather popular."

"What else is in the satchel?"

"There's a notebook."

Milton flicked through the pages. "These are odds. I suspect Kelly liked the dogs... What's this?" He squinted at the page to which he'd just turned. "Snuff Box."

"Snuff Box what?"

"That's it. Just Snuff Box."

"Could be the name of a greyhound," Rowland suggested.

"Yes, I suppose. But he hasn't written any other names down."

"Perhaps it was a particularly sure bet," Clyde said. "Anything else?"

"A tin of tobacco, cigarette papers, a razor and a couple of shillings."

Rowland helped himself from the tray of sandwiches that had been delivered from the kitchen. "So, what do you think?"

"Those blokes in the Royal seemed to know Kelly was a Communist."

"And they seemed rather irate about it."

"Do you think they could have killed Kelly?" Rowland was sceptical. "Cutting a man's throat seems a fair way removed from a drunken bar brawl."

"They didn't seem plastered," observed Clyde.

Milton straddled his chair. "Do you remember the hard nuts from the New Guard and that group of Charles Hardy's? The bastards who killed your uncle, who tried to tar and feather me and beat the hell out of you?"

"Yes, of course, but the New Guard is fading, Campbell's caught up with his new political Party, and Hardy's too busy being a senator to incite vigilante mobs…"

"Exactly my point. What do you suppose the militants who were in the Fascist Legion are doing now Campbell's lost interest? Do you think that after spending the last few years convinced they were all that stood between Australia and the Red Army, beating people up for sport, they've just gone home and learned to play euchre?"

"No… perhaps not."

"You know, I'd wager that without the likes of Campbell and Hardy, the hard nuts would have nothing to hold them back."

"Good Lord, man, you're not suggesting Eric Campbell and Charles Hardy were in fact moderating influences?" Rowland was already shaking his head.

"Yes, I am, Rowly. Campbell and Hardy saw themselves as respectable men. Neither wanted to be associated with murder."

Rowland looked to Clyde. Milton was prone to becoming carried away, but Clyde had always been reason personified.

"I think what Milt's saying, Rowly, is, we shouldn't assume the clowns from the Royal are incapable of cutting a man's throat." Clyde poured himself a cup of coffee from the pot delivered with mixed sandwiches. "All those right-thinking men of the Fascist Legion haven't disappeared… and perhaps they haven't retired."

Rolling up his sleeves, Rowland clipped a sheet of cartridge paper to the board on his easel.

"What are you doing?" Milton asked.

Rowland retrieved his jacket from the hook by the door and pulled his notebook from the breast pocket. "I thought I'd make some proper drawings of those fellows in the pub while they're still fresh in my memory."

"Why?"

"I could send them to Delaney. And if these chaps are anything more than your standard bar room thugs, the police might be able to identify them." It was the state's worst kept secret that the New South Wales police force had its own operatives spying on many of the numerous Fascist and Communist groups. Indeed, Rowland had first met Detective Delaney when they were both undercover in the New Guard.

"Marjorie Curtis may be able to identify them if they're local," Milton added.

"I'm not setting foot in that flaming doll room again," Clyde said quickly.

Milton ignored Clyde. "It might be worth showing Major Jones, too. Of course we may have to come up with some vaguely plausible explanation as to what we were doing in Queanbeyan."

And so Rowland drew likenesses of three of the men, using the quick sketches he'd made in the pub as well as the recollections of Clyde and Milton to build what amounted to hand-drawn mug shots. With no newspapers involved, there was no need for the faces to be beautiful.

Edna found them in the makeshift studio late the next morning. Milton and Rowland were playing cards, Clyde was working on a sketch of Parliament House.

"What on earth did you get up to?" Edna demanded, scrutinising each of them in turn.

They'd cleaned up from the previous night's fracas but bruises could not be washed away so easily.

Milton told her what had happened in heroic detail. Accustomed to him, the sculptress ignored the self-serving embellishments without comment. "Dolls? Gosh! How many?"

"Bloody hundreds!" Clyde threw his hands in the air. "I tell you, if it turns out Marjorie Curtis slit Kelly's throat I wouldn't be surprised."

Milton laughed. "She's harmless… just lonely and a little obsessed. I have a cousin who collects ashtrays—has hundreds, doesn't even smoke."

"What are you going to do with the bag? Does Mr. Kelly really have a mother waiting for it?"

"No, I made that up. He's married though." Milton picked up his hand and considered the cards.

"Oh… that's a problem."

"Why?"

"You can't send his widow a bag containing photographs of other women. That'd be cruel."

Milton's brow furrowed. "I'll speak to Comrade Howells. He knew Kelly."

"Perhaps these women were the reason Kelly was keen to get out of here," Rowland mused. "Juggling three would be awkward and quite possibly dangerous."

"We don't know that all three were current," Clyde noted. "But I do see what you mean."

"How was your evening, Ed? Did you have a good time with the Ainslie tennis set?"

"It was lovely," Edna replied. "Mr. Ley took us on a private tour of Parliament House."

"Ley?"

"Yes, he and Mrs. Brook are in Canberra to meet with old political colleagues apparently. And so is Mrs. Roche. She's a little put out that you haven't been to see her yet."

"I would have said it's rather fortunate I haven't, since it appears she's no longer in Yass," Rowland replied.

"She said she'll have to come here since you're so determined to be coy."

"When?"

"This afternoon."

"I'm sure we can manage to entertain her."

"Actually, I can't. I'm playing croquet this afternoon." Edna smiled. "The Canberra Croquet Club plays on the lawns right here. Maggie Brook is a member... she's invited me to play."

Milton snorted. "Wait till she realises you cheat!"

"I don't cheat!"

"You always cheat!"

"Because the three of you gang up on me!"

"How exactly did Ley give you a private tour of Parliament House? He's not a parliamentarian anymore," Clyde asked before the exchange escalated.

"It was pretty late—there was no one else there except the cleaners, and a couple of clerks. Mr. Ley seems to know how to get in."

"He broke in?"

"Of course not! One of the clerks let us in—Mr. Ley knew him," Edna said. "Nobody inside seemed surprised. It's not a bank, after all."

Rowland might have asked more about the clandestine tour if Edna had not decided then that she should change her attire for the afternoon's sport.

"Is there such a thing as a croquet outfit?" Clyde asked as the sculptress dashed out.

Rowland shrugged. On the occasions they'd played croquet on the lawns of *Woodlands* there'd been no dress code. They had swung mallets in whatever they happened to be wearing at the time the fancy to play took them. On moonlit nights they'd played in pyjamas and dressing gowns, much to the horror of Mary Brown. But the Canberra Croquet Club would possibly have more exacting standards.

When the reception desk rang to inform him that a Miss Jemima Roche was waiting in the hotel foyer, Rowland was alone. Milton had decided to return to Queanbeyan to show Marjorie Curtis the photographs they'd found in Kelly's carpetbag, as well as Rowland's sketches of the men they'd encountered at the Royal.

"If any of them are locals, she may recognise them."

"Do you think it's safe?" Clyde had been uneasy.

"I won't go into the Royal."

"I'm not worried about those jokers—I meant Marjorie's parlour."

"For an artist, you're very easily unsettled by the unconventional, Clyde old mate."

In the end Clyde had decided to accompany Milton in case the poet needed an ally against either thugs or dolls. Rowland suspected the excursion had been concocted to allow him to be alone with Jemima Roche. He wasn't quite sure if he was grateful.

Jemima was seated on one of the reception's chesterfields, her legs crossed, her head bent over the leaves of a letter. Rowland paused to take in the elegance of her. She looked up and smiled as he approached.

"Hello, my darling."

"Mrs. Roche."

"Oh do stop that... you can call me Jemima or my love—nothing else will do." She took his hand and pulled him down beside her. "Do you know what I'm reading?"

"No idea."

"Your letters, from *that* summer. Do you want to see?"

Rowland flinched. Jemima Roche seemed determined to torture him with his youthful indiscretions. "No, I don't."

"Don't be silly, Rowly... you were so sweet. I found them among the things I had at Grandmama's. I'm not going to let you forget."

"It appears. How is your Grandmama?"

"A little frail, but as sharp as ever. She caught me up on all the district gossip. She says you're far more scandalous these days than I ever was."

"I see."

Jemima leant towards him and whispered, "Apparently some of the local pastoralists call you Red Rowly."

Rowland started to laugh.

"That's better," she said. "You always did have a lovely laugh." Jemima stood and held out her hand. "Come on."

"Where are we going?"

"It's such a splendid day—I'm taking you on a picnic."

Jemima led him out to a sky blue Riley and waited while he opened the driver's side door for her. He climbed into the passenger seat and allowed her to take him where she would. Jemima had selected a lone willow tree by a pool where the Cotter and Paddys Rivers met, beneath which to spread out a picnic blanket. Under her direction, Rowland took a large, generously stocked basket from the back seat and they settled to share sandwiches, chocolate cake and bottles of ginger beer. The day was cool despite the sunshine and the sky was cloudy but not threateningly so. Filtered through the new green of recently unfurled leaves, the light under the canopy of the willow was soft.

They reminisced about picnics they'd had back in Yass. Jemima read from Rowland's letters until he grabbed them from her, swearing to destroy the excruciatingly sentimental adolescent missives.

"Don't you dare! They're mine!"

"A man's got to defend his dignity, Jem."

"Rowly!"

He sighed, handing them back. "Very well, go ahead."

Jemima pressed the letters to her breast. "They remind me of that lovely, magical summer. Long before I met Oswald and everything went so terribly wrong." She told him then of her marriage to Oswald Roche. "He was very suitable you know. Father liked him a great deal. But it turned out he was more like your father than mine."

Rowland tensed. His father had been brutal. Jemima knew that. Could that be what she meant? "Jem—"

"I don't want to spoil this spectacular day talking about Oswald," she said abruptly. She pushed him down so that he was lying back on the blanket, and stretched out next to him. They watched the clouds as they had years ago. "Grandmama tells me you were arrested last year."

"Yes. I was."

"Why?"

"The police thought I'd shot my father."

"All those years ago?"

"Yes."

"Did you?"

"No."

"Nevertheless, I wouldn't have blamed you if you had. Some people should be dead!"

Rowland said nothing.

"If I needed help, you'd want to help me, wouldn't you, Rowly?"

He rose onto one elbow and looked at her. "You're not going to ask me to kill someone, are you, Jem?"

13

PERSONAL

---◆---

VICE-REGAL

Her Excellency Lady Isaacs, accompanied by Miss Helen Hughes, was present at the Canberra Croquet Club on Saturday afternoon, and presented the prizes won during the croquet season.

The Sydney Morning Herald, 3 July 1933

Milton Isaacs watched Marjorie Curtis' face carefully as she shuffled through the photographs that had been stowed in James Kelly's carpetbag. The poet was alone with the lady in her doll-lined parlour, Clyde having elected to stay with the car.

"We thought we probably should let Jim's lady friends know that he's passed away," Milton said. "Do you by any chance recognise any of them, Miss Curtis?"

"This here is May Dwyer; and that's Sally Burton. I'm afraid I don't know the other woman. Perhaps she goes to the Catholic church."

"I beg your pardon?"

"These ladies," Marjorie handed him two of the photographs, "are devout members of the congregation at St. Clements every Sunday. The other one I don't know. As I said, she might be a Roman."

"Do you know why Mr. Kelly had their photographs?" Milton asked tentatively.

"I'm sure I don't know, Mr. Isaacs. Let me assure you, I run a respectable establishment. No visitors after four o'clock and never in the bedrooms."

"Of course, I didn't mean to imply anything improper."

Marjorie made a funny little cooing noise. "Of course you didn't—you're too much a gentleman." She smiled, trying to compensate for her earlier shortness. "I can tell you this, Mr. Isaacs, May Dwyer and Sally Burton are both of them married."

———

Jemima Roche laughed. "You're far too tall to be an assassin, Rowly. You'd be spotted straightaway." She pushed herself up and kissed him gently, enjoying his bewilderment. "I just wanted to know if you still cared what happened to me."

"Of course I do, Jem. Are you in some kind of trouble? With what do you need my help?"

Her face grew grave. She fingered his tie absently.

"I'm not sure I can go on this way…"

Startled he sat up and put his arm around her shoulders. "Jem…?"

She gripped his lapel and looked up into his eyes. "I'm so desperately bored!"

He groaned, falling back as she laughed.

She pinned him down, and pressed against him. "Boredom is very serious. Grandmama has me trapped drinking tea with the withered old crones from the Red Cross. If it wasn't for Tommy and Maggie taking me out occasionally…"

"You could always leave, Jem. You're not a child anymore."

She frowned. "I need to be remembered in Grandmama's will and she wants to have constant company in her twilight years."

"I see."

"Do you not like girls anymore, Rowly?"

He choked. "What?"

"Well here I am, by all accounts a beautiful woman, and I'm throwing myself at you. Most men would have ravished me by now; you haven't even loosened your tie."

"For the love of God, Jem, we're in a public space."

Jemima smiled impishly. "There's that shy boy again. I have missed him."

Rowland kissed her this time. He wasn't sure if it was to shut her up or to prove himself, or because he wanted to. Even after all these years, her lips were familiar, they yielded easily to his.

When he pulled away, she drew him back. "There's no one here but you and me, Rowly." She attended to his tie herself, and then the buttons of his shirt. "Oh my," she said tracing the scar on his chest with her hand. "You'll have to tell me the story of this someday... but not now."

"Jem..."

Silencing him with another kiss, she slipped out of her dress, removing her chemise and undergarments with a similar seductive expertise. And Rowland was mesmerised. Caution fell away.

Her body had changed, become more curved, though he'd never really known it in quite this way before. Even as he made love to her, Rowland wasn't sure if he was falling in love with Jemima Roche again, or just falling. She'd always had that effect. Always been able to hold him in thrall.

Edna lined up her shot. She was losing rather badly but that didn't bother her. It was only Milton to whom she could not bear to lose. Her shot went awry once more.

"Oh dear!" Maggie Brook shook her head. "Never mind, Eddie old girl. Sometimes it just takes a while to get your eye in, and sometimes the blasted ball won't co-operate regardless!"

Edna stood back on the pretext of watching and learning from Maggie Brook's excellent technique. She was distracted. Rowland had left with Jemima Roche a couple of hours before. Edna had waved from the croquet lawn but he'd been too focused on Jemima to see. The sculptress wasn't sure if she really liked Mrs. Roche. There was something about the woman that made her uneasy.

Perplexed by her own reaction, Edna did wonder if she was jealous. She knew she had no right to be. Rowland Sinclair was her best friend, a spirit so kindred she couldn't bear to lose him, and for that she had made the decision long ago that she would not allow herself to fall in love with him, that she would not permit him to love her. It was too dangerous. It was not that she didn't think she could love Rowland enough, but that she feared she'd love him too much... at the expense of everything else, including her art.

Edna was determined to only love men she could put aside when there was work to be done. Rowland Sinclair was not that kind of man. So, instead, she occupied herself with the likes of Bertie Middleton who expected nothing more than a passing passion.

But to want Rowland to do the same was being unfair. He was not like her—he'd always been something of a romantic. Edna wondered if she should leave, to ensure that Mrs. Roche did not get the wrong idea. Still, she wanted instinctively to protect Rowland from Jemima... perhaps it was more than simple jealousy.

Maggie Brook had been very kind and attentive. She'd introduced Edna to the club members as "an artist of considerable renown", feigning shock that they didn't know her work and implying that their cultural educations were lacking. She didn't mention Thomas Ley at all in the polite social exchanges, presumably because he still had a wife. Despite her current circumstances, there was a confident decorum about the former politician's mistress.

She did enquire of Edna about Rowland and the Sinclairs in general. Edna assumed the interest was pursuant to Thomas Ley's ambitions to re-enter parliament. Wilfred Sinclair was influential in conservative politics.

"We must see if we can invite him to supper while we're all in town," Maggie said when Edna mentioned that Wilfred was in Canberra. "Do you know where he's staying?"

"No, I'm afraid not. Perhaps Rowly—"

"Oh don't give it another thought." She lowered her voice to a whisper. "Tommy will be able to find out... he still has all manner of connections in Canberra."

Edna glanced around quickly to make sure their conversation was private before she said, "If you don't mind my asking, why did Mr. Ley ever leave politics? He seems to miss the cut and thrust of it so very much."

Maggie sighed. "Stanley Bruce," she said angrily. "Tommy wasn't from the right sort of circles. He's from very humble beginnings. Mr. Bruce made it clear he was no longer welcome and Bruce was the prime minister of the day."

"Oh, I do see. That's terrible."

Maggie hooked her arm through Edna's. "Come on, old bean, let's finish this game. And then I believe some liquid refreshments are in order. I've told Tommy to fetch Mr. Middleton and pick us up."

"I'm not sure I should. Rowly wanted to—"

"Oh I don't expect Mr. Sinclair will get away from Jemima so quickly. They were very much in love once. He proposed to her you know."

"Really?" Edna was startled both by the fact and her own dismay.

"She turned him down, but I expect she's sorry she did. They are very suited, don't you think—both from good pastoral families. I'm sure Mr. Wilfred Sinclair will be delighted with the match."

Edna doubted that Wilfred would approve of a divorcee however illustrious her family, but on that she did not comment. "Are you saying Mrs. Roche wants to marry Rowly?"

"Oh my giddy aunt, I've let the cat out of the bag, haven't I? Jemima will be vexed with me. You won't say anything will you, dear? I confess I'm an insatiable romantic... and they do make such a handsome couple."

***

It was dark by the time Rowland returned to the Hotel Canberra. He went directly to the studio in search of his holy trinity: canvas, paint and solitude. Events had taken a rather unexpected turn. Rowland thought most clearly with a brush in his hand and he certainly needed to think now. He was not unhappy—far from it. He had no desire to be a monk and Jemima Roche was beautiful and spirited; she had been his first love and his confidant. She seemed to want nothing more from him beyond the affair she had told him they would have from the first. Perhaps it was her bloody-mindedness on that count that unsettled him. Rowland had met women with similar motivations before, but rarely had they had such a sense of purpose. It was not so much that Jemima knew him well, but that she was willing to use whatever she knew. Jemima Roche seemed to observe few boundaries.

"Rowly, you're back!" Clyde and Milton walked through the door.

Milton grinned. "What did you and Mrs. Roche get up to?"

"A picnic," Rowland replied.

"How very civilised."

Rowland said nothing. He wasn't sure if civilised was the right word.

"Would you care for a drink?" Clyde asked.

"I would rather. Where's Ed?"

"She and Middleton made up a foursome with Ley and Mrs. Brook."

"How'd you go with Miss Curtis?"

"Ask Milt." Clyde handed Rowland a glass of gin. "I stayed with the car and listened to the radio well out of the reach of those flaming dolls."

"You're a bloody coward." Milton took the photographs out of his pocket, as well as the folded sketch of the men from the Royal. "Miss Curtis recognised two of the photographs. May Dwyer and Sally Burton—both married. Clyde and I found out where they lived and called on them. Both deny any knowledge of Jim Kelly—they didn't even recognise the name."

"It makes sense they would deny it, I suppose."

"Yes, perhaps... but you know, Rowly, I think I believed them."

"And the sketches?"

"Miss Curtis didn't know them but, blowed if there wasn't a picture of this bloke," he pointed to one of the faces, "on May Dwyer's mantle."

"Husband?"

"Maybe."

"So doesn't that make it more likely that May Dwyer was involved with Kelly? It would explain why Mr. Dwyer was so angry."

"Maybe. But these were nice addresses, respectable, decent church-going ladies... hardly the type to consort with a godless Communist."

"I wouldn't count on that, Milt."

"Bluey Howells swears that Jim Kelly was devoted to his own wife," Milton persisted.

"So why then would he have the photographs?"

Clyde turned the photographs over and pointed to the embossed studio mark. "They were all taken at the same place."

"Well that's not surprising. How many studios could there possibly be in Queanbeyan?"

"Sunshine Studios are not in Queanbeyan, Rowly, they're in Canberra. Eastlake, to be precise."

"Is there a photographic studio in Queanbeyan?" Rowland held the photo up to the light to inspect the mark.

"Two."

"That is a little bit of a coincidence, then."

Clyde peered around the easel to see what Rowland was working on. A sketch of Jemima Roche in dilute paint, a loose jumble of lines and yet the likeness was unmistakable. Clyde sensed something in the detail of the painting. There was a kind of intimacy in the line work. He knew Rowland well enough, had watched him work often enough, to tell when he was painting a lover.

"Exactly where is *Mr.* Roche, Rowly?" Clyde asked.

"I don't know. From what Jemima says the marriage was over years ago." Rowland sensed the disapproval in Clyde's voice. He wasn't particularly surprised. As much as Clyde accepted the unconventional morality of the artistic circle in which he now lived, he was still vaguely Catholic.

Milton shook his head, grinning. "A divorcee... and here we were thinking you probably couldn't shock Wilfred any further."

The mention of Wilfred reminded Rowland that his brother had intended to invite Jemima to dine at *Oaklea*. He couldn't possibly know she was divorced. Which seemed a little odd... that kind of scandal was usually disseminated with singular efficiency via established lines of gossip.

"Wilfred's pretty good at keeping you out of the newspapers. Perhaps the Fairweathers have their own protector of skeletons."

Rowland smiled. It was, he thought, an apt title for a very necessary role.

"Don't you know this Roche chap?" Clyde asked. "I thought your lot always married each other."

"I can't say I remember anyone called Roche," Rowland replied, thinking. "But I've not moved in the right circles for a while."

"There is that at least," Milton muttered.

Clyde placed a canvas on the other easel, setting out his brushes and colours in pedantic order. His technique was as neat as Rowland's was chaotic. Working in the same studio was something of a challenge. He positioned the easel as far as possible from Rowland's so that his own work did not get splattered with the almost violent manner in which Rowland wielded his brush.

Milton settled in the armchair between them with a tall glass of gin. "So what now?"

"I have to duck back to Sydney for a couple of days." Rowland grimaced. He didn't like abandoning his friends when they still had no clue who killed James Kelly. But it was necessary.

"Mrs. Roche?" Milton asked, grinning.

Rowland smiled. "No. I have to see a man about a plane."

"Who?"

"Chap called Edwards. He came in on the *Monterey* a couple of days ago to see his aeroplane win the MacRobertson Air Race."

"Gotta love a confident man. But why would he give his plane to you?"

"From what I understand, the race has already cost him a fortune... even if his plane does win. My offer might go some way towards mitigating those expenses."

"How much is that going to cost?" Clyde groaned. "You volunteered to fly Egon to the congress, not to underwrite the entire exercise. Look, mate, we know you want to help but we also know you're not a Communist."

Rowland laughed. "You might be in the minority. I have it on good authority that they call me Red Rowly."

Clyde stared at him. "Red Rowly? My old mum used to make that for pudding on Sundays."

"That's a jam rolly," Milton corrected. "A Red Rowly is just as sweet but a threat to democracy nonetheless."

There was an unmistakable gleam of excitement in Rowland's eyes. "Edwards' plane is the *Grosvenor House*, Clyde, a de Havilland Comet—there are only three in existence. To be honest, I'd pay a fair bit just to have a chance to fly her. Getting Egon back to Melbourne in good time is a bonus."

"What if she doesn't get here on time or at all?" Clyde asked. His concerns were well grounded. The MacRobertson Air Race from London to Melbourne was the longest in the world. It was understood from the outset that many craft would never make it to the finish line.

"In that case, I'll take Doris."

"*The Rule Britannia*!" Clyde was alarmed enough to use the aircraft's actual name. The Gipsy Moth was not fast. She would need at least twenty-four hours flying time between Fremantle and Melbourne.

"It's not ideal," Rowland conceded. "But I can carry fuel in the passenger cockpit on the way over and we'll have tailwinds on the way back. By my estimates, it's still faster than the train."

"You'd better go see Edwards." Clyde finally abandoned his disquiet about the cost of procuring the Comet. "Doris will be pushing it. No point killing Egon in the attempt to get him there on time."

14

HERE TO SEE FINISH

OWNER OF BRITISH PLANE EXPECTS TO WIN BIG AIR RACE

AUCKLAND, Monday

The hope that the machine he owns will win the Centenary air race was expressed today by Mr. A. O. Edwards, managing director of Grosvenor House, London, who is on his way to Melbourne. This machine is a specially designed De Havilland Comet, and will be piloted by C. W. Scott and Captain Campbell, two of the best pilots in England. It has a guaranteed speed of 200 m.p.h. and, according to Mr. Edwards, the pilots propose to take four hour shifts during the day with shorter shifts at night.

Daily Examiner, 2 October 1934

Colin Delaney waved from beneath the sandstone clock tower at the University of Sydney.

"Good to see you, Rowly," he said as he shook the artist's hand. "Sick of Canberra already?"

"I'm just back for a meeting—thank you for seeing me, Col."

"Not at all. I'm sorry I had to drag you out here. MacKay insisted I personally check the security with respect to this poor girl. They have her here, you know." He took a cigarette from the case in his pocket and lit it. "People filing through to see the body like it's some kind of sideshow. Though I must say they preserved her quite successfully, if you could ever call such a ghoulish thing successful."

"I take it you still don't have any idea who she is?"

"No. There have been all sorts of claims of course, from one of Tilley's girls to the Tsar of Russia's youngest daughter. Nothing that holds up under scrutiny." The cigarette glowed red as he inhaled. "I'm rather glad it's not my case anymore. Still... poor wretch."

They found a hotel near the university which provided both refreshment and a modicum of privacy. Rowland told Delaney what he knew about the murder of James Kelly.

"So the murder weapon ended up on the prime minister's desk." The detective scratched his chin. "Blimey! Good thing the secretary caught it... I'm not sure old Joe Lyons' heart could have taken it." He took a sip of his beer, licking the froth off his upper lip contentedly. "Do they know from where it was sent?"

"I gather not... of course, Major Jones isn't necessarily bringing me into his confidence."

"Yes, I suppose he wouldn't."

"As far as I know, it would have had to have come from within Parliament House or the Secretariat Building."

"But even if the killer worked in the Secretariat Building it seems silly to take it there only to send it back." Delaney signalled for another round of drinks. "No, I suspect it was sent from within the House... someone who didn't want it to be found on them."

"In which case, it must have been sent immediately after the murder itself."

"Makes sense." Delaney tapped the coaster as he thought. "Who would be able to get into the House after hours?"

"All manner of people, I believe. As Ed tells me, it's not a bank."

"But still, it makes it unlikely that the killer was some disgruntled husband whose wife was playing up."

"I suppose that's true."

"Look, Rowly, I'll see if I can find out what the various Canberra forces are up to on this and why Jones is involved. Are you sure Kelly was not a spy of some sort?"

Rowland shrugged. "Not sure, but I've been told he was simply there to keep an eye on the machinations of parliament from the public gallery."

"But the Federal Parliament doesn't resume for a week or so."

"Part of me suspects that the Communists forgot about that when they sent him. They're more passionate than organised."

Colin Delaney's face became grave. "Don't you believe it, Rowly, old mate. And you be careful what you get involved with. If someone's decided to kill Communists, then I think your slate might just be marked."

Rowland Sinclair returned to *Woodlands House* after leaving Delaney. If Mary Brown was surprised to see him she gave no indication. It was, after all, her duty to ensure the house was ready whenever the family chose to be there.

Lenin, however, was not nearly so composed. One of Edna's rescued cats also seemed pleased to see Rowland... the others ignored him entirely.

He went through his correspondence. Again, no invitations to submit. A letter and postcard from his mother written on board the SS *Marella* and posted from Fremantle. She wrote that she had been able to follow the developments surrounding the identity of the Pyjama Girl via the ship's news service. What developments, Rowland wasn't sure. Elisabeth Sinclair wondered if the mysterious body might belong to the upstairs maid at *Oaklea* who vanished into thin air the year before. Rowly laughed. Far from vanishing, the girl to whom his mother referred had left Wilfred's employ to marry the local blacksmith. Elisabeth asked to be remembered to Mr. Isaacs. The letter was addressed to Aubrey Sinclair.

Rowland ate dinner in his studio, in the company of Lenin and a ginger cat. He was struck with how quiet and virtually lifeless *Woodlands House* was in the absence of his friends. He had become accustomed to the noisy good humour and calamity of them, the philosophical arguments, the easy camaraderie.

He had barely seen Edna in the day or two before he'd left. Between them, Middleton and Mrs. Brook seemed intent on monopolising her company. Rowland missed her.

Lenin climbed onto the couch beside him and burrowed his long nose under his master's arm. Rowland took out his notebook and began to sketch from memory: Marjorie Curtis and her dolls, Major Jones, Thomas Ley and Jemima. Inevitably though, he returned to drawing Edna Higgins.

Rowland stood as Albert Octavius Edwards approached the table at which he'd been waiting. The London hotelier was solidly built and stylishly attired. His dark double-breasted suit was sharply and precisely creased; a blue silk pocket handkerchief matched his tie.

"Mr. Edwards," Rowland offered his hand. "How d'you do, sir?"

"Very well, Mr. Sinclair. Very well indeed." The Englishman's handshake was firm.

Edwards took a seat and cast an assessing eye over the table setting. He sniffed a little derisively before shaking out the napkin himself. "I can't bear small napkins," he said irritably. "A napkin should be Irish linen at least sixteen inches square. Anything else is the mark of a lesser establishment."

They ordered from a nervous waiter. Edwards critiqued the menu and the wine list before he selected. Rowland prudently ordered the same meal as his guest.

"So, Mr. Sinclair," Edwards said once the first course was served. "Why is it that my airman, Scott, owes you a good turn?"

"I met Charles Scott in the boxing ring several years ago, Mr. Edwards. We're old friends. He doesn't owe me anything. On the contrary, I'm now indebted to him."

"Yes, you are." Edwards held up his silverware to the light before using it to taste the soup. "Scott asked me to meet with you as a personal favour. What can I do for you, Mr. Sinclair?"

"I understand that funding *Grosvenor House* has been a rather expensive exercise, sir."

"Yes, of course. Even if Scott and Black win, as I'm sure they will, the endeavour will be quite the loss-making venture. A stroke of publicity genius, but financially, very unsound."

"I have a proposition for you, Mr. Edwards."

"Let's have it then, Mr. Sinclair."

"I find myself in need of a fast and proven plane for a few days in early November. I was hoping to buy yours."

"What?"

"I assume you won't need it after the race. I'd like to purchase it."

"Do you have any idea how much a de Havilland Comet would cost, Mr. Sinclair?"

"I do have an idea what you paid for it, Mr. Edwards."

"If *Grosvenor House* wins the MacRobertson she'll be worth a great deal more."

"And if she doesn't, a great deal less. I'm offering you a fair price regardless of the outcome."

Edwards picked up his glass and drank, taking a moment to consider both the quality of the wine and the proposition before him. "I must say, Sinclair, many men would find your audacity quite outrageous. I rather like it."

"So you'll sell me the plane?"

"Only if she doesn't win."

"But—"

"In the much more likely circumstance that she does win, I'll lend her to you for an appropriate compensation."

Rowland stopped, surprised. It was a reasonable solution. And so they negotiated a price with the genteel civility one would expect of gentlemen.

"Can you fly a plane, Mr. Sinclair? The Comet is not your standard pleasure craft."

"I've acquired my aviator's licence. Kingsford Smith taught me to fly. And Charles tells me he's willing to familiarise me with the instruments of the *Grosvenor House* after the victory party."

Edwards wiped his mouth with the offending napkin. "I suspect taking instruction from Mr. Scott after a victory party would not be conducive to the health of either yourself or my plane... and waiting for him to sober up may take a while. Best he show you as soon as he lands. Can you be at Flemington for the finish?"

"Yes, of course."

"And you're not planning to do anything illegal with my Comet, are you?"

"No, sir, nothing illegal."

"Then as our American cousins would say, Mr. Sinclair, we have a deal."

Milton Isaacs and Edna Higgins were shown into the office of the newly appointed Minister for Interior Affairs. The fact that he had an office was indicative of the Member for Wentworth's senior position in the government. Most representatives had only their respective Party rooms in which to meet constituents.

The Honourable Eric Harrison was not especially happy about the intrusion; he had a great deal to attend to without losing time having impromptu cups of tea with constituents on some kind of grand tour of the capital. Still, one did not snub the Sinclairs. He exhaled and put on his hustings face. It was a necessity of democracy.

Milton felt a little underdressed for the meeting. On Clyde's insistence he had donned one of Rowland's suits—well cut, but entirely unremarkable, a straitjacket of conservative conventionalism. It was undeniably the uniform of admittance to the capitalist establishment, bespoke, expensively tailored from the finest British fabric. Still, it was almost unbearably dull.

In truth, Milton had not expected his slightly duplicitous request for an audience with his local representative to be met. He had telephoned for an appointment more in jest than anything else. But as he was not a man to waste an opportunity to advocate for social justice, he had prepared a list of concerns, and what amounted to a treatise on their solution for discussion with the Honourable Eric Harrison. Clyde and Edna had tossed a coin to see who would accompany him. The sculptress had lost.

Silently, the poet sized up the politician. Once a stalwart of the short-lived All for Australia League, Harrison had been collected in a harvest of transitory right-wing parties which, along with a sprinkling of disaffected Labor men, made up the conservative United Australia

Party. He bore the air of a man who knew his political star was on the rise and thought it not before time.

Shown into the small office, they took the chairs to which they were directed.

"Thank you kindly for taking the time to see us, Mr. Harrison," Edna leant forward and placed her hand on his desk.

"A pleasure, Miss... Higgins. Though I can't imagine what an attractive young lady like yourself would find to interest her in politics."

"In politics, nothing, Mr. Harrison. In democracy, a great deal."

"I see." Harrison cleared his throat and looked to Milton. "I understand you have some concerns, Mr. Sinclair."

"Isaacs," Milton corrected. "Elias Isaacs. Mr. Sinclair was called away unexpectedly. I've come in his stead."

"As his representative?"

"Not at all. As his fellow constituent. Since you had put aside this time to meet with a constituent, I assumed it wouldn't matter which constituent that was." Milton's smile was wide-eyed innocence itself.

Harrison glared at him. "This is a little irregular but since you are here, what can I do for you, Mr... Isaacs, was it?"

Milton nodded, taking a sheaf of papers from his inside breast pocket. "I have a number of concerns for the Commonwealth Government. First and foremost, I must most strenuously complain about the folly that was the Ottawa Agreement. Clearly, since our Imperial masters do not feel at contractual liberty to trade favourably with the Dominions, it was a farce from the first. What on earth did you people think you were doing signing us up to such a ridiculous folly?"

Harrison's mouth moved silently, stuttered, and finally blustered a somewhat coherent if feeble defence.

Milton moved on to monetary reform.

Harrison recovered somewhat and argued with more certainty.

Milton had some suggestions for the alleviation of unemployment, the facilitation of industrial harmony, and working hours.

Harrison became angry. "Mr. Isaacs, if you have come here to put the Labor cause—"

"Not the Labor cause, Mr. Harrison, my cause. And you represent me, sir! So go to Mr. Lyons and the other members of the UAP and jolly well represent!"

"Milt..." Edna warned.

"Mr. Isaacs, it behoves you to remember that the United Australia Party has just been returned to government on the basis of our sound and credible policies, and not those of the Labor Party! Now you and Miss Higgins will have to excuse me... I have rather a lot to do today."

"Just one more matter, Mr. Harrison. The *Melbourne Herald* reports that we will have the privilege of a visit from a most eminent speaker next month, a gentleman by the name of Egon Kisch. Don't you think it behoves the government to organise some kind of reception? A drinks party, perhaps something simple in the gardens?"

Edna sighed.

Harrison looked like he might explode. "Did you say Kisch... Ewart Kisch?"

"Egon... not Ewart." Milton smiled. "I believe he's quite famous on the Continent. Certainly better known than the king's third son whom every arm of government seems desperate to fete."

"How dare you, sir! Your words come very close to treason!"

Milton snorted.

"And what's more, the Commonwealth is not in the habit of throwing soirees for known Communists!"

Milton banged the desk. "You are my representative, sir. I demand you put my request to the parliament."

"Why that's absurd!"

"And here I was thinking that you'd been won over to democracy despite your dalliance with the All for Australia League."

Harrison was truly furious now. "I believe it would be prudent for you to leave before I'm forced to have my secretary call security and have you arrested for... for... have you arrested!"

"A fine way to treat a constituent!"

"You would do well, Mr. Isaacs, to reconsider your present course. I don't know what you call democracy, but it does not entitle you to march in and demand of a Minister of the Crown that he entertain a known dissident who has already been deported and banned from the United Kingdom!"

Milton stopped. "Yes, well thank you, Mr. Harrison. It's been a pleasure." He stood. "Keep up the good fight and all that, old bean." He opened the door for Edna. "We'd best let you get on."

"Good day to you, Mr. Harrison," Edna said sweetly.

Harrison stared after them as they waved cheerio and disappeared down the corridor.

15

FEDERAL MINISTRY

PERSONNEL ANNOUNCED
MR. HARRISON THE SURPRISE

Mr. W.M. Hughes Included

The new Federal Ministry was announced tonight, by the Prime Minister as follows:

Prime Minister and Treasurer: Mr. J.A. Lyons.

Minister for External Affairs and Territories: Sir George Pearce.

Attorney-General: Mr. R.G. Menzies.

Minister for Defence: Mr. Archdale Parkhill.

Minister for Trade and Customs: Colonel T. White.

Vice-President of the Executive Council and Minister for Health: Mr. W.M. Hughes.

Postmaster-General and Minister in Charge of Development: Senator A.J. M'Lachlan.

Minister for Commerce and Industry: Mr. F.H. Stewart.

Minister for the Interior: Mr. E.J. Harrison.

Assistant Treasurer: Mr. R. Casey.

Minister without portfolio directing trade treaties: Sir Henry Gullett.

Minister without portfolio in charge of repatriation and War Service homes: Mr. J. Francis.

Assistant Minister for Commerce and Interior: Senator T.C. Brennan.

Assistant Minister until the conclusion of the royal tour: Mr. C.W. Marr.

The only surprise was the inclusion of Mr. Harrison in the Cabinet. He represents Wentworth.

Wagga Wagga Daily Advertiser, 11 October 1934

"Would I be right to suppose you had some purpose in goading Mr. Harrison into losing his rag?" Edna whispered as she and Milton walked down the main stairs, avoiding the spot on which they knew Jim Kelly had died. For some reason it seemed disrespectful to step there.

"I was simply raising some very valid concerns, Ed. But apparently Egon has been banned in the United Kingdom."

"Does that matter?"

"I'm not sure. But the fact that Harrison is aware of it before Egon is anywhere near this country makes me wonder about the source of his information."

"He's the Minister for the Interior—isn't it his business to know?"

"Harrison's only been minister for a few days. A week ago he was a backbencher." Milton stroked his short beard, his brow furrowed. "Arthur Howells thought there was a spy in the movement."

Edna smiled. "Of course there is. The police have spies everywhere. I wouldn't be surprised if Mary Brown was a member of the New South Wales police force!"

"That'd explain a few things."

"What do you think will happen, Milt?"

"The Lyons government will try to revoke Egon's visa or something equally daft. But the movement's ready for that, though it would be handy if we could tell the barrister under what authority they will seek to exclude him."

"The movement has a barrister?"

"I don't think he's on a retainer but if Egon is prevented from landing there's a former judge of the High Court ready to act on his behalf. But, as I said, that's not our greatest worry."

"And what is?"

"I don't believe Kelly was killed by a disgruntled husband. I think he was killed by someone who knew he was a Communist."

"Why?"

"There was a Communist badge pinned on his lapel."

"So..."

"He was undercover—our signal was the red scarves. Why would he wear a red star badge?"

"Maybe he wasn't that bright," Edna countered. "We've never met Jim Kelly, Milt; how could we begin to guess what his motivations were?"

"The badge was pinned too low on the lapel." Milton tapped his own lapel just above the jacket button. "I don't think Kelly would have worn a pin at all, let alone in such an odd position. No, I suspect the killer left it there to make sure the police knew full well that Jim was a Communist."

They stepped out together to cross the street, their arms entwined, their heads together.

"We need to visit Sunshine Studios and establish why Kelly had those photographs—Ed! Watch out!"

The black Ford Tudor had been travelling on the other side of the road, which is why they hadn't noticed it until it swerved towards them. The sound of its engine rose to a roar as it accelerated. Milton pushed Edna out of the vehicle's path just a breath before the Ford's grille impacted with his body. He flew over the bonnet and landed in a motionless, crumpled heap on the bitumen. Screams and shouts and the screech of tyres as the Ford reversed and sped away.

Rowland strode into the Canberra Hospital. The moment he arrived back at the Hotel Canberra, the concierge had informed him that Mr. Isaacs and Miss Higgins had been involved in an accident. He hadn't waited to ask for details. He spotted Clyde first.

"Where are they, Clyde? What the hell happened?"

"A hit and run... Milt took the brunt of it. Ed's a little bruised from the fall, but they say she'll be all right."

"What fall?" Rowland asked, confused.

"Milt shoved her out of the way. The car hit him."

"And Milt?"

"A dislocated hip. He hasn't come round yet."

Rowland cursed.

Clyde nodded. "Quite. The police have been taking Ed's statement. They left just before you arrived. We should be able to go in now."

Edna smiled to see them. Still in a hospital gown, the grazes on her arms were visible, as was the bruise on her forehead. "I fell on some gravel," she said. "I don't know why they're making a fuss." She embraced them each in turn. "How's Milt? They won't tell me anything." Her voice broke.

"I'll find out," Rowland promised, kissing her hand.

He left her with Clyde and went in search of someone who could update them on Milton's condition. He managed to speak to a doctor who assured him that the poet, while seriously injured, was not in danger. The bones in his hip had been realigned under anaesthetic.

It was a couple of hours before they were allowed into Milton's room.

He was awake, but groggy with pain medication. Eventually the staff asked them to go.

"Mr. Isaacs is not in any danger," the matron said as she ushered them out. "The doctors simply want him to rest. You can come back in the morning."

Edna shook her head. "Someone tried to kill Mr. Isaacs, Matron. What if they try again?"

"The police didn't say…"

"They are convinced it was an accident." She looked earnestly at the nurse. "But it wasn't. It really wasn't."

The matron frowned. "You need to rest too, Miss Higgins. Clearly you're still distraught."

Rowland handed his car keys to Clyde. "Please take Ed back to the hotel. Make sure she rests. I'll look out for Milt."

"I'm sorry, sir, this is a hospital," the matron puffed to her full volume.

Rowland stepped away from his friends, and towards her. "I do realise it's an imposition, Matron," he said quietly. "But I fear that Miss Higgins will fret for Mr. Isaacs' safety, and, considering the shock she's just had, the worry might impede her recovery… I'll just sit outside Mr. Isaacs' room… I won't disturb him."

"You'd sit in a chair all night just so Miss Higgins won't be upset?" The matron glanced at Edna. With burly Clyde's arm about her, she looked very young and pale. And she was close to tears.

"It would set all our minds at ease."

The matron sighed. "Perhaps you can sit in his room… as long as you don't disturb him." She folded her arms over an ample breast. "I will not have you cluttering my corridors by loitering outside Mr. Isaacs' door."

"Thank you."

Rowland paused to farewell Clyde and Edna. He resisted the impulse to take the sculptress in his arms and handed her his handkerchief instead. "I'll keep an eye on Milt, you mustn't worry."

"The car swerved from across the road and accelerated to hit us, Rowly." She took his hand in both of hers. "You be careful."

"I will. You try and rest and I'll see you both tomorrow."

Rowland settled in the easy chair beside Milton's bed. Despite her initial resistance to the idea, the matron brought him a pillow and a blanket.

"Thank you, Matron, you're very kind," Rowland whispered. "But I wouldn't be much of a bodyguard if I fell asleep."

"As you wish, Mr. Sinclair. If, however, you disturb my nurses in their duties you will have to go. I've asked one of the younger nurses to bring you some supper."

Once again Rowland thanked her.

Milton's legs were elevated in traction, his hips packed in ice and surrounded by counterweights. Rowland winced, glad his friend seemed as yet oblivious to any pain. He did not for a moment doubt Edna's claim that this had been no accident.

A young nurse brought in a cup of tea, some sandwiches and a bowl of jelly. She checked on Milton and chatted to Rowland as he ate.

"Mr. Isaacs will be all right, sir." She responded quite willingly to his enquiry. "There weren't any fractures and the doctors were very happy with the realignment. He'll be able to walk on crutches in a week or so." She adjusted Milton's pillows. "They say he saved Miss Higgins life. One doesn't often think of a Communist being heroic."

Rowland looked up sharply. "How did you know Milt was a Communist, Miss...?"

"Owens. The badge on his jacket." She giggled. "And when he was coming out of the anaesthetic, he started singing that Communist song—the one about the flag—at the top of his voice. Nearly scared Neville, the wardsman, half to death. The doctor thought it was best to give him something to calm him down."

"Neville?"

"No, Mr. Isaacs."

"I see."

Whatever it was that had been administered to Milton it was a number of hours before he was awake enough to be coherent. At first he just cursed a string of profanity through gritted teeth.

Concerned, Rowland stood to summon a nurse. Milton called him back.

"Rowly, is that you?"

"Yes. What can I do?"

"I dunno. What the hell happened?"

Rowland told him what he knew.

"So Ed's all right?"

"She is, thanks to you, old boy. Do you remember anything?"

"I remember the car swerved onto our side of the road. Nothing after that." He raised his eyes to his feet suspended well above his head. "I must say I'm a little surprised to wake up slung up like a brace of rabbits."

"Are you in a lot of pain?" Rowland asked.

"I'm not sure. My nether regions are pretty bloody cold."

"That'll be the ice… I'll call someone."

"No, never mind about that. What did the police say?"

"They're sure this was an accident… Milt, were you wearing a Communist badge today?"

"Of course not! I'm not daft." Milton paused, closing his eyes against a wave of pain.

"God, Milt, I should call the doctor—"

"No. I'm all right. Just have to remember not to move—at all." He caught his breath. "The only reason I got into see bloody Harrison was because he thought I was you. I'm hardly going to announce I'm a member of the proletariat by wearing a badge."

"That's what I thought. Nurse Owens mentioned there was a badge on your jacket when they brought you in." Rowland hoped Milton would not become too agitated by the news.

The poet started, swearing as the movement told. "Like Kelly."

"Yes." Rowland did call for a nurse this time.

It was the matron who responded. He waited as she attended to her patient, making notes in a clipboard and extending a kind of firm maternal sympathy. "I'll fetch the doctor and see about something more for the pain, pet," she promised as she left the room once again.

Rowland pressed Milton's shoulder. "We'll get to the bottom of this, Milt. I'll organise professional security in the morning and, until then, I'm not going anywhere."

"Look, comrade," Milton said urgently. "You'll have to send word to Howells. He can't send anyone to replace me and he'll need to warn anyone else he has stationed here."

"I'll send a telegram tomorrow morning."

"I need to speak to Clyde."

"Why?"

"Because he's a Communist and you're not."

"You don't trust me?"

Despite everything, Milton smiled. "I trust you with my life, mate. I just don't want to make things awkward for you."

The doctor arrived then. He seemed a little surprised to see Rowland, but aside from a pointedly raised brow, he said nothing. Rowland watched Milton's face visibly relax as the morphine took effect.

Clyde and Edna arrived early the next morning. The sculptress looked herself again, the grazes on her arms covered by the drape of a short navy cape, the bruise on her face disguised by the jaunty set of her hat. She came in with a bunch of pungent gardenias, but Rowland could only smell roses. It might have been her perfume or simply an association, he wasn't sure. Even after all these years, there was a familiar stirring in his chest at the sight of her.

"Oh, Rowly, you look exhausted!" Edna said as he rose from the chair in which he'd spent the night watching for anything untoward, and ready to fight.

Clyde placed the keys to the Airflow into his hands. "You go back to the hotel and grab a shower and a kip. We'll keep an eye on Milt."

"He wants to speak to you about something... remind him before they give him another dose of pain medication."

Clyde nodded.

Before he left the hospital, Rowland asked the nurse for the clothes Milton had been wearing. "I'll have them cleaned for when Mr. Isaacs is ready to leave."

"That's good of you, sir." He was given a large paper bag marked "Isaacs".

Back at the Hotel Canberra, Rowland pulled a Communist badge from the breast welt pocket of the jacket of what looked very much like one of his own suits. The badge had a new minted shine to it. Other than that, there were no identifying marks. He showered quickly, ordered coffee and toast, and then made some telephone calls.

He rang through to Major Harold Jones and explained events such as he knew them to be. "Someone appears to be trying to kill Communists, sir."

On the validity of that conclusion they argued for a time. Jones suggested that it might be best if Milton returned to Sydney.

Rowland agreed. "Unfortunately the nature of Mr. Isaacs' injuries are such that he will not be able to travel for at least a week."

A further exchange of differences in opinion. Finally, Jones grudgingly agreed to provide two men at the hospital until such time as Milton was physically able to leave the capital.

Next, Rowland arranged for a telegram to be sent to Arthur Howells, advising him that Milton had been injured and that there was reason to believe that Communists in the capital, or at least in the vicinity of the Federal Parliament, were in danger.

He slept for two hours then, before returning to the hospital.

He was surprised to find that the men Jones had promised had arrived so promptly and in such number. There were two officers in place outside the hospital and another three inside. There seemed to be a general state of excitement about the place.

The matron bustled past. "You should have given us some warning, Mr. Sinclair," she said, beaming. "We could at least have shaved him."

"I beg your pardon?"

"Mr. Isaacs' visitors... it's quite the honour. We couldn't be more excited if it was the Duke of Gloucester himself." She scurried off before he could enquire as to the identity of these illustrious visitors.

He wondered if he should wait outside but curiosity got the better of him and he ducked his head into Milton's hospital room.

16

BRUCE-PAGE AGAIN?
NO THANKS

————————◆————————

MYSTERIOUS RESURRECTION MOVES

BUT GENIAL AMATEURS TOO COSTLY

LYONS WON'T BE DITCHED FOR
THE "CALAMITY TWINS"

Strange undercurrents are flowing in the political world. A subterranean movement is being engineered to ditch Joseph Aloysius Lyons, Prime Minister of the Commonwealth, and bring back Stanley Melbourne Bruce and Earle Page as his cobber in a new U.A.P.- U.C.P. Coalition Government.

AND IF STANLEY MELBOURNE BRUCE IS UNWILLING TO ACT, SOMEONE ELSE CAN BE PUT UP AS THE COCONUT. IT DOES NOT REALLY MATTER WHO IT IS. BECAUSE THE OBJECT OF THE FINESSE IS TO MAKE EARLE PAGE THE DICTATOR OF POLICY.

Truth, 24 June 1924

"Mr. Sinclair, there you are!" The familiar warmth of Ethel Bruce in an elaborate hat greeted Rowland as he walked into the room. She left Milton's bedside and manoeuvred her way towards Rowland.

"Mrs. Bruce," Rowland said as first she shook his hand, and then, deciding that would not do, embraced him.

"I cannot tell you how much I've missed you all since our caper in London!"

"Ethel..." Stanley Bruce cleared his throat. "Ethel... unhand the boy."

Ethel Bruce flapped a hand in her husband's direction. "Oh, Stanley. We're old friends, comrades in arms."

"Splendid to see you again, Your Excellency," Rowland said smiling.

"Edna was just telling us what a hero Mr. Isaacs was," Ethel said.

"*Is*," Milton declared. "I'm not dead."

"Of course not, Mr. Isaacs!"

"How are you, Milt?" Rowland asked.

"No change, no pause, no hope. Yet I endure."

"Shelley." Rowland smiled, relieved. Milton did not look comfortable, but his face had lost the pallor of the previous day, and he was apparently well enough to steal poetry once again.

As Ethel Bruce exchanged news with Edna and Clyde, and fussed over Milton, Stanley Bruce spoke quietly to Rowland. "Miss Higgins seems to be of the opinion that Mr. Isaacs' injury was not accidentally caused."

Rowland nodded. "Yes."

"I believe Wilfred has made you aware of the crude item which was delivered to the prime minister's office via the Lamson tube system."

"Yes, he has."

"I am, of course, mindful, Rowland, of your predilection to undertake your own amateur investigations—"

"I see."

"I do not intend to dissuade you. Lord knows if Wilfred couldn't talk sense into you, I am unlikely to meet with success." Australia's eighth prime minister shook his head. "As you may remember, my good wife is also predisposed to play the sleuth when the opportunity arises. I would prefer it if you did not encourage her on this occasion."

Rowland's lips twitched. "I see."

"Do we understand each other, Rowland?"

"I doubt Mrs. Bruce will follow my direction, sir."

Bruce sighed. "No. Mrs. Bruce doesn't follow directions." He emphasised his next words. "Just don't encourage her. It's unseemly for the wife of the Australian High Commissioner to Britain to be solving murders like some Belgian detective."

Rowland glanced at the new copy of Agatha Christie's recently released *Murder in Three Acts* sitting on the table beside Milton's bed. He assumed it was a gift from Ethel Bruce, who like the poet was a fan of the genre. "I'll do my best, sir, but I doubt Mrs. Bruce will be affected by a simple lack of encouragement on my part."

"Yes, quite," Bruce conceded.

Ethel Bruce collected her handbag from where she'd left it on the bed. "We should be on our way now, Stanley, before Mr. Isaacs gets too tired." She considered Milton for a moment. "Kate was so hoping you'd all come out to *Oaklea*... perhaps when you're up and about, Mr. Isaacs."

"I'll drop in on my way to Melbourne," Rowland promised.

"You pulled it off then?" Clyde asked grinning.

Rowland nodded. He had not previously had the chance to inform his friends that he'd been successful in securing the Comet.

"Well done, Rowly!" Milton too applauded, albeit gingerly.

"What have you pulled off, Mr. Sinclair?" Ethel Bruce enquired curiously.

"Rowly has bought himself a new plane, Mrs. Bruce," Clyde said.

"And it's in Melbourne?" Ethel said.

"It will be, I hope," Rowland replied. "The aircraft in question is competing in the MacRobertson Air Race so I'll need to be there at the finish to claim her."

"How very exciting," Ethel clasped gloved hands. "But you shall miss all the excitement here. The Duke of Gloucester will be opening parliament, and I believe there will be a grand ball that evening."

"Ethel, my dear..." Bruce opened his pocket watch pointedly.

"Yes, yes, we must be off to luncheon." Ethel made a face. "There's nothing like the talk of Imperial markets and the gold standard to aid digestion."

And so they bade Mr. and Mrs. Bruce farewell. Ethel assured them she would return as soon as she could, and insisted Edna promise to report any "developments" directly to her.

"Major Jones may think he's in charge of CIB..." Milton murmured.

The Bruces departed, pausing to shake hands with the hospital staff who it seemed had forgotten Stanley Bruce was no longer prime minister.

Edna placed her hand gently on the poet's forehead. "Would you like us to leave too, so you can get some sleep, darling?"

"God no! We have developments to deal with!"

Rowland and Clyde begged a couple of extra chairs from the matron. Still glowing after having exchanged pleasantries with Stanley Melbourne Bruce and his charming wife, she was happy to indulge them.

Milton had already told Clyde and Edna about the Communist badges, and their implications.

"I've let Arthur know that the government is communicating with London about Egon," Clyde said.

Rowland assumed that was the communication out of which Milton had been careful to keep him. He was grateful. Not that he thought the message was of great import, but he would have

164

struggled with reporting to the Communist Party on the activities of government, however trivial.

"How do you know they're talking to the government about Egon?" he asked.

Edna told him about their meeting with Harrison.

"Good Lord, are you sure he didn't run you down?" Rowland murmured as Edna described Milton's ludicrous demands for representation.

"It's possible," Milton replied gravely.

"I was speaking in jest, Milt. The Member for Wentworth did not try to kill you with a Ford Tudor."

Milton frowned. "You're right," he said in the end. "Harrison's much more likely to drive a Rolls-Royce... can you instruct a chauffeur to run a man down?"

"I don't know," Edna replied. "I don't think Mr. Johnston would follow such a direction, but Wilfred's chauffeurs might and Mary Brown definitely would."

They lapsed briefly into a discussion of which of the Sinclair servants could be successfully instructed to kill. It was generally agreed that Rowland's housekeeper could indeed be so directed but by Wilfred rather than Rowland, who had never had real control of his staff.

When the homicidal potential of the staff had been adequately explored, Rowland told them about his conversation with Jones and the director's promise of men to guard the hospital.

"Good," Milton said. "Since you don't have to be my personal security, you'll be able to find out who's been trying to knock off Reds."

"And how do you suggest we do that?"

"Sunshine Studios. There's something odd about those photos."

Rowland agreed. "It might allow us to establish why Kelly had them."

"Rowly and I will go this afternoon," Edna decided. "I can pretend I want to have some portraits taken."

"Ed, did you see who was near Milton after the accident?" Clyde asked.

Edna closed her eyes to recall. "Police, Parliament House staff, a couple of people trying to help and the ambulance. Why?"

"Well, one of those people pinned a Communist badge to Milt's jacket."

Rowland nodded. "We're not talking about one person then."

"What do you mean?"

"Well, the driver of the Ford Tudor didn't stop to pin a badge on Milt—he had to be acting in concert with someone."

Milton shifted against the pillows. Edna stood to adjust them for him. "That makes sense. We're not talking about random, opportunistic murders… Communists are being targeted."

"How do you suppose they knew Milt was a Communist?" Clyde pondered. Milton did not hesitate to declare his politics but in the streets of Canberra, wearing one of Rowland's suits, he was hardly wearing a sign.

"The men in the car clearly knew whom they were looking for," Edna said quietly.

"Men?" Rowland said sharply. "You saw them?"

"I saw that there were two men." She shook her head. "I wouldn't recognise them."

"They must have known that Milt was going to be at Parliament House," Clyde added.

"I wasn't supposed to be at Parliament House," Milton said. "Rowland Sinclair had the appointment."

Rowland groaned for many reasons. "So they're not targeting Communists…"

"Not necessarily. You're Red Rowly, remember." Milton pointed at Rowland. "Before you even think about flogging yourself over this, mate, bear in mind that I'm quite put out that they wouldn't try to run me over in my own right."

"Don't worry," Clyde muttered. "I'm sure someone will soon."

"The point is, Rowly," Milton continued, "you need to be careful. Don't assume it's just we bona fide Communists in their sights. You know Howells is convinced there's a rat in the movement. They could well know that you're the man we're relying on to get Egon to the congress."

Sunshine Studios at Eastlake was a thriving photographic studio which specialised in formal portraits. The modest office was gloomy and cluttered. Dusty frames exhibited examples of the studio's work. On the counter stood price lists for anything from passport pictures to wedding portraits.

Edna enquired of the gentleman behind the counter about having her portrait taken.

"We offer a very reasonable service, Madame," he said enthusiastically, "and we come highly recommended. Will it be just of yourself, or perhaps you and your husband would prefer to be taken together?"

"Oh just of me," Edna said, smiling. "My husband doesn't like being photographed."

"Who'll have copies of the photographs you take?" Rowland asked gruffly. "I don't particularly fancy my wife's photo being stuck on your wall as an advertisement!"

"Well... I'll... I'll just have to fetch Mr. Banks."

"Please do."

The man disappeared through a door into what Rowland assumed was the studio. Edna peered behind the counter before returning to link her arm through his in a manner that was quite conjugal. Rowland winked at her. Somehow they seemed to always fall into masquerading as husband and wife when called upon to play a part. Perhaps it was because married couples raised less suspicion.

The man who emerged through the door was no more than forty. Dapper and well-groomed, he moved and spoke smoothly. "Good afternoon, sir, madam, George Banks at your service."

"How d'you do, Mr. Banks. Rowland Sinclair. May I introduce my wife?"

"Charmed, thoroughly charmed. As a photographic artist, Mr. Sinclair, can I tell you that I would be very excited to make your wife's portrait. Madame, the planes of your face are perfect!"

Rowland frowned. "I am concerned about the privacy of any prints." He glanced pointedly at the portraits on the walls.

"Oh no, Mr. Sinclair, let me assure you that the portraits on our walls are there only with the consent of the subjects. Most of our clients consider it an honour."

"I'm afraid Rowly's far too proper, not to mention jealous, to allow that." Edna gazed adoringly at her supposed husband. On cue, Rowland placed his arm possessively around her shoulders and tried to look as tyrannical as possible.

"Well of course. If it bothers you, we shall never use your wife's portrait for display."

"How can we be sure?" Rowland demanded. "Do your clients receive all printed copies?"

"Well yes, we only keep the negatives on file in case you should want a reprint at some later date."

"And where are these files, Mr. Banks? Who has access to them?"

"I'll show you." Banks opened the door to the adjoining studio.

Rowland and Edna walked through. The room was long, naturally lit through lateral windows just below the ceiling. The walls were hung with backdrops, some neutral, others exotic. Plinths and urns, ostrich feather fans, draperies, armchairs, chaises and a stuffed toucan, all ready to add visual interest to a portrait. The back wall of the room was lined with wooden filing cabinets, each drawer labelled with a letter.

"All our negatives are filed here under the client's name."

"So you could make an extra print at any time?"

"Yes, Smithy does most of the darkroom work."

"The gentleman we met at the counter?"

"No, no, that's Pete Wilks. Smithy only comes in the evening. He's a bit of a night owl and it means we don't get in each other's way."

"I see," Rowland said. "I will say, Mr. Banks, you do come highly recommended."

"Can I ask by whom, Mr. Sinclair?"

"Chap who used to do some work for me by the name of Jim Kelly."

For just the briefest moment, Banks looked startled. Almost immediately he smiled again. But Rowland had caught it. "I can't say I recall a Mr. Kelly. But please extend him my thanks for the recommendation."

Rowland took Edna's hand. "We've taken up enough of your time, Mr. Banks."

Banks stood back so they could walk past him through the door. "Shall I ask Pete to make you an appointment for a portrait, Mrs. Sinclair?"

"What do you think, dearest?" Edna blinked beseechingly at Rowland.

"I'll consider it," Rowland replied.

Edna laughed. "Don't you worry, Mr. Banks. I'll persuade him."

Rowland sighed as if she were an incorrigible child. To the gaping photographer he said, "We'll be in touch."

17

VOGUE OF THE "THRILLER"

From Horace Walpole to Edgar Wallace—and After

People of all times have asked for exciting stories, whether they were told or written. Horace Walpole set a model for terror tales of a new type by writing in the 18th century the "Gothic" romance "The Castle of Otranto." He had many imitators among writers in Germany, France, and England. Edgar Allan Poe developed the story of mystery in a new way by introducing the detection of crime in such tales as "The Mystery of Marie Roget." His French detective, Dupin, was undoubtedly one of the ancestors of Sherlock Holmes.

Dickens treated of detective work in his records of Inspector Bucket and in "Hunted Down"; but it was a younger novelist of that time, Wilkie Collins, who invented a new variety of crime story, letting the reader learn the truth gradually from the uncomprehending statements of a number of characters. After the great vogue of the Sherlock Holmes stories of a later period there was not much demand for "thrillers" until the novels of Edgar Wallace became the fashion.

Ingenuity is shown by a number of the writers of "thrillers," and some of them have a good share of literary ability. Most of the writers prefer to reserve the full solution of the mystery for the last chapter, but a few think that even greater interest can be imparted to the story by telling the reader the secret at the beginning, and letting him observe the mistakes and the fresh efforts of the investigators. Among the most accomplished writers of "thrillers" are Agatha Christie, Dorothy L. Sayers, G.D.H. and M. Cole, Ronald Knox, and Valentine Williams...

The Argus, 8 December 1934

A handful of people still lingered around the Airflow when Rowland and Edna returned to it. Rowland was becoming accustomed to his motorcar's almost celebrity status. He had to admit she was an unusual-looking automobile. He answered a few questions and the curious soon moved on.

Edna waited until they were both in the car before she spoke. "What do you think, Rowly?"

"It seems any of them could have made extra copies of the portraits. Banks did appear to react to Jim Kelly's name."

Edna nodded. "Yes, I saw that too."

"So let's assume Banks sent Kelly the photographs," Rowland said trying to set events in a logical sequence. "Or that he at least knew Pete Wilks had done so. I still can't fathom why."

Edna wrinkled her nose. "They were hardly the kind of photos men generally collect. And Mr. Banks makes those too."

"He what?"

"Mr. Banks takes photographs of nude models."

"How do you know?"

"I saw a pile of postcards behind the counter... taken using his backdrops and props." She smiled. "They're not unlike your paintings."

Rowland suppressed an instinct to defend his work against a comparison with pornography.

The sculptress laughed as she saw the unspoken affront in his eyes.

He continued. "So we can probably conclude Kelly was not procuring portraits of entirely attired women for the purpose of titillation... not when there was more conventionally erotic material close at hand."

"Probably," Edna said thoughtfully. "Rowly, what would you do if you came across another man—a stranger—with a photograph of your wife?"

"You or some equally imaginary but hypothetical wife?"

"The latter."

"I'd ask him to explain himself, I expect."

"And if he also had a picture of Milton's wife and Clyde's?"

"I don't know... the notion's somewhat bizarre."

"Would you be angry?"

"Very possibly."

"I do wonder if Mr. Kelly was sent those photographs in the hope that the husbands of the women in them would take offence." She tapped his arm excitedly as a thought occurred. "Perhaps their husbands are Communists."

"I'm not sure I follow, Ed."

"Perhaps the intention here was to make Mr. Kelly's fellow Communists distrust him."

Rowland nodded slowly. It was plausible. "But how would they know he had the photos?"

Edna's shoulders slumped. "They wouldn't, of course. Darn, I thought I was on to something."

Rowland smiled at the open disappointment on her face. He tried to help. "What if Kelly was enticed to do something with the photographs that alerted the husbands? If they were Communists, it's quite possible Kelly knew them."

Edna sighed. "Maybe it doesn't matter anyway."

"What do you mean?"

"Well, the point is that it looks as though someone was attempting to at least discredit Mr. Kelly, and possibly place in him in danger of retribution by a husband who thinks he's been cuckolded. But perhaps it didn't work." Edna's shoulders straightened again. "Perhaps whoever sent the photographs decided to take more direct action."

"As convoluted as that is, it does make a strange sort of sense." Rowland turned over the Airflow's engine. "I wonder what Major Jones would make of Sunshine Studios."

"You're going to tell him?"

"Yes." He glanced at Edna. "I'm going to have to leave for Melbourne soon, Ed. Though with Milt in hospital—"

"Don't be silly, Rowly. Clyde and I can take care of Milt. You go collect your aeroplane and fetch Egon back to Melbourne."

He reached over and took her hand as he spoke. "I want you to be careful... please. I hate leaving when I know you could all be in danger. As soon as Milt is able to travel get him back to *Woodlands*."

Edna smiled. "Major Jones has two men stationed at the hospital and that matron is pretty formidable. We won't let anything happen to him."

"I'm not only worried about Milt. You and Clyde need to watch your backs too."

For a moment Edna looked defiant and then her eyes softened. "We'll be careful, but promise you will be too."

Rowland laughed. "Me—"

"This new plane, Rowly, is it safe? How can you be sure it'll make it to Fremantle in one piece?"

"I'll only be able to take the *Grosvenor House* if it makes it to Melbourne from London. Melbourne to Fremantle will, by comparison, be child's play." Enthusiasm crept into his voice. "The Comet is the fastest plane in the world, Ed."

"But you've never flown a Comet, Rowly."

"I can't imagine it'll be all that different to flying any other twin engine... just faster with any luck."

Edna shook her head. There was no point trying to reason with
Rowland about modern vehicles of any sort. Despite nearly dying
in the Mercedes, he seemed to believe a steering wheel made him
invulnerable. She said as much and he pointed out that aeroplanes did
not have steering wheels.

Bertram Middleton was waiting for Edna at the hospital. He leapt
out of the visitors' lounge in a manner so sudden and unexpected that
Rowland reacted instinctively to protect the sculptress. He had the
man by the collar before he realised his mistake.

"Middleton!" He lowered his fist. "For pity's sake…"

Ignoring Rowland, the journalist straightened his attire and
embraced Edna. "I just heard what happened. Why didn't you let me
know?" He brushed aside her hair to inspect the bruise on her brow.
"Oh my darling, are you sure you're all right?"

"I'm perfectly well, Bertie. It was poor Milt they ran down."

"Thank goodness for that!"

"I beg your pardon!"

Rowland left them to it. He spoke to the matron who reassured
him that Milton was sleeping peacefully, and then he popped his head
into the room to see that Clyde too was dozing in the armchair by the
bed.

He stood in line to use the public telephone. The two people
before him were brief and as there was no one lined up behind him
he was able to make his calls in relative privacy. He called through to
Arthur Howells first.

"Rowland? What's wrong? Has Milton taken a turn for the worse?"

"No, Bluey. He seems much stronger today, in fact. I'm calling
about something else entirely." He told Howells about Edna's theory

that the photographs they'd found in Kelly's bag had been sent to cause trouble with their subjects' husbands, who might or might not be Communists.

"What are their names?" Howells seemed to realise what he was asking.

"Dwyer and Burton."

"Yes. They are members of the Queanbeyan branch. Quite active in the Trades and Labour Council. Kelly had photographs of their wives?"

"Yes. But I doubt the poor chap had ever met the ladies. Otherwise I presume he would have recognised them as the wives of his comrades."

"I'll get in touch with Dwyer and Burton. See what they have to say."

Rowland made a second call then to Detective Delaney. Luck was with him again and he was put through immediately. He updated Delaney on what had happened.

"Bloody hell! Is Milt all right?"

"He will be, we're told."

"Have they tracked down the car? The driver?"

"No, neither. The Canberra Police are treating it as a hit and run."

"I see." Delaney sighed. "Look, Rowly, they're sending me to Canberra for the duke's visit—to represent the CIB or some such nonsense. In the meantime, I'll make some enquiries."

"Can't ask fairer than that, Col."

"Give Milt my best and the rest of you watch yourselves. God only knows what you've stumbled into this time."

Finally, Rowland telephoned Major Harold Jones. The crisp, vaguely bored voice informed him that the director was not available.

When Rowland returned to Milton's hospital room, he found Edna, Clyde and the injured poet deep in conversation. They were poring over a newspaper.

"Where's Middleton?"

"I sent him to buy Milton some fruit." Edna handed Rowland the newspaper. "Page three, top left-hand corner."

Rowland opened the broadsheet. An article about *Black Magic*, the de Havilland Comet to be flown by Jim and Amy Mollinson. "Wrong plane," he said smiling. "I'm waiting on the *Grosvenor House*. There are three Comets in the MacRobertson."

"We know," Clyde said. "They only started testing the Comets a couple of weeks ago..."

"The *Grosvenor House* will have to get here before I take her, Clyde. Presumably that won't happen unless her engines are in good order."

Clyde snorted. "You've flown with Kingsford Smith, Rowly—you know those blokes will tie the wings back on with their neckties to limp a plane home. There are no guarantees. If something goes wrong while you're up there alone—"

"You're not suggesting I pull out?" Rowland's tone made it clear that was not an option.

"No, but I should go with you."

"You want to fly the plane?"

"No, you can do that," Clyde replied. "But I understand engines, and I'll be a second set of hands. If something goes wrong that'll be useful, I imagine."

"Possibly, but we can't both leave Milt—"

"I'm not in any danger, Rowly," Milton said firmly. "The mongrels in the Tudor were set on removing a Communist from the vicinity of Parliament House. That's been achieved, for the moment at least. Nobody's going to come after me now."

"They cut Kelly's throat, Milt."

"At Parliament House. And we should also bear in mind that the blokes who ran me down probably thought I was you. Someone needs to watch your back."

"When's Egon due in Fremantle?" Edna asked.

"The sixth of November."

"And how long will the Comet take to get there?"

"About six hours, I believe."

"So you'll want to leave for Fremantle by—but probably not earlier than—the third." Edna counted the days on her fingers. "A day to get there, a day to rest and a day just in case."

"That sounds about right."

"Well, in that case, Clyde will have plenty of time to meet you in Melbourne. Milt will be back on his feet, or at least on crutches, and we'll be home in Sydney before the end of the month."

Rowland groaned. Somehow everything had become very messy.

"Tell me, comrade," Milton propped himself up on his elbows, biting his lip as he did so. "When do you need to head to Melbourne to claim the *Grosvenor House?*"

"The race doesn't even start till the twentieth, so I have a few days."

Despite his current condition, Milton's dark eyes glinted. "Well, let's use that time to figure out who killed Kelly and then tried to do me in."

Clyde sighed. "We can blame this," he said, picking up the volume of Christie's *Murder in Three Acts* that Ethel Bruce had brought in that morning. "We really shouldn't let him read anything but the Bible."

Rowland grimaced. The Bible was probably uncalled for.

"For an artist you have very little imagination." Milton reached out to snatch back his book.

"We might as well try to find out what we can," Rowland said, smiling. "At the very least it might motivate Jones to treat this as something more than a traffic accident." He told them what he and Edna had discovered at Sunshine Studios and his subsequent conversation with Arthur Howells.

"I wonder what Mr. Kelly was really doing here," Edna murmured. "Parliament's been in recess. What on earth could he have been doing for the past month?"

Clyde sighed, deciding to let Edna and Rowland in on what he and Milton already knew. "Howells says Kelly was trying to recruit members."

"In Canberra?"

"In the House. Kelly thought if he could bring a few staff members over to the cause, well then, we might learn a darn sight more than we would in the public gallery."

Rowland flinched. "Was he successful? Actually, forget I asked that. I really don't want to know."

Milton smiled. "Of the hundreds of people who clean, and cater, and maintain the Federal House, surely you'd expect one or two of them to be amenable to the workers' cause."

"Mr. Ley seems to believe the gentlemen of the Labor Party are all Communists," Edna added, thinking briefly of the erstwhile politician's discourses on the topic at dinner.

"He said that?"

"It's a favourite subject of his."

"If they were Communists," Milton muttered, "perhaps Jim Kelly's death might be treated as more than an unfortunate deposit of litter on the steps of democracy."

18

POLICE FORCE

◆————◆

Leaving for Canberra
DUKE'S VISIT

SYDNEY, Tuesday

Fifty uniformed men will leave Sydney on October 22, as part
of the police force to be present when the Duke of Gloucester
arrives at Canberra.

It was announced that the following members of the CIB
will go to Canberra for the Royal visits: Detective-Sergeants
Kennedy, Lawrence, Delaney, and Baker, and Detectives
Buckley, Crampton, Wilson, and Bodol.

The Maitland Daily Mercury, 16 October 1934

Although parliament had not yet resumed, the Federal House
was gradually filling. Newly elected members and senators had
arrived and were orienting themselves with the building in which they
would conduct the important business of government. Re-elected
representatives renewed acquaintances with colleagues and briefed
journalists. Ministers settled into offices and the remainder worked
from their respective Party rooms.

"I wonder who's policing the rest of Canberra," Clyde said quietly
as they walked in through the main entrance.

Rowland nodded. There did indeed seem to be a large number of peace officers patrolling the House. Members of the New South Wales Police Force were also present in number. "Probably something to do with the impending arrival of the Duke of Gloucester," he murmured.

"Of course." Clyde sighed. "A murder or two might upset His Majesty's delicate sensibilities."

They took particular note of the copper piping of the Lamson tubes, visible at various points.

"Where are the sending stations?" Clyde asked.

"We'll ask, shall we?" Rowland spotted the long-limbed Usher of the Blackrod as he strode out of the Senate chamber. "Mr. Broinowski, might we have a moment, sir?"

Broinowski turned stiffly on his heel. "Oh, yes, Mr. Sinclair the younger, and Mr. Watson Jones."

Rowland was more than a little impressed that Broinowski recalled their names after such a brief introduction. He shook the public servant's hand.

"We assume you're here about Mr. Sinclair's roses." Broinowski's manner was as upright and direct as his appearance.

"Wil's roses?"

"Yes, for the Parliamentary Rose Gardens. We were hoping that Mr. Sinclair could see his way clear to donating four varieties of red, two white cultivars and a yellow floribunda."

"I'm sure that won't be a problem," Rowland replied smoothly. Wilfred's enthusiasm for roses bordered on the obsessive. *Oaklea*'s rose beds were extensive and lovingly tended. If Broinowski wanted bushes, they would no doubt be found. "But to be honest, Mr. Broinowski, Clyde and I were just curious about the Lamson tubes."

The Usher of the Blackrod's eyes narrowed suspiciously. "And what is your interest in the Lamson tube system, gentlemen?"

Rowland decided on honesty. "We were wondering from where the razor sent to the prime minister's office might have been sent."

Broinowski's eyes darted anxiously as he beckoned for them to follow him. "The unfortunate incidents of the past days are not something we would wish to cast a shadow over the wonderful occasion of His Majesty's visit," he said brusquely, motioning them into the hallway.

"A friend of ours found the body. And then someone ran him down in front of the House a couple of days ago."

"Yes, I am aware of the accident—"

"With respect, Mr. Broinowski, it was not an accident."

Broinowski stared at them for a moment. "There are five possible locations from which the weapon might have been sent. Only one is in an area open to the public." He pointed them towards the Parliamentary Library. "Items may be despatched from the Parliamentary Post Office behind King's Hall."

"So the razor must have been sent from within the House?"

"That is correct."

"So you think the weapon was sent from the Parliamentary Post Office?"

"That, gentlemen, is a matter for the police."

"Blackrod! Why hello, old man! How tremendous to see you."

Rowland saw the slight widening of Broinowski's eyes before he turned. Thomas Ley approached with his hand extended.

"Good Lord, Sinclair!" Ley glanced at Clyde. "Mr... forgive me..."

"Watson Jones," Clyde said.

"Mr. Watson Jones!" Ley clapped Clyde exuberantly on the back.

"Mr. Ley," Broinowski's tone was measured. "I had heard you were back."

Ley grinned and winked broadly. "Can't get anything past Blackrod here. Nothing happens in this place without his say so."

On this Broinowski did not comment. "Can I help you, Mr. Ley?"

"No thank you, Blackrod. I'm just reacquainting myself with the House and calling in on old colleagues. I've missed this place!"

Broinowski nodded. "If you'll excuse me, gentlemen, I must get on."

"Capital fellow that Blackrod," Ley murmured as they watched him continue on his way. "Now, Sinclair, Jones, what brings you gentlemen here, and where is the lovely Miss Higgins? I've told young Middleton that he better marry her quick smart before some other young buck beats him to it!"

"We were curious about the Lamson tubes," Rowland said, leaving everything else aside.

"The tubes! Why would you be interested in the tubes?"

"Just curious about how they worked," Clyde said. "Rowly was thinking about having some installed at *Woodlands* so he can send instructions to the servants."

"Oh, I see." Ley seemed to miss both the look on Rowland's face and the jest in Clyde's voice. "It is an efficient system when things don't get stuck. You wouldn't believe what people try to send through the tubes. I have heard of the odd bottle of stagger juice being so despatched."

"An act of kindness, no doubt," Rowland said.

"I trust you don't mean that, Mr. Sinclair. It would be a sorry state of affairs if we couldn't rely on sober government."

Ley began a passionate monologue on the benefits of temperance. He may have detained them in this conversation for some time had Stanley Melbourne Bruce not appeared with a gentleman Rowland recognised as Robert Menzies. The Honourable Thomas Ley tipped his hat curtly to the newcomers and, with a hasty farewell, was on his way.

With his mind still on Ley's noticeably awkward exit, Rowland introduced The Honourable Robert Menzies to Clyde Watson

Jones. Menzies' history with the Sinclairs was long, though Rowland had first met him only the previous year when he'd still been Deputy Premier of Victoria. Wilfred Sinclair, on the other hand, had known the newly elected Member for Kooyong since 1920, when they had both vied for the hand of a Miss Patty Leckie.

Rowland congratulated Menzies on his election and his subsequent appointment as the Federal Attorney-General. "Why thank you, Mr. Sinclair. I am looking forward to the challenge of the federal stage."

"Actually, Rowland, may I have a private word?" Bruce asked pleasantly. "It won't take a moment."

"Of course. Excuse me, gentlemen."

Rowland stepped out of hearing with Bruce.

For a moment, Bruce didn't seem to know how to begin. That alone aroused Rowland's curiosity. In the end, Bruce opened with a question that quite surprised him.

"When exactly did you return to Australia after completing your studies in Oxford?"

"Late in 1927."

"I must say, I find it extraordinary you don't seem to be aware of Mr. Ley as a Member of Parliament."

Rowland's brow rose. "I must confess I didn't really have any interest in politics then." He was almost wistful. Life was definitely simpler when he'd been able to ignore politics. "Did Mr. Ley do something of particular note?"

Bruce hesitated. "Men who stood against Mr. Ley, politically or otherwise, had an unfortunate habit of either dying or disappearing mysteriously. There are those who believe Mr. Ley was somehow involved in their fates."

Rowland stared at the diplomat. "You're not serious!"

"If I were to jest, Rowland, I assure you, it would *not* be about Thomas Ley."

In truth Rowland could not imagine Stanley Melbourne Bruce would jest about anything at all. "So you're saying Mr. Ley is a murderer?"

"Not at all. I am simply saying that I had very good reason to suggest that he was no longer welcome on the coalition benches."

"I see."

"Tell me, Rowland, are you aware of a speaker by the name of Egon Kisch?"

Rowland regarded Bruce thoughtfully. So this was the transaction. Information for information. "Yes. He's a capital fellow."

"You know him?"

"I met him in Germany."

"Are you aware that he intends to come here?"

"Why, that's excellent news. I look forward to meeting him again."

"What do you know about Kisch, Rowland?"

Well aware that Bruce was no fool, Rowland replied carefully. "He's a journalist, I believe."

"What do you know about his politics?"

"I know the Nazis didn't like them."

Bruce maintained his gaze and then he seemed to relent. "How is Mr. Isaacs today?"

"On the mend, I believe."

They returned to the stilted conversation that Menzies and Clyde had been trying valiantly to maintain in their absence. It appeared the artist and the attorney-general had little to discuss. With reason now to end the interaction politely, they took their leave of one another thankfully.

Rowland told Clyde of Bruce's revelations and probing questions as they walked down the main stairs to the road.

"Ley's a murderer?" Clyde was astonished.

"Bruce didn't say that exactly, but clearly he believes there are definite grounds to suggest he is."

"Jesus, Mary, and Joseph… he doesn't even drink!"

"Probably explains it then."

"Rowly, does it occur you that—"

"*Willowview* where we met Ley is just off the Howlong road where that poor girl was found? Yes, I did wonder about that."

"And Ley was in Canberra when Jim Kelly was killed. One helluva coincidence?"

"We were in both places at relevant times too," Rowland reminded him. "Why would Thomas Ley wish to kill either of them?"

"We have no idea who the Pyjama Girl was… perhaps he had a reason. Has anyone seen Mrs. Ley? She seems to be conveniently absent while the Honourable Mr. Ley swans about with his mistress."

Rowland paused and considered the possibility. He shook his head. "No, the girl I saw was young… no older than Ed. She wasn't Mrs. Ley."

"Even so, Rowly."

"And Jim Kelly? Why would Ley kill him?" Rowland asked, resolving in any case to speak to Delaney about the erstwhile politician.

"Ley was the New South Wales Minister for Justice in the twenties—while you were still abroad. He had a harsh reputation— sent an insane man to the gallows if I remember correctly."

"It's a bit of a long bow between refusing to grant mercy and cutting a man's throat, Clyde." Even as he said it, Rowland recalled that Ley had taken his dining companions on a tour of the Federal House after hours.

"Ley was an arch-conservative, Rowly. Anti-Communist, anti-Catholic and anti-alcohol." Communist, Catholic, occasionally intemperate Clyde warmed to his subject. "If what Bruce suggests is true…" He shook his head. "Perhaps he's become more direct since leaving parliament… expanded his selection of victims beyond his political enemies."

"Middleton seems quite enamoured of the man." Rowland frowned and he thought of how much time Edna had been spending with Ley and his mistress through the writer. "We may need to have a quiet word with Bertie."

The hill upon which St. Andrew's had been constructed was being grazed by sheep. Rowland was glad they'd left the Airflow in the relative safety of the Parliament House parking lot. In his experience, rams occasionally took exception to motorcars. Every now and then a carelessly parked automobile fell foul of a belligerent ram on *Oaklea*.

Workmen were installing stained-glass windows into the sanctuary in preparation for the Gothic-styled church's opening in September.

One of the stonemasons broke away when he spotted the two gentlemen in suits walking up the hill, and proceeded down to meet them. And so it was in the shadow of St. Andrew's spire, among a flock of milling sheep, that Rowland and Clyde shook hands with Bill Dwyer. The meeting with the aggrieved husband of May Dwyer had been arranged by Bluey Howells who had already informed the man that Jim Kelly had not been seducing his wife.

"I never killed him," Dwyer said at the outset. "I sure wanted to break his nose, but I never killed him."

"We're not here to accuse you, Mr. Dwyer," Rowland assured him. "We just want to work out what exactly happened. What made you suspect Jim Kelly was having an affair with your wife?"

"Because of the photograph." Dwyer's remorse was obvious. "He had her picture. We'd just had them taken at a studio a couple of months before. I thought my May must've given it to him as a memento."

"But how did you know he had a photograph of your wife? Did he tell you?"

"No." Dwyer flinched. "I got this letter… from someone who called themselves a 'concerned friend'."

"What precisely did the letter say?"

"In a nutshell, that May was meeting Jim Kelly while I was at work… that she'd given him a photograph." Dwyer shook his head. "I don't mind saying I was played for a fool. I didn't believe it, I didn't want to believe it… but I went over to Jim's and looked."

"Miss Curtis let you in?"

"No, Jim slept on the sleepout off the back verandah. I knew he stowed his bag under the bed. I found the photograph and one of Jake Burton's wife and Robert O'Brien's. I figured Kelly must have been doing the rounds."

"Surely your wife—"

"I didn't say nothing to her." Dwyer blanched. "I didn't want to tell May that Kelly was using her like some common trollop. I figured my May must've been in love with him or something. She likes novels, you know. Whatever she'd done, I didn't want to humiliate her. I blamed Kelly."

"And Burton and O'Brien?"

"Poor old Burton cried like a baby when I told him. He'd got a letter too."

"Did he speak to his wife?"

"I don't think so. He's afraid of her. We were both hell-bent on blaming Kelly for all of it."

"What about O'Brien?"

"Now he was real mad. Don't know whether he confronted his wife—he left the Party, hates Communists now."

Clyde took the drawings of the men from the Royal from inside his jacket. "I spoke to your wife. She'd never heard of Kelly… but a picture of this bloke," he pointed to a single portrait, "was on your mantle."

Dwyer nodded. "That's Bobby O'Brien—my brother-in-law... the wife's brother." He glanced at the other sketches. "These blokes used to be New Guard, but now they're just Commie-bashers at large."

Clyde pressed the man's shoulder. "Thank you, comrade. We know this can't have been an easy matter to talk about."

"I'm a bloody fool. I made sure Jim's name was mud. Poor bastard. We were played like violins."

19

CANBERRA HOSPITAL

Built on the most modern lines in accordance with the ideals of the Federal Capital, the Canberra Hospital has been condemned in the Commonwealth Parliament as badly and unhygienically administered. Comment was so strong from Labour Senators that the Minister for Health has agreed to an investigation of its affairs. The hot water system is alleged to cease functioning in the early evening, preventing adequate washing and sterilisation. In fact, it is said that the instruments are sterilised in the most primitive way in a kerosene tin over a small fuel stove.

Northern Star, 18 December 1934

Clyde faltered in his stride as they neared Milton's room at the hospital. A step or two ahead of Rowland, he saw into the room first, and under his breath he cursed. And so Rowland had been warned that there was some cause for alarm when he first sighted Thomas Ley standing at the foot of Milton's hospital bed.

The lawyer turned. "Mr. Sinclair, Mr. Isaacs! You're back! Well that makes my offer rather redundant, I suppose."

"What offer?" Rowland asked, stepping into the crowded room. Maggie Brook stood by the open window smoking. Edna sat on the end of Milton's bed and Bertram Middleton hovered near her. The patient himself had been released from traction and was sitting upright, propped up by pillows.

Bertram Middleton explained. "Mr. Ley was very kindly offering to stay with Mr. Isaacs while the rest of us stepped out for a spot of luncheon."

Milton rolled his eyes. "I've already told them that I don't need a nursemaid."

"How are you, Milt?" Rowland removed his hat.

"Much improved, comrade."

Ley's smile waned for a split second. And then it was back. "Perhaps you and Mr. Jones would care to join the others," he said congenially. "Maggie has found a wonderful restaurant at Eastlake."

"Rowly and I have already eaten," Clyde lied.

"Well then," said Middleton. "You and I can take the ladies to luncheon, Tom."

Edna's eyes were fixed on Rowland's. "Actually, I'm not feeling quite myself. You'll forgive me if I don't come to lunch either."

"Nonsense, I'm sure it's just being cooped up in here that's making you feel queasy." Middleton scowled as he noticed the direction of her gaze. "You need to take some fresh air, and indulge in some proper sustenance. I really must insist, Eddie."

Edna smiled but there was a flash of green steel in her eyes. "No, you really mustn't. I'm afraid I couldn't eat a single morsel right now."

"But Eddie…"

"You go and have a lovely meal, Bertie. Milt isn't supposed to have more than three visitors at a time anyway."

"I'll stay."

"No really, darling. Go. I need to talk to Rowly before he leaves for Melbourne anyway."

Ley glanced at Rowland. "You're off to Melbourne?"

"Yes… business, I'm afraid."

"Don't you worry, Sinclair. We'll look after Mr. Isaacs in your absence." Ley beckoned Maggie Brook. "Shall we go to luncheon then, my dear? I'm famished." He hooked his arm through his mistress' and bade them all a robust farewell.

The couple had already stepped into the corridor when Middleton began to vacillate about leaving again. Rowland reached the end of his patience. He pulled the writer aside. "For pity's sake, man, the lady has asked you to go. Don't tempt me to throw you out."

Edna winced.

"How dare you!" Middleton rose up furiously, his fists clenched. Rowland responded with a look of almost amused derision that served only to further incense him, and for a moment Middleton looked ready to swing.

"Bertie!" Edna grabbed Middleton's hand and pulled him away from Rowland. "Don't be so jolly silly. You should go. This is a hospital."

"If that's what you want, Eddie." He looked sullenly at Rowland, and then kissed Edna fiercely. "You're not fooling me, Sinclair," he said as he stalked out.

For several moments there was silence in his wake.

"You're going to have to do something about that bloke, Ed." Clyde glanced out of the window to make sure they had in fact gone.

Milton smiled. "To tell you the truth I was hoping he'd refuse to leave. I'm getting a little desperate for entertainment."

"Bertie doesn't mean it. He's just..." Edna sighed. She sat back on Milton's bed, being careful not to disturb his leg. "All right, you two, what's going on? I hope it was worth sacrificing lunch. I'm famished!"

Rowland closed the door before recounting the conversations with Broinowski and Bruce.

"He killed them?" Edna said horrified. "Why isn't he in prison?"

"I presume he wasn't caught."

"Physically or legally?" Milton asked.

"Both, I expect. He left the country at the height of the speculation, but Bruce was at pains to point out that it was nothing more than speculation. There's no proof Ley killed anyone—it could just be that the good Lord likes him and helpfully strikes down anyone who gets in his way."

Clyde snorted. "I doubt very much that the Almighty would aid and abet a politician… let alone a Protestant."

"What if he's innocent of all the murders?" Edna said quietly. She looked at Rowland. "He could well be. You were."

"He might be," Rowland conceded. He had, as Edna alluded, been falsely accused in the past. Perhaps Ley too had an unfortunate habit of being in the wrong place at the wrong time.

"What are we going to do?" Edna asked.

"Let's be cautious. It might be best if we proceed as if Ley is a killer," Rowland said carefully, "at least until we know he's not."

Edna nodded.

"Ley seemed to be pretty keen to get Milt on his own when we arrived," Clyde pointed out.

"Yes, I thought that was a bit odd at first too," Milton said. "But then I put it down to my natural charm. Mostly it's women that want to get me alone but—"

"Ley may just have to get in line to cut your throat," Clyde murmured.

"How soon do you think you'll be fit to travel, Milt?"

The poet smiled. "Let me show you something." He rolled gingerly onto his side and gradually swung his legs over the edge of the bed. He held up his hand as Rowland moved to help him. "Just give me a second, comrade," he said as he paused to gather himself. Then he grabbed the iron bedhead and very slowly pulled himself to his feet.

Edna clapped and Milton accepted the applause with his customary aplomb. "I think I could get out of here tomorrow."

Rowland moved to lend Milton his shoulder. "I'd have Johnston fetch you in the Rolls but you might be more comfortable if I book you a private sleeping compartment on the train. You can recuperate properly at *Woodlands*."

With his weight on Rowland's shoulder, Milton took a couple of tentative steps. "I'm game."

"We'll organise a wheelchair," Rowland said, frowning, unsure if he was pushing Milton too hard. He feared sitting upright would prove quite painful for the poet.

"Stop fussing, Rowly." Milton read the concern in his face. "It might be a bit soon for footraces, but I'll be all right."

"I don't think it's just Milt we should be worrying about." Clyde folded his arms. "Did you see Ley's face when Milt called you comrade?"

"Milt calls everyone comrade."

"Ley doesn't know that."

"I'll be leaving for Melbourne as soon as I put you all on the train to Sydney, in any case," Rowland said, though he didn't for a moment believe he was in any danger.

Edna's brow furrowed slightly. "What about your Mrs. Roche, Rowly? She seems to spend a great deal of time with Mr. Ley and Maggie. Shouldn't you—"

"I'll warn Jemima when I'm in Yass." He dragged a hand through his hair as he contemplated the conversation. "She's going to suspect I'm mad."

"That's not quite what I meant," Edna said.

"Jemima's not involved in this, Ed."

"Are you sure, Rowly?"

Milton laughed. "Don't listen to Ed, she's jealous!"

Rowland stopped, surprised.

"I am not!" Edna said furiously.

Milton grinned. "Of course you are. You've become used to being the most beautiful, outrageous woman in the room... and then Jemima Roche comes along and makes you look positively conventional."

"Don't be ridiculous!" Edna glared at the poet.

Rowland observed their interaction. The sculptress seemed more genuinely upset by the accusation than she'd ever been by such teasing. But surely Milton could not have struck a chord. Edna wore her beauty easily, carelessly. She was not vain, or insecure. And to Rowland's mind, she remained the most beautiful woman in any room. "What do you mean, Ed?" he asked gently.

"Just that..." She faltered. "Nothing. I don't mean anything."

Clyde remained at hospital that night while Rowland returned to the hotel to pack all their belongings for the following day's departure. Rowland made telephone calls and sent telegrams to ensure his friends would travel as comfortably as possible and be met at Central Station. He rang through to *Woodlands* to arrange for a room to be prepared on the ground floor for Milton's use and a nurse to be engaged for his ongoing care. Finally, he telephoned Delaney and informed him about Sunshine Studios, the letters Dwyer, Burton and O'Brien had received, and Thomas Ley.

"Lemonade Ley!" Delaney exclaimed at the last. "He's back in the country? Bloody hell... I had no idea."

"I take it that what Bruce told me has legs."

"Big hairy legs, Rowly. If I recall, a politician called McDonald—Fred or Frank—disappeared after alleging Ley tried to bribe him. Then Hyman Goldstein was found dead on the cliffs off Coogee after campaigning against Ley in the wake of the Prickly Pear Poisons fiasco, and then some chap appointed to investigate the matter mysteriously, not to mention conveniently, fell overboard and drowned."

"But there was nothing to sustain a prosecution?"

"I'm afraid Ley's rather too clever for that. There was nothing we could pin on him... but there was talk."

"His wife lives in Melbourne, doesn't she?"

"I know what you're getting at, Rowly, but Mrs. Ley is too old to be the poor girl we've got in formalin. Still, we'll look into this tennis party old Lemonade hosted... make sure that was not the last place anyone was seen."

"Thank you, Col. You will let me know if anything—"

"Actually, Rowly, I did a little digging after our last conversation. The commissioner has been receiving letters from a group who call themselves the Commonwealth Legion. The letters list the names of people they claim are Communists and whom they demand be arrested for treason. They write specifically of the national capital being overrun by a Bolshevik conclave."

"Surely that's just the usual conservative rhetoric?"

"The commissioner has written it off as that. But the more recent letters have been quite militant in demanding action—the usual allegations of a partisan police force and what may be read as a threat of direct action."

"Do you know who this group is?

"The letters are signed D. King, but the name isn't known to the police. I don't suppose you remember a D. King from your time undercover with the New Guard?"

"No, but I was introduced to only a handful of Campbell's inner circle. There were fifty thousand men in the New Guard and it was not the only Fascist army." Rowland was mentally filing through the names he remembered. "I'll speak to Wil." Perhaps D. King was from the Old Guard. It would explain why he had not before come to the attention of the police. In contrast to the New Guard, the Old Guard had been astutely clandestine in its dealings, maintaining secrecy with Masonic vigilance and discipline.

"Do you want to tell me what you'll be doing in Melbourne, Rowly?"

Rowland answered carefully. He trusted Delaney but he had no wish to put the detective in an awkward position. "I thought I'd catch the end of the MacRobertson Air Race. I'm thinking of buying a new aeroplane."

"I'm surprised that new-fangled contraption you're driving can't fly."

Rowland laughed. He gathered that the Airflow's streamlined shape was a little avant garde for Delaney's traditional tastes. "She'll grow on you, Col."

Edna accompanied Rowland when he went to see Major Jones—given the circumstances, neither was willing to leave the other alone. The Canberra Chief of Police was working late to ensure that the visit of the Duke of Gloucester would be without incident. He was heartily pleased that Rowland Sinclair and his companions were leaving. Jones did not believe they were involved in the murder of the Communist, James Kelly, but they did seem to be the eye of the storm. A Detective Delaney from the Sydney Central Investigation Bureau had telephoned with information about some photographic studio in Eastlake. A few basic enquiries had revealed that this Delaney had long been associated with Sinclair. Jones shook his head. God save the Commonwealth from well-heeled polo players who fancied themselves sleuths.

Rowland asked about the running down of Milton Isaacs.

Jones informed him that neither the Ford Tudor nor its occupants had been found. "You must understand, Mr. Sinclair, the population of Canberra is comprised of many transients and the territory border is never far away. I suspect Mr. Isaacs was the victim of an inebriated driver who, on realising he'd run someone down, fled into New South Wales. We've informed the authorities in that state, of course, but I'm afraid it's out of our hands now."

"And Mr. Kelly's murderer?" said Rowland coldly. "Did he flee across the border too?"

Jones' face was unreadable. "Quite possibly."

"I expect you're aware that Mr. Thomas Ley is in Canberra."

"I most certainly am." Jones said nothing more.

Rowland gave up. It was probably optimistic to hope Jones would take them into his confidence.

"I'm afraid I haven't had the chance to contact Mr. Mildenhall about his photographs," Edna said as Jones stood to show them out.

"Did you take many yourself, Miss Higgins?"

"A few, Major Jones, but I've come to the realisation that I would need to stay much longer to understand this city and photograph her properly."

"Then we shall look forward to your return, Miss Higgins." Jones showed them to the door of his office. He spoke quietly to Rowland after Edna had stepped through. "I'll have a man on the train back to Sydney as a precaution, but that's the best I can do, Mr. Sinclair."

Rowland shook Jones' hand. "Thank you, sir. We'll manage the rest."

20

CANBERRA

———◆———

As it appealed to me on the occasion of my first visit to
Australia's Federal Capital.

On September 28, 1934
(By J.F. O'Connor, in the Inverell "Times")

...One remarkable feature of the Garden City is its wonderful
rosery; it is called the National Rose Garden and is ten acres in
extent, with two further sections, which, together, comprise six
acres. The main portion of the National Rose Garden contains
approximately 5000 rose plants, presented by associations and
citizens from far afield, roses having been given from all quarters
of the world. In season, this is a wonderful site. Just here, I feel
how futile it is to attempt to give a complete description of the
beauties of Canberra...

Glen Innes Examiner, 25 October 1934

The whistle sounded and Bertram Middleton ran frantically onto
the platform just as the train to Sydney departed. He was able
to wave farewell to Edna Higgins but that was all. Disappointed and
furious, he spotted Rowland Sinclair. The fact that Sinclair had not
departed as well only made him more angry.

"Sinclair!"

"Mr. Middleton, how are you?"

"Not well, Sinclair, not well at all! You've seen to that!"

Rowland blinked. "I'm sure I don't know what you mean."

"You're jealous! That's it, isn't it? That's why you sent Miss Higgins away. Banished her like some fallen woman to a nunnery!"

Rowland smiled. He knew it wouldn't help the situation, but he couldn't help it. "*Woodlands House* is hardly a nunnery."

Middleton swore at him.

Rowland attempted to calm the man. "I didn't banish Miss Higgins, Middleton, she's looking after Mr. Isaacs—whom you well know is like a brother to her."

"She didn't say goodbye!"

"I don't believe she had time." Rowland tried to be kind despite an urge to see the writer off once and for all. "Her decision to decamp was made rather hastily. I believe Miss Higgins left you a letter…"

"Indeed!" Middleton pulled the pages of Edna's missive from his pocket. "She says I should be careful of Tommy Ley! What cock and bull story did you tell her, Sinclair? You've said something, libelled Tommy to frighten her away from me." He pointed at Rowland. "You couldn't seduce her with your wealth and your fast cars and your flaming blue eyes so you decided to frighten her into your arms! You low, conniving bastard."

"You're making a fool of yourself, Middleton." Rowland turned to walk away.

Middleton grabbed Rowland's shoulder, yanking him back. But Rowland was ready for the punch. He ducked and jabbed reflexively. Middleton's fist met clean air, Rowland's didn't. Someone called for the station master.

Rowland offered his felled opponent a hand. Cursing, Middleton refused to accept it, scrambling to his feet, wiping a bloody nose. "I won't forget this, Sinclair. This isn't over. Eddie will see what a two-face mongrel you are!"

By the time the ancient station master and his assistant had fought a path through the gathering crowd to investigate the commotion, both men were on their way. Rowland was more disgusted than angry and strangely relieved that he now at least had good reason to dislike Bertram Middleton.

The oak trees which lined the long winding drive of *Oaklea* were luminescent with the green of new leaves. Lambs bounded after their mothers in the lush surrounding paddocks. The occasional ewe wandered onto the drive, unhurried by the oncoming Chrysler Airflow as it negotiated the stock grids that separated the lambing and grazing paddocks. Rowland was content to slow for each crossing beast. The countryside had always worn Spring well.

As the homestead came into view, he could see Ernest, who it seemed was home from school, watching for him on the entrance stairs, with two-year-old Ewan. Rowland climbed out and waited by the car for his nephews to run over. Ernest reached him first.

"Uncle Rowly." Ernest stuck out his hand. "How d'you do?" He gestured back to Ewan who was scrambling to catch up. "You know my brother, Ewan, of course."

Rowland shook Ernest's hand. "Yes, I believe we've met." He smiled as his godson stumbled towards him with arms outstretched. "How are you, mate?"

"Up! Rowly, up!"

Rowland heaved Ewan onto his shoulder.

"*Uncle* Rowly," Ernest told his brother sternly. He sighed, mortified as a seven-year-old could be by his uncouth relation.

"Rowly!" Ewan echoed smugly.

Rowland laughed. "Good thing he has you to apologise for him, Ernie."

"Does Daddy apologise for you, Uncle Rowly?"

"Regularly."

Rowland allowed Ernest to lead him into the house and shout an announcement of his arrival. Mrs. Kendall, *Oaklea's* longstanding housekeeper, emerged from the parlour. "Goodness me, Master Ernie, you're in fine voice this morning." She paused to look at Rowland, her eyes moistening at the sight of him.

"Oh Mr. Rowland, don't you look well!"

Rowland set Ewan down and embraced the motherly servant, aware that he'd not been back to *Oaklea* since the accident that had been reported as fatal. "I'm fighting fit, Mrs. Kendall."

"I was so worried—"

Rowland wished he'd come back sooner. The tension between him and Wilfred had made it easier to put off any excursion to Yass, at least until he'd purchased an automobile in which to undertake the trip. But he should have known how news of his accident would distress Alice Kendall, who'd treated him like one of her own for as long as he could remember. "Not a scratch on me, Mrs. Kendall... there was nothing to be worried about."

"Mr. Sinclair telephoned to tell us, of course... but oh, it's good to see for myself." She clasped his face between her hands and beamed.

"It's marvellous to see you too," Rowland replied sincerely. Alice Kendall was what he missed most about his childhood.

She wiped her eyes and gathered herself. "Look at me, waylaying you like some bandit when you'll be wanting to see your brother. Mr. and Mrs. Sinclair are taking tea in the conservatory."

"Uncle Rowly!" Ernest said impatiently.

"Up!" demanded Ewan.

Alice Kendall straightened his tie and patted down his lapel. "Away with you before Mr. Sinclair dismisses me for keeping you too long."

Rowland laughed, convinced Wilfred would sooner get rid of him than Mrs. Kendall, especially now. They'd not parted well, and he was honestly not sure he'd be welcome.

He threw Ewan over his shoulder once again and followed Ernest down the hall. The conservatory at *Oaklea* overlooked the extensive rose beds behind the house, and beyond that the less formal structure of the new gardens designed by Edna Walling. In the nine months since Rowland had last been back, the young plants and vines had established and structures had weathered into their surrounds. Also visible from the conservatory was the wing reconstructed after the blaze that had razed it.

A linen-draped table was burdened with tea, scones and butterfly cakes. Upon a second table, more than two-dozen vases each held a different rose. Wilfred was holding a bloom up to the light as he and Kate scrutinised it.

"Uncle Rowly's here!" Ernest declared.

Kate Sinclair turned before her husband. "Rowly!" She moved to allow her brother-in-law to kiss her cheek. "We are so glad you're here," she said meeting his eye. "It's been too long and the boys have missed you terribly."

"Rowly's just passing through," Wilfred said curtly.

"No!" Kate objected. "You must stay. You really must."

"I—"

"Please, Uncle Rowly," Ernest begged. "Maudie's had puppies and Gilbert's got a tooth."

Rowland hesitated. "I could leave tomorrow morning, I suppose..."

"It's settled then!" Kate said firmly. "We'll have you for one night at least."

Ernest cheered. He pulled Rowland's hand. "Come on, Maudie's puppies are in the shed… "

"Ernie! For heaven's sake let your uncle enjoy a cup of tea first." Kate smiled nervously, as she tried to compensate for the fact that Wilfred had not yet said a word. "Wil and I were just choosing roses for the gardens at Parliament House."

"Mr. Broinowski did mention it."

"A lovely idea, don't you think, Rowly? Roses from our garden will be growing at Parliament House. Rose growers from all over the region will be donating cultivars…" Kate looked desperately at her husband.

Wilfred carried on comparing blooms. "Yes. It'll be a truly excellent garden, I'm sure."

"And how is Mr. Isaacs, Rowly?" Kate asked. "Ethel said he was being very brave."

Rowland smiled. "He's well on the mend—walking on crutches. Clyde and Ed are taking him back to Sydney today."

"So soon? Is he well enough to travel?"

"He says he is."

"Oh, Rowly, you could have brought him here to recuperate. We're a lot closer than Sydney and you are all always welcome."

Wilfred cleared his throat.

"That's very kind of you, Kate." Rowland regretted that his sister-in-law was caught between him and Wilfred. Kate was by nature peaceable. She'd always suffered when the Sinclair brothers went to war against each other. "I might head down to inspect these puppies before the day gets away." Rowland ruffled Ernest's hair.

"Harry's back from the snow leases at the moment," Kate offered. "You might find him somewhere about the place."

"He's at the cottage." Wilfred did not look away from his roses. "I will telephone him to expect you."

"Thank you, Wil," Rowland said carefully. He looked down at Ewan.

"Up!" The child stretched out his arms.

"I thought so."

They took the Airflow to the shed, not because the distance warranted it, but because Rowland's nephews wanted a ride. Rowland turned on the radio so there was music for the five-minute journey.

Maudie's puppies were barely two weeks old, consigned to a large basket in the shade of the machinery shed in the care of their mother. A working dog, Maudie was a tolerant parent, allowing Rowland and the boys to handle her squealing progeny without complaint. Ernest had given each of the six puppies a name, though it was clear to Rowland that the boy couldn't tell one from another. It didn't matter. Rowland presumed each dog would claim a name in time.

When they pulled up beside the accommodations reserved for the *Oaklea* managers, Harry Simpson was waiting on the verandah of his cottage. He was an arresting figure, taller even than Rowland and broad. His dark skin was almost glossy. An easy wide smile carried into the dark blue of his eyes.

"Gagamin!" he boomed, meeting Rowland on the steps. He shook his hand and slapped his back at the same time.

"It's so very good to see you, Harry," Rowland replied. While Harry Simpson had a permanent home on *Oaklea*, he did not always remain, and so finding him there was a happy chance. As Wilfred's most trusted man, Simpson managed the other Sinclair properties from time to time, or went wandering in the custom of his people.

The Wiradjuri stockman had been raised on *Oaklea* in the company of the Sinclair boys. The same age as the late Aubrey Sinclair, his relationship with each of the brothers was close and strong. Rowland would have done anything for him.

"Hello, Mr. Simpson." Ernest ran up the steps. "Are you going fishing? Can I come, please?"

Simpson nodded. "Your father and I might go out tomorrow. We could put up with you, I reckon, but you'd have to bring the sandwiches."

Ernest nodded solemnly.

And so they sat on the squatters' chairs on Simpson's verandah with enamel cups of tea, ginger beer for the boys, and a damper which the stockman had proudly baked himself. Simpson entertained them with tales of the high country. Only later, when they stood leaning shoulder to shoulder on the verandah railing, watching Ewan and Ernest picking dandelions in the grass, did Simpson broach the subject of Wilfred. "So what are you and Wil bluing about this time, Rowly?"

Rowland told him quite honestly about the fiasco of his last art exhibition and the personal offence Wilfred had taken to it.

Simpson grimaced. "Just keep your head down, Rowly. You know what he's like. He'll cool down."

"The thing is, Harry, I can't keep my head down at the moment."

"What do you mean?"

"I'm involved in something that I suspect Wil won't like at all."

"Then why are you doing it?"

"It's important."

Harry Simpson sighed. "In the end you've got to be your own man, Gagamin."

Rowland said nothing for a moment, and then he asked Harry Simpson for a favour. "When this all comes out, would you tell Wil that I wasn't trying to defy or embarrass him? It's just what I had to do."

"That bad, is it?" Simpson asked.

"I don't think so... but Wil might."

21

BABY'S FIRST TOOTH

"George," exclaimed Mrs. Young to her husband, with a radiant smile, "baby has a tooth!"

"Has he?" was the response, in a tone which betrayed no emotion.

"You don't seem surprised."

"I'm not surprised. All babies have first teeth. If ours didn't have any I'd manage to work up some excitement—maybe."

"I thought you'd be ever so pleased and happy about it."

"No; I don't see that it's any occasion for especial congratulation. The baby has my deepest sympathy."

"What for?"

"For having his first tooth. He has just struck the opening chapter of a long story of trouble. Pretty soon he'll have other teeth."

"Of course he will."

"Every one he cuts will hurt him. Then his second teeth will come along and push these out. That will hurt him again. Some of the new ones will grow crooked, as likely as not, and he will have to go to the dentist and have a block and tackle adjusted to them to haul them into line. Then he'll cut his wisdom teeth. They will hurt a lot. After that he'll have to go to the dentist and let him drill holes and hammer until his face feels like a great palpitating stone quarry. I shouldn't like him to go through life without teeth. But I may say that I don't see any occasion for the customary hilarity over an event that means so much in the way of sorrow and humiliation."

Camperdown Chronicle, 14 March 1933

When Rowland returned to the *Oaklea* homestead with his nephews, he discovered that the Bruces were also back from a morning in Canberra visiting old friends and colleagues. And so, they were to be a party for dinner, the eminence of which dictated that they would be dining formally.

Rowland found his dinner suit had been laid out in the bedroom that had been his as a child. He showered and changed, wondering whether his friends had reached *Woodlands House* without incident. He might have telephoned then, had not Ernest Sinclair knocked on his door to remind him that he had not yet seen Gilbert's tooth. An immediate visit to the nursery was necessary to rectify the oversight. Not yet a year old, the youngest of Wilfred's brood had not seen his uncle enough to know him. He gazed at Rowland suspiciously with the dark blue eyes which seemed to mark all the Sinclair men.

"Gil doesn't do much yet," Ernest confided. "But he's not as embarrassing as Ewan."

"Give him time, Ernie mate."

Rowland bade his nephews goodnight, promising he would see them in the morning before he left, and proceeded to the drawing room for pre-dinner drinks.

With the Bruces present, the tension between Rowland and Wilfred was mitigated somewhat by the simple fact that it was not absolutely necessary that they speak directly to each other.

Over a five course supper, Wilfred and Stanley Bruce chatted about the price of wool and the animosity of Prime Minister Lyons. It appeared that Lyons felt Bruce's presence in the country was destabilising to his leadership. Consequently, the current visit of Australia's High Commissioner to the United Kingdom had been kept low key and unofficial. Ethel Bruce spoke to Kate and Rowland about snippets of gossip and her own investigations into who had run down Milton Isaacs. She had, it seemed, telephoned Major Jones herself to ensure that he was expending all efforts to identify the culprit and bring him to justice.

Stanley Bruce broke into the conversation. "Sadly, unlike your rather extraordinary automobile, Rowland, black Ford Tudors are not at all unusual, and so finding that particular vehicle may prove difficult. In any case, it's best left to the relevant authorities."

Rowland was reminded of Bruce's earlier request.

"I had the pleasure of Mrs. Roche's company for tea the day before yesterday," Kate volunteered shyly. "She's a childhood friend of Rowly's who's just returned to *Meredale* next door," she added for Ethel Bruce's benefit. "We had such a delightful time. She's quite beautiful, so very charming, and she was wonderful with the children."

Rowland looked up, a little startled. If he didn't know better he would think his sister-in-law was matchmaking again. Kate Sinclair was committed to seeing him settled happily with a suitable girl, but Jemima Roche was a divorcee.

"It's very sad that she was widowed so young."

Rowland quite admirably kept the surprise from showing on his face. Widowed? He realised suddenly that Jemima had never said she was divorced, just that her marriage had been unhappy. He'd made that assumption.

"Yes, a most tragic circumstance," Ethel agreed. "But still, perhaps, as she's young and pretty, Mrs. Roche will be able to remarry, someday."

Rowland sipped his wine as he listened to what he guessed was a prearranged conversation to press the case for Jemima Roche. Clearly, Mrs. Bruce had been recruited to the cause.

"I did telephone to ask Jemima to join us for dinner today," Kate went on. "But I'm afraid she left for Melbourne yesterday."

"What a coincidence!" Ethel glanced knowingly at Kate. "You're on your way to Melbourne, aren't you, Mr. Sinclair? Perhaps you might see her there."

Rowland smiled. "Perhaps."

"What exactly will you be doing in Melbourne, Rowly?" Wilfred asked sharply.

"I'm going down to see the finish of the MacRobertson Air Race."

"I must say I find that hard to believe," Wilfred said, almost under his breath.

Rowland replied evenly. "I've always had an interest in aircraft, Wil."

"Yes, but I've never known you to go anywhere without those friends of yours before." Wilfred glared at Rowland from the head of the table. "Just what are you up to?"

"Oh for goodness' sake, Wilfred," Ethel chided. "I would have thought it was perfectly obvious why your brother is rushing to Melbourne!"

"I'm sure we have no idea what you're talking about, Ethel," Bruce said, shaking his head.

Ethel sighed. "How like a man—not a romantic notion in your head! Rowland is pursuing Mrs. Roche."

Rowland choked on his wine.

"Is that true, Rowly?" Wilfred asked.

"Great Caesars, no."

"Oh my giddy aunt, you don't expect a young man to declare himself to his family before he speaks to his intended? That's really too old-fashioned." Ethel was quick to Rowland's defence once again. "Look at him. Poor boy is mortified. You men really have no subtlety in matters of the heart." She raised her glass. "Let us say no more about it, apart from wishing the happy couple good luck."

When the ladies left the gentlemen to brandy and cigars, Rowland excused himself to take some air on the verandah. The evening was cool. Indeed it was the kind of clear, sparkling night that hinted at a late frost—a concern for the new lambs. Rowland smiled at himself.

Despite his best efforts to avoid all things agricultural, it seemed his brother had managed to impart at least that skerrick of pastoral insight.

He turned as he heard someone step onto the verandah behind him.

Wilfred Sinclair cupped his hands to light the cigarette he held between his lips. He replaced the lighter in his pocket and inhaled before he spoke.

"Kate is expecting you for coffee in the parlour."

"Wil, couldn't we—"

"Just come in and drink coffee," Wilfred said coldly.

"Wil!" Kate Sinclair closed the verandah door after her. "I've had enough. This can't go on!"

"Katie, this matter is between Rowly and me."

"No, Wil, listen to me. Whatever he's done, this is your brother! This is the man who ran into a blazing house to save our son. I don't care that his friends are Bohemians or Communists, I truly don't care what he paints…"

Kate was crying now. Rowland looked on, horrified. He had never heard her disagree with Wilfred ever before. "Kate, it's not Wil's fault—"

Wilfred embraced his wife. "It's all right, Katie. Of course, you're right."

"This can't go on, Wil."

"I know, I know." He wiped her tears with his own handkerchief.

Rowland turned away. He felt intrusive, guilty.

"You go back to Ethel and Stanley," Wilfred said quietly. "I'll talk to Rowly."

"Oh, Wil, I'm so sorry." Kate hesitated now. "I didn't mean to make such a fuss."

"No, my darling. You are perfectly correct."

Kate slipped back into the house and left the Sinclair brothers alone.

Rowland spoke first. "Wil, I'm sorry. I had no idea Kate—"

"She's right, Rowly. I've been taking your stubborn idiocy too personally."

"I'm sure that's not what she said." Rowland smiled faintly.

"It's what she should have said." Wilfred stubbed out his cigarette. "You're a damnable fool, and sometimes your behaviour is so utterly disgraceful that I forget that you were willing to go to prison in my stead, and that if not for you and your disreputable friends we would have lost Ernie and Ewan last year."

"They're my nephews, Wil."

"And they are my sons."

Rowland hesitated. He did not want Wilfred to forgive him only to feel betrayed when his involvement with Egon Kisch was discovered. "Wil, we shall disagree again, you know that. I will do things that you... that you won't approve of, that you won't understand."

Wilfred stared at him. "No doubt."

"I have to do what I think is right, Wil."

"That's dangerous rhetoric, Rowly. Your personal conscience does not eclipse your obligation to this country, to its laws."

"I assure you I'm not a Communist and I'm not a traitor. I'm not doing anything illegal."

Wilfred flinched. "My God, Rowly, just what are you involved in? Why are you going to Melbourne?"

Rowland shrugged. "You could call it a romantic notion."

"I could have you committed, you know," Wilfred muttered. "I should just have you committed and be done with it."

"That might be even more embarrassing than my paintings."

"Don't count on it."

Rowland broached a new subject tentatively. "Did you by any chance know the fellow Jemima Fairweather married, Wil? Do you know how he died?"

"Ozzie Roche? Yes, I escorted Mother to the wedding—you were abroad, of course. He was from Western Australia, I believe. A banker of some sort. They went to America after the wedding." Wilfred frowned as he tried to recall. "He died in an accident, I think. I can't tell you much more than that." Wilfred lit another cigarette. "Do you intend to ask Jemima Roche for her hand?"

"Not especially."

"It might be time for you to give up your ideas of Miss Higgins. Aside from the fact that she's entirely inappropriate, Rowly, she won't have you. The Fairweathers are a very respectable family. Sometimes a man's got to admit defeat and move on."

Rowland said nothing.

Wilfred studied his brother. "You might find that relinquishing your absurd infatuation with Miss Higgins will allow you to have the proper regard for a more suitable young woman."

"Proper regard?" Rowland laughed. "I have a *proper regard* for the law, the Queensberry rules, and the king. I'd hoped to have rather more for my wife."

Kate opened the door again. "You're talking," she said, obviously relieved. "Stanley thought we might play a round of cards, if you're finished."

Wilfred placed his hand on Rowland's shoulder. Perhaps it was to demonstrate to Kate that they had indeed reconciled, or perhaps it was because her appearance served to remind him that his young wife enjoyed much more than his proper regard. It was in any case as effusive a gesture of fraternal friendship as Wilfred Sinclair was ever likely to make. "Capital idea, Katie."

22

CENTENARY AIR RACE

Scott Leads to Darwin

Numbers of planes have flown over Roma since Saturday on their way to Charleville for the purpose of witnessing the result of the Centenary Air Race at that town. Visitors have also travelled from all quarters by car. On Monday four planes passed over Roma from the east, and the only plane left in Brisbane on Tuesday was the Qantas mail plane. Charleville residents are suffering from stiff necks owing to watching the visiting planes over the town.

The great race began from Mildenhall at 6.30 a.m. on Saturday, when the first plane, piloted by the Mollisons took off, and was followed at intervals of 45 seconds by the others. All machines were in the air within 18 minutes.

Mr. and Mrs. Mollison reached Bagdad, the first compulsory stop in the speed race, at 7.10 p.m. Saturday, having flown non-stop from Mildenhall, the distance covered being 2553 miles. Scott was the next to land at 9 p.m., nearly two hours behind Mollison, and he was followed by Parmentier (Holland) at 11.50 p.m., Roscoe Turner (U.S.A.) at 2 a.m. Sunday, Cathcart-Jones (England) at 5.12 a.m., and the Dutch Pander at 6 a.m.

The Mollisons departed at 8.40 p.m., and Scott took off about 40 minutes later. The Mollisons made a perfect landing at Karachi at 4.45 a.m. Sunday, and after staying an hour took off again, but were forced to return 10 minutes later owing to some mechanical trouble. Scott went on from Bagdad to Allahabad, and reached that stopping place at 9.18 a.m. In an interview he said he and Black were very tired, but were determined to proceed within half an hour, flying direct to Singapore.

> Scott arrived at Singapore with a lead of about 1500 miles over his nearest competitor, and arrived at Darwin at 9.30 p.m. Monday, Australian time, having been 52 hours 34 minutes on the journey from England.
>
> Parmentier was in second place, with Roscoe Turner third, and the Mollisons following.
>
> *Western Star and Roma Advertiser,*
> *24 October 1934*

The influx of visitors into Melbourne for the centenary celebrations, as well as the Spring Racing Carnival, meant finding accommodation was difficult. Rowland had eventually secured a suite at the Federal Hotel in Collins Street only because a late cancellation preceded his enquiry.

The newspapers spruiked the impending conclusion of the MacRobertson Air Race, which was expected to be won by the following day. The *Grosvenor House* was in the lead. For the first time Rowland began to believe Edwards' claim that she would triumph. It seemed he would have the privilege of flying the Comet, but he would not be able to keep her.

The next day, over fifty thousand people had gathered at the Flemington racecourse to welcome the *Grosvenor House* which had crossed the final mandatory checkpoint at Charleville in Queensland that morning. The crowd was undaunted by the inclement weather. After all, the clouds blocked the sun and made it easier to gaze skyward for the race winner.

Rowland turned up the collar of his overcoat against the rain as he waited at the nearby Laverton aerodome with the aeroplane's owner and various race officials. He had already settled Edwards with a significant sum in accordance with their agreement. Though the sum was of no great consequence to the Sinclairs, Rowland had been careful to take the funds from the profits of a lucky investment he'd made in Hugh McIntosh's Black and White Milk Bars in Britain. That money was more truly his than any funds he drew through the Sinclair Trust. He was cognisant of the fact that his brother would not only disapprove, but also object to this latest venture, and, with that in mind, he did not want to make Wilfred an indirect sponsor of Egon Kisch's visit.

The Comet would cross the finish line over Flemington and then land at Laverton. The pilots would be taken back to the racecourse to be cheered and acclaimed, but before that, Charles Scott would give him a Cook's tour of the *Grosvenor House*.

"You won't have long," Edwards warned. "The public will be anxious to receive the pilots, but then you've flown de Havillands before."

Rowland nodded. The *Rule Britannia* was a de Havilland Gipsy Moth and he had also piloted a Gipsy Six.

"From what I understand the engines are just upgraded versions of the standard Gipsy Six," Edwards said, already puffing on a celebratory cigar. "But Scott will be able to tell you all that. Oh yes—I believe there was a problem with one of the port engines... lost power over the Timor Sea... you should probably ask Scott about that. I say, here it is!"

Rowland's eyes were already on the red Comet which had come in low over Flemington in a final flourish. Long-nosed and thin-winged, the *Grosvenor House* was gloriously streamlined. There was no doubt she was designed for speed. Her landing gear lowered and she touched down in a cloud of spray on the wet tarmac.

"Come along, Sinclair." Edwards raised his umbrella and walked out as the plane taxied to a stop.

The cockpit canopy was opened and the airmen clambered out. Limping, Scott leant heavily on Black. There was, by that time, a number of people gathered around the Comet and for several minutes the triumphant pilots were subsumed in back-slapping congratulations.

"Rowly!" Scott staggered over to shake Rowland's hand the moment he could break away. "How are you, old chap?"

"Utterly impressed, if you must know. Congratulations, Charles! What the hell have you done to yourself!"

"Cramp." Scott's voice was husky. "Had to compensate for uneven power levels between port and starboard by pressing the bloody rudder the whole way... but you'll know all about that too soon." He introduced Rowland to his co-pilot Tom Black. "Rowly's an old chum. He's taking the plane out in a few days. We've got about ten minutes to show him how to fly her."

Black was a smaller man than the burly Scott, and more reserved. He accepted Scott's declaration without question.

"How long have you been licensed?" Scott climbed up to look at the cockpit. He groaned, stretching out his right leg. The rain thankfully had eased to a general mist. Below them, race officials, Edwards and various aeroplane mechanics drank champagne and toasted the win.

"About eighteen months."

"Have you flown a twin-engine before?"

"Yes, once or twice."

"Are your affairs in order?"

"Yes, I believe so."

"Good show! Let's introduce you to the red lady then."

In the next fifteen minutes the pilots imparted as much information as they could. The cockpit was snug and, as a result, Scott warned, the instruments on the right fuselage wall were quite awkward to use. To Rowland's relief, the main instrument panel was conventional.

"The forward view is very poor—absent really," Scott advised. "You'll have to weave slightly to actually see where you're going."

"The port engine was seizing so we throttled it down," Black told him. "The engines are easy to synchronise but if you happen to raise her tail too quickly on takeoff she'll swing hard to the right."

"Take her for a taxi if you get a chance," Scott said. He glanced behind him. Two de Havilland D60 Moths were being readied to fly them back to Flemington for the official public reception. "Tom and I have to go make speeches." He shook Rowland's hand. "Good luck, old bean. Give me a call if you need me to take her through her paces with you. I'd be happy to lend a hand if I'm not too drunk."

Melbourne was a city in multiple celebration. It was one hundred years old; the Great Air had been won; and soon they would welcome the Duke of Gloucester. Between them, Scott and Black and Prince Henry had pushed the as yet unidentified Pyjama Girl out of the headlines. Rowland returned to the hotel in Collins Street each evening in an excellent temper.

As Scott suggested, Rowland had taken the *Grosvenor House* out, familiarising himself with her peculiarities while taxiing about the Laverton aerodrome. The cockpit was snug for a man his height, but it was not an unreasonable discomfort. His infatuation with aircraft was now at a point that he probably would have flown her if the cockpit had been half the space.

He had settled in to spend that evening absorbing the Comet's flight manual when the telephone call from reception came through.

"There's a Mrs. Jemima Roche to see you, sir. Shall I send her up?" The manager's tone made it clear that sending unchaperoned ladies up to a single gentleman's suite was not hotel policy.

Rowland hesitated. "No, I'll come down. Thank you." In all the excitement, he had forgotten that Jemima was in Melbourne. He paused only to pull on his jacket and rebutton his waistcoat before heading down to reception.

She met him on the landing between the first and second floors.

"Rowly!" Jemima threw herself into his arms. The feather boa draped across her shoulders slipped to the floor revealing the low cut of a beaded bodice. "There you are! I've been waiting for simply ages." Rising onto the tips of her toes, she whispered into his ear, "That officious chap at the desk told me I wasn't allowed to come up and surprise you."

Rowland picked up the boa. "Hello, Jem. What are you doing here?"

"What kind of question is that?" She stood back and crossed her arms indignantly. "I tell you I'm simply dying of boredom and you sneak away to Melbourne without me!"

He smiled. "I believe you got here before me."

"Well yes, technically," she said, rolling her eyes. "Bertie Middleton telephoned me at Grandmama's to inform me that you were planning to go to Melbourne, and Emily was going for the centenary celebrations, so I thought, why not!"

"How helpful of Middleton."

"I can only assume your Miss Higgins mentioned your plans to him. And, of course, Bertie has his own reasons to throw me in your path."

"I beg your pardon?"

"Oh, Bertie has a notion that if you were spoken for, then he would be allowed to speak for Miss Higgins."

"I see." Rowland suppressed a rise of ire at Middleton's presumption, and at Middleton more generally.

"Bertie mentioned you assaulted him like a common hooligan." Jemima ran her finger along his jawline. "Who knew you could be such a brute!"

At that moment Rowland would have quite liked to punch Middleton again.

"Aren't you glad to see me?" Jemima seemed suddenly unsure of herself.

Rowland smiled, forgetting about Middleton. "Of course I am. I'm delighted. Just a little surprised." He kissed her hand. "How did you know where I was staying?"

"Tommy Ley made some enquiries for me."

Her mention of Ley reminded Rowland that he was yet to talk to Jemima about the former politician's dubious past. "We should step out for supper, I think."

Jemima's eyes sparkled. "Shall we go dancing?"

"If you'd like."

"I'll wait while you change," Jemima said pointedly. "You do have a dinner suit here, don't you?"

Parer's Crystal Café on Bourke Street had for decades enjoyed a reputation as one of Melbourne's premier restaurants. The venue was lavishly and elegantly furnished in a distinctly European style. Gilt-framed mirrors, Spanish chandeliers and fountains all contributed to the hotel's exotic style.

The maître d' greeted Jemima Roche by name and with compliments. He took their coats to the cloakroom, before escorting them to a table draped with white linen and set with embossed silverware.

They ordered dinner and took a turn on the dance floor while they waited for the first course to arrive.

"Whatever possessed you to go to Canberra, Rowly?" Jemima asked as they stepped into a waltz. "It seems a strange, dull place to holiday."

"I don't know—it was quite interesting in the end."

"Only because you found a corpse!"

Rowland's brow rose.

"Tommy Ley told me," she added when she saw the question in his eyes. "He says the police suspected Mr. Isaacs for a while... before someone tried to kill him too."

"Mr. Ley is well informed," he said. "But that's not the reason I found Canberra agreeable."

She smiled. "Well I am glad to hear that. I told you it would do us both good."

"Yes, you did."

"Do you think you could fall in love with me again, Rowly?"

Startled, Rowland said nothing for a moment. There was an underlying vulnerability in the question that Jemima rarely allowed anyone to see. "Do you want me to?"

"Not really." She was coy confidence again. "I just like to know that you could."

He laughed. "Yes, then, I could. In fact I might be."

"Come on," she led him off the dance floor. "I'm famished."

Over an elegant supper they talked of the many things they'd missed when their lives moved apart. Jemima ordered champagne and insisted he drink the greater portion.

"A lady should not be more drunk than her gentleman," she declared. "That would be positively common!"

In a mood to celebrate his procurement of the Comet, Rowland obliged. Jemima asked about the swastika-shaped scar she'd seen when he made love to her by the rockpool. He told her about Germany and London, of what had happened to him and how he'd escaped and how he'd changed. Tentatively he broached the subject of Thomas Ley's dubious past. On that score, she would not hear him.

"Good Lord, Rowly, that's just idle gossip. Tommy was a politician. According to rumour they're all philandering drunkards."

"True, but not often murderers."

"Who told you this nonsense?"

"Jem—"

"You told me yourself that you've been suspected of murder too. Should I be worried you'll stab me with your fish knife?"

"I just want you to be careful."

"Thomas Ley has been nothing but kind to me!" she said fiercely. "And he's an excellent solicitor!"

Despite himself, Rowland smiled slightly. He remembered Jemima as ferociously protective.

Jemima saw the smile; she guessed the memory in his eyes and her face softened. "You're thinking about that day at the Crookwell polo match, aren't you? When your father was being absolutely beastly to you." She laughed. "The look on his face when I told him what an ogre he was! He stormed off in a terrible huff."

Rowland winced. "Yes, you were—"

"Your knight in shining armour! Don't you dare say I wasn't!"

"No, I wouldn't dare." He studied her face. It was beautiful. There was a strength to the set of her jaw, a determination, but once or twice he'd seen a fleeting shadow of desperation cross it.

"Whatever happened to this chap you married, Jem? How did he die?"

She stared at him, her eyes widening, before they filled with hot tears. "Damn you, Rowly! Why would you bring that up?"

Startled, he handed her his handkerchief. "Jem, I'm sorry."

"I loved him in the beginning, Rowly. I didn't in the end... but that doesn't make it easier."

He grabbed her hand across the table. "I'm sorry. I didn't realise... I won't ask you about him again."

She took a deep breath and told him about the West Australian businessman she'd married, a man who'd squandered everything they'd owned and who turned out to be unkind and cruel.

Rowland tensed, remembering Jemima's allusion that her husband had been more like his father than hers. He pressed her hand. "Dammit, Jem, I wish I'd been there to help."

"You're here now," she said quietly.

━━━━━━━━━━━   ━━━━━━━━━━━

Rowland locked the door behind him. The premier suite on an upper floor of the Windsor Hotel overlooked Spring Street. He and Jemima had walked from Parer's after an evening that had extended into the early hours with champagne and dancing. Rowland had, of course, intended simply to see her safely to her hotel and return to the Federal, but by the time they'd arrived at her door, less noble impulses had won the day.

If Rowland had stopped to examine his involvement with Jemima Roche, it might have concerned him that his most passionate feelings about her were nostalgic. But he didn't stop. He allowed her to lead him into the bedroom, and he accepted when she invited him into her bed.

Whether it was the champagne, their past, or just a present desire for one another, they were lovers that night. When finally, they lay spent in each other's arms, Jemima laughed softly. "It's fortunate you already have a reputation as a rake, Mr. Sinclair. I don't want to be the woman that destroyed your good name."

"Rest assured, Jem," Rowland said drowsily, "my good name was destroyed long ago."

Almost asleep, he did not notice the relief in her eyes.

In the morning they woke as friends, enjoying each other but without the awkwardness or the excitement of new discovery.

"I really should be on my way," Rowland said, kissing her gently as he climbed out of bed. "I'm meeting Clyde's train and I'd rather not do it in the same clothes I was wearing last night."

"But you look so handsome in a dinner suit."

"Clyde has less formal tastes."

"Are you afraid he'll tell Miss Higgins?"

Rowland laughed. "Not at all."

Jemima clasped her arms around her knees as she watched him step into his trousers. "Why have you not made an honest woman of Miss Higgins, Rowly?"

Rowland continued dressing. "Ed isn't interested in being made honest."

"You know what I mean. Why on earth do you allow that girl to get about with Bertie? Declare yourself, Rowly! Demand that she have you!"

Rowland didn't deny his feelings, as awkward as it was discussing them with the woman with whom he'd just spent the night. "That wouldn't be the way to win Ed."

Jemima sighed. "Stay and take breakfast with me. You must. Anything else would be bloody ungentlemanly!"

"That's hardly language for a lady, Jem." Rowland pulled on his shirt. He smiled. "Yes. Of course."

Jemima reached over and kissed him. "Good, there's something I need to talk to you about. I'll have them send something up. What would you like?"

"Just coffee," Rowland replied, preoccupied with finding his studs and tie.

She telephoned to order a Continental breakfast for herself and "a pot of coffee for Mr. Sinclair".

If it had been anybody other than Jemima, Rowland might have wondered at the lack of discretion in the request. He got dressed while she languished naked on the bed, chatting nervously about this and that in a manner that piqued Rowland's curiosity about what it was she really wanted to talk about. He asked her as much.

"There's something I have to confess."

"I would have thought it fairly clear that I'm not a priest, Jem."

"Stop it. This is not funny."

"Sorry, Jem, I am listening."

"I can't be serious when I'm naked. Pass me the dressing gown in the bathroom, will you?"

Rowland took the Chinese silk robe from the hook beside the bathtub. There was a knock at the door.

"That'll be the girl with breakfast. Will you let her in, Rowly?"

Rowland tossed Jemima her robe and walked through the sitting room to collect the tray. An explosion of light blinded him as soon as he opened the door. As he blanched, the door was shoved hard against him and two men burst into the suite. Jemima screamed. More flashes. Rowland grabbed one of the intruders. The other ran at him, slamming him against the wall and kneeing him in the ribs for good measure; another flash and they were gone.

Rowland cursed, moving immediately to check on Jemima as he tried to blink the dazzle out of his eyes. "Jem, are you all right?"

She pulled the robe more tightly closed. "Yes... they were taking photographs."

Rowland stopped. "What? Why?"

"Well how the hell would I know, Rowly?"

"Yes... I'm sorry." Rowland locked the door to the suite.

Jemima sat down on the bed, pale. "They were from the newspapers," she whispered. "My God, Grandmama..."

Rowland slammed his fist against the wall as the full horror of the intrusion dawned. Publications like *The Melbourne Truth* specialised in exposing adulterers in flagrante, ruining people to titillate the masses.

But neither he nor Jemima was married. "There must be some mix-up, Jem."

Jemima swallowed. "Mix-up?"

Rowland tried to remain calm, though he was furious. "A bachelor and a widowed lady behaving unchastely is probably not scandalous enough to warrant this—"

"You'd better go now, Rowly."

"Jem, I'm sorry. I had no idea who was outside the door."

She shook her head, her hands trembled uncontrollably. "You'd best go now."

Rowland didn't question her anger, her panic. His reputation had long since been compromised, though not quite in this way... and in any case, he was a man. It would be Jemima Roche upon whom the public scorn would be heaped. "I'll speak to Wil—get him to throw our solicitors at this..."

"No, don't you dare!" Jemima stuttered. "I don't want Wilfred to know... this is too awful. Just go, Rowly."

"Jem... please."

She turned her back on him. "I'll talk to Tommy. Get out of here, Rowly, before you make it worse."

"You know where to reach me..." he said, unsure now of what to do.

"Goodbye, Rowly."

23

SHOCK FOR WIFE

◆━━━━

Private Detective Was Old Friend

(From "Truth's" Canberra Rep)

WHEN Mrs. Florence Merle Ginn was a friend of Henry Joseph Dykes, an inquiry agent, she little thought that later he would find her in Centennial Park in the arms of a man who was not her husband. But that this had occurred was disclosed at the hearing of the petition for divorce of William John Ginn from his wife, Justice Dethridge presiding, in the Queanbeyan Supreme Court last week. Leon Pezet, of Bondi, was named as co-respondent.

Ginn stated he was 28 and was married at Canberra on October 26, 1933, to Florence Merle Williams. After marriage they went to Cooma, but something occurred there that aroused his curiosity and a disagreement with his wife followed. She returned to Sydney and he employed Dykes to watch for developments.

Having received a letter he came to the city, and there one night with Dykes he saw Pezet and his wife leave a house in Anglesey Street, Bondi, and go to Centennial Park.

They followed and found his wife lying under a tree with Pezet. Dykes, giving evidence, said he knew Mrs. Ginn before her marriage. When he and the husband found her and Pezet under the tree, Mrs. Ginn said to Dykes, "I didn't think you'd do a thing like this. I thought you were a friend of the family." Dykes said he replied, "I didn't think you would either, and I wouldn't have believed it only I saw it with my own eyes."

> Justice Dethridge: I find the adultery proved and grant a decree nisi, returnable in one month on the assurance that respondent and co-respondent desire to marry as soon as possible.
>
> *Truth, 20 October 1935*

"I appreciate the effort, Rowly, but now I feel decidedly under-dressed." Clyde shook his friend's hand warmly as he met him on the platform. He noted the slightly dishevelled state of Rowland's dinner suit. Another all-night victory party no doubt. "I expect you've been celebrating with Scott."

"Not quite," Rowland replied.

Clyde's smile faded as he detected a note of despondency in Rowland's voice. "What's happened? Is there a problem with the Comet?"

"No. The *Grosvenor House* will be ready to go as soon as she's serviced."

"Then what?"

The whine and chug of trains approaching and departing the platform made any conversation challenging, and this was not something Rowland wished to discuss in a public place. He led Clyde out to the Airflow and recounted the events of the last day in the privacy of the vehicle's cabin.

"I assume they were from the *Truth*. Unless I can do something to stop it, Jemima and I will be in the headlines tomorrow."

Clyde groaned. "Jesus, Mary, Joseph, and all the flaming saints! Whenever I begin to think my love life is a disaster, you come along and show me that it could be a whole lot worse."

Rowland dropped his head onto the steering wheel. "What am I going to do, Clyde? This will destroy Jem, humiliate her publicly. God, what was I thinking?"

Clyde pressed Rowland's shoulder. There was not a lot one could say. This was one helluva dog's breakfast. But there was a solution. So drastic that he felt like a heel even offering it. "You could, of course, marry her."

"What?"

"If you marry her—quickly and quietly—then this becomes an invasion of privacy as opposed to an exposure of vice. Eloping with a divorcee is scandalous, but in comparison—"

"It seems she's widowed, not divorced."

"Really? Even better. Nothing to see at all."

Rowland was silent. He tried desperately not to think of Edna. This was the honourable thing to do. The only thing to do. "Would you stand up for me, Clyde?"

The question startled Clyde. He hadn't really expected… "Yes, of course, mate."

Rowland turned over the engine. "I'd better change. One shouldn't propose marriage in yesterday's shirt."

─────────────────────

Rowland put down his razor and wiped his face. He did not look long enough at his own reflection in the shaving mirror to see the growing panic in his eyes. Knotting the tie he'd slung around his collar, he stepped out of the ensuite to join Clyde. "It's too early for a drink, I expect?"

In his Sunday suit, Clyde stood ready for whatever was required of a best man. "Not today." He opened the cocktail cabinet built in to a corner of the room, and poured gin and tonic water into two tumblers. "To your happiness, old mate," he said, raising his glass.

Rowland drank. He did love Jemima Roche. He did.

Clyde swirled his drink. "One detail puzzles me, Rowly. How did the photographers know where you were?"

Rowland considered the question. "I've no idea. There were two or three photographers taking pictures for the society pages at the restaurant, but I'm sure they weren't the same bastards who burst into Jem's suite." He fiddled nervously with the knot in his tie. "Perhaps someone from the hotel noticed us go up and informed a contact at the papers in return for some sort of gratuity."

"Do you want to call *Woodlands* before we do this?"

"No." Rowland was definite. He could not bear Edna being happy for him. "Let's go get Jemima and find a clergyman."

Knowing the number and location of Jemima's suite, Rowland did not need to call at the reception desk. He and Clyde went up directly.

He was a little surprised when Thomas Ley opened the door. "Mr. Sinclair! What are you doing here?"

"I'm here to see Mrs. Roche."

"About what happened this morning? Don't look so alarmed, my boy. I'm Jemima's solicitor, you know."

Rowland and Clyde walked into the suite. Ley closed the door behind them. Jemima was seated in the club chair, fully dressed, smoking a cigarette held in a thin Bakelite holder. She was still pale.

"Jem, could we possibly have a word alone?" Rowland asked, his misgivings allayed by a sudden desperation to put things right.

"Under no circumstances!" Ley said. "Being alone in this suite with Mrs. Roche is what has led us to your current predicament. That and the devil's drink."

Rowland glared at Ley.

Clyde intervened. "We may have a solution... a way out of this situation."

Ley folded his arms. "Let's have it then?"

"Mr. Ley, would you kindly get out?"

Perhaps it was the flint in Rowland's tone that made the ex-politician reconsider the wisdom of pushing him. "Mr. Watson Jones and I shall wait in the bedroom—with the door open."

Rowland held off until they were at least out of sight. He tried to ignore the fact he and Jemima were not alone. They didn't have time for anything else.

He knelt and took her hand. "Marry me, Jem. The scandal won't exist if you're Mrs. Rowland Sinclair."

For a moment Jemima was overcome. She put her hand to his cheek. "Oh God, you're so sweet... but I simply can't..."

"Jem, I realise there's nothing remotely romantic about this proposal, but I do love you. I have loved you since I was fifteen."

She smiled, though her lips were unsteady. "But not the way you loved me when you were fifteen. I know you, Rowly. And I told you all I wanted was an affair."

"But this is the only way—"

"I can't marry you, Rowly. I'm already married."

Rowland dropped her hand. "What?"

"Oswald isn't dead. And we're not divorced."

"You lied—"

"No. Never. Not to you. I didn't ever say I was divorced... you assumed that... until you decided that I was widowed."

"Semantics!" Rowland said angrily. "You deceived me, Jem, and you jolly well know it."

She paused. "Yes, I suppose I did. I had good reason, Rowly."

"What possible reason could you have?"

"Oswald won't grant me a divorce unless I assume the blame. Unless I am the adulterer of record. You said your reputation was already destroyed, Rowly... you said you'd help me."

"For God's sake, Jem, why me, why now?"

"I can probably best answer that." Thomas Ley walked back into the room. Rowland stood.

"What you must understand is that Mrs. Fairweather is a grand old lady—nearly ninety years old, and she's not as well as she used to be. If she passes away while Jemima is still married, then Oswald Roche will be entitled to at least half of the estate."

"He's already squandered everything I had from Papa. I will not let Oswald do the same with Grandmama's estate!" Jemima said hotly.

"I don't understand." Rowland stepped away from her.

"Unfortunately, your picnic in Canberra wasn't witnessed by anyone." Ley sighed. "I informed Mrs. Roche that she would be far better creating the requisite evidence in an establishment such as this, where the staff could attest to a gentleman's presence, his breakfast order and so forth."

Rowland turned back to Jemima in horror. "*You* called the papers?"

"No! This was supposed to be discreet. Being the latest scandal in the *Truth* will destroy everything. And what's more, it'll destroy Grandmama."

"Yes," Ley agreed. "The papers are going to cause a number of problems."

"You see, darling," Jemima pleaded with Rowland. "I was simply planning to name you in the divorce proceedings... it would have been relatively quiet. It would have been the truth. It's how it's done."

Rowland was reminded that Jemima Fairweather had never let anything stand in her way. He admired that once. "Why didn't you simply tell me, Jem? Why did you have to trick me into this?"

"I wasn't sure you'd perjure yourself, or knowingly take a married woman to bed. I didn't have time to take the risk that you had become morally upstanding since I knew you last. I couldn't see the harm, Rowly... your Miss Higgins doesn't look like the type who'd be overly sanctimonious about where you'd spent your nights. I thought perhaps it might make her jealous, and then we'd all do well out of this."

Rowland shook his head. He had thought to marry this woman. He noticed the bags near the door for the first time. "Where are you going?"

"Back to Yass. Perhaps I can prevent Grandmama disinheriting me, or dying of shame when she learns of the *Truth's* little exposé. Either would be unfortunate. If I ever find out who called the newspapers, I'll kill them myself." She put out her cigarette and stood. "Please don't hate me, Rowly. I honestly didn't believe I was at risk of breaking your heart… not really."

"You've made a complete fool of me, Jem."

"I do adore you, Rowly. I wasn't pretending about that… and we had fun, didn't we?"

"Jem, do you not realise the consequences of this?"

"You said your reputation was already destroyed, that you wanted to help me."

"I would have helped you if you'd just asked me."

"If it makes you feel any better, Mr. Sinclair," Ley said almost proudly, "this little charade was my idea. We had intended to just hire a gentleman to play the 'evidence' but when you happened upon my little tennis soiree at *Willowview* and Jemima told me about your past affection, I realised you would do so much better."

"Why?" Rowland demanded frostily.

"Oswald Roche is fully aware that Jemima is Mrs. Fairweather's heiress. Consequently he's exceptionally reluctant to co-operate with divorce proceedings. I thought the involvement of a name like Sinclair might help him amend his attitude."

Rowland struggled to keep his temper. "What the devil are you talking about, Ley? Why would the Sinclair name make a jot of difference?"

"Aside from the fact that Wilfred Sinclair is a powerful man, your name, Rowland, has come up in connection to a number of suspicious deaths: your father; Isobel Hanrahan; Orville Urquhart; Lord Alfred Dawe; Charles Hayden; and the list goes on. It was only your brother's influence and intervention that prevented you from being charged with the attempted assassination of Eric Campbell." Ley smiled about the room, a man pleased with his own cleverness. "I hoped the thought of you—a potentially dangerous and volatile man—being involved with Mrs. Roche might dissuade Oswald Roche from trying to make life difficult."

Speechless, Rowland stared at Ley.

"Perhaps, Mr. Ley, the poor chap might have been more frightened if, instead, *you* were involved with Mrs. Roche," Clyde said casually.

To this, Ley's reaction was quite extraordinary, given the circumstances and the accusations he had just levelled at Rowland. "How dare you, sir. I'll have you know I have prosecuted men for less defamatory and scurrilous insinuations. I demand you retract immediately!"

Rowland addressed Jemima. "I believe this man is dangerous, Jem. He is at the very least a fool. All you had to do was ask me. I would have found a way to help you."

"By despatching Oswald as you have others, I suppose," Ley said imperiously. "We didn't want to resort to that."

Jemima wiped a stray tear from her cheek. "I'm so sorry, Rowly…"

"Jemima," Ley said sternly. "Do not be taken in by this man. He's ruthless. I'm told he killed a woman once. A Miss Isobel Hanrahan who was in fact carrying his child—"

Rowland punched him then. Ley went over, his arms windmilling as he fell. He landed on the floor between the settee and the smoking stand.

Clyde did not move. The blow was inevitable. If anything, too long in coming, but he'd always considered Rowland more restrained than most men.

Without another glance at Ley, Rowland moved to grab one of Jemima Roche's suitcases. "When are you heading back to Yass, Jem?"

"My train leaves in an hour."

"Good. We'll take you."

"But Tommy—"

"I'm not leaving you here with him. Either you let me take you to the station or I'll have to call the police and we'll have to explain this whole sordid mess to them."

Clyde picked up the second bag and opened the door. With a tentative glance over her shoulder at Ley, who sat nursing a bloody nose, she stepped out into the corridor. "You'll pay for this, Sinclair!" Ley promised as Rowland and Clyde followed her out.

Jemima Roche checked out of the Windsor. Rowland Sinclair settled her account.

They did not speak to each other until they reached the station, and then only as Jemima's train was boarding.

"If the court asks me, I will not deny that I spent last night in your bed," he said quietly.

Jemima looked up into his face and, though she smiled, her eyes were moist. "I didn't warn the newspapers, Rowly. You have to believe me. Grandmama will be furious."

"I'll see if anything can be done about the *Truth*," Rowland replied. He had no desire to be the rag's tawdry headline either.

"What will you do?"

"I'm not going to kill anyone, Jem, if that's what you're worried about," Rowland said irritably. A whistle for last boarding. "You'd better go. Good luck, Mrs. Roche."

"I am sorry, Rowly."

"Yes, so am I."

24

BACKER OF COMET PLANE LOST MONEY, BUT IS SATISFIED

EXPECTS CHANGES BEFORE S.A. CENTENARY

While C.W.A. Scott and Campbell Black are objects of hero worship in Adelaide equally with the rest of Australia, the man who made their success in the air race possible arrived unheralded in the express from Melbourne today. He is Mr. A.O. Edwards, the owner of Grosvenor House, London, and the nominator of the red Comet plane in which the epoch-making flight to Australia was made. The race was as much an adventure to Mr. Edwards as it was to his pilots. He left London with no more tangible evidence that he was the owner of an aeroplane than a photograph of the factory drawings of the design, and an agreement with two aviators, who were almost strangers to him, to fly it to Australia. "To win success in such circumstances was a wonderful thrill—one that could be expected only once in a lifetime," said Mr. Edwards today. "My confidence received a jolt only once, and that was when they telegraphed me from Darwin to have a mechanic waiting at Charleville."

Mr. Edwards said he lost money over the venture, but he was well content. The gold cup for the air race would have a place of honour in his hotel, where it would be a constant reminder of Australia and the event. In spite of his outlay on the venture Mr. Edwards has not had a ride in the Comet. He is not a pilot, but likes air travel.

News, 5 November 1934

Clyde returned to the suite and opened the door tentatively. He'd left Rowland to telephone Wilfred in private, and stayed away for more than an hour to be sure. He wasn't certain how Rowland would come out of the conversation.

Rowland was standing by the window, staring out.

"How was it?" Clyde asked.

"Humiliating." Rowland folded his arms and leant back against the architrave. "Wil's setting our solicitors upon the *Truth*, and pulling what strings he can with the paper's editors."

"Will it work, do you think?"

"We'll know tomorrow morning when the papers come out."

"Was Wilfred livid?"

"Incandescent."

Clyde winced. Rowland's frayed relationship with his brother had only just begun to recover. "I'm sorry to hear that, mate."

Rowland frowned thoughtfully. "To be honest, he was not as incensed with me as he was with the *Truth*."

"Really?" Clyde scratched his head. "Did you tell him everything?"

"Yes, I thought I owed him that since I was asking him to clean up the mess. He's been a lot angrier about my paintings than he was about this."

"Perhaps he's mellowing."

"I wouldn't count on it."

"Well, perhaps he's just relieved you didn't marry her."

Rowland smiled, as he considered how Jemima's penchant for misbehaviour would sit in the polite and proper pastoral and polo society of his brother. "Could be."

Clyde regarded Rowland critically. "Are you all right, Rowly?"

"Yes." Rowland moved to take his hat from the rack by the door.

"Are you sure? It would have been a shock to discover Mrs. Roche was—"

"It shouldn't have been," Rowland said. "A shock, I mean. Not with Jem involved. I'd just forgotten to expect it."

"How could you possibly expect this?"

Rowland tried to explain. "Jem was never one to contemplate consequences. She was never there to see them. When we first met, she gave my father one helluva dressing-down." He shook his head, still a little awestruck by the memory of it. "She was magnificent! I loved her for it. But I also paid for it."

"I see." Clyde knew how brutal Henry Sinclair had been towards his son. He could only imagine what Jemima's stance had cost Rowland. "Did you tell her?"

"God no—I was in love with her, Clyde." Rowland adjusted the band of his hat distractedly. "Or I thought I was."

Clyde nodded sympathetically. "We all thought we were in love at fifteen, mate. It's the age for it."

Rowland smiled. "You probably chose better than I did."

"If you think Sister Benedict Michael sounds like a good choice."

"Good Lord! You are joking."

"Sadly not," Clyde said gravely. "I was ready to fight the Almighty for her."

Rowland's smile broadened. "What happened?"

"My old mum found out and dragged me to confession by the ear." Clyde grimaced. "I reckon I wasn't the first boy to confess about Sister Benedict Michael because Father Murphy was quite understanding. He dished out a few Hail Marys as penance and Mum barged into the confessional booth to complain that it was not enough."

Laughing now, Rowland opened the door.

"Where are we going?" Clyde asked.

"I think it's high time I introduced you to the *Grosvenor House*. You can tell me more about Sister Benedict Michael on the way."

Edwards' mechanics had been through the engines of the *Grosvenor House* searching for the fault that had caused the loss in pressure which had necessitated flying the Comet at half throttle. They'd found nothing.

"She seems to be in perfect order, Mr. Sinclair."

"Are you sure?" Clyde said, rolling up his sleeves. "Let me have a butcher's."

Knowing that Clyde Watson Jones was to be Rowland Sinclair's co-pilot, the engineers took him through the workings of the plane. Clyde listened intently and asked questions which demonstrated his affinity with motors. Rowland had been given a similar orientation. If there was an emergency, they would have only their own know-how with which to extract themselves.

While Clyde wasn't technically licensed to fly a plane, he had flown the *Rule Britannia* often with Rowland in the second cockpit. The paperwork was simply a formality.

They spent an hour poring over the engines, examining and re-examining anything that might have caused the problem experienced by Scott and Black.

"I don't suppose we could take her up, Rowly?"

Rowland pointed at the small crowd of reporters at the edge of the aerodrome. "It'll be news if she does anything other than taxi, Clyde. I was hoping to keep a low profile. I don't want to chance Edwards reneging on our agreement."

"Fair enough. You sure you can fly this thing, mate?"

"I'm sure *we* can fly her."

"You're going to have to pilot solo on the way back," Clyde reminded him. From Perth, Egon Kisch would take the second cockpit and Clyde would return on the train. As far as they knew, the Czechoslovakian journalist could not fly a plane.

"By then, we'll know each other," Rowland said, running his hand along the aeroplane's thin single wing. "Good Lord, she's beautiful."

Clyde agreed without reservation. "Bloody gorgeous!" He chuckled. "There was a black Comet and a green one, wasn't there? You did well to pick the *Grosvenor House*, Rowly. No one will believe bringing Egon Kisch to Melbourne in a red aeroplane wasn't an orchestrated act of propaganda genius."

They climbed into the cockpit and, after making the requisite checks, the chocks were removed and they taxied the plane around the tarmac. The exercise allowed Clyde to familiarise himself with the configuration of the instrument panel and become accustomed to the tightness of the cockpit and the lack of forward view. They finished just after sunset, exhilarated, eager to try her in the clouds when the time came.

In a buoyant mood despite the trials of the day, they took supper at the Café Florentine. While Rowland had not forgotten that the morning's edition of the *Truth* might bring disaster, he was able to put it out of his mind... substantially at least.

Indeed, it was Clyde who brought the situation back to his thoughts as they enjoyed the Italian-styled cuisine of the popular restaurant.

"Do you really believe Mrs. Roche when she says she didn't inform the newspapers, Rowly?" he asked as he passed a small basket of freshly baked bread appreciatively beneath his nose.

"Yes. She was genuinely distressed at the idea of her grandmother discovering the... indiscretion."

"Then who? Ley?"

"I'm not sure it would serve his purposes either. I stayed the night in Jemima's suite. I didn't sneak in and she mentioned my name when she ordered breakfast. Even if I'd tried to deny being there, she has ample evidence. Ley is Jem's solicitor… I don't suppose he wanted to see her unnecessarily humiliated."

"Unless he enjoyed the idea."

"I'm not sure I follow."

"I've been asking around at Trades Hall about Thomas Ley. They say that when he was Minister for Justice, he relished sending men to hang… revelled in the fact that they knew he had the power to grant reprieve. They say he's an evil bastard."

The consternation showed on Rowland's face. "Bloody hell, I hope not. He's still Jem's solicitor."

"If it isn't Ley, or Mrs. Roche herself, who was aware the pair of you would be in the Windsor compromising yourselves last night?"

"As I said, Clyde, we weren't sneaking about. There's probably some member of staff at the Windsor who keeps an eye out for scandalous pairings and informs the *Truth* for some kind of consideration."

"Possibly." Clyde was not entirely convinced. "Well, look at it this way, Rowly. At least you're not married on top of everything else."

"It was you, my dear friend, who suggested I marry her," Rowland reminded him.

"I did. But I'm still glad you didn't have to go through with it." Clyde wiped sauce from his chin. "I realise you must feel a bit deflated about how it all turned out, mate, but I believe you dodged a bullet."

Rowland smiled. "Would it be ungentlemanly of me to admit I was relieved?"

"Yes."

"I'd best not admit it then." Rowland raised his glass. "I am glad you're here, old boy."

Clyde was still asleep when Rowland stepped out to buy the paper. The hotel customarily provided the *Melbourne Age* with each guest's breakfast tray. The *Truth*, however, was not the kind of publication supplied by establishments such as the Federal.

Rowland turned up his collar and pulled down his hat against the drizzle. He vaguely remembered a paperboy stationed at the corner of Bourke and Spencer. Though he had not mentioned it to Clyde, his greatest concern was that Edwards might, on seeing the story, consider Rowland Sinclair an inappropriate man with whom to associate the name of *Grosvenor House*.

It began to rain a little more heavily and Rowland cut through an alley to save time. Most shops were still shut, and the hour and the weather combined to keep the streets deserted. Perhaps it was the rainfall that cloaked the second set of footsteps until he was in the alley. Rowland stopped and turned on his heel. The man behind him sidestepped past, and continued on his way. Rowland relaxed. The situation was making him edgy. Two more sets of footsteps behind him... It appeared the citizens of Melbourne were finally emerging for the day.

And then the man in front of him stopped abruptly; the two behind him did too. Rowland tried to get past but the first man blocked his path.

"Can I help you?" Rowland lifted the brim of his hat so he might see the man's face. No reply but for a nod. Not for him—a signal. A blow to the kidneys from behind, hard and targeted; an arm locked around Rowland's throat dragged him backwards. A fist flew into his ribs and another to his jaw. As he stumbled he felt the hold about his neck loosen just a little and the instinct honed in the boxing ring took over. Twisting, he swung back and connected, following with a punch that crunched the soft bone of someone's nose. But numbers were against him. A crushing blow to the back of the neck and Rowland's knees buckled. He gasped as he became aware of a piercing pain in his side. Blood, thinned by the rain, ran freely through his fingers as he clutched the wound, still not sure what had happened. He reached up and grabbed the tie of the man before him and yanked with all his strength. Strangled profanities and the man fell. A clatter as a knife was dropped. Someone kicked Rowland in the back now, until he was completely down. His head cracked against the path. The world began to lose focus. He thought he heard Edna crying, Wilfred calling his name. His enemies lined up: Eric Campbell, Henry Alcott, Ernst Röhm, Blackshirts and Brownshirts, the Fascist Legion in their black hoods and capes. The glint of a blade held high. And then a shout—familiar somehow.

Scuffling and more shouts. "Bastard's got a gun!"

Rowland struggled to stay conscious. A growled whisper in his ear, "You're dead, Rowly."

"Leave off, you mongrel, or I'll shoot!" Clyde's voice.

The grip on his collar released. Scrambling. Rain. Agony.

"Rowly!" Clyde's face came out of the blur. "My God, you're bleeding!"

"I'm all right." Rowland kept his hand pressed against his side. "Just help me up."

Clyde put his shoulder under Rowland's arm and pulled him to his feet. "We must inform the police—" He looked around for help. There was no one.

"Let's… get back to… out of this flaming rain." Rowland swore as he tried to take his own weight.

"Rowly, you can't walk—"

"I'm all right," Rowland said again through gritted teeth. They had to get back before he became too light-headed to walk.

Reluctantly, Clyde agreed. The hotel was only a couple of hundred yards away, there wasn't a policeman in sight and he could hardly leave Rowland in order to find one. He was mindful that Rowland's assailants could very well return.

And so they staggered back, Clyde's determination and broad shoulders keeping Rowland on his feet, the driving rain washing away any trail of blood.

The concierge responded to their arrival with what Clyde believed was appropriate alarm, and Rowland felt was unnecessary panic and arm waving. As the presence of a bleeding man in the reception area was distressing other guests, he had Rowland helped to his suite while he sent for medical assistance.

Rowland fell into the settee. Cursing, he took his hand away from his side to inspect the damage. All he could see was a bloody waistcoat. The pain was searing. He began to shiver uncontrollably.

Clyde sent the porters who'd all but dragged Rowland up to the third floor suite to check on the promised doctor, and helped his friend to remove his coat and jacket, both of which had been pierced.

"Bloody hell, Rowly, I think you've been stabbed."

"That's what it feels like." Rowland opened his waistcoat and lifted his shirt, swearing under his breath as the wound was revealed.

Clyde used a towel to stem the bleeding, trying to stay calm as the white cloth turned rapidly red. He applied a damp facecloth to the graze on Rowland's brow where his head had hit the concrete. "Who were those blokes, Rowly?"

Rowland shook his head. "I've no idea…" He doubled over. "God, that stings…"

The concierge came puffing in with a doctor who, after cutting away Rowland's waistcoat and shirt, confirmed that the trouble was indeed a stab wound. While he worked, he introduced himself as Dr. Featherstone. He didn't ask how the wound came to be inflicted, but proceeded as if treating stab wounds was a perfectly ordinary part of a hotel doctor's duties. The blade had pierced about three inches into Rowland's flesh. An excruciating examination of the wound left Rowland incoherent, but established that the blade tip had not broken off, and, whether by divine intervention or dumb luck, there was no evidence that the knife had damaged any vital organs. Rowland had, however, lost a reasonable volume of blood. Repair required some rather unpleasant needlework.

"As agreeable as this suite is, Mr. Sinclair, I recommend you spend the next couple of days in a private hospital," Featherstone advised as he packed the wound with gauze and secured it with bandages. "I've closed the lesion but it may start bleeding again if it's disturbed."

Rowland refused politely. "That won't be necessary, Dr. Featherstone... I can recuperate perfectly well here."

"This is an hotel, Mr. Sinclair! The chamber maids are not trained as nurses."

"I don't need a nurse, Dr. Featherstone, but I can retain one if I need to. Please don't be concerned."

Featherstone employed the next ten minutes in a quite strident attempt to convince him otherwise, listing the potential consequences of refusing hospital care, before relenting. "As long as we're agreed that you are acting against my explicit advice," he said cantankerously. "I'm likely to lose my position if you bleed to death in the hotel."

Rowland smiled weakly. "We are agreed. And I give you my word that if it looks like I might exsanguinate, I shall have Mr. Watson Jones remove me from the hotel premises forthwith."

"Bed rest is vital to your recovery, Mr. Sinclair—I cannot speak more plainly. Anything but immobility will be positively dangerous."

"I understand, Dr. Featherstone."

"Well then, I shall call back this evening to clean the wound and check the dressings. You'll forgive me if I refuse to give you anything for the pain, Mr. Sinclair."

"What?" Clyde demanded. "What kind of sadistic tin pot—"

"The pain will keep you from doing anything other than resting as recommended," Featherstone said resolutely, almost smugly. "If that does not suit you, then you may go to hospital, as I suggested."

"That seems fair." Rowland didn't argue. His brother had, in any case, instilled in him a suspicion of morphine. Having served with men who'd been ruined by addiction to the painkillers so often administered too liberally on the battlefield, Wilfred was vehemently opposed to the use of the drug if the pain in question might be borne by stoic determination.

Once Featherstone had departed, Clyde poured Rowland a glass of whisky as an alternative painkiller. "Medicinal," he said placing the drink on the occasional table before his friend. "I know you hate the stuff but it's effective."

Rowland drank, spluttering as the liquor caught in his throat.

"We should notify the police," Clyde said.

"Do you have a firearm on you, Clyde?" Rowland vaguely recalled shouts about a gun. He wasn't sure how much of his memory was real.

Clyde patted his pocket. "Actually, I have yours."

"Mine?" Wilfred Sinclair had given Rowland his old service pistol years before, ostensibly to shoot Communists. Rowland kept the Webley revolver in a box under his bed.

"After what happened to Milt in Canberra, I thought it mightn't be a bad idea," Clyde said. "I grabbed it before I left Sydney."

"How did you know I needed help this morning?"

"I was looking out the window when you left and I noticed three jokers take off after you… I figured they were up to no good, so I took the gun out of my bag and set off in the same direction. I was in the next block when I heard the commotion in the alley."

"For heaven's sake, don't mention the gun to the police."

"Why ever not?"

"You don't have a licence for it."

"Oh, I didn't have time to load it. I just waved it around. If they hadn't baulked, we would have been in serious trouble. "

Slowly, painfully, Rowland sat forward. "I should find another shirt," he said pushing the hair out of his face.

"Steady on, Rowly. You look like hell."

A knock at the door.

Clyde answered it, to admit two sturdy members of the Victorian Police Force. Constables Meggit and Brown were attending on the request of hotel management who'd reported that one of their guests had been assaulted in the street. Brown, who seemed very young, turned noticeably green at the sight of the blood-soaked towel and the similarly stained remains of Rowland's waistcoat and shirt.

"Please sit down, Mr. Sinclair," Constable Meggit said as Rowland tried to get to his feet.

Afraid Brown could well faint, Clyde removed the towel and clothing out of his line of sight. Aware of Rowland's preference for being fully dressed in public, heightened by a self-consciousness of the swastika-shaped scar on his chest, Clyde returned with a fresh shirt. Rowland redressed while answering questions.

"They knew your name?" Meggit asked thoughtfully, on hearing Rowland's account of the last whispered threat.

"Yes."

"And Mr. Watson Jones saw them follow you from this location?"

Clyde nodded.

"So this was not a random robbery but a carefully planned assault." Meggit frowned. "Do you have enemies, Mr. Sinclair? Did you recognise any of these men?"

"I don't think so... I'm afraid I can't recall much of it clearly..."

"Why not?" Meggit sounded almost offended.

Rowland shrugged. "I hit my head when I fell and everything got hazy and quite confused after that. I can only bring one face to mind clearly."

Meggit looked at him strangely but did not pursue the line of questioning. "It's possible that this is an inside job."

"I beg your pardon, Constable."

"A gang member planted in the employ of the hotel. He identifies wealthy guests and alerts fellow gang members who set upon and rob the gentleman when he leaves the hotel at a time conducive to such criminal activity. There was a similar operation working out of the Windsor last month, though not with the level of violence we find here." Meggit seemed pleased with his reasoning, and quickly became committed to it. Every detail Rowland mentioned seemed to his mind to confirm the operation of a gang connected to the hotel somehow.

He terminated the interview soon after, and signalled Brown to follow as he departed to question the staff.

Rowland got to his feet. "I need a tie, and a jacket."

"Why?"

"Standards, old boy. I can't step out without a tie."

"Don't be an idiot, Rowly. You've been stabbed."

"I'm not going dancing. Just back to that alley." Rowland tested his movement tentatively.

"Now? What the hell for?"

"I'm hoping I'll remember more if I go back. I'm not sure, but I think the knife fell…"

Clyde shook his head. "Not a knife. When I caught up to you, some bloke was about to slash you with a razor. It was still in his hand when they bolted."

"I couldn't have been stabbed with a razor, Clyde. There must have been another knife and I'm sure it fell. Perhaps they didn't retrieve it. It may tell us something."

"Why didn't you tell the police?"

"I only just remembered." Rowland blinked, still trying to clear his head. He wasn't thinking straight. "Perhaps I should just get them back."

"I'll go," Clyde decided. "If I find anything, we can tell Constable Meggit then. You stay here and try not to bleed."

"What if those blighters are still about the alley?"

"If they are, you're not going to be much use in your present condition, mate. I'll keep my eyes peeled."

As he left, Clyde locked the suite door. He spoke to no one on the way out, lest doing so would alert the wrong people that Rowland was alone. Whatever the constables thought, it was clear to him that someone had tried to assassinate Rowland Sinclair.

25

WOUNDS

———◆———

Wounds and cuts should be attended to at once. Above all, they must be kept clean, and should be washed at once in warm water with some absorbent cotton, or other soft material. Deep, punctured wounds, from nails, broken glass, splinters, etc., require thorough opening out and cleaning by a physician, or lockjaw may develop. While waiting for his arrival, wash the wound with peroxide of hydrogen and bandage a wet compress over it. When there is much bleeding, place a piece of absorbent cotton or clean linen over the wound and apply firm pressure with the thumb or finger, until the bleeding stops and the cotton adheres. Then apply a light bandage.

Warialda Standard and
Northern Districts' Advertiser, 17 April 1933

It had ceased raining when Clyde stepped out into Collins Street. The sun shafted occasionally through the clouds, falling in concentrated beams upon a city sparkling after the recent deluge. Clyde inhaled. Rain smelled different in the city. In all the years he'd lived in Sydney, he'd not got used to that. He walked briskly towards the scene of the morning's incident, keen to return to Rowland as soon as possible. The threat worried him as much as the attack. Whoever these men were, they were unlikely to be happy with their failure to kill Rowland Sinclair.

Clyde reached the alley and went directly to the place on the footpath where the assault had taken place. The blood had been washed away but he was sure about the location. He walked the footpath slowly, searching for a knife, checking the gutters, and casting his eye in all directions. There was nothing. Perhaps Rowland had misremembered the knife falling or his assailants had simply retrieved it.

"Mr. Watson Jones! What exactly are you doing here?" Meggit and Brown strode towards him.

"Mr. Sinclair wondered if his assailants might have dropped something." Clyde continued scanning the footpath. "He's not in any condition to search himself, so I came in his stead."

"We'd thank both you and Mr. Sinclair to leave any investigation to the proper authorities."

"Well since you're here, perhaps we could all look."

"What exactly is your relationship to Mr. Sinclair, Mr. Watson Jones?" Brown asked.

"I'm his... motor mechanic."

"Not many men travel with their mechanics. It's a little unusual, wouldn't you say?"

"Mr. Sinclair is very attached to his automobile."

"I see. Did you and Mr. Sinclair have a falling out recently?"

"Me and Rowly—no—of course not."

Brown read from his notebook. "The concierge saw Mr. Sinclair leave at precisely twenty past five this morning. He noticed the time because it was remarkably early to be seeing a guest up and about. According to him, Mr. Sinclair seemed distracted and in a hurry. Then he claims to have seen you leave the hotel no more than ten minutes later. You were, according to him, running. The concierge saw no one else."

Clyde took a step back. "Surely you don't think..."

"We've no evidence to substantiate the existence of the three men Mr. Sinclair claims attacked him. It would not be the first time that a disagreement between a gentleman and his... mechanic... became overheated."

"Surely Rowly might have thought to mention it, if I'd stabbed him."

"Perhaps he might have if we'd interviewed him without you present. Or perhaps he was genuinely trying to cover for his... mechanic."

Clyde was a little disturbed by the manner in which Brown seemed to pause before saying the word mechanic. "Mr. Sinclair and I sent for the police—that seems like a funny way to cover up a crime."

"Our records suggest that the concierge telephoned the station, sir."

"Why would I be here looking for evidence?" Clyde persisted in trying to make them see reason.

"Perhaps you're here making sure that there is no evidence."

Clyde's temper flared. "This is flaming absurd!" He pointed at Meggit. "First you have some ridiculous notion about criminal hotel personnel and then you—" he turned his gaze to Brown "—decide to trump him with an even more ludicrous theory that I overpowered and stabbed my best friend because we argued!"

"What exactly was the nature of this argument?" Brown asked, unperturbed by Clyde's tirade.

"There was no argument," Clyde said wearily. "Now if you're quite finished gentlemen... since you are both here, I'm a little concerned that Mr. Sinclair, in his impaired state, is alone in his hotel room with a mob of assassins on the loose!"

The door into the suite was still locked. Clyde let himself in. He was aware that storming away from the officers as he had might have made him look guilty of something, but it was better than *being* guilty of assaulting an idiot policeman. At least they hadn't arrested him.

Rowland startled awake as he entered. "Clyde…"

"You should be lying down, Rowly," Clyde muttered as Rowland shifted painfully in the armchair. "And you should probably eat something too, replace the blood you lost. I might see if they have stout."

Rowland ignored his concern. "Did you find the knife?"

"No, but I did run into Constables Meggit and Brown inspecting the scene as it were."

"Oh, did Meggit find his crooked concierge?"

"No, their latest theory is that I stabbed you in some kind of tiff."

Rowland bolted upright, then fell back suppressing a curse. "What?" he said weakly.

Clyde explained the constables' thinking.

Rowland laughed, regretting it as he did so. He winced. "You said you were my mechanic? Clyde old man, I'm afraid that sounds like some kind of appalling euphemism."

Now Clyde paled. "How's your side?" he asked, desperate to get his mind off what exactly the constables might have assumed. "It hasn't started bleeding again, has it?"

"It hurts like the blazes, but whatever Featherstone did it seems to be holding."

"Well you look like death warmed up. And we need to get you well enough to fly the Comet in a week."

"I'm on the mend."

"Doesn't look that way. Go lie down, Rowly. I'll book a call through to Delaney and let him know the latest. Maybe Major Jones has made some progress. And then we'll work out what we're going to do."

――――――――― ―――――――――

True to his word, Clyde telephoned Central Police Station in Sydney and spoke with Colin Delaney who had returned from Canberra just the day before. Concerned, the detective advised them to come back to Sydney.

"We can't for a few days, Colin."

"Why not?"

"You probably shouldn't ask."

"What are you and Rowly up to, Clyde?"

Clyde didn't respond.

Delaney cursed. "At least you're with him rather than Milton. God knows what trouble he could get into with Isaacs."

Clyde booked another trunk call through to *Woodlands House*. When he was eventually connected, he told Edna everything—from Jemima Roche and her scheming to Thomas Ley, and finally the assault on Rowland.

Edna was, as he expected, distressed by the news. "Are you sure Rowly is all right, Clyde? You know how he is…"

"Dr. Featherstone is coming back this evening, Ed. If Rowly's condition is any worse I'll take him to the hospital whether he likes it or not."

"Is he taking it easy? How's his colour? Is he in much pain?"

"Steady on, Ed," Clyde said calmly into her panic. "He'll be all right. I'll make sure."

Edna took a deep breath and then said quietly, "Were the photographs in the paper?"

"The paper—Good Lord, we forgot all about that!"

"Is he terribly sad, Clyde?"

"About what?"

"Mrs. Roche."

"Not terribly. This was just a bit of a fling, Ed."

"He asked her to marry him."

"Only because he had to."

"It's not the first time. He's proposed before."

"You know, Rowly... he probably thought it impolite not too." Clyde sighed. "Look, Ed, I'm pretty sure it's not his broken heart that's causing him the most pain."

"Oh God, poor Rowly, just stay with him... please... just in case."

Clyde reassured her that he would. "How's Milt?"

"Much better. Leaping about on crutches. Mary's spoiling him rotten."

"Mary?" Clyde was surprised. Mary Brown had always appeared to regard Milton as some thieving, drunken tramp whom Rowland had brought home as an exotic house pet.

"I don't understand it either," Edna confessed. "Perhaps Mary feels sorry for him. She's never been this nice to Rowly."

"Perhaps we should all throw ourselves in front of speeding cars."

The sculptress' voice became thick and strained. "You will be careful won't you, Clyde? They might have killed Rowly if you hadn't arrived."

"We'll be careful, Ed. I promise."

Clyde hung up. He stood tapping his fingers pensively against the receiver. Edna was rarely spooked. The very fact she was made him uneasy too. He debated with himself over the next call. Still unsure, he looked in on Rowland, relieved that his friend was finally asleep. Though he appeared to be resting normally, Rowland seemed pale. Clyde supposed being stabbed would do that.

Clyde returned to the sitting room and picked up the telephone once more. He called through to *Oaklea*. Wilfred Sinclair was in a hurry, late for a meeting in Canberra, and he was surprised to receive a call from Clyde Watson Jones. While Wilfred's opinion of his brother's Bolshevik unemployed friends had mellowed somewhat, he rarely engaged directly with any of them.

"Mr. Watson Jones, what can I do for you?"

Suddenly Clyde wasn't sure where to begin. "I'm in Melbourne with Rowly, sir."

"Is this about the *Truth* debacle?" Wilfred asked irritably. "I was assured the article would not run."

"To be honest, sir, we haven't seen the paper."

"What's going on, Mr. Watson Jones? Where's Rowly?"

Clyde told him then what had happened that morning.

"Why is my brother not in a hospital?" Wilfred roared.

"The hotel doctor patched him up, Mr. Sinclair."

"He didn't graze his knee—he was stabbed!"

"Rowly's certain he'll be fine, sir. He doesn't want to go to hospital."

"Oh for the love of God!" Wilfred said, exasperated. "I'm assuming, Mr. Watson Jones, that you are able to drive that hideous new automobile of his."

"Yes, of course."

"Then put him in it and drive up to Yass. I'll make sure he gets the medical care he needs."

"I'm afraid Rowly won't do that, sir."

"Why not? The bloody air race is over!" Wilfred paused. "Why exactly is my brother in Melbourne?"

By now Clyde heartily regretted his decision to telephone Wilfred. "He came for the air race, sir... and now I'm not sure he's fit to travel."

"You said he wasn't in danger."

"He's not," Clyde was getting flustered now. "The doctor's prescribed bed rest and Rowly's a bit tender... a long car trip might be too much."

Wilfred cursed. "Where is Rowly now?"

"He's sleeping—he lost a fair bit of blood."

"Instruct him to telephone me here at *Oaklea* as soon as he's fit to do so."

"Yes, sir."

"Thank you for informing me, Mr. Watson Jones. I'm genuinely comforted by the knowledge that he's with you and not that long-haired buffoon!"

———————   ———————

When Rowland finally woke, Clyde insisted he eat. To this end, Clyde ordered Scotch broth and chocolate cake from the hotel kitchen. Rowland regarded the tray, amused. It seemed like an odd combination.

"My old mum used to say that red meat was good for the blood," Clyde explained.

"But broth?"

"Mum would make broth whenever we were poorly."

"I see." Rowland didn't really think he was unwell enough to warrant broth, but he knew better than to question the wisdom of Clyde's mother. "And the cake?"

"I like cake. I tested them both. I think they're all right."

"For salt?" Rowland asked, confused.

"For poison."

Rowland grinned. "Clyde—"

"If someone in the hotel is involved in this, they could well decide that adding strychnine to your soup would finish the job."

"I'd better eat it then since you've risked life and limb to check it."

"How are you feeling, Rowly?" Clyde cut into the steak and kidney pie he'd ordered for himself.

Rowland began with the cake. "A bit battered," he admitted, "but not bad considering." He pulled aside his shirt and looked down at the site of the wound. A penny-sized spot of blood had penetrated the gauze but it was not widening. "I don't think it's started bleeding again. I'll be flying fit in a few days."

"I telephoned Wilfred," Clyde said quickly.

"Whatever for?"

"I thought I should let him know about this morning. He's your brother after all…"

"What did he say?"

"He'd like you to telephone him as soon as you're able. He seems a little concerned about what you're doing here."

"You didn't—"

"I'm not a bloody fool."

"Sorry—of course." Rowland rubbed a hand through his hair. "If Wil suspects what we are doing, he'll jolly well find a way to make sure we never take off."

"Does he know Egon is coming?"

"Bruce does, so I expect he's shared that information with Wil."

Clyde sighed. "Eat. You can deal with Wilfred later."

Rowland polished off the cake and then began on the broth. It was not as bad as he'd feared. "I don't suppose you've seen the *Truth* today?"

"Actually curiosity got the better of me and I sent one of the bellboys out for it after I spoke with Wilfred. I don't know what your brother did, Rowly, but there's nothing about you or Mrs. Roche—not yet anyway."

"Well that's something, at least."

Anticipating a lecture demanding he go to hospital, Rowland waited until after Featherstone had visited that evening to telephone Wilfred. As the physician had expressed relief that he had not died, Rowland was able to report quite truthfully that the doctor was pleased with his condition, and slightly less truthfully that a hospital would be a laughable overreaction. He tried to keep the conversation light, telling Wilfred about Melbourne's preparations for the Duke of Gloucester. "There's a fortune to be made in bunting and flags, Wil. We should think about diversifying."

"Have the police any clue as to who stabbed you, Rowly?" Wilfred ignored his brother's attempt to change the subject. He could in any case hear the strain in Rowland's voice.

Rowland told him about the attending constable's theory of a gang of thugs connected to the hotel somehow, and, as an afterthought, the newfound suspicion of Clyde. Wilfred also thought that absurd. "That Isaacs fellow, perhaps—but not Mr. Watson Jones. Exactly which of your enemies do you think might have done this, Rowly?"

"I do wonder about Thomas Ley."

"Why would he want to kill you?"

"He was a little upset with me when we last parted." Rowland recounted his most recent meeting with Ley, and the manner in which it ended. To his surprise, Wilfred did not chastise him for punching the erstwhile politician.

"It's possible," he said instead. "From what I understand Thomas Ley is a particularly dangerous man to cross."

"It could also be the same mob who murdered Jim Kelly and ran Milt down," Rowland ventured tentatively.

"You keep telling me you're not a Communist," Wilfred said tersely.

"Clearly the message is not getting out."

"For pity's sake, Rowly..."

"What can I tell you, Wil? Some people may well have decided my politics by the company I keep."

"There are more Communists in this country than I care to contemplate, Rowly. Why is it that you and your friends are the ones they want to kill?"

"Kelly wasn't a friend, but you do raise a good point," Rowland said thoughtfully. "Who would want to kill Milt and me in particular? Perhaps looking at that might help us find them."

"Ethel mentioned you were buying another aeroplane." Wilfred's question was anything but casual.

"That was just a whim, Wil. The excitement of the air race, you know… made me want a fast bird."

"So you didn't buy an aircraft?"

"No, of course not." Somehow, even over the telephone line, Rowland felt his brother's scrutiny. He wondered if Wilfred could tell he was leaving something unsaid.

"I want you to recuperate at *Oaklea*. We'll have to return to Melbourne for the dedication, but you'll be able to convalesce here first."

Melbourne's Shrine of Remembrance was to be dedicated by the Duke of Gloucester on Armistice Day. Wilfred would attend in various official capacities as well as that of a decorated veteran. The National Congress of the Movement Against War and Fascism had been intentionally scheduled for the same day, to urge the public to consider the cause against conflict when the generation the country had lost was at the forefront of people's thoughts.

"You will be attending the dedication." Wilfred read into his brother's silence.

"Of course." Rowland elected to respond as if Wilfred had asked a question.

"Rowly, I hardly need to remind you that our brother fell in the Great War; that he died for this country. Whatever else you're planning, you will be at the dedication. Do you understand me?"

"Bloody hell, I'm not a child!" Rowland bit his lip against a sudden awareness of pain. He tried to resist the rise of blood which seemed to compromise his ability to deal with the constant sharp ache where the blade had pierced.

"I won't have you disrespect Aubrey's memory!" Wilfred barked.

Rowland spoke slowly. "Aubrey was my brother too, Wil. For God's sake, I still miss him." He stopped to catch his breath. "You don't have to order me to attend the dedication! I'll be there."

"Come back to *Oaklea*, Rowly. We'll attend the dedication together. I'm sure Aubrey would have liked that." Wilfred's voice was conciliatory but wary.

Rowland closed his eyes as he wondered what Aubrey would have thought of what he was doing. "I'm not sure I'm up to a long car trip, Wil."

"What are you up to, Rowly?"

"Not a great deal… I'm under doctor's orders to move as little as possible."

"Well, see that you do just that!"

26

CRAMP

The best immediate remedy for cramp is friction with the hand or, better still, with the soap, chloroform, or opium liniment. Any disorder of the digestive organs ought, of course, to be attended to. Some persons find relief to the immediate attack of cramp by tying a band of some kind tightly round the limb, between the affected part and the body, while others are in the habit of standing upon some cold substance. The first process is perfectly safe, and may be tried; the second certainly is often effective, but is not devoid of danger. Active friction is quite the best temporary remedy.

Warialda Standard and
Northern Districts' Advertiser, 26 February 1934

"Mr. Sinclair..." Momentarily startled, Clyde admitted Wilfred Sinclair and Dr. Frederick Maguire to the suite.

"Good afternoon, Mr. Watson Jones. Freddie and I thought we might drop in and check on Rowly," Wilfred said brusquely. He removed his bowler and cast his eyes about the suite.

"Yes... of course..." Clyde stuttered, folding up the map spread out on the card table, from which he had been plotting their route to Fremantle. It was a ten-hour drive from Yass. Wilfred must have set off not long after he'd last spoken to Rowland. "Rowly's in the bedroom. Can I offer you gentlemen a drink?"

"We'd best look in on Rowly first." Wilfred opened the door to the bedroom and Maguire stepped in ahead of him.

Rowland was as surprised as Clyde had been by his brother's arrival. Wilfred had always produced Maguire like some kind of medical genie he kept in his fob pocket, but both men would have needed to come from Yass at least. "What on earth are you doing here?" he asked as he tried to sit up.

"Stay where you are, Rowland," Maguire instructed, opening his medical bag.

"I just so happened to have some business matters to attend to in Melbourne," Wilfred said. "We thought we'd make sure that your newfound fear of hospitals wasn't going to see you end up in the morgue."

"I'm not afraid of—"

"And if you're well enough to travel—then you can come back with me." Wilfred kept his eyes on Rowland's face.

Maguire placed a thermometer under Rowland's tongue and removed Featherstone's dressings to inspect the wound. He pressed on Rowland's stomach. "I'll thank you not to bite my thermometer," he said as Rowland tensed against his touch.

The doctor removed the instrument and held it up to the light to see the reading. "You've a temperature," he murmured. "How much pain are you in?"

"It's tolerable as long as I don't move." Rowland had no intention of returning with Wilfred. And now he wondered how much Wilfred knew or suspected.

Maguire felt around the wound.

Rowland gasped and tried to pull away. Wilfred watched on.

"Did Dr. Featherstone check that the blade hadn't broken off?" Maguire posed, still prodding at the wound.

"Yes, sir, he did," Clyde said quickly. "He made absolutely sure."

"I suspect you have a mild infection." The surgeon reached into his bag. "I'll need to irrigate and clean the wound. It should be done twice a day from here on in."

"I'll make arrangements for a nurse to attend to you at *Oaklea*," Wilfred said. "Bloody ridiculous to be hiding out in a hotel like some criminal."

"Wil, I can't—" Rowland said.

"I could give him some morphine," Maguire offered. "It should make him more comfortable for the journey."

"Absolutely not!" Wilfred replied.

"You're not drugging me just so you can drag me back to *Oaklea*," Rowland growled. "I'm staying here, Wil."

"Why? Why are you so determined to stay? After this fiasco with the Roche woman, I would have thought you'd be happy to leave!"

"Why are you so determined to confine me to Yass? What are you afraid I'll do?"

"Don't be absurd, Rowly! You're seriously ill."

Rowland sighed. "Look, Wil, I'm all right… but it hurts like the devil when I move. Being rattled along in the back of your Rolls for ten hours will be pure torture."

"I believe you'll find a Rolls-Royce does not rattle," Wilfred said coldly.

"You know what I mean. If I feel able in a few days, Clyde and I might attend the Melbourne Cup. But for the moment, I'm just going to lie here and feel sorry for myself."

"If I could have a quiet word…" Maguire beckoned Wilfred to follow him into the sitting room. They spoke in hushed tones for several moments.

"Very well, Rowly," Wilfred said, returning to the room. "Freddie seems to agree that it would be ill-advised to move you at present. I'm due back in Melbourne on the ninth. In the meantime, he'll speak with this chap Featherstone to ensure you're being looked after properly."

"For God's sake, try not to offend him," Rowland muttered, expecting that Maguire would do just that. He coughed, cursing as the movement seemed to tear open the wound anew.

Wilfred contemplated his brother. He hesitated. "Perhaps something for the pain is warranted…"

Rowland shook his head. "No. I'll manage."

Wilfred nodded. "Good man."

Maguire and Wilfred departed not long after, with warnings about infection and over-exertion. Clyde pulled a bridge chair up beside Rowland's bed once they'd gone. "What the hell was that about?"

"Wilfred suspects we're up to something, I expect. He came down to lock me up in *Oaklea* until Armistice Day."

"Are you all right?"

Rowland smiled. "I was playing it up a bit. Had to make sure Wil wouldn't insist I go back with him."

"Crikey, mate, I was getting worried that I'd let you lie here in agony for a day and a half."

Rowland held his side gingerly as he sat up. "Don't get me wrong—it hurts, but not as much as I made out," he said slowly.

"What now?"

"I'm going to have to lie low until we leave." Rowland grimaced as he contemplated a week in the hotel room. "I wouldn't put it past Wil to have me watched. No doubt he'll have Featherstone on his payroll by the end of the day."

It was barely light at the Laverton aerodrome. Clyde and Rowland had arranged to take off in the early hours to ensure they attracted as little attention as possible. Now six days after the stabbing, they had decided they couldn't delay any longer. The daybreak drizzle ensured that even the most dedicated reporters had not thought to stake out the Comet in the hope of an impromptu visit by Scott or Black. Despite their best efforts, however, a small crowd had gathered to see them off: Arthur Howells, John Fisher, and Nettie and Vance Palmer represented the Movement Against War and Fascism. A young woman and a man leaning heavily on a walking stick also stood on the edge of the tarmac.

Edna Higgins and Milton Isaacs had come down on the train the day before. Milton had been determined to be at the MAWF congress in any case, and Edna had wanted to see for herself that Rowland was fit to fly. They found both Rowland and Clyde in the hotel suite going over flight plans and memorising routes. Rowland's wound appeared to be substantially healed and clearly the arrival of the sculptress was a tonic in itself. And so they'd all spent the previous evening exchanging news and playing cards, and rekindling the excitement of what they were about to do.

Milton had taken the extra bed in Clyde's room. Refusing to deprive Rowland of his bed, on the account of his recent injury and the impending flight, Edna had settled on the couch with pillows and blankets. Even so, she'd padded into Rowland's room in the middle of the night. Rowland was not particularly surprised by the intrusion. Edna had a habit of visiting in the dead of night when she had something on her mind. And he'd sensed she had something on her mind.

"Rowly... Rowly, wake up."

He'd opened his eyes to her face as she knelt beside his bed. "Ed..." It was not so dark that he could not see the familiar planes of her countenance and, for a moment, he'd allowed himself to simply look at her. Then he'd sat up and moved over so she could sit beside him.

"I have to know, are you dreadfully upset about Mrs. Roche?"

He smiled, touched that she was so concerned. "No. Not anymore. Jem and I were more a memory than anything else."

"It was Bertie," she blurted. "Bertie called the papers."

"Middleton... How did he—"

"I told him you were in Melbourne, Rowly. I'm so sorry."

"Good Lord, Ed—it's not your fault." Rowland shook his head, perplexed. "Knowing I was in Melbourne doesn't explain how he knew I'd be with..." He faltered.

Edna smiled. She could sense his embarrassment. "I suspect Mrs. Roche might have told him of her intentions, Rowly. Bertie spoke to some of his journalist friends about it."

"But why?"

"He's an idiot and it seems he's frightfully angry with you."

Rowland sat up. "Rather lousy thing to do to Jemima, just because he was cross with me."

"As I said, he's an idiot."

"Yes, I knew that."

"I'm so sorry, Rowly."

"It's certainly not your fault he's an idiot."

"But I am sorry, especially if what he did came between you and—"

"Ed, sweetheart, Jemima simply used me to establish grounds to petition for a divorce. That was all."

She reached out and touched his cheek. "That's... are you all right?"

"Perfectly well. I was quite relieved when she refused my proposal, if truth be told."

"Well marriage is a rather drastic solution," Edna nudged him. "What were you thinking?"

"It was Clyde's idea." He took her hand and kissed it. "Honestly, Ed, my pride's a little bruised, but my heart is perfectly intact."

Her eyes moved to the place under his ribs where she knew the stab wound to be. "And what about the rest of you?"

"Never better. Healed."

"Show me," she said, unwilling to take his word on this. In Edna's experience the men she lived with were wont to complain excessively about head colds and dismiss the life-threatening.

He turned on the lamp beside the bed, and lifted his singlet so she could see for herself. At Rowland's insistence, Featherstone had removed the stitches that day, earlier than he would otherwise have done so. The area was quite bruised, a little inflamed, and if Rowland was honest, very tender, but the wound was closed.

Edna touched the still livid scar. "Gosh, Rowly, you were frightfully lucky. If the blade had been angled upwards, it would have punctured your lung. You wouldn't have been able to make a sound."

"Perhaps that was their plan," Rowland said, mildly distracted by her touch. Her hand was cool on his skin.

"I stepped out with a soldier a couple of years ago. Special operations or so he claimed," Edna said thoughtfully. "He told me once that if you wanted to kill a man silently, you stabbed him in the lungs from behind so he couldn't scream, and then cut his throat."

"He told you that?"

"It sounds macabre out of context. I suspect he was using the demonstration as an elaborate if rather transparent ploy to get his arms around me." Edna smiled at Rowland's obvious alarm. "He was quite sweet really. What I mean to say is that the men who attacked you might have been in the army at some point."

Rowland nodded slowly. There had been a kind of efficient order to the way he'd been corralled and restrained. If the blade had hit his lung, he probably would not have been able to fight back as he had. Still, there were many men who'd seen service, who would be trained in the rigours of hand-to-hand combat. The observation did not really narrow the field. Despite returning with a detective inspector on two occasions, Meggit and Brown had not made any progress on the identity of his attackers either, though they had at least abandoned their ridiculous suspicions of Clyde.

Edna frowned. "Are you sure you're well enough, Rowly? Perhaps—"

"Yes," he said firmly. "I wouldn't risk the *Grosvenor House*, let alone Clyde's life, if I wasn't able to fly. Whoever those mongrels were, they're not going to be able to reach me at 19,000 feet."

A letter from Oswald Roche delivered to the hotel had made Rowland wonder if the attack had, in fact, nothing to do with anti-Communist thugs or Ley. The missive was outraged and vitriolic, pledging to reveal Rowland as a blackguard of the worst kind to make him understand the consequences of dealing immorally with another man's wife. Reminded of how desperate Jemima had appeared to be rid of her husband, he'd telephoned Wilfred and asked him to check on her. It seemed to him that Jemima Roche had become involved with at least two very dangerous men.

But now, as they were about to climb into the cockpit of the fastest aeroplane in the world, Rowland forgot about murderers and husbands. Exhilarated, he kissed Edna's cheek. "Isn't she beautiful, Ed?"

Edna laughed, quite accustomed to his tendency to become besotted with machines and gadgetry. She reached up and wrapped a white scarf around his neck, tucking its ends into the front of his leather aviator's jacket. "For luck," she said. "Fly safely, Rowly, and come back to us."

"Our Rowly's the type of the wise who soar but never roam," Milton said sagely as he hobbled up to shake Rowland's hand. "True to the kindred points of heaven and home."

"I'm not sure what that means, but it's Wordsworth." Rowland took Milton's hand, warmly. "You're sure you can drive?" he asked, frowning.

The sculptress and the poet would stay with Max Meldrum in Olinda. The artist's home in the Dandenong mountains, it had been decided, was safer than a city hotel with Rowland's attackers still unidentified and at large. Milton and Edna would take the Chrysler Airflow with them.

"Without a second thought, Rowly." Milton twirled his walking stick, using the handle to push his hat into a more jaunty angle. "I just keep this to look distinguished. It's a rather stylish accessory, don't you think? Gives one a rather well-heeled air... it seems only the working classes are content to limp."

Rowland and Clyde farewelled the Kisch Reception Committee, thanking Meldrum particularly for welcoming their friends into his home. The illustrious artist waved off their gratitude in his way. Edna demanded they all pose for photographs. There was a momentous air about the endeavour that precluded any recognition of risk, any contemplation of failure.

Edna kissed Clyde goodbye, and ceremoniously wrapped a second silk scarf over the top of the woollen one he was already wearing. She stood back to inspect them, snapping another picture. "You both look so very dashing."

The small crowd applauded as Clyde climbed onto the wing and opened the cockpit canopy.

Rowland lingered. There was something about farewells at dawn. It seemed to suspend propriety for just a moment. The drizzle had formed tiny auburn ringlets around Edna's face. Her eyes were bright and, even in the rain, he could smell the faint rose of her perfume. She embraced him one final time and, gently, he kissed her in a way that was possibly inappropriate. The representatives from MAWF applauded once more. Edna laughed. "Whoever said you weren't a showman, Rowland Sinclair?"

Rowland pulled on his flying helmet and climbed into the first cockpit. Perhaps it was because Milton had just stolen from

Wordsworth that the words of the bard came to him now. Bliss was it in that dawn to be alive. But to be young was very heaven.

***

The *Grosvenor House* took off from Laverton aerodrome just after five o'clock on the morning of 4 November. The *R.M.S. Strathaird* was due to deliver Egon Kisch to Fremantle on Tuesday the sixth, Melbourne Cup Day 1934, and Rowland would fly him back to Melbourne by the eighth.

They'd plotted a flight plan which took them over land rather than the more direct route over water, so that they would have more options if there were problems. As it was, they were flying via Mildura, Port Augusta, Forrest, Kalgoorlie and Merredin. They would land only in Forrest to break the seven-hour flight. Capable of flying 2500 nautical miles without stopping, the *Grosvenor House* would not require refuelling and the break would be only for the comfort of her pilots.

In the cockpit the noise of the engines was such that Rowland and Clyde could only communicate with each other by shouting. Initially, they were excited enough that the requirement was no great chore, but after an hour or so they fell into silence, each privately revelling in the Comet's speed.

It was over Mildura that the *Grosvenor House*'s port engine lost pressure and began seizing. Clyde cursed. Rowland reacted quickly. Given Scott and Black's experience, he'd been prepared for the possibility. He recited Scott's instructions out loud as he throttled down the port engine and manually pressed the rudder with his foot to equalise the power levels. The aircraft settled.

"Good show, Rowly!" Clyde shouted, crossing himself thankfully.

Rowland bit his lip. He hadn't anticipated how the consequent position of his leg would impact the injured muscles in his side. The pain began sharply but gradually eased to a dull burn. He dismissed the discomfort, sure that it would abate as he became accustomed to the strain.

They approached Forrest, a little behind time due to throttling back the engines. Rowland signalled to Clyde that he would fly around the airport first as the Comet's design left it with almost no forward view. Briefly he pressed his hand to his side trying to ignore the ache. He'd deal with the wound shortly, but first they'd have to land. He brought the *Grosvenor House* down gradually, locking his eyes on a peripheral view of the runway's edge as he reduced speed. The scorching conditions combined with a light crosswind to make keeping wings level a challenge. Rowland felt for the runway, and the plane touched down with a jolt. A cold sweat dampened his forehead as he worked the throttles and the stick to bring her to a controlled, if less than perfect, halt.

Clyde popped the canopy and got out first. He stared at Rowland. "What's wrong? You look like hell."

Rowland took the hand Clyde offered him and dragged himself out. "I'm still a little sore," he said, not wanting to alarm his friend. "I think I may have pulled a muscle trying to keep pressure on the rudder."

"We'll swap places for the next leg." Clyde watched carefully as Rowland hobbled down from the wing. He looked pointedly at Rowland's side. "Are you sure you're all right?"

Rowland nodded, his hand over the site of the wound. "It's holding. I just need a breather."

A settlement rather than a town, Forrest was located on the longest stretch of straight railway in the world. It was flat country just inside the border of Western Australia. The hostel at the airstrip provided accommodation and meals for passengers stopping overnight on the passenger air service between Perth and Adelaide. Its restaurant boasted cuisine "worthy of any city hotel". It was here that Clyde and Rowland stopped for luncheon.

Rowland removed his jacket, stuffing the scarf Edna had given him into the pocket. It was warm—an arid desert heat mitigated a little by Forrest's proximity to the ocean. Being out of the cockpit was a relief. A cursory examination revealed no new bleeding, and Rowland decided that the pain which had almost incapacitated him in the cockpit was a symptom of the wound "healing". They ate, buoyed by the fact that, despite all the drama and difficulty of the past weeks, they were finally on their way to collect Egon Kisch. Rowland had been secretly sure that Wilfred would discover his plans and find a way to scuttle the endeavour. But there was nothing Wilfred Sinclair or anyone else could do to stop them now.

In Forrest it seemed they were able to discuss the intrigues of both Canberra and Melbourne with a kind of temporal and emotional distance.

"Do you suppose that Oswald Roche orchestrated the attack on you?" Clyde asked as he tucked enthusiastically into roast lamb and potatoes.

"If he knew somehow what Jem was up to—maybe." Rowland rubbed his leg under the table. "It seems an impersonal way to do it. If some chap seduced my wife, I'd want to kill him myself, not despatch hired thugs to do the job."

"But that's you," Clyde said. "You're a bit of a romantic about such things." He pointed his fork at Rowland. "I suspect there are many blokes who'd be quite happy to let others do the dirty work."

Rowland cut into his steak. "Sadly we have nothing to connect the attack to Roche or, for that matter, Thomas Ley."

"What did they sound like, Rowly?"

"What do you mean?"

"Were they likely to have been your lot, or workers?"

Rowland tried to remember. Men tended to swear with the same inflection. "It was hardly 'I say, Sinclair old bean, you're a dead fellow'... but I think they were what you keep insisting is my lot."

"Don't be offended, Rowly—the Good Lord wouldn't have given you all poncy accents if He didn't want us to tell the difference." Clyde paused to savour the excellent gravy which graced his potatoes. "I think we can agree that your garden variety thugs-for-hire don't normally retire to the club for an aged malt after stabbing a man."

Rowland laughed. "You're beginning to sound like Milt."

"That's uncalled for, mate," Clyde said tersely. "The question is: what would cause gentlemen to attempt to murder you?"

Rowland told Clyde then of his conversation with Edna the night before. "I didn't register it until Edna mentioned what that assassin fellow of hers had told her, but the men in the alley did seem to know what they were doing. If they hadn't missed my lung, it would have been over very quickly and quietly."

Clyde leant back in his chair as a thought occurred. "How do you know one of those blokes *wasn't* Oswald Roche?"

"Because..." Rowland stopped. "I don't. You're right. I wouldn't know Oswald Roche from a bar of soap. He might well have been there."

"When we get back, ask Mrs. Roche if she has a photograph of her husband," Clyde advised. "And ask her if he saw service. You do remember what the blokes in the alley looked like?"

"One of them at least," Rowland said grimly.

"Good." Clyde went back to his meal. "Perhaps Roche, too, is a romantic."

27

BETTING IN HOTEL

TWO MEN FINED

William Armanasco (24), clerk, and Ernest Cuffe (24), labourer, were each fined £5, with 4/6 costs, at the Fremantle Police Court yesterday on a charge of having used the National Hotel, Fremantle, as a place for betting on July 25. Mr. H.J. Craig, S.M., was on the Bench. Mr. C. Greif pleaded not guilty on behalf of the accused, and Sergeant Nisbet prosecuted.

Constable Douglas, stationed at Perth, said that at 2.30 p.m. on the date in question he went to the National Hotel, Fremantle. He saw the two accused outside. Armanasco received money from a number of men, while Cuffe was holding a book. At 4.10 p.m. they entered the front bar of the hotel and witness followed. He heard the names of a number of horses mentioned and finally a man mentioned the name Sociable. He gave some money to Armanasco and Cuffe wrote in the book. Witness arrested the accused and took possession of the book. The last entry was the name Sociable. Armanasco said "Let the other chap go. I will take the blame."

Cross-examined by Mr. Greif, witness said he could not remember the names of any horses other than Sociable that were mentioned.

In defence, Armanasco said that he went into the hotel for a drink. The only money in his hand when he was arrested was the change from the barman. The only time a horse was mentioned was when a friend told him a "good thing." He denied having said that he would take the blame.

Cross-examined, he said that he had a considerable amount of money with him, as he had been collecting rents. Cuffe admitted having made bets in the street, but denied having done so in the

> hotel. Four men, who said they were in the hotel at the time, supported the evidence of the accused. "Why you went into the bar I don't know. You were likely to get the publican into trouble," the Magistrate remarked in convicting the accused.
>
> *West Australian, 4 August 1934*

Rowland brought the *Grosvenor House* to land at the Maylands aerodrome, a couple of miles north of Perth, early in the afternoon, west coast time. They had landed at Merredin en route to allow Clyde to rest his cramped leg and then swapped places once more. Clyde had taken the opportunity to temporarily modify the throttle pedal with a block of wood and the final hop had consequently been considerably less painful for Rowland than the first. Katharine Prichard had organised for a vehicle to be waiting for them at the aerodrome.

Before leaving the rudimentary terminal, Rowland made arrangements for the aeroplane to be refuelled and serviced for the flight back. On the ground, the scarlet Comet was attracting a great deal of confused attention—many people assumed the two men who emerged from her cockpit were Scott and Black.

Clyde chatted with the aircraft engineers from the MacRobertson Miller Aviation Company. Partly owned by Macpherson Robertson, the confectionary millionaire behind the Great Air Race, the airline had recently moved its offices to Perth and operated a number of aircraft from Maylands. As such, its employees took a fraternal interest in the race winner. And, of course, to airmen, the *Grosvenor House*, one of only three Comets in existence, was of itself a celebrity.

Horatio Miller, Robertson's partner, was particularly curious as to how Rowland and Clyde got hold of the Comet.

"We didn't steal it," Rowland assured him. "I hired it from Edwards for a little job we have out here."

"Mr. Edwards hired out the winner of the Great Air Race?" The scepticism showed plainly on Miller's hawkish features.

"She hadn't won when we made the deal," Rowland replied. He smiled. "If the *Grosvenor House* had been stolen, surely you would have heard by now?"

Miller grinned as he conceded the logic of Rowland's defence. "Well, considering she's family of sorts, I'll have my blokes take special care of her."

"Much appreciated, Mr. Miller."

"Though we might need to take her up to check the oil pressure problem—so we can fix it." Miller winked.

Rowland laughed. "Naturally. I'm sure Mr. Edwards will be delighted if you can remedy the problem. Do whatever you need to. I'll be happy to cover any expense."

They took their leave of Miller and his airmen, confident that the *Grosvenor House* was in capable, not to mention enthusiastic, hands. Rowland was unsure from where Katharine Prichard had procured the battered Oldsmobile she'd left for them, but with a little coaxing and cranking Clyde was able to get the motorcar to start. After the speed of the Comet, the rattling momentum of the tourer seemed archaic, but the short journey was undertaken in anticipation of reunion with an old friend and so the lumbering progress did not vex them unduly.

With a stop in Perth to get their bearings and despatch telegrams of their safe arrival to Melbourne, the twenty odd miles to Fremantle took them the best part of an hour and a half to traverse. They checked into the National Hotel in the High Street to await the *Strathaird's* arrival. The decorative, four-storey building with its wide wraparound verandah occupied a prominent corner. The hotel epitomised all the fruits and affluence of the gold boom, offering its primarily pastoralist clientele a retreat of quality and lavish elegance. In these surrounds,

Rowland and Clyde did look a little rough, still in flying suits, their jawlines shadowed after nine hours in the confines of the *Grosvenor House*'s cockpit. The concierge offered to send a barber to their suite as he signalled for a porter to take their bags. Though mildly irked by the sniffing condescension in the man's manner, Rowland accepted.

There were bags waiting when they got up to the suite. With minimal room in the Comet for luggage, they'd had the foresight to send their clothes and toiletries on ahead by train. Clyde would take it all back with him, leaving only whatever luggage Egon Kisch had to be squeezed into the limited space of the aeroplane.

An hour or so later, they were able to come down to the dining room, showered, shaved and appropriately attired. After satisfying their stomachs from the extensive menu, they decided upon a stroll about the port city to stretch muscles which had been cramped one way or another throughout the flight.

"Are you in pain?" Clyde had noticed Rowland wince as he stood from the table.

"No. Not at all." Rowland took his hand away from his side. "It twinges occasionally, that's all."

Clyde frowned. "Maybe we should have a doctor look you over before the return flight… just to be sure."

"Nonsense. I'm perfectly well."

Clyde sighed. They still had no idea who had stabbed Rowland, or who had run down Milton. Jim Kelly's death was also a mystery which would have to wait until they got back. It seemed there was enough trouble about already, and yet they were about to invite a great deal more.

They explored Fremantle by streetlight, walking down to the port for which the town was famous, enjoying the salt breeze that blew in from the Indian Ocean. Perhaps it was the knowledge that it was not the Pacific, but they felt a world removed from Sydney.

Rowland raised the subject of Edna and Milton. The sculptress and the poet seemed much closer to danger than they, and this fact played on his mind.

"Bluey Howells has promised to keep an eye out for any sign of trouble," Clyde said, though he too was noticeably uneasy. "First sign of anything amiss and he'll move them from Meldrum's."

Rowland loosened his tie, his eyes narrowing as he stared past Clyde's shoulder. "That can't be…" he said quietly.

"What can't be?" Clyde turned in the direction of his gaze.

Rowland began walking. "Come on." He broke into a run. Clyde bolted after him.

Rowland slowed about a block away, stopping on the corner and looking in all directions.

"What?" Clyde gasped as he caught up. "Who did you see?"

"One of those blaggards from the alley," Rowland said, frustrated by what seemed to be empty streets.

"Here? Are you sure?"

"Yes… well almost." Rowland began to doubt himself now. "What the hell would he be doing here?"

"Maybe it was just some bloke who looked a bit like him," Clyde suggested. Rowland had, after all, been accosted and stabbed less than a week ago. It was likely he was a bit jumpy.

"I suppose," Rowland said dubiously. Perhaps his mind was playing tricks.

"Did this bloke see you?"

"Yes. I assumed that's why he took off."

"We should be getting back to the hotel." Clyde glanced over his shoulder. If Rowland's assailants had indeed traversed the continent in pursuit of him, then they were probably quite determined to kill him. If that was the case, standing in a dark, empty street was possibly ill-advised.

They walked towards the hotel in silence, listening for footsteps or any sudden approach. It was not until they approached the National's entrance that they saw three men standing on the other side of the crossroads. Now Clyde recognised two of them. Rowland could only be certain about one, though another seemed familiar… but that was enough.

Clyde grabbed Rowland's arm as he moved to cross the road. "Whoa, Rowly, what the devil are you doing?"

"I'm willing to wager that one of those bastards stabbed me, Clyde. Thought I'd have a word."

Clyde pulled Rowland back. "Have you taken leave of your senses? They still outnumber us and God knows what they're armed with this time."

"We can't just carry on as if nothing happened!" Rowland said angrily.

"We could call the police?" Clyde reasoned. The three men had not moved. They stood with their arms folded, watching.

Rowland cursed. Clyde was right, of course. Confronting these men would be foolhardy to say the least. "Let's go in."

They walked into the hotel foyer and waited there, half expecting the men to follow them in. After a minute or two Rowland looked out through the doorway.

"They're gone," he said, unsure if he was relieved or disappointed.

"We should telephone the police," Clyde said.

Rowland shook his head. "What would we tell them? We still have no idea who those chaps are… or where they are."

"I don't know, mate." Clyde was unhappy but he had to admit Rowland had a point. They had no real information to give the police. No crime had occurred in Western Australia and they could not prove that the men they'd seen were wanted in Victoria. Clyde took off his hat and rubbed his hair. "We're just going to have to be bloody careful, Rowly," he said. "Until you and Egon get on that flaming plane, you don't go anywhere without me... and we make sure those mongrels don't have a chance to corner you again."

"Seems fair." Rowland exhaled. The important thing now was to get Egon back to Melbourne. He could not allow the consequences of his personal indiscretions to prevent Kisch from bringing his message to Australia.

They locked the door of the suite and secured it further by wedging a chair, chocked by two bibles, against the handle. Exhaustion countered the disquiet which might otherwise have kept them from sleep. By morning, after having slept soundly, the unexpected presence of Rowland's attackers seemed less of a threat. Breakfast was taken over reminiscences of their last meeting with Kisch in their anticipation of the great man's arrival.

They made their way down to the dock where the *Strathaird* was due to disembark its passengers mid-morning. They were among many who made their way towards the water to welcome family and lovers, or to join the ship when it sailed for Melbourne. Clyde stayed close to Rowland in the crowds, half a step behind so he could watch his friend's back. Rowland too kept his eyes out for the faces of the men who'd attacked him.

They pushed their way to the gangplank as the First Class passengers left the ship. The Tourist Class passengers, of which Egon Kisch was one, would disembark next. Rowland watched for the journalist while Clyde stood behind him, remaining vigilant for assailants. Smartly dressed men and stylish women were followed by a succession of less chic passengers—families with small children, single men and groups of young women. But no small dark man with a thick moustache. A couple of hours later, there was still no sign of Egon Kisch.

A gaggle of reporters, recognisable as such by the cameras which hung on their hips, stepped onto the gangway from the dock. Hearing one of their number say something about "Keesh", Rowland stopped the last of them.

"Excuse me, sir, I don't suppose you could tell me why you and your colleagues are boarding?"

The reporter regarded him suspiciously. "What's it to you?"

"Is it to do with a man named Egon Kisch?"

The reporter's brow rose. "So it's got out already."

"What's got out?"

"The government's banned the Commie stirrer. They're not going to let him off the bloody ship."

28

HERR KISCH

Reasons For Exclusion
MR. MENZIES' STATEMENT

MELBOURNE, Wednesday

Referring to the action of the Commonwealth immigration authorities in preventing the Czechoslovakian novelist, Herr Egon Kisch, from landing at Fremantle yesterday, the Federal Attorney-General (Mr. Menzies) said that the Commonwealth felt under no obligation to admit persons of this type.

Herr Kisch was excluded from Great Britain because of his subversive views and his association with Communist organisations.

Mr. Menzies said that the case had been dealt with by the Cabinet before his appointment as Attorney-General, and he could not indicate whether it would be reviewed.

Mr. Menzies said that Mr. J. Griffin, a New Zealand delegate to the all-Australia congress against war and Fascism, had been prevented from landing in Sydney for the same reason. "Mr. Griffin is known to have Russian affiliations," he added.

The Kisch reception committee in Melbourne, which passed a resolution of protest last night, decided to hold a public meeting of protest tomorrow night.

The Sydney Morning Herald, 8 November 1934

"Wil's worked it out," Rowland said with absolute certainty. "He's somehow figured out we were intercepting Egon Kisch's ship at Fremantle."

Clyde swore. He had no doubt that Rowland was correct. Wilfred Sinclair had outmanoeuvred them. "Dammit! What the hell do we do now?"

"We'd better see if we can get a message to Arthur." Rowland glanced up towards the ship. It was unlikely that Arthur Howells would be able to receive and send instructions before the ship left port at the end of the day. He cursed his brother's influence; his quiet, elegant power. Even if Kisch was permitted to leave the ship in Melbourne, he would be too late for the National Congress against War and Fascism. Rowland could almost hear Wilfred laughing at him.

Clyde swore again, though this time he was staring past Rowland and up the gangway. Rowland turned in the direction of his gaze. The three men they'd seen the night before were boarding the *Strathaird*, carpetbags in hand.

Rowland moved quickly, speaking to the crew officer who stood at the bottom of the gangplank. He asked to be allowed on board to speak with Egon Kisch.

"I regret to inform you that Herr Kisch has been detained by Customs, sir. He won't be speaking to anyone for a while. And I'm afraid I can only allow passengers on board."

Undeterred, Rowland pressed on. "The three gentlemen who just boarded, I'm absolutely certain we're acquainted. I don't suppose you recall their names?"

The crewman checked through the passenger list attached to his clipboard. "Messrs Smith, Brown and Lamb. Shall I give them your card, sir? They'll be travelling with us to Melbourne."

"No need," Rowland replied. "I'll be joining the ship for the leg to Melbourne myself."

"Very good, sir. We look forward to welcoming you aboard the *Strathaird*."

"What now, Rowly?" Clyde asked as Rowland strode away from the dock.

"We're going for a cruise," Rowland replied. "Those jokers weren't after me in particular. This is about stopping Egon from speaking."

Clyde sighed. "What about the *Grosvenor House*?"

"I'll see if Miller or one of his pilots can fly it back for us. It has to be in Sydney by the tenth for some exhibition or other."

They went straight to the hotel to collect their luggage. "We didn't bring dinner suits," Rowland murmured as they hastily repacked the bags.

Clyde laughed at him. "I don't think they dress for dinner in Tourist Class, Rowly, and if we're going to keep an eye on Egon we can't be travelling First Class, old mate."

Rowland grimaced. "Capital."

He telephoned through to Maylands aerodrome and spoke to Miller, explaining that they were unexpectedly delayed. "I'm afraid I'll need someone to fly the Comet back to Sydney for me."

"I don't think you'll have trouble finding volunteers, Sinclair." Miller chuckled. "We might have to draw straws… bugger it, I'm the boss. I'll take her—one of the other blokes can cover me."

"I'd appreciate it, Mr. Miller." Rowland spent a few moments telling Miller about the issue with the port engine, but it seemed the pilot was well aware of the problem.

"I've taken her up," he confessed. "My blokes have resolved the problem, and if it recurs, I know what to do. I don't know what's delaying you, Sinclair, but I reckon it must be mighty important if you're willing to give up a chance to fly that bird again."

"I'm afraid it is, Mr. Miller."

As they were checking out, Rowland arranged for a telegram to be sent to Howells, outlining the sudden change of plans, and another to Edwards, informing him that Miller would be flying the *Grosvenor House* to Sydney. The concierge assisted them in the purchase of two tickets for the *Strathaird*, and though he sniffed in his way, he said nothing about the Tourist Class fares Rowland purchased. Finally, they called in at the Gentlemen's Outfitter in High Street to purchase extra shirts, undergarments and ties to see them through the additional days on board the ship. Rowland assumed that even Tourist Class would have dress standards of some sort.

They made their way back to the dock and boarded. Many of the continuing passengers, who had disembarked for a day in Fremantle or Perth, were returning now. The purser in charge of allocating cabins in Tourist Class was in a bit of a flap. It seemed the men who were sharing Herr Kisch's four-berth cabin had seen the evening paper and were now demanding alternative accommodations.

"You cannot expect me to live with a spy?" A gentleman in shirtsleeves showered the harried crewman with projectile spittle as he shouted. The purser wiped his face with a handkerchief.

"This man might cut our throats as we sleep!" The second irate passenger sounded like an Englishman. "This is an outrage!"

Rowland saw his opportunity. "I say, if it would help, Mr. Watson Jones and I would be happy to share digs with this Herr Kisch fellow." He smiled at the spitter and the Englishman. "We could arrange an exchange. You gentlemen could have our berths."

"Why that's tremendously kind of you!" The Englishman addressed the purser. "I believe that solves the problem, my good man. These gentlemen have no objection to sleeping with a spy."

"Are you sure, sir?" the purser asked.

"Indeed we are," Rowland replied. "We're quite happy to share a cabin with Herr Kisch."

"Thank you." The purser made the necessary changes to his allocation chart. "I'll speak to the captain about refunding part of your fare," he whispered once the spitter and the Englishman had set off to find their new cabin.

"That won't be necessary," Rowland said. "Mr. Watson Jones and I consider it quite an honour to share a cabin with a journalist of international renown."

The purser hesitated. "You have seen the newspaper, haven't you, sir? Herr Kisch has been banned from setting foot on Australian soil."

"Probably an administrative error," Rowland said. "I'm sure it'll all be cleared up before we reach Melbourne."

The purser directed them to the Tourist cabins on the lower decks. They proceeded down four levels below the main deck.

"Good Lord! We must be below the jolly waterline." Rowland ran a finger around his collar. With each floor they descended it became noticeably warmer.

Clyde grinned. "Welcome to the world of the proletariat, old mate."

They made their way down what seemed a never-ending corridor of identical doors. A young crewman with a cleaning trolley emerged out of the cabin which would be theirs.

"Oh, hello," Rowland said. "Could you possibly tell us if we have the right cabin? We're sharing with Herr Kisch I believe."

The boy nodded. "Yes, sir. I was just cleaning up after the Customs officers. They made rather a mess."

"Why?"

"They were searching the cabin, sir."

"For what?"

The boy shrugged. "Herr Kisch has the bottom bunk on the right. Mr. Quinlan sleeps on the bunk above him," he informed them helpfully.

The cabin was compact to say the very least: a set of bunks along each of two opposite walls, between them a dresser, a sink and a single chair. It was oppressively warm. There was no window through which to glimpse the outside world, let alone catch a breeze. But then, Rowland recalled, they were below the waterline. Rowland noted the large boots at the end of the bed. If the rest of Mr. Quinlan was commensurate with the size of his boots, the cabin would be cosy indeed.

"You take the lower bunk, Rowly," Clyde said, in deference to Rowland's recent injury. They unpacked hastily into the bottom two drawers of the dresser, which it appeared the previous residents had cleared earlier in their determination to not share a cabin with a spy.

"We'd best find Egon," Rowland said.

"What about the clowns calling themselves Smith, Brown and Lamb?"

"Perhaps I should have a word to the captain about them." Rowland's eyes darkened. "Have him notify the police."

"I wouldn't do that just yet, Rowly. If the captain doesn't believe you, he'll have *us* thrown off the ship and Egon will be at their mercy. Wait till we've left port at least."

"You could be right," Rowland agreed. He looked about the small cabin. It was certainly a change from the staterooms to which he was accustomed.

"Come on, mate," Clyde said opening the door. "You'll find the lower classes spend as much time out of their cabins as possible."

They made their way back up four flights of stairs to the lower deck. Rowland caught sight of the purser who had assigned their rooms. "Mr. Watson Jones and I were wondering if we should introduce ourselves to our new cabin-mates. I don't suppose you know where Mr. Kisch is, Mr...?"

"Tonkin, sir. I believe Mr. Kisch was in the Customs processing area, Mr. Sinclair. But I'm afraid you can't go up there."

"Why not?"

"It's the First Class saloon, sir. Tourist passengers are only permitted for the presentation of passports and the like."

"I see."

"The second class smoking room is just through the doors, sir. I can send a message to Mr. Kisch that you'll meet him there, if you'd like."

"That won't be necessary, thank you, Mr. Tonkin. I'm sure we'll become acquainted with him in due course."

Clyde grinned as they watched the purser set off about his business. "Never thought I'd see the day a Sinclair was refused entry to First Class. I feel for you, mate."

Rowland rolled his eyes. "Come on. I have a fairly good idea where the First Class saloon is."

"You heard what he said."

"I'm sure passengers get lost all the time. You're not going to give in to a bit of social segregation are you? What kind of self-respecting Commie are you?"

Clyde laughed. "Lead on, then, mate."

Rowland adjusted the knot of his tie as they stepped onto the upper deck. Unlike most of the passengers on the warm lower decks, he and Clyde still wore their jackets. Rowland's waistcoat was buttoned, and there was a certain accustomed confidence to the manner in which he strode among the First Class passengers, tipping his hat at the ladies. Clyde was less at ease but not obviously so. With any luck, no one would think to ask about the actual status of their tickets.

The First Class saloon was on F Deck, amidships. Although the Tourist Class saloon was on the same deck, but aft with the galley between, direct transgress by passengers between the two saloons was prohibited. Crew members politely redirected Tourist passengers who transgressed towards the First Class saloon. Movement in the other direction rarely occurred.

Consequently Clyde and Rowland found it necessary to take a somewhat convoluted route to the exclusive saloon. Still, they did find their way eventually via corridors and staircases hidden from public view.

The dining saloon itself was modern and elegantly appointed. There were fewer tables fitted into the space and the flower arrangement on each table was more elaborate, but otherwise, it was not all that different from its Tourist Class equivalent.

"You're paying for a better class of people, not facility," Clyde whispered, laughing.

"Not in my experience," Rowland muttered.

A diminutive man in a boxy double-breasted suit was sitting at a table by himself, smoking. His face was kind despite the bristling black moustache that seemed to dominate his features. This was Egon Kisch. All the tables around him were conspicuously empty but for one, at which sat two police officers. Passengers at far-flung tables cast dark glances in the Czechoslovakian journalist's direction and conversed in whispers behind upheld menus.

When he saw Rowland and Clyde making their way towards him, Kisch jumped to his feet so exuberantly that the policemen rose from their seats too. "Mr. Sinclair, Mr. Jones!" He shook their hands and kissed their cheeks, so great was his joy to find friends in the First Class saloon. "What are you doing here, my mates?"

"We're escorting you to Melbourne," Rowland said quietly.

"You blokes will accompany me as far as Melbourne," Kisch corrected. "Your Mr. Menzies has refused me entry. It's a fair cow. I am a bloody dangerous émigré! See how the good people keep their distance. Bloody oath!"

Rowland glanced at Clyde, wondering why on earth the journalist was speaking like a Czechoslovakian jackaroo.

"Your friends at MAWF will challenge the exclusion, Herr Kisch," Clyde said, raising his brows in response. "In the meantime, we will make sure you're safe."

Kisch smiled broadly. "Good-oh!"

Rowland laughed now. He couldn't help it. Clyde too hung his head and chuckled.

Kisch was not offended. "I have been learning Australian," he said proudly. "Mr. Quinlan has been a bloody wonderful tutor in this… he is what you call a dinky-di Aussie. He has schooled me in the use of the great Australian adjective. Too right."

Watchful passengers tutted disapprovingly at the sight of two men rendered helpless with laughter as they sat companionably and openly with the dangerous Communist spy. In time, the policemen prepared to disembark before the *Strathaird* put to sea. They reminded Kisch once again that "Any attempt to set foot on the soil of the Australian Commonwealth would involve very serious consequences," before moving to escort him back to his cabin, where he was to remain until the ship had left port.

Rowland spoke to a waiter and, after slipping the boy a note, procured a bottle of Scotch and another of brandy. "I noticed there was no drinks cabinet in the cabin," he explained when Kisch enquired. "We have rather a lot to talk about."

29

GIRL'S £10,000 CLAIM AGAINST SEPTUAGENARIAN

———————◆———————

ALLEGED BREACH OF PROMISE

MET ANOTHER ON LINER STRATHAIRD

(From "Truth's" Melbourne Office)

One of the most sensational breach of promise actions ever launched in court is at the present moment attended by an "if" for if Mrs. Stewart Dawson, one of Sydney's best-known matrons, at present on a pleasure trip abroad, can be found, she is to have material evidence taken from her on commission.

The action is being brought by Miss Ethel Wynne Roberts, until recently Mrs. Stewart Dawson's lady companion, against "Small Arms" Emanuel Abrahams, one of the richest Jews in Australia, and who a few years ago was involved in the greatest taxation sensation of the age.

SHE IS CLAIMING £10,000 DAMAGES FOR ALLEGED BREACH OF PROMISE OF MARRIAGE.

It is alleged that, while they were both passengers on the steamer Strathaird on her trip out from England in September, 1933, the elderly Jew whispered fatal words into her ear and then repudiated them.

Truth, 18 November 1934

Being too tall to sit on one of the lower bunks without hitting his head on the bed above, Rowland was allowed the cabin's only chair. Clyde and Kisch sat on the beds. Clyde dispensed Scotch for himself and the journalist, but for Rowland, who detested all forms of whisky, he poured a generous tumbler of brandy. They toasted, first, their reacquaintance. They had last met in the most dire of circumstances, and so the fact that they were alive to drink together was reason enough for celebration.

The Australians told the reporter of their escape from Germany to France and then England, of their attempts to inform the British Government of the atrocities that the Nazis were committing against their own people, and of their efforts to warn anyone in authority who'd listen of the serious danger the Fascists posed. Few had listened, fewer had heeded. They'd come home to find Eric Campbell, Commander of the New Guard, launching a political Party, inspired by Hitler's Nazi Party, to legitimise and promote Fascism in Australia.

"And has he succeeded, this Herr Campbell?" Kisch asked.

"He hasn't faced an election as yet," Rowland replied.

"Then we cannot be complacent. Bloody oath we cannot!"

Rowland smiled as he loosened his tie in the warmth of the windowless cabin. Egon Kisch had, it seemed, embraced the Australian vernacular with almost religious zeal. "Well we're glad you're here, Egon."

"But I am not here! I am currently just some bloody bloke observing the Australian coastline from a ship!" Kisch sighed. "I have come all this way to not set foot on Australian soil."

"I expect your friends in Australia have already briefed King's Counsel to issue a writ of habeas corpus," Rowland assured him.

"I am sure your Mr. Menzies would prefer Kisch's bloody corpus to Kisch that lives."

"Perhaps not only Mr. Menzies," Clyde added. They told the journalist then of Smith, Brown and Lamb, recounting their experiences in Melbourne as well as the encounter in Fremantle.

Egon was aghast. "These men, they have already stabbed you, Rowland?"

"I'm afraid so."

"Is that not frowned upon in your country?"

Rowland laughed. "Yes, generally. But regrettably, these gentlemen have avoided apprehension by the police."

"And now the bloody bastards are on board the *Strathaird*."

"Yes."

"Can you not have the ship's captain arrest them?"

"It may be difficult," Clyde admitted. "We have no proof that they stabbed Rowly or that they intend you any harm."

"But Clyde and I will be here to protect you," Rowland promised.

"They've already stabbed you once," Kisch said glumly. "That does not make me confident."

"Nonsense." Rowland topped up the Czechoslovak's glass. "The fact that I am not dead should assure you that they are not particularly competent assassins." He thought it best not to mention the fate of Jim Kelly at this point.

Kisch drank. "Enough. Enough of my troubles," he said. "Tell me, my mate, how is the bloody beautiful Miss Higgins? I hope you will inform me she is no more Miss Higgins, but Mrs. Bloody Sinclair."

Rowland coughed as the brandy caught in his throat. "Ed?"

"Yes. I remember clearly that you were in love with her."

Clyde stifled a guffaw.

"Miss Higgins is still very much Miss Higgins," Rowland said carefully.

"My commiserations, cobber. Perhaps if you had brought her with you. Lovemaking is a popular pastime on the ship." He slapped

Rowland on the back as he confided, "One simply has to say 'Let's go have a look at the Southern Cross'." He shook his head. "One grieves for the lonely men of the northern hemisphere who must find love without the erotic power of these five stars. It is no wonder you put them so proudly on your flag!"

Chuckling, Clyde proposed a toast to the Southern Cross. Rowland wasn't sure if romantic utilitarianism was in fact behind the constellation's presence on the flag, but it seemed as good a reason as any. He wondered fleetingly what Edna was doing. With Smith, Brown and Lamb on board, perhaps she and Milton were safe.

The cabin door opened and a very large gentleman in shirtsleeves and no tie loped into the room. "G'day, Eegone," he boomed with a voice as large and relaxed as his person. "Who the hell are these blokes then?"

Egon Kisch introduced Stanley Quinlan, a Mallee farmer who was making his way back to Australia after taking polo ponies to India.

Rowland offered the farmer his hand. "How d'you do, Mr. Quinlan?"

Quinlan pumped his hand and then Clyde's.

"This is the gentleman who has been my personal tutor in all things Australian." Kisch's eyes twinkled mischievously.

"Would you care for a drink, Mr. Quinlan?" Rowland asked.

"Would I what! What are you blokes doing down here? We're about to set sail... everybody's on deck with streamers and such." He winked. "The ladies seem to think it's flaming New Year's Eve!"

Egon told his cabin-mate the sorry story of his exclusion from an entire country. "To be banned from England is one thing... it is such a small country, but to be banned from the Antipodes is an exclusion from half the world!"

"Well that's a fair cow! Why the hell have they banned you, mate?"

"They say that I am a dangerous Communist activist."

"Oh." Quinlan shrugged. "Bugger."

They spent the next hour or so becoming acquainted with Stanley Quinlan. The young farmer was returning penniless after a great adventure abroad. At six foot four inches tall, he was what Kisch called an "awe-inspiring Australian giant". He had the slow, easy manner of the Mallee from which he hailed and spoke in the colourful vernacular which seemed to so delight the Czechoslovak. He had taken Kisch under his large wing, teaching him to "speak" and telling the curious journalist what he could about his country and his countrymen. He seemed to think he could overcome the government exclusion by simply issuing a personal invitation and threatening to "flatten" anyone who didn't welcome his "little mate".

Without going too far into the details of the matter, Rowland did warn him that there might be men on board who wished Egon ill, and who had boarded for the purpose of inflicting it.

"Just point the bastards out, mate." Quinlan flexed his enormous fist. "Tell yer what, Eegone, if anyone gives you any trouble, you shout 'Watch out, I am a boxer and I'll break your bloody jaw' and I'll come running and do it for you."

When the bottles were empty, the party of four made its way to the Tourist dining saloon for dinner, at which they were encouraged to sign up for the various social activities offered on board. Clyde and Rowland dutifully placed their names beneath Egon Kisch's for quoits, shuffleboard and deck tennis, all the while vigilant for any glimpse of the three men from the alley whom they suspected had boarded to assassinate the journalist.

"Can you see them, Rowly?" Clyde whispered.

"No," Rowland said uneasily. "I've seen no sign of them since we came on board."

"I don't suppose they'd be in First Class?"

"What would be the purpose of that?"

"The First Class decks are exclusive, Rowly. Tourist Class doesn't need to be."

Rowland stopped. Clyde was right. One didn't expect First Class passengers to sneak into Tourist. That direction of movement was probably not monitored particularly. "We need to find out where the hell they are," Rowland muttered.

"We could take a gander at the passenger list."

"That'll only tell us they're on board... we know that."

Clyde checked his watch. Service in the First Class dining saloon began in half an hour. "We could go over and have a look."

Rowland grimaced. "Not without dinner suits, but we could try at breakfast. We won't be as conspicuous then."

"What exactly are you proposing we do, Rowly?"

"I want to find out who the devil these jokers are, why exactly they're here."

"They're unlikely to simply tell us."

"The three of them mightn't." Rowland studied the menu. "But one on his own might."

"You want to abduct a man from First Class?"

"I want to have a word with a man in First Class."

"What's going to stop the other two bumping off Egon while we're on the upper decks chatting?"

Rowland glanced at Stanley Quinlan who was explaining in some detail how he would bring down a steer with his bare hands.

Clyde nodded. "Fair enough." He sighed. "I don't suppose we'd do better speaking to the captain."

"If he doesn't believe us, we could end up in the brig, which would leave Egon with only Stanley to look out for him."

"I expect you're right."

And so dinner was had in the Tourist saloon. Their table seated only four and so they were not called upon to socialise outside their Party during the meal. Egon Kisch's new notoriety as a banned political agitator might have made socialising difficult in any case. Rowland could sense the hostility directed at the journalist from various quarters. A table of Italians near the window seemed to be taking particular exception.

Live music in the First Class saloon was piped across, and soon couples stood to dance. Egon and Clyde smoked and Rowland took the notebook from his pocket to sketch. He drew loosely, without breaking contact between his pencil and the page—silhouettes of dancing couples, young stewards from the subcontinent, and in greater detail, the faces at his table. Stanley Quinlan asked a girl from the neighbouring table to dance. She accepted, giggling excessively in response, and Rowland wondered if the Mallee farmer would take her to view the Southern Cross.

Before they left the dining saloon, Rowland found a purser and procured a passenger list. Egon was keen to stretch his legs upon the promenade deck before retiring and so they accompanied him, ever watchful for Smith, Brown and Lamb. Rowland felt they were being watched but that may have been because, thanks to that day's newspaper headlines, every passenger had cause to look askance at Egon Kisch. On many occasions the journalist's friendly salutations were snubbed, mothers pulled their children away as if he may devour them. All this obviously hurt the Czechoslovak though he tried to make light of it.

They retired to the reading room where, in the comfort of armchairs positioned for intimate conversation, the rebuff of fellow passengers was less noticeable.

"We'd better have a look at this passenger list then, Rowly," Clyde said as a steward brought coffee and cognac.

Rowland handed over the booklet, and Clyde thumbed through the names. As Smith and Brown were such common names he looked instead for Lamb. "As I thought," he said triumphantly. "They're in First Class."

Kisch sighed. "At least I will be murdered by a gentleman."

Clyde continued browsing through the list. He stopped at a name. "They've got you listed in First Class, Rowly. Must be force of habit." He handed the open booklet to Rowland.

Rowland squinted at the tiny print. He put down his coffee and sat up. "This isn't me, Clyde."

"Oh, of course." Though not as common as Jones, there were other Sinclairs.

"Good Lord, what's she doing here?" Rowland said, still staring at the list.

"Who?"

"Mother. This listing is for my mother and Aunt Mildred."

"Your mama is on board?" Kisch asked.

Clyde took the booklet back. "I thought Mrs. Sinclair wasn't due home till next month."

"She isn't." Rowland was worried now. "She should still be in Ceylon. Dammit, I hope she hasn't become unwell."

Clyde understood the extent of Rowland's concern. While Elisabeth Sinclair had been quite well since taking up residence in *Woodlands*, she'd suffered a number of breakdowns in the past.

Rowland stood. "I think I might just check on her."

"Rowly..." Clyde was torn. Of course Rowland had to go, but they couldn't leave Kisch entirely unprotected. He rose uncertainly.

"You stay with Egon," Rowland said. "I'll be perfectly safe on my own."

"They've tried to kill you once already, Rowly; we don't know that they've given up."

"I'll speak to one of the officers," Rowland replied. "Explain that my mother is currently residing in one of the staterooms. I expect they'll escort me up."

"I will be safe in the cabin, my mates," Kisch interrupted. "Do not concern yourselves about my welfare."

"It's the whisky we're worried about, Egon." Rowland smiled. "We're not leaving you alone with a new bottle." To Clyde, he said, "I'll be careful."

Clyde checked his watch. "One hour, Rowly, and then I'm going to hide Egon under the bed and come after you."

Rowland grinned as an image of Clyde doing just that flashed upon his inner eye. He saw them to the door of their cabin and then, finding one of the ship's officers on deck, he explained the situation.

"Are you saying you had no prior knowledge of your mother being on board, sir?"

"I only joined the ship in Fremantle. My mother wasn't expected back until next month. I'm concerned that her change of plans might mean she's unwell."

"And she's in a First Class stateroom?"

"Yes."

"Very well, sir. If you'd care to follow me, we'll see if Mrs. Henry Sinclair is willing to receive you."

The First Class staterooms were located amidships on D Deck. Rowland followed the officer, a Mr. Webster, to the appropriate door and waited as he knocked. The door was answered by one of two nurses who had accompanied his mother abroad. She looked directly past Webster to Rowland. "Mr. Sinclair! As I live and breathe! What are you doing here, sir?"

Now satisfied of the veracity of Rowland's claim, Webster left them to it.

"Mrs. Sinclair is just having a sherry with your aunt," the nurse said, glancing over her shoulder.

"Perhaps you'd better let them know I'm here," Rowland suggested, not wanting to shock the elderly ladies unduly.

"Nonsense, there's nothing wrong with your mother's heart! Seeing you will do her the world of good."

"Maggie…" Rowland heard his mother's voice. "Who is that at the door?"

30

TOURIST CLASS OPPORTUNITY

Homeward bound travellers are offered an exceptional opportunity to enjoy an economical, comfortable voyage by using the Tourist Class of the P. & O. Company. The new 22,500 ton steamers "Strathnaver" and "Strathaird" carry special Tourist Class facilities, in addition to their First Saloon, and the Royal Mail Steamers "Mongolia" and "Moldavia" are exclusively reserved for this method of sea travel. Fares, subject to exchange:—1st Saloon, from £96; 2nd Saloon, from £80; Tourist Class, from £39.

Australian Christian Commonwealth,
9 September 1932

Rowland stepped into the stateroom. It was spacious, furnished in English Manor style with large porthole windows. Elisabeth Sinclair and her sister-in-law, having not long returned from dinner, were formally attired and sparkled with jewels. They sat together on a floral upholstered settee with glasses of golden sherry.

"Hello, Mother, Aunt Mildred."

"Aubrey!" Elisabeth Sinclair said. "Good Heavens! What are you doing here? Have we arrived in Sydney already?"

Mildred glared at him in horror. Rowland half expected his aunt to shoo him out.

He explained that he'd boarded the ship at Fremantle. "I didn't realise you'd both be on board... thought you'd be in Ceylon for the rest of the month." He kissed his mother's cheek. "I hope this doesn't mean you're unwell."

"Unwell!" Mildred exclaimed. "Elisabeth has never been in better health. We were having a truly splendid time!"

"Then why did you cut your trip short?"

"I thought we'd been away quite long enough to make hearts grow fonder," Elisabeth replied, smiling coyly.

Inwardly Rowland cringed; outwardly he showed no sign that he'd even noticed his mother's coquettishness, or suspected the object of it.

"Sit down, Aubrey, and let us hear your news," Elisabeth commanded.

"Where are your rooms, dear boy?" Mildred enquired. She looked him up and down. "I'm surprised we didn't see you at dinner, but judging by your attire you did not go down."

Rowland smiled. "I did actually, but dinner suits are not compulsory in Tourist Class."

Mildred gasped and placed her sherry glass down firmly. Elisabeth looked confused. "What is a Tourist Class, Aubrey?"

"What has happened to bring you so low that you would do such a thing, Rowland?" Mildred demanded.

Rowland laughed. "Nothing at all, Aunt Mildred. I'm travelling with friends whose tickets are Tourist Class."

"What friends, Aubrey?" Elisabeth asked enthusiastically. "Is Mr. Isaacs on board?"

"I'm afraid not. Mr. Watson Jones is here though."

"Oh. How nice." Elisabeth sighed.

"Really, Rowland!" Mildred's mouth tensed and pulled closed like the neck of a drawstring bag. "Tourist Class! Your dear departed father would have been mortified! You may as well be sleeping in the servants' quarters."

"I'm perfectly comfortable, Aunt Mildred."

"Well I'd say that's more alarming than anything else!"

Elisabeth Sinclair attempted to change the subject. "Mrs. Kenneally, in the stateroom across the way, says there's a spy on board. Imagine that!"

"Apparently he's some dreadful Bolshevik; and a foreigner no less!" Mildred said. "We'll probably all be murdered in our beds."

"I wouldn't worry too much, Aunt Mildred. He's travelling in Tourist."

"You've seen him?" she gasped.

"Indeed, I have."

"Oh how terrifying!" Mildred clutched her hands to her breast. "We'll have to speak to the captain about moving you to a cabin in First Class—there's nothing else for it. You're in danger!"

"That's not necessary, Aunt Mildred," Rowland said calmly. "I know Herr Kisch rather well. He's a sterling chap."

Mildred responded as though he'd just admitted to consorting with the devil. "Oh my Lord, did you hear that, Elisabeth?" She looked up and entreated the ceiling. "Dear Henry, how merciful that you are not here to see your son cavorting with godless Communists. It would have broken your devout and gentle heart."

Rowland winked at his mother. "I assure you, Aunt Mildred, cavorting is the furthest thing from my mind. Perhaps when we get back to Sydney…"

Mildred rose to full outrage. "Do not be smart, young man. Regardless of the dissolute company you keep, you remain Henry Sinclair's son—raised as a gentleman! There are expectations, proprieties. People look to us to maintain certain standards."

Elisabeth smiled and took Rowland's hand. "I've always found Aubrey an excellent picker when it comes to choosing friends, Millie. Why Mr. Isaacs is charm itself. It's no wonder that there's an Isaacs at Government House."

"I'm not sure they're related," Rowland said, though he knew there was nothing that would dissuade his mother from the notion that Milton was some nephew of the governor-general. It was quite possible the idea had originated with the poet in any case.

"Nonsense, there's a strong family resemblance," Elisabeth insisted.

"We met an old chum of yours this evening," Mildred said, deciding that quite enough had been said about Milton Isaacs. "Fortunately not all your friends travel in Tourist."

"An old chum of mine?"

"Yes, Aubrey." Elisabeth took over the story. "It was that lanky boy who would spend the school holidays with us at *Oaklea* on occasion. His father was a doctor or dentist or some such thing. What was his name, Millie? Henry... Henry Alcott."

Rowland stiffened. Henry Alcott and Aubrey Sinclair had been childhood friends. They'd served together in the Great War. Aubrey had died and Henry had returned home not quite right. When Rowland had last encountered him, Alcott had joined the Fascist Legion, a ruthless clandestine arm of the New Guard which specialised in the brutalisation of suspected Communists. It was now a little more than two years since Henry Alcott and two other men had nearly beaten Rowland to death. But, of course, his mother didn't know that. Wilfred had used his connections and influence to cover the incident up—ironically to keep Rowland out of gaol.

"Are you sure?" Rowland said finally.

"Yes, I am. He's a grown man now, of course, and he has a simply awful scar on his face, but it's the same boy."

"Did he tell you what he was doing on the *Strathaird?*"

"No, he didn't. We really didn't speak for all that long... he just paid his respects." Elisabeth appeared to become bored of the subject. "Really, Aubrey, why don't you just speak to him yourself?"

Mildred was waspish. "I expect Rowland's embarrassed to be travelling in Tourist, Elisabeth."

Rowland ignored his aunt. "Look, Mother, it might be best if you avoid Henry."

"Good Lord, why?"

"Well I can't really say in this company." Rowland scrambled for a reason. "Let's just say he's not the kind of chap with whom I wish my mother to be acquainted!"

Both Mildred and Elisabeth gasped.

"I thought there was something unsavoury about the man," Mildred whispered. "He was wearing a white dinner jacket."

Rowland checked his watch. His hour was almost up. "I'd best get back. I'm delighted to see you both so well." He kissed his mother and his aunt, though the latter offered her cheek reluctantly.

"You must join us for dinner, Aubrey," Elisabeth declared.

He smiled. She seemed genuinely pleased to see him even if she didn't know his name. "I'm afraid I didn't bring a dinner suit, Mother... but I will call by again, and if you require me, you need only speak to one of the crew." He left the two old ladies to contemplate how a man could possibly travel without a tailcoat let alone a dinner suit, and walked out into the adjoining corridor.

As he passed the doors to the other five staterooms aboard the *Strathaird*, he wondered if any of them was occupied by the three men from Melbourne. It would be a conspicuous way for assassins to travel, but perhaps that was a disguise in itself. He needed to think about the presence of Henry Alcott. Surely it couldn't be a coincidence. His mother and aunt had mentioned meeting Alcott only that evening. Perhaps he too had joined the ship in Fremantle with Smith, Brown and Lamb.

Rowland made his way back to the lower decks, arriving at the cabin just as Clyde was making plans to go find him. "Rowly, thank God!"

"Is Quinlan not back, yet?" Rowland asked rather redundantly. A man the size of Quinlan could not possibly be in the tiny cabin and remain unseen.

"The Southern Cross," Kisch said knowingly. "How is your dear mama, Rowland?"

"She seems well and in fine spirits," Rowland replied. He locked the door. "Clyde—Henry Alcott's on board."

"What? I thought he'd... actually I'm not sure what I thought had happened to the bloke. I just didn't expect we'd ever see him again."

"Who is this Alcott?" Kisch asked. The expressions of his cabin-mates left him in no doubt that the man's presence was not welcome.

Between them, Rowland and Clyde told him of their association with Alcott, such as it was.

"And he was never punished for trying to kill you?" Kisch asked, astounded.

"It was complicated," Rowland admitted. "In the end both Alcott and I stayed out of gaol."

"And you have not seen him since?"

Rowland shook his head. "I understood he'd gone to Queensland. Perhaps he's returning to Sydney—though he appears to be taking a rather circuitous route."

"Do you think it has anything to do with Egon?" Clyde asked.

Rowland leant back against the frame of the bunks. "Delaney mentioned some new group of Fascists who'd been writing letters to the Commissioner complaining about Bolsheviks in Canberra. The letters were signed by D. King... I didn't place it at the time."

Clyde sat up. "As in Diamond King?"

"I don't understand," Kisch shook his head violently as if he were trying to dislodge whatever it was that prevented him from understanding.

Rowland explained. "Henry Alcott was once a member of a vigilante group called the Fascist Legion whose mission was to set upon and brutalise Communists. The identities of individuals within the group were kept secret by wearing black robes and pointed hoods, but they identified themselves and each other with playing cards. Alcott was the Diamond King." He shrugged. "Perhaps Smith, Brown and Lamb have joined him in some resurrection of the Fascist Legion."

"Terrific. Now there are four Fascist lunatics on board!" Clyde muttered.

"At *least* four Fascist lunatics," Kisch corrected despondently. "A child, a small child, threw a stone at me today!"

"Good Lord!" Rowland said, frowning. "Where did the little brat get a stone out here?"

Despite himself, Kisch smiled.

Clyde rubbed his face wearily. "So what do you think is going on, Rowly?"

"Milt said something a while ago... The Fascist Legion, and all their like-minded friends, didn't simply disappear when Eric Campbell's New Guard lost momentum." He lay back in his berth with his hands behind his head. "To be honest, I haven't given Alcott much thought in the past two years. But once he was angry enough to kill me."

"Having Ed fire on him might have brought on an epiphany," Clyde said without any real conviction.

"Miss Higgins tried to shoot this man?" Kisch was growing increasingly alarmed by the revelations of his cabin-mates.

"To save me," Rowland said.

"Sadly, she shot Rowly instead," Clyde added.

"It was an accident," Rowland explained. "She's rather prickly about the subject. Best not mention it to her." He rolled over onto his side. "My point is... actually it was Milt's point originally, but I tend to think he's right. The men in the Fascist Legion did not stop being Communist-hating thugs in 1932. I expect the way it all turned out only exacerbated Alcott's particular animosity against me."

"I'm not sure I understand," Kisch interrupted. "Was not this Alcott your late brother's comrade? Why then does he wish to murder his friend's brother?"

"I believe Alcott felt I was betraying both my family and my brother's memory by mixing with the likes of Milt and Clyde."

"I see." Kisch pulled at his moustache, twirling one end as he absorbed the situation. "So these bloody bastards... they are after you?"

Clyde shrugged. "I can't see why Smith, Brown and Lamb would have come on board if they were just after Rowly. How long has Alcott been on board, Rowly?"

"Mother and Aunt Mildred only encountered him for the first time this evening, so my guess is Fremantle."

"Do you think these men knew that Egon would be banned?"

Rowland shook his head. "Haven't the foggiest. But they'd know now... so presumably their only purpose for boarding, once it was clear that Egon had been banned, is to ensure he never sets foot on Australian soil, one way or another."

Egon sighed.

"Don't worry, Egon," Clyde nudged the dejected activist. "The Kisch Reception Committee will be unleashing all kinds of hell on your behalf."

Stanley Quinlan returned to the modest cabin at about midnight. Rowland admitted him, with Clyde standing by ready to fight should it not be Quinlan. The farmer, having successfully shown a young lady the Southern Cross several times that evening, was in an excellent temper, if a little tired. He climbed onto the bunk above Egon, cursed at his boots as he pulled them off, and murmured a grateful prayer before falling almost immediately into a noisy slumber.

It was also Stanley Quinlan who woke them the next morning with another prayer spoken aloud before he rolled out of his bunk.

"What time is it?" Rowland murmured, part question, part complaint.

"It's gone five o'clock, mate," Quinlan answered. "Get a move on, you blokes. Time to storm the washroom before the hordes get up."

Quinlan, it seemed, advocated the rural custom of early rising to beat the congestion at morning ablutions. And so it was, half asleep, that the three Australians and the Czechoslovak used the baths and shaving basins. They were finished before the halls began to fill with half-dressed men and women in gaudy silk kimonos, and they could only commend the farmer's timely tactics.

As they made their way up to the Tourist dining room for breakfast they discussed their strategy for the day. It was decided that Stanley Quinlan would stay with Egon that morning in the Tourist smoking saloon where there would be plenty of people at their correspondence, playing cards, or completing crosswords as they smoked. Rowland and Clyde intended to slip into First Class to locate Smith, Brown and Lamb, and perhaps to ascertain what Alcott was up to.

They left Egon and Stanley eating breakfast with a real estate agent from Darwin and a fifteen-year-old Indian lad travelling alone to Melbourne for the International Scout Jamboree. When they were stopped by a crew member at the entrance to the First Class dining room, Rowland told the white-gloved steward that he and Clyde had been invited to join his mother and aunt for breakfast. A moment to check with Mrs. Sinclair and they were seated.

"We must have forgotten we invited you to join us at breakfast," Mildred said, squeezing lemon onto her pancakes.

Rowland grinned. "We are adequately dressed, I hope, Aunt Mildred."

Mildred sniffed. Elisabeth Sinclair was so delighted to see them that she was not inclined to quibble over invitations. Instead she chatted happily to Clyde of the tropical flowers she had painted in Singapore and Ceylon. Rowland scanned the dining room as it started to fill. Of course, not all the five hundred odd First Class passengers would breakfast at once and so he was not particularly surprised when he didn't spot any of the men he sought. Quietly, Rowland enquired of the nurses who travelled with his mother about her health.

"Don't you be worrying, Mr. Sinclair," Maggie O'Hara said as she piled smoked salmon onto her English crumpet. "Mrs. Sinclair is in very good health and for the most part she knows her own mind. Despite what she says, this trip has done her the world of good."

"And her decision to return early?"

"Your mother missed Mr. Isaacs terribly... and you too of course, sir."

Rowland laughed. "I see."

"Rowly." Clyde's eyes flickered to the entrance. Rowland followed his gaze. One of the three, Smith, Brown or Lamb—of course they had no idea which—and Henry Alcott. Deep in their own conversation neither man looked in their direction.

Rowland moved to stand. Clyde reached out and pulled him down. "Not a good idea, Rowly."

Rowland said nothing. His eyes flashed furiously.

"If we start something here," Clyde warned under his breath, "the captain will have us in chains before we know it."

Still Rowland did not respond, his gaze fixed on Alcott.

"Rowly, I'm serious. This is not the time to settle the score."

Rowland gritted his teeth, frustrated. In their present company he was denied even the small satisfaction of cursing. "Yes... you're right, of course."

"Do you think they know we're aboard?"

Rowland shrugged. "Perhaps not. We're not on the passenger manifest having purchased our tickets so late. The gentlemen we swapped with are probably still listed as sharing Egon's cabin."

"That could be to our advantage," Clyde said, still concerned his friend would challenge Alcott.

Rowland was not so sure. "Knowing Egon is not unprotected might give them pause."

"What are you proposing, Rowly?"

"Why don't we join them?" Before Clyde could reply or, more likely, protest, Rowland made their excuses to his mother and aunt. "We'd best go say hello to Henry Alcott since he's on board."

"I thought you said he was undesirable," Mildred said sharply.

"He is," Rowland replied. "But unless I speak with him, he's likely to keep bothering you ladies. I believe he's looking for investors for one of his schemes."

That was enough for Mildred who, as Rowland well knew, had learned by experience to be wary of gentlemen looking for finance.

And so they took their leave and walked briskly towards the table at which Alcott and his companion were seated.

"Alcott. It's been a long time," Rowland said brusquely as he took a seat. Clyde grabbed the fourth chair. "I don't believe you've met my friend—Clyde Watson Jones."

Clyde nodded. "Charmed."

Alcott was visibly startled. His companion rose. Clearly neither gentleman had been expecting to see Rowland Sinclair.

"Sit down." Rowland met the man's eye. "Are you Smith, Brown or Lamb?"

Glancing at Alcott, who nodded, the man resumed his seat and admitted, "Lamb."

"Well, Mr. Lamb, I thought it might be best if we had a chat with you and Mr. Alcott, since we're all here."

"What do you want, Rowly?" Alcott said frostily.

Rowland leant back in his chair, refusing to be hurried. "I'm curious. Was it you who stabbed me in Melbourne, Mr. Lamb?"

Lamb smiled and sipped the glass of whisky beside his eggs and bacon. "I don't know what you're talking about, Sinclair."

"You're here for Kisch?" Alcott accused. "You haven't learned have you, Rowly? Still backing the wrong horse."

"Perhaps." Rowland kept his eyes on Alcott; Clyde watched Lamb. "He's been excluded, Henry. So you can leave him alone."

"I suppose you're going to tell me that your Commie friends are happy to leave it at that. That they'll be content to accept the decision of the sovereign government of the Commonwealth of Australia." Alcott laughed. "I'm afraid we're not so daft as to rely on you bloody Red mongrels to accept the king's laws. You'll find that many good men live by an oath to protect those laws."

"The king's laws also protect Egon Kisch," Rowland snarled.

"We wouldn't dream of breaking the law, Rowly. Of course, from what I've heard, there are accidents at sea all the time."

"Do you really think you'd get away with that, Henry?"

"Oh, you wouldn't believe what I've got away with, Rowly."

Clyde intervened as the tension rose. "The fact is, Mr. Alcott, we're not going to let you anywhere near Egon Kisch without making a great deal of noise."

"You may find, Jones, that many of our fellow passengers will become suddenly deaf in circumstances related to a dangerous Communist agitator here to cause trouble and destroy the Australian way of life."

31

NATION-WIDE COMMEMORATION

ARMISTICE DAY OBSERVANCE IN ALL STATES
DEDICATION OF VICTORIA'S MEMORIAL
DUKE'S PART IN IMPRESSIVE CEREMONIAL

Armistice Day, commemorated throughout Australia since that fateful day in 1918, was remembered in church observance in all States yesterday. From the vast concourse of 300,000 who watched the Duke of Gloucester dedicate the Shrine of Remembrance in Melbourne to the tiny hamlets of Tasmania, Armistice Day, 1918, marking the cessation of four years of war, was recalled vividly, and coupled with the recollection was the fervent hope that its continued observance would remind a nation of its duty to those affected by war, and would strengthen the will for peace.

Victoria's centre of commemoration—marking a solemn climax to an impressive Royal tour in the State—was the scene of amazing orderliness and precision. His Royal Highness, accompanied only by leaders of the State and representatives of returned soldiers, entered the Inner Shrine, unlocking the formidable door with a golden key, and reverently placed on the Rock of Remembrance the wreath despatched in Royal keeping by His Majesty the King. Afterwards the Duke of Gloucester dedicated the Shrine.

The Mercury, 12 November 1934

When the *R.M.S. Strathaird* moored at Adelaide, it was greeted by what seemed to be the entire population of the city on an outing to see the controversial stranger, shake his hand and take his photograph. German farmers, now living in the districts surrounding Adelaide, stood on the dock to greet him. A jostling, excited gaggle of reporters boarded, each in hope of an interview with the great man. Kisch was consequently obliged to give what amounted to a press conference, in the middle of which he received a trunk call from the *Melbourne Star*.

All this, Egon took in his stride, speaking with wit and passion and not a little showmanship. He spoke of celebrated German writers who were persecuted and murdered by the Nazis. He told the crowd of the inquisitorial methods of the Gestapo, about men who were tortured to death in concentration camps and of great minds languishing still behind barbed wire. He spoke of Ernst Thalmann, leader of the German Communist Party, who had once received six million votes as a candidate for president, but who despite or possibly because of this, had been kept in solitary confinement since May the previous year, forbidden even to read or write. Kisch told the crowd then of the ten thousand anti-Fascists who had suffered the same fate. He gave them an account of the German workers who had been beheaded or "shot while attempting to escape". And he gleefully punctuated his address with the liberal use of the Australian adjective which delighted him so. In this way Egon held court on the deck for the time the *Strathaird* was moored in Adelaide.

Throughout, Clyde, Rowland and Stanley Quinlan remained within reach of the Czechoslovakian journalist, watching the crowd for any sign of trouble. Alcott and his associates were present on the deck, but the tight press of journalists and photographers made it impossible to get too close.

"What do you think?" Clyde murmured to Rowland as Kisch described the brutality of the German regime.

Rowland watched as the reporters hung off Kisch's every word, scribbling in their notebooks, nodding unconsciously as they did so. Since they had escaped from Germany, Rowland had himself carried the same message but he'd found no audience. "I think that it's worth doing whatever is necessary to allow Egon to speak, to be heard by as many people as possible. They're actually listening to him, Clyde."

Clyde braced Rowland's shoulder companionably. He knew how hard Rowland had tried to make people understand what was happening under the Nazis, how much he had risked to do so, but though Sinclair connections had given Rowland access to the highest offices, he had been dismissed as a hysterical troublemaker working to a Communist agenda. Of course that was also what the Lyons government claimed of Egon Kisch, but the circumstances of the journalist's arrival were, it seemed, creating a great deal of public interest.

Even so, the Kisch Reception Committee was unsuccessful in its attempts to have the ban on the Czechoslovak lifted so that he could disembark in Adelaide, and the liner cast off with Egon Kisch still aboard. The *Strathaird* continued its journey towards Melbourne, and was still at sea when the National Congress against War and Fascism opened with only an empty chair for its principal speaker. This failure they all felt keenly.

"We did everything we could," Clyde said as they commiserated with Kisch in the Tourist saloon.

"I don't know," Rowland murmured. "Perhaps we should have made a run for it in Adelaide."

"Don't be daft—they would have arrested us all."

"But Egon would have been in Australia. As it is the *Strathaird* is our prison."

On board, attitudes towards Kisch had become more hostile since the stop in Adelaide. Newspapers collected in the port revealed the furore the activist was causing. His friends in the reception committee—now called the Kisch Defence Committee—had issued a writ of habeas corpus and charged the captain of the *Strathaird* with kidnapping. Many passengers chose sides and it was no longer just the four men from First Class about whom Rowland and Clyde were concerned. A group of Italians took the journalist's stance against Fascists rather personally and employed every chance to make their discontent known. Stanley Quinlan remained loyal to his friends, happy to defend Kisch with his fists whenever the opportunity rose, and it was he who quite enthusiastically became the journalist's champion against the Fascisti when fisticuffs broke out.

Rowland and Clyde rarely left Kisch's side, wary of any attempt to lure one or both of them away. Alcott and his men seemed always close at hand, watching and waiting for any relaxation of the guard around Egon Kisch. On Armistice Day, however, Rowland slipped back to the First Class decks to see his mother, who was affected this year, as she was every year, by a melancholia she did not understand. It was as close as she came to allowing herself to admit she'd lost a son in the Great War. She held onto Rowland, and convinced herself again that he was the brother he so resembled.

Rowland, for his part, did not deny her that comfort and he kept his own grief to himself. The thought of Wilfred standing alone at the dedication of the memorial in Melbourne churned in his gut. He'd promised he'd be there, he'd wanted to be there. He didn't know how he was going to explain this choice to Wilfred.

On a whim, because his mother was reluctant to let him go, and perhaps because the idea was so abhorrent to his Aunt Mildred, Rowland escorted Elisabeth to the Tourist saloon to meet Egon Kisch. The thrill of being introduced to a dangerous spy seemed to shake the sadness which pressed upon her.

"Where is your poppy, Herr Kisch?" she asked, noting that the journalist did not wear one.

"My dear lady, I am an opponent of war. I cannot commemorate it."

"We commemorate the fallen, not the war, Herr Kisch."

"No, it is a fair point," Kisch said before Rowland could step in. "I commemorate the fallen by opposing war and Fascism, Mrs. Sinclair."

"I believe you're here to agitate against Germany, Herr Kisch."

"Not at all, madam. I am here to agitate *for* Germany, against the Nazis into whose hands she has fallen. Against the Fascists who are a threat to the peace of the world."

"But how do you suppose we oppose the Nazis without a war, Herr Kisch?" Elisabeth's grey eyes were clear and sharp. "They are, after all, Germany's elected government. We can hardly send them to bed without supper!"

Egon sighed. "I am not sure, dear lady. But I know this: one cannot prevent war by closing one's eyes to the persecution of one's fellows. That is not the way to peace."

Rowland was a little surprised by the clarity and confidence with which his mother debated the journalist. Having never heard her speak of politics before, Rowland found himself somewhat fascinated. His father would never have tolerated Elisabeth having opinions on the subject. Perhaps she'd just become accustomed to keeping them to herself, and her sons, having never heard them, had made the mistake of assuming they didn't exist. In her calm logic, her sceptical conservative argument, he heard Wilfred, though he doubted his brother would ever have given Egon Kisch a hearing. Perhaps Elisabeth Sinclair's willingness to do so was due to the fact that she'd been living with Communists for much of the year.

Kisch made his case passionately but gently and with respect. For that he had Rowland's gratitude.

"Do not mistake me, Herr Kisch. I do not like war any more than you. I sent two sons to the Great War." She reached for Rowland's hand. "Aubrey and his brother Wilfred both answered the Empire's call and I thank God they both returned. But we are all British. We do what must be done."

Egon glanced at Rowland but said nothing, sensing the fragility behind Elisabeth's conviction. Instead of arguing further, they took tea and talked of shipboard activities and gossip. Elisabeth told Egon of the as yet unsolved case of the Pyjama Girl and shared with him her theory of the crime. She spoke also of her great friend, a poet, who, like Egon Kisch and the governor-general, was a Jew.

"Will you be leaving the ship in Melbourne tomorrow, Herr Kisch?" Elisabeth asked as she prepared to return to First Class.

"I fear not, Mrs. Sinclair."

"It does seem a shame to come all this way, and never set foot on Australian soil."

Egon sighed. "I am assured, madam, that that will not be the case. By the time the *Strathaird* reaches Sydney, Kisch will be free!"

"Well, if that is the case, Herr Kisch, you must join us for dinner. That would be splendid, wouldn't it, Aubrey?"

A Mrs. Joan Rosanove came aboard from a launch as the *Strathaird* neared Port Melbourne. She demanded to see her client, whom, she informed the captain, the crew and the man in question, was Egon Kisch. When given access to the journalist, she explained that she was his counsel in the case against Mr. Carter, the captain of the *Strathaird*.

Rowland watched the interview unobtrusively, recording it in his way. The barrister was striking, exuding a natural confidence in the law and her ability to navigate it. In strong lines, he sketched, capturing the strength and poise of her presence as she explained the legal process to Kisch. Her focus remained on her client and she ignored Rowland entirely. She explained that once the *Strathaird* was moored, a Justice of the Peace would come on board with a Mrs. Jane Aarons who would declare before him that she had met the journalist years before to establish Egon Kisch's identity for legal purposes. Without telling him directly what to do, or asking whether he actually knew Mrs. Aarons, the barrister made it clear that it was imperative Egon recognise her in return. Mrs. Rosanove would then appear in the Supreme Court of Victoria to demand a decree nisi and the discontinuance of Kisch's detention on board.

When the liner moored, Rowland realised why the barrister had taken the precaution of boarding early via launch. The *Strathaird* was circled by small boats manned by anti-Fascists with banners and flags bearing slogans demanding the release of the political prisoners of the Third Reich. Young activists raised their oars chanting "We want Kisch". Although no person or delegation was permitted on board to see Egon Kisch, visitors eager to shake his hand boarded by claiming they wished to see one of the other passengers named in the manifest. The liner was inundated. Among the visitors were Members of Parliament, Senator Arthur Rae and Dr. Maloney M.H.R.; the Kisch Defence Committee; and the President of the Australian Railways Union. The *Strathaird* was plastered with stickers declaring "Kisch Must Land!" With the journalist surrounded now by so many friends and admirers, Rowland and Clyde could relax. The atmosphere on board was revolutionary and, as meetings were organised, they were pushed to the side.

They farewelled Stanley Quinlan who disembarked to return to the Mallee with tales of his brush with a spy. He charged Rowland and Clyde with "looking out for his little mate" as he set off down the gangplank.

"Rowly!" Edna and Milton pushed through the crush of excited people towards them. Rowland grabbed the sculptress' hand and they fought their way out of the heart of the crowd, finding a quiet place behind the stairs to the upper deck.

"Well, comrades, you did it!" Milton said, shaking their hands and clapping their shoulders jubilantly.

"Not quite," Rowland said. "We missed the congress and Egon still can't disembark."

"The papers are full of the 'Raging Reporter'," Milton replied. "And Griffin got back in."

"Who's Griffin?"

"The other delegate, from New Zealand. He was banned too. But he came in anyway."

"How?"

"He caught another boat and got into the country wearing horn-rimmed glasses. Apparently they make you unrecognisable. He's currently the most wanted man in Australia!"

Rowland's mind flickered to the Pyjama Girl whose killer remained at large. And yet it seemed it was a man preaching peace for whom the police were hunting most earnestly.

"Banning Kisch and Griffin has turned them into celebrities," Milton continued. "This is bigger than the congress would ever have been!"

Edna embraced them both. "We can go home now. This is all over finally."

"*If* Mrs. Rosanove is successful in getting Egon released," Clyde cautioned.

"I say, isn't this a happy reunion?" It was Alcott's voice.

Rowland looked up. Alcott leant over the bannister, smiling, but his eyes glinted furiously.

Edna gasped as she recognised him.

"Don't be too smug, Sinclair. Your man hasn't got off this barge yet. I promise you he won't."

"We'll let the courts decide, shall we?" Rowland said, placing his arm protectively around Edna. He could feel her shaking.

"You could always have your tart start shooting people again."

Rowland flared, reaching up and grabbing Alcott's collar.

Clyde seized Rowland's shoulder before he could pull Alcott over the bannister. "Don't, Rowly. He's trying to get you thrown off the ship. Let it go, mate. We're not finished."

A pause, and then Rowland released Alcott and stepped back. Alcott straightened, adjusting his tie which had been reefed awry.

A cheer as the crowd responded to Kisch.

"It's over, Alcott," Milton said coldly. "Egon Kisch is here, Australians want to hear him speak. Whatever the hell you and your band of Fascists were trying to do, you've failed."

"Fortunately, Isaacs, the Commonwealth of Australia is not yet in the hands of Stalin, and your Bolshevik mongrel friends are not welcome. If Mr. Menzies fails to keep him out, I assure you there are good men who will step into the breach."

"This is ridiculous," Clyde murmured. "Rowly, we need to speak to the police."

"Yes, perhaps you should do that." Alcott's lip curled. "I'm sure they'd be happy to learn what exactly you're doing on the *Strathaird*. Perchance they'll deport you as well."

"*Perchance* I'll just let Rowly deck you," Clyde snarled.

"Sinclair, Jones… I wondered where you fellas had got to!" Arthur Howells elbowed his way through the crowd towards them. He shook their hands warmly. "Egon said you've been watching his back."

Rowland glanced back at the stairs. Alcott had disappeared in the moment they'd looked away. He told Howells that the men who had attacked him were on board.

"Someone stabbed you? You didn't say…"

"To be honest, Bluey, I didn't think it was related to Egon or the congress," Rowland said a little sheepishly.

Howells' brow rose, but he didn't pursue the matter. "The problem is that the powers that be are well aware that Egon's friends wish to come on board and are consequently very reluctant to sell tickets for the journey to Sydney at this stage. We're trying but I don't know that we'll be able to get anyone else on board if the courts don't release Egon."

"What are you going to do if they don't?"

"Well the next stop is Sydney. We'll appeal to the Supreme Court of New South Wales and, given that New South Wales customarily makes a point of disagreeing with Victoria, we stand a good chance."

"That's it?" Rowland asked sceptically.

"Don't fret, comrade. There's a groundswell of support for Egon, and with it contributions to the cause. We're briefing King's Counsel. We'll get this bloody ban overturned."

Rowland glanced at Clyde. "So we're staying."

Clyde nodded. "Looks that way."

"No!" Edna protested. "Henry Alcott nearly killed you once, Rowly. He's dangerous. Can't someone else—"

"We'll be all right, Ed," Rowland said calmly. "Henry and his chums only take on a man on his own. We'll make sure that none of us, including Egon, are ever alone."

"Surely you can organise someone to help." Edna appealed directly to Howells.

Howells shook his head. "There are a hundred blokes who'd happily stand between Egon and the Fascists but we can't get them on board."

Rowland took the sculptress' hand, aware that she had been deeply shaken by seeing Alcott again. "We can't leave Egon on his own, Ed."

Edna bit her lip. "No… of course not."

"Hopefully we'll all disembark tomorrow, but if not, it'll only be a couple of days until we make port in Sydney."

Milton too was distressed. The danger to his friends was exacerbated by the fact that he could do nothing to help. Without a ticket he would have to leave Rowland and Clyde to deal with Alcott and his cronies as best they could.

That evening, the case being heard at the Supreme Court of Victoria was adjourned to recommence the next day. On board the *Strathaird* the party continued with Egon Kisch as the guest of honour. The visitors to the ship from shore remained. Impromptu speeches were the order of the day or more accurately the night.

They all watched the dawn together from the open deck. Howells found them again and assured Rowland that Egon Kisch would be surrounded by friends and protectors until the ship left port. "Go get some sleep, comrade. Once we're gone it'll be up to you and Clyde."

32

BANNED NOVELIST

———◆———

To Take Legal Action
EGON KISCH'S ALLEGATIONS

MELBOURNE, Monday

Allegations that passengers on the *Strathaird* had made it
unpleasant for him when it became known that he would not
be permitted to land in Australia were made by the celebrated
Czechoslovakian novelist and lecturer, Herr Egon Kisch, when
he reached Melbourne on the liner today.

Shortly after the vessel had berthed, Herr Kisch consulted
a barrister and there is a possibility of his commencing legal
proceedings as a result of imputations which, he alleges, have
been made against him personally by the Commonwealth
authorities who were responsible for having the ban placed
upon him.

National Advocate, 13 November 1934

Rowland woke with Edna curled beside him. Having escaped the
commotion of the open decks to the cabin, the four of them had
talked into the early hours, exchanging accounts of the days since they
parted, until, exhausted, they'd all fallen asleep.

Unsure of the time, Rowland lingered where he was, watching the
sculptress sleep. In time her dark lashes fluttered open. At first, she

simply stared at him, trying to remember how she'd come to be lying beside him. Then slowly she smiled. "We must have dropped off."

Rowland checked his watch. It was nine in the morning. Clyde stopped snoring and stirred in the bunk above them. Edna looked for the shoes she'd kicked off the night before.

Rowland rubbed his chin, wondering if they would beat the crowds to the shaving basins this morning. "I'm looking forward to having a private bathroom again," he murmured. "If I could bribe that flaming judge to overturn this ban I would."

"It's all been worthwhile whatever he decides," Milton said cheerfully. "The papers have really picked up on Kisch and Griffin since the ban. Fisher's done an excellent job with publicity." The poet retied the cravat of which he had divested himself at some point the previous evening. "Not all the coverage has been in favour of them, but our men won't come and go unnoticed. Now tidy yourselves up and we'll see if your mother is back from shore leave."

Rowland smiled ruefully. "She would have been delighted to see you. But I'm afraid Wilfred took her and Aunt Mildred off the ship not long after we made port—I expect he wasn't thrilled with the idea of his mother sharing a ship with Egon Kisch."

"Wilfred? Did you speak to him?" Edna asked gently.

"No, I didn't know he was coming. One of the stewards told me after the fact."

"Did he know you were on the *Strathaird* too?"

"Yes, he left me a rather blunt note."

"Oh Rowly..."

He placed his arm about her shoulders. "It's all right, Ed. Really. I'll deal with Wil once we sort out the rest of this mess... He might have calmed down a little by then."

Consciously, in an attempt to take Rowland's thoughts from this new rift with his brother, they returned to the conversation during which it seemed they had fallen asleep: the as yet unsolved murder of James Kelly.

"The culprit's got to have something to do with Parliament House," Milton declared as he washed his face in the small hand basin. "Kelly died and I was run down there."

Rowland buttoned his waistcoat. "Actually I've been thinking about the razor in the Lamson tube—the one that ended up in the prime minister's office."

"What about it?"

"What if it wasn't intended to threaten Lyons? Suppose the killer simply placed it in the tube to get rid of it?"

"Surely there are better places to dispose of a weapon," Edna said, running Rowland's comb through her hair. "He had to know it would be found."

"That's true, but putting it in the Lamson tube did buy him time."

"What are you saying, Rowly?"

"Well, the killer would only need to get rid of the weapon immediately if there was a chance he'd be caught with it—if he was there when the police arrived."

"Hiding?" Clyde tried to pinch the crease back into his trousers.

"Maybe not." Rowland turned to Milton. "When you found the body, Milt—"

"There was the guard!" Milton exclaimed, following Rowland's line of thought. "The Commonwealth Police security guard, or whatever he was!"

Clyde stopped. His brow furrowed. "Hold on, wasn't that guard's name Smith?" He looked at Rowland. "I know every crook calls himself Smith but—"

Realisation then, finally and suddenly. "Yes," Rowland slammed his fist on one of the upper bunks, frustrated that he'd not seen it sooner. "It was him." Rowland had recognised only one of the three men they'd encountered in Fremantle as one of his attackers. Another had seemed familiar... but it was not from the attack, though he'd not realised that till now. That man had been the peace officer at Parliament House. Smith. "Confound it! How did we not recognise him?"

"We did," Clyde said. "We just didn't place the bastard."

"Are you saying one of the policemen actually killed Mr. Kelly?" Edna asked.

"Perhaps. At the very least, he helped the man who did." Rowland turned back to Milton. "You said he arrested you..."

"He handcuffed me and then went into the building to telephone for help."

"He might have placed the weapon into a Lamson tube then, knowing full well parliament wasn't sitting. He probably thought he had time to retrieve it from the prime minister's office before Lyons returned."

"One of the constables who guard Parliament House came over to help when Milt was run down," Edna said. "He got there first."

"And left the badge on Milt's lapel!" Rowland dragged a hand through his hair as he thought. "He would have seen you go in to meet Harrison and recognised you from the night Kelly was killed... perhaps he got a message to whoever was driving the car."

"Bloody hell!" Milton murmured, as the cold-blooded, calculated nature of both attacks became clear.

"What about you, Rowly?" Clyde asked. "They didn't pin a badge on you in Melbourne."

"You interrupted them," Rowland replied. "Perhaps they didn't have time."

"And Alcott?"

"He might have been there when I was attacked."

"You didn't say anything—"

"I thought I was hallucinating… but perhaps he was there."

"What do we do?" Edna pulled on her gloves, ready for whatever was required. "You can't stay."

Rowland slipped on his jacket. "We must, Ed. You and Milt need to get to Harold Jones. If we notify the Victorian Police they're likely to simply conclude this is a ploy to get Egon off the ship."

"You want me to drive back to Canberra?" Milton said dubiously.

Rowland hesitated. A telephone call from a known Communist would probably be regarded sceptically if it was taken at all. But it was at least an eight-hour drive to Canberra and there was no guarantee that Major Jones would take Milton any more seriously in person.

"Get in touch with Delaney if you can. Actually, better still—talk to Wil."

"Wilfred?" Milton gagged. "Have you lost your mind? Comrade, your brother's the enemy, not to mention that he's furious with you."

"Don't be absurd!" Edna intervened. "Wilfred doesn't want Egon in the country, but he's not a Fascist, Milt. And he knows what Mr. Alcott did before."

"I don't know…" Milton shook his head. "I can't see Wilfred Sinclair caring who killed Kelly."

"But he would care about who stabbed Rowly."

"Wil would not condone assassination." Rowland spoke with a quiet certainty that was more than mere fraternal loyalty. "These men are not his lot."

"We don't even know if he's still here. He might have taken your mother and aunt back to Yass already."

"No. If I know Wil he'll want to be here to see the ban enforced."

Milt sighed. "He's not going to listen to me anyway, Rowly."

Rowland grimaced. That much was true. At the best of times, Wilfred tolerated Milton under sufferance. He'd be unlikely to receive the poet now.

"I'll speak with Wilfred," Edna said. "He's too civil to throw me out."

Rowland and Clyde returned to the cabin to shower and shave, having decided that it was now time to speak to the captain of the *Strathaird* about the Fascists in First Class. Clean-pressed suits and faces clear of stubble would at least prevent the man concluding they were intoxicated.

Milton and Edna were on their way to find Wilfred, to tell him about Alcott and Smith in the hope that his connections would see the information fall into the right hands. But, in the meantime, the captain needed to know that there were murderers among his passengers, particularly if their intended victim was forced to stay on board.

Unfortunately, it seemed that the captain, too, was ashore, dealing with actions against him for kidnapping. The officer in command of the moored liner listened attentively, made many notes and promised to raise the matter with the captain when he returned. Until then, he regretted that he could do nothing.

Rowland and Clyde found Egon Kisch still talking to visitors and well-wishers in the Tourist smoking room. Knowing that he had not returned to the cabin the night before, they couldn't help but be in awe of the Czechoslovak's stamina. Indeed his wit seemed, if anything, to be sharpened by fatigue.

Arthur Howells shook his head to signal that they had still heard nothing about the outcome of the trial. And so they settled in the comfortable lounge chairs and waited. They had platters of sandwiches brought in rather than adjourning to the dining room for luncheon. The trays had been cleared away and they were taking coffee when the siren sounded to tell all the visitors it was time to go ashore. The *Strathaird* was leaving.

An officer came into the smoking room to inform Egon Kisch that his application before the Supreme Court had been dismissed, that his detention on board the *Strathaird* had been declared legal, and, further, that he was ordered to pay costs.

Egon took the news on the chin, soothing the outcry of his friends who were being ushered off the ship, and wishing them farewell. "I will come out on deck to wave as the ropes are cast off," he promised.

A young steward approached Rowland. He shouted in his ear to be heard over the siren. "Excuse me, sir. A Mr. Sinclair has asked to see you before the ship leaves. He's waiting for you on the lower afterdeck."

"Wilfred Sinclair?" Rowland shouted back.

"Yes, sir. I'm afraid you'll have to hurry. Visitors must be ashore in the next ten minutes."

Inwardly, Rowland cheered for Edna. It seemed even his brother was not immune to the persuasive charms of the sculptress. If Wilfred would use his influence with the authorities perhaps they could do something about Alcott and his minions. Quickly letting Clyde know, he made his way to the lower afterdeck, preparing himself for Wilfred's fury. Rowland sighed—he would apologise. He did owe his brother an apology. But he did wonder what he could possibly say.

The afterdeck seemed deserted when he reached it. Rowland stepped out of the stairwell, wishing the siren would stop already before they were all rendered deaf.

The rope snapped around his throat and pulled tight from behind, bringing him down, as it cut off his breath. The gag was tied before the rope was released, while he was still reeling from lack of oxygen. They secured his wrists behind his back before they started laying into him.

33

EGON KISCH

———◆———

Writ of Habeas Corpus
APPLICATION MADE

MELBOURNE, Monday

Application was made today to Chief Justice Irving by Mrs. Joan Rosanove, barrister, on behalf of Egon Kisch, for an order nisi calling on Captain Carter of the Strathaird to show cause why a writ of habeas corpus should not be issued requiring him to produce Kisch before the court.

His Honour granted the application.

In the event of the order being made absolute a writ will be issued, and Mr. Justice Irving will then determine whether Kisch shall be released or remain in the captain's custody.

Warwick Daily News, 13 November 1934

Clyde gave Rowland ten minutes before he too made his way down to the lower afterdeck. It was not that he was alarmed by the length of his friend's absence—in his experience, Wilfred's tirades could last for days—but he expected that Rowland might need a friendly shoulder and they also needed to get back to Egon before the last of his supporters were herded off the *Strathaird*.

A muffled warning alerted him to the impending ambush as he came out of the stairwell—he turned, but too late. The blade was at his throat, Alcott's voice in his ear. "We've got Sinclair. Give us any trouble and you're both dead Reds." He laughed. "Dead Reds..." he said again, louder so his companions could hear. "That's quite good."

Clyde was dragged back behind the lifeboats, where they were almost completely hidden from view, the knife still at his throat lest he consider shouting for help. He saw Rowland then, face down on the deck, bleeding from a gash above his ear, conscious but clearly dazed. His wrists had been tied behind his back, a crude gag had worked loose and the man they knew as Lamb knelt over him with a blade against his spine. Rowland's eyes met Clyde's. Angry. Panicked.

Clyde was jerked back as he tried to reach his friend. "You won't get away with this, Alcott," he said with more hope than conviction.

"That's the difference between us and the Commies," Alcott said as Clyde was pushed down on the deck beside Rowland. "We're not trying to get away with anything—to get around laws, to sneak into countries. We're proud of our part in the defence of this country."

"Not wearing hoods this time, then," Clyde murmured, reminding Alcott of the bizarre costume of the Fascist Legion.

He gasped as someone kicked him in the back. It had probably not been a good idea to remind Alcott of past failures. He tried reason. "Look, Alcott—"

"That's Mr. Alcott to you... or sir. Bloody Commies never had any manners."

Gritting his teeth, Clyde tried again. "Mr. Alcott, the ban's been upheld. Egon Kisch has not been allowed to land. This is not necessary—you've won."

"Perhaps," Alcott said. "Or perhaps you people will manage to have him released at Sydney. We're not taking that chance."

Rowland's voice was hoarse. "You'll make him a martyr, Henry."

"I think not. When Kisch disappears just as the *Strathaird* leaves Melbourne, it will be assumed that he simply came ashore illegally as his comrade Griffin did. The police will hunt for a while to no avail and Australians will feel that they've been taken advantage of, made to look fools... I think you'll find the tide will turn."

"And us?" Clyde asked, realising that they could not be allowed to live if Alcott's plan was to work. "How are you going to explain what happened to Rowly and me?"

Alcott shrugged. "Perhaps you went ashore with Kisch, perhaps you left to fight for Stalin, perhaps you got drunk and fell overboard... I don't think many people will care."

"Let's just finish them now," Lamb snarled. Rowland felt the prick of a blade against the skin of his back.

"Later," Alcott snapped. "Blood on the deck may arouse suspicions."

"What then?"

"We send Casey to Kisch with a message that Messrs Sinclair and Watson Jones want him to meet them on the lower afterdeck. And then we take care of all three of them."

Clyde snorted. "Egon's not an idiot."

"He has no friends left on board," Alcott said. "He'll be most eager to find his valiant protectors, and even illegal Commie spies seem to take a steward at his word."

Rowland cursed. The steward with the message from Wilfred. Egon's words came back. "*At least* four Fascists." He'd been right. There were clearly more than four. For all they knew, the captain could be one of Alcott's men.

Alcott grabbed Rowland's hair and pulled back his head. "I told you two years ago that you'd get yours eventually, Rowland. My God, Aubrey would have been disgusted with what you've become! I can't tell you how sick I feel when that doo-dally mother of yours calls you Aubrey."

Rowland bristled. He was thankful Wilfred had insisted his mother and aunt leave the ship.

Alcott unbuttoned Rowland's waistcoat with his free hand, smiling as he did so. He found the precise spot the blade had entered and it was here that he pressed. Rowland bucked and cursed. Clyde struggled to help his friend, but Lamb and another man kept him pinned. Alcott continued and eventually Rowland's body grew limp as he lost consciousness. Desperate to stop the attack, to bring help, Clyde shouted "Fire!"

Lamb punched him in the face.

Brown kicked at Rowland's unmoving form. "Blimey… did you kill him?"

"I wouldn't have thought so." Alcott shrugged. "Not yet anyway."

Smith called from the stairwell. "Passengers!"

Startled, Alcott and his men moved to hide their prisoners, tying Clyde's hands hastily, and gagging him before dragging them both into one of the tarpaulin-covered lifeboats. Voices in the stairwell. Rowland was lifted quickly into the lifeboat and gagged, but there was no time to do anything more. He was, in any case, unconscious. "Either one of you clowns makes a sound, we'll kill the other one as well as anyone within hearing," Smith promised for safe measure.

The tarpaulin was resecured over the top of the lifeboat and Clyde found himself in darkness, and out of sight of anyone who should wander onto that part of the afterdeck. Rowland came to, fully aware of what had happened. The faint had not been complete. At first neither he nor Clyde moved at all, certain that Alcott and his associates would happily carry out the threats they'd made.

A final siren told them that the last of the visitors had left the *Strathaird*. Kisch would begin to wonder where they were. Casey the steward, if he was in fact a steward, would be sent to fetch the journalist now.

Then slowly, Rowland rubbed the side of his head against the bench built into the lifeboat, catching the gag and dragging it down. He paused to gather breath, to gird his will. The stab wound he'd thought healed, burned anew. They could no longer hear conversation from outside. He hoped that meant Alcott and his men had stepped away. "Clyde?" he whispered.

"God, Rowly, are you all right?" It seemed Clyde too had got free of his gag.

"Yes. Are you facing the wall of the boat?"

"Yes."

"Good. I'm going to try and turn over without making a sound so I can untie you."

Rowland moved slowly, painfully alert to any creak or shuffle.

It took several minutes of fumbling to free Clyde's hands but finally the bonds came loose. "What now?" Clyde whispered.

"If we stay here, we're dead men." Rowland lifted the tarpaulin a crack and peered out. "Just Smith," he said. "The others must have gone after Egon."

"What do you reckon, Rowly?"

"We rush him… hope for the best."

"Let's go then."

A deep breath, and Rowland ripped off the tarpaulin as they launched out of the lifeboat. Smith reacted quickly, pulling a revolver from his jacket. "No you don't." He levelled the weapon at Rowland.

Rowland dodged to the right and, as Smith's gaze and the gun followed, Clyde came from the left, grabbing Smith's hand before he could discharge the weapon. Rowland stepped in and swung, connecting with Smith's jaw. The gun was dropped and skittered across the deck. Shouts as the commotion alerted Alcott and the others who were amidships.

"Oh bugger!" Clyde spotted Egon Kisch near the rail with Casey in steward's uniform.

Rowland and Clyde bolted towards him, shouting, but Alcott and his men were ahead of them. The ship began to move away from the pier, its horn sounding.

Rowland grabbed Alcott. Clyde threw himself at Lamb.

"Egon!" Rowland's voice was still hoarse.

Clyde's was not. "Egon, run!"

Kisch took in what was happening. Rowland and Clyde were doing their best to hold back what seemed to be half a dozen men, but they were outnumbered. In panic, he looked for the steward.

"No!" Clyde struggled out of a headlock. "Run!"

But Kisch was cornered. He backed away and, with nowhere else to go, climbed on to the rail. Casey grabbed for him, his hand swiping air as the banned journalist jumped. There were screams from the pier.

Rowland and Clyde tried to get to the rail.

Smith and Casey grabbed Rowland, restraining him as Alcott's fists flew into his ribs. Winded, both physically and with the horror of what he'd just witnessed, Rowland was struggling. Lamb and Brown held Clyde down on the deck, pummelling him with equal vigour. And then, from the pier, some eighteen feet below them, they all heard the shout. "If you have arrested me on shore, you have no right to put me back on the ship!"

Egon.

Stewards finally began to emerge from the stairwell to investigate what had happened on the afterdeck. And then the police arrived.

Alcott faltered. Rowland and Clyde rallied. Though they still had no idea what exactly had happened, they knew at least that Kisch had survived. The fight had not yet been lost.

Despite their protests, Clyde and Rowland were confined to the infirmary until the captain was able to resolve the dispute between themselves and the passengers from First Class. Knowing that Egon was off the ship and probably surrounded by supporters on the pier, they complied with less protest than they might have otherwise. The partially healed knife wound below Rowland's ribs was spotting blood. Alcott's assault had, it seemed, ruptured the new scar.

A young nurse treated the area with iodine. "I think Doctor should have a look at this."

Rowland felt the ship move. "What on earth—"

"We're setting sail," the nurse informed him.

Rowland re-buttoned his shirt, alarmed. "We have to get off!"

"I'm afraid it's too late, sir. We won't be stopping till Sydney now."

Rowland groaned. Still, the main thing was that Kisch had finally landed on Australian soil.

"What happened to Mr. Alcott and his friends?" Clyde asked. "Did the police take them ashore?"

The young nurse seemed surprised. "No, sir. They've been confined to their staterooms until the captain has a chance to resolve the dispute between you gentlemen."

Clyde glanced at Rowland. "But they were trying to kill us, not to mention Herr Kisch!"

The nurse sniffed. "Herr Kisch has only himself to blame if he has broken his leg. Nobody asked him to jump."

"He's broken his leg?" Rowland asked. "To which hospital was he taken? Can we send him a radiogram from on board?"

"He *claims* to have broken his leg. Of course he would. Well, he wasn't taken to a hospital."

"They couldn't possibly have taken him straight to a police station after such a fall," Clyde said sceptically.

The nurse laughed. "No. They took him back on board. The doctor's attending to him, but there isn't a lot he can do without an X-ray machine."

"What?" Rowland regarded her with growing dismay. The relief of knowing Egon Kisch had made land, that he was safe, evaporated. In its place the realisation that both Kisch and the men who wished to assassinate him were still on board; even worse, he and Clyde were trapped in the infirmary and Egon could no longer even run.

Rowland dismissed the throbbing pain below his ribs, telling himself that it was not that bad. He demanded to see the captain immediately. "You tell Captain Carter," he said angrily, "that since the court has seen fit to leave Egon Kisch in his control, I intend to hold him responsible for the gentleman's safety!"

"But…"

"Where exactly is Herr Kisch? Surely if the man has broken his leg he should be here in the infirmary?"

"Even if his leg was actually broken, there's nothing the doctor can do for him, sir. He was taken to his cabin."

"Good Lord, that's barbaric! What the devil are you people thinking?"

"Nobody asked Herr Kisch to jump," the nurse said again. "It's entirely his own fault."

Rowland rubbed the back of his neck, appalled. "Unlike Mr. Kisch, we are not under arrest, so if it's all the same to you, we'll wait for the captain in our cabin."

"The captain said you weren't to leave—"

"You have my word as a gentleman that we will not leave the cabin until we've seen Captain Carter."

"I don't think…"

"And if another passenger feels unwell?" Rowland asked, trying to reach her with reason. "You can hardly deny him medical attention because the infirmary is being used as a prison."

The nurse wavered. He stepped past her to the door and opened it. There were a couple of stewards outside. Hardly security—they could not, either of them, have been twenty years old. If that was all that was keeping Alcott and his men confined, Egon Kisch might be dead already.

"Excuse me, gentlemen, if you don't mind stepping aside we will be adjourning to our cabin."

The young stewards were plainly startled. They looked to the nurse for direction. She shrugged. "Escort them to the cabin. I'll inform the captain."

34

A NEW
"NEW GUARD"

It is unlikely that investigation will show the slightest foundation for the story that there has been brought into being an organisation known as the Commonwealth Legion which is arming itself with rifles and machine guns. But the statement having been made in the Senate it becomes the duty of the Federal Government to investigate it and, in particular, to ascertain whether or not military equipment is getting into hands for which it is not intended. Senator Collings, of Queensland, tabled last week a document alleged to be a report of the Legion, described as a Fascist organisation. In that document, which was typewritten and unsigned, were set out the aims and activities of the organisation and the location of arms belonging to it. According to the Senator its strongholds are Queensland and New South Wales. An unsigned, typewritten document is not much upon which to go, and it might be thought that it should be ignored by those in authority; but if it is allowed to go unchallenged it will quickly take on the appearance of authenticity and the at present unsubstantiated legion will be "an armed force of many thousands ready to use force to create a Fascist dictatorship." The Minister of Defence has promised that he will enquire at once into the statements insofar as they affect the distribution of military equipment. If these statements are incorrect the rest of the story may be discounted. Whether Senator Collings' "disclosure" is a matter for action or mirth hinges on the one point as to arms.

Examiner, 19 November 1934

Wilfred Sinclair was not in a mood to speak with any of his brother's Bolshevik friends. He might have refused to see them altogether if his mother had not already admitted the pair to his suite at the Windsor. When Wilfred strode in, he found Edna and Milton taking tea with Elisabeth Sinclair and her sister-in-law. He may have asked Isaacs to leave immediately, but the presence of the ladies made it difficult to do so in a manner the long-haired layabout may have understood.

"Mr. Sinclair," Edna stood as he came in. "May I have a word, please?"

"I'm very busy, Miss Higgins."

"I really must speak with you, Mr. Sinclair." There was something in her tone that told Wilfred she was prepared to be difficult.

"Mr. Sinclair," Milton began.

"Very well, Miss Higgins," Wilfred ignored Milton. "If you'd care to come with me. Perhaps we can speak in the other room."

"Oh yes," Elisabeth chirped. "Do chat elsewhere. Mr. Isaacs was just about to recite for us."

As Milton entertained the old ladies, Wilfred and Edna stepped into an adjoining office. Furnished with an ornate, green leather inlaid desk and captain's chairs, the room was designed to accommodate those guests who needed to conduct business from the Windsor, in a manner befitting.

He invited the sculptress to take a seat. "What can I do for you, Miss Higgins?"

For a moment Edna didn't know quite where to start. "Henry Alcott is on the *Strathaird*," she blurted.

"I beg your pardon?"

Edna told him everything as she knew it. Wilfred listened silently.

"You see, Mr. Sinclair, Rowly didn't plan to board the ship. He meant only to fly Egon back to Melbourne... but when he saw the men who had stabbed him board he didn't have a choice."

"I think you'll find he did have a choice, Miss Higgins. He chose poorly."

Edna was not going to allow that. "He did not!" she said, flaring. "He chose exactly as you would have done if one of your friends was in danger, if a man who once saved your life needed help! He chose exactly as any decent man would!"

"Where is Rowly now?" Wilfred said after a moment.

"He's still on the ship... with Mr. Watson Jones."

Wilfred opened his briefcase and extracted the evening edition of the *Age*. "Have you seen the newspaper, Miss Higgins?" He pointed out the item.

Edna scanned the article. "Oh my God! Herr Kisch jumped... He's here?"

"If you read on, Miss Higgins, you'll see that he has been returned to the *Strathaird*."

"But he's hurt!"

"The Supreme Court of Victoria dismissed his appeal. The ban has been upheld."

"Regardless, Mr. Sinclair, we are a civilised country!" Edna said fiercely. "We take injured people to hospital—we don't press-gang them onto ships!"

"Calm yourself, Miss Higgins. It's possible that if Kisch attempted to leave the ship, Rowly may in fact have disembarked more successfully."

"Rowly wouldn't leave the ship without Herr Kisch. Not while Mr. Alcott is aboard."

Wilfred stood and moved to look out of the window. "Committed," he muttered under his breath. "I should have him jolly well committed!"

"I think prison would be more appropriate. Mr. Alcott is a very dangerous man."

"I was talking about Rowly, Miss Higgins."

"Oh."

Wilfred sighed. Noting the alarmed width of Edna's eyes, he added more assuringly, "I'll have a message sent to the ship somehow, warn the captain that Alcott is not what he may appear. I expect Captain Carter will be delighted to know that he has more than one criminal on board!"

"Herr Kisch is not a criminal," Edna interrupted. "Unless you were talking about Rowly again…"

Wilfred paused, surprised that he was more amused than irritated by the sculptress' impertinence. "I fear both gentlemen may be relying on technicalities in that regard."

Edna smiled.

Wilfred continued before the exchange could thaw more than he wished. "I'll have Alcott and his men removed from the ship in Sydney one way or another. But Rowly may have to resign himself to disembarking without Herr Kisch, unless he plans to sail on to Europe!"

———————   ———————

Rowland and Clyde found Egon Kisch in one of the lower berths of the cabin. A linen sling had been secured to the bed above so that he could pull himself up. Someone had helped him undress and change into a nightshirt. He lay on top of the blankets—unable to bear the weight of any covering on his injured leg. The limb in question was red and blue, and untreated. Kisch's forehead was covered in a sheen of sweat, and his eyes were glazed with pain and fever.

Rowland cursed.

"This man needs immediate medical attention," he told the stewards, who remained outside the door.

"The doctor's been to see him, sir. Nothing can be done without an X-ray machine."

"That's not good enough. The man's in agony."

"Nobody asked him to jump, sir."

Frustrated, Rowland closed the door. This was unbelievable. Melbourne was marking its centenary with an act of medieval cruelty.

Clyde held a glass to Egon's lips so he could drink.

"*Merci*, Madame Denise," Kisch said.

"Egon, it's me—Clyde."

Kisch responded in French.

"What did he say?" Clyde asked Rowland.

"Something about a room and an aviator," Rowland replied. "He seems to think you are his landlady."

"Herr Strauss!" Egon waved Rowland over. "I know, I know... you have never yet sent a man to the gallows... but I tell you, I don't want to see Ussakowski or Trebitsch..."

Clyde glanced at Rowland who could only shrug. It seemed Egon was hallucinating. Perhaps the doctor had given him something for the pain, or perhaps it was the fever.

They did what they could to make him comfortable, which was little enough. Aside from whisky, conversation was all they could offer to distract him from the pain. Egon continued to address them as Strauss and Madame Denise, and they did not argue.

In time, someone knocked on the door of the cabin. Rowland answered while Egon complained about the noise of the typewriters. A young woman's voice responded to Rowland's precautionary enquiry on the caller's identity. Once admitted, she claimed to have been sent by the Kisch Defence Committee to stay with Egon Kisch. She offered as proof a ticket to New Zealand which she had purchased to get around the *Strathaird*'s refusal to carry coastal passengers, as well as her Party identification. It appeared the committee was concerned that Egon would be transferred to another ship at sea and disappear before the liner reached Sydney.

"My name is Gwendolyn, comrades."

Egon seemed to regard her as a rather pleasant apparition.

She assured him that she was real, and informed them that an appeal would be lodged in Sydney, the prospects of which were considerably brighter. Further, she continued, a draft of the speech Egon was to give the congress, and which he had passed to Bluey Howells earlier, would be printed as a pamphlet to be distributed in Sydney before the *Strathaird* arrived. The news seemed to cheer Egon somewhat. Finally, and most triumphantly, Gwendolyn informed them that Gerald Griffin, the other banned delegate who had snuck back into the country, was addressing a group of Newcastle miners that very night.

"Won't he be arrested?" Clyde asked.

"We have taken precautions," Gwendolyn said, smiling. "In any case the police are unlikely to arrest Comrade Gerald in a room full of miners."

It was midnight when Rowland walked Gwendolyn back to her cabin.

"Please be careful," he warned. "There are men aboard intent on harming Egon and anyone who may help him."

"I have not approached him on deck, Mr. Sinclair. I have been nothing but a fellow passenger."

"Until this evening when you brought comfort to an injured man. Please be careful Miss—"

"Gwendolyn," she said firmly. "If you cannot call me comrade, then it must be Gwendolyn. I promise you, Rowland, I will not put myself at risk."

The message from the captain was delivered via a steward early the next morning. Captain Carter was happy to grant Mr. Sinclair's request for a meeting, but it would have to be in his office.

Having already been led into one ambush by a steward with a message, Rowland refused, sending a return missive through the same steward that it would be more convenient if the captain came to him. Some minutes later, the steward knocked again.

"Captain Carter regrets that he cannot attend your cabin at this time. He would be happy to receive you at noon if that is more suitable for you, sir."

Rowland cursed, exasperated. "Tell him I'll be there."

"What are you doing, Rowly?" Clyde asked once the steward had gone. "Alcott and his mates will simply throw you overboard at noon instead."

"I'm not going at noon—I'm going now. If that message was from the captain I'll be unfashionably early, and if not I won't be wandering into a trap."

"I don't know, Rowly..."

Rowland glanced at Egon who was muttering about typewriters again. "There's got to be something more they can do for him, Clyde. If the captain won't come here..."

Clyde groaned. "I still don't like it. Be bloody careful." He sighed. "I wish we'd thought to bring your gun."

Rowland grimaced. "I'm not sure an act of piracy would help matters." He grabbed his hat from where he'd tossed it on the upper bunk, turning away to wince as that careless extension of his arm incited a piercing pain in his side. There was nothing to be gained by having Clyde worry further. Egon Kisch's injury was more pressing. "I won't be long."

As most of the passengers were at breakfast, the corridors and stairwells seemed deserted. Rowland remained wary, moving quickly but cautiously towards the exclusive First Class B Deck on which Captain Carter had his office. As the steward had been heading there to deliver his message, Rowland assumed he would find the captain in.

Once again his attire and his lack of interest in the opulence of the deck ensured his presence in this part of the ship was not particularly noticed or questioned. As he neared the captain's quarters, Rowland saw there was a number of stewards standing outside the door. He relaxed a little—he would have help in the event of another ambush… unless of course all the stewards were Fascists. He dismissed the thought as unlikely—the stewards were for the most part youths from the subcontinent where Fascism was almost unheard of.

"Captain Carter summoned me," Rowland told the steward standing before the door.

The young man glanced nervously at the door. "The captain—"

"I'll just go in and see what he wants, shall I?" Rowland opened the door before he could be stopped.

The cabin was decorated in an ostensibly maritime tradition: an imposing desk heavy enough to resist the motion of the sea, shelves filled with leather-bound volumes and models of sailing ships, oak-panelled walls and porthole windows.

The office was large enough to accommodate the several people within. Carter sat behind his desk flanked by two officers. Also in the room were Henry Alcott, Lamb, Smith and Brown, as well as another three stewards.

Rowland paused at the threshold as they all turned towards him.

Carter cleared his throat. "Mr. Sinclair, I presume. You're early."

Rowland said nothing, his eyes on Alcott.

"We have a situation, here, gentlemen," Carter continued. "Mr. Alcott contends that you, Mr. Sinclair, and your companion, Mr. Watson Jones, are Communist operatives sent on board to either sabotage or seize my ship."

Rowland laughed. "Two unarmed men? I hardly think we're likely to storm the bridge and take control, Captain Carter. As for sabotage... the notion is preposterous!"

"Regardless, I do not take any threat to my ship or its passengers lightly."

"With the greatest respect, sir, perhaps then, you should have allowed Herr Kisch to be taken to a hospital."

Carter's moustache bristled. "Mr. Alcott and his companions have volunteered to take you all into custody until we reach Sydney."

"For the sake of our fellow passengers," Alcott said calmly. "And for your own safety, Mr. Sinclair."

Rowland took a step back but the door had been closed behind him. "Mr. Alcott has no authority to take anyone into custody."

Alcott spoke up. "My friends and I are members of a league of gentlemen loyal to king and country, sworn to defend the Commonwealth against acts of Communist terror. We offer you our services with respect to the Communist agitator Kisch and his comrades."

"Mr. Alcott and his minions are Fascists!" Rowland said angrily. "Their intention is to execute Herr Kisch, myself and Mr. Watson Jones. Acceding to this request, Captain, will make you complicit in the murder of your own passengers!"

"Will it indeed?" Carter said coldly. Alcott smiled.

35

AUSTRALIA'S WAY WITH UNDESIRABLES

Gentlest Treatment in World

Amidst the tangle of accusations levelled at the Federal Government for its allegedly harsh treatment of two recent arrivals who desired to enter this country after it had been made very clear to them that they were not wanted here, many people have been inclined to lose sight of the fact that not only does Australia possess the fairest immigration laws in the world but that she also administers them with a courtesy to those concerned which is unknown in any other country.

...Australia's Immigration laws rest basically upon the Immigration Restriction Act passed in 1901 and subsequently amended. This measure provides for the prohibition of the entry into the Commonwealth of persons who have failed to pass a dictation test in any prescribed language, who are likely to become public charges, are insane or suffering from infectious diseases, or have been convicted of an offence not of a political nature, and have not served the sentence passed upon them. The real barb of the Act lies in the first provision, for by means of the dictation test the authorities have power, theoretically at least, to exclude anybody whose presence in the Commonwealth is not desired.

NO NATIONS NAMED

Nowhere do the Immigration laws of Australia discriminate against or even mention any specific nationality as being barred from the country, and in this they exhibit a tactfulness and a diplomacy lacking, from the American laws, which say in unequivocal words that Japanese shall not come into the United States, a fact which has led to bitter and burning resentment in Japan, where there is no feeling at all against the Commonwealth's machinery of exclusion. Actually Australia, which was the first country to adopt the dictation test, long ago succeeded by these means in solving a problem which has perplexed many foreign Governments at different times. There have been occasions in the Commonwealth's history when the dictation test has enabled officials to get around obstacles which might have otherwise been insurmountable. One of them was nearly thirty years ago when a minor potentate from a Malayan State set out to visit Australia, this country's Government having already been warned from London that he was likely to prove anything but an acceptable guest. In due course he arrived at Sydney, where it was tactfully explained to him that the law required everybody coming into Australia to pass a dictation test. A foolish law, of course, the officials explained, adding, with infinite diplomacy, that since he had spent some time at Oxford he would of course have no difficulty in passing it. Smilingly the potentate said that he was ready for the test and it was given to him—in modern Greek. He failed to pass and was informed by the officials that they were desolated with grief but could not land, the law being the law. In the following ten minutes the newcomer said some hard things about Australia and its laws, but when the steamer sailed the next day he was on board...

The Telegraph, 22 November 1934

The *Strathaird's* captain pressed his fingertips together, regarding the men standing before him thoughtfully. "Mr. Alcott's offer struck me as both patriotic and obliging. Certainly Mr. Kisch's antics have caused no end of trouble."

"For pity's sake, man!" Rowland exploded. "These men are murderers!"

"Settle down, old boy," Alcott said, stepping towards Rowland. "You'll be treated fairly if you don't resist."

"Go to hell, Henry—"

"Just a minute, Mr. Alcott." Carter signalled the stewards to step between the two. "While I was initially inclined to accept your offer, I received a telegram this morning warning me that you and your colleagues are wanted for questioning with respect to attacks on people in Canberra and Melbourne."

"Propaganda from one of Kisch's Communist friends, no doubt!" Alcott barked.

Carter spoke evenly. "Mr. Wilfred Sinclair is certainly not a Communist, Mr. Alcott. In any case, his telegram was confirmed by another from a Detective Delaney of the New South Wales Police Force."

"Why, this is outrageous! Scurrilous, slanderous allegations!"

"I have decided, Mr. Alcott, that the only way to ensure the safety of everybody concerned is to confine all parties to their cabins until we make port in Sydney, at which point the matter will be one for the police."

For a moment it looked as though Alcott and his men would resist. The crewmen responded by flanking each of the passengers and displaying, if not unholstering, their weapons. It seemed they were not ordinary stewards but armed security. Simmering, Alcott conceded and the four men were accompanied back to their First Class accommodations.

"Captain Carter," Rowland said before he too was escorted to his cabin. "Herr Kisch is in a lot of pain. I understand that there is no X-ray equipment on board, but surely there's something that can be done?"

"I'll speak to the ship's doctor, Mr. Sinclair," Carter said gruffly. "There's nothing more I can do."

In the end Rowland returned to his friend with only a few sleeping powders, but it was something.

And so, the next day was passed confined to an airless cabin with a man in agony, while the liner made her way to Sydney. Aware that their situation may have been a good deal more perilous had Captain Carter accepted Alcott's version of events, they bore it without further protest. The *Strathaird* found herself trapped in Darling Harbour in much the same way that she had been delayed in Melbourne while lawyers argued over whether Egon Kisch should be allowed to land. Miss Christian Jollie Smith and Mr. Piddington, K.C., came to his bedside to discuss his case. At extraordinary expense, an X-ray machine was installed on the ship and Egon Kisch's leg finally treated and plastered. Henry Alcott and his men disembarked and disappeared before Colin Delaney could question them. Rowland and Clyde's vigilance was relieved, at least temporarily, by dozens of Egon Kisch's supporters who once again boarded to fill the infirmary from where the man himself spoke to the press and made his case directly to the Australian public. Among the visitors to the infirmary was the fugitive Gerald Griffin who spoke with his fellow delegate and wrote a letter on *Strathaird* letterhead before eluding the authorities and vanishing once more. Rowland couldn't help but wonder if the New South Wales Police really wanted to capture him.

"Someone murdered a young woman and set her alight, Rowly," Delaney admitted. "We'll catch that bastard first."

Edna and Milton also joined them on board. Rowland kissed the sculptress' cheek. "You and Milt probably saved our lives," he whispered. "Thank you."

"You should be thanking Wilfred." She embraced him tightly and noticed him flinch. "What have you done?" she demanded, pulling back to look at him.

"I'm just a little sore." Rowland resisted the urge to clutch his side.

"We should find you a doctor."

"No—I'm perfectly well… how was Wil?"

"He was… is quite cross," she said, clearly aware that Rowland was trying to avoid the subject. "You seem pale, Rowly." She turned to Clyde. "What happened to him?"

Clyde glanced at Rowland. "Perhaps you should have that wound looked at again now that Egon's safe."

"As soon as we disembark," Rowland promised. The injury was increasingly uncomfortable but not yet intolerably so. He expected a doctor would simply instruct him to rest… which he would, as soon as the "Raging Reporter" was finally on Australian soil.

The case of Egon Kisch continued to be debated through that day and the next. Miss Jollie Smith ran back and forth between the court and the *Strathaird* infirmary to clear up points of fact and law. Finally, on the afternoon of 16 November, just after the infirmary had been cleared of visitors, the message came that the Supreme Court of New South Wales had ordered the release of Egon Kisch.

The halls and decks of *R.M.S. Strathaird* rang with cheers and heartfelt renditions of "For He's a Jolly Good Fellow". The residents of *Woodlands House* celebrated too, not just for the release of Egon Kisch but also their own. They had done their part and now they could go home.

Amidst the joyous furore they could only watch from a distance as Egon Kisch was lifted onto a stretcher and carried down the gangway to the long-awaited shore.

"Have you ever seen such a showman?" Clyde murmured as Egon waved to the crowd.

And then, on the dock, Egon's triumph turned to confusion. He was bundled into a police car and taken away, leaving bewildered supporters and the excited press in his wake.

"What the blazes..." Rowland began.

Milton was already moving, swinging his walking stick to create a path through the crowd. "They'll take him to Police Headquarters—come on!"

They were not alone in following Kisch to the station, and like his other supporters and the press, they were denied admittance while the Czechoslovak was carried into the reception room. The best they could do was peer in through the forecourt window with dozens of others. Egon was clearly furious as they searched his suitcase and questioned him on its contents.

"What the hell's going on?" Milton asked.

"I'm not sure," replied Rowland who had the added vantage of his height in observing what was happening. "They've just given him a paper and pen... perhaps they're trying to get him to write a confession of some sort."

Suddenly Egon shouted loudly enough for those behind the window to hear: "In Gaelic language? You want me to submit to a dictation test in Gaelic? It is stupid and unfair to test me with this. It will make Australia a laughing stock!"

"For the love of God," Rowland said. "They're making him sit an entry test in Gaelic."

"Can they do that?" Clyde asked outraged. "Can you see what's happening now, Rowly?"

"Egon's throwing away the pen... they've given him another one... he's refusing to take it." Rowland shook his head incredulously. "The constable's reading again."

"That doesn't sound like it did the last time," Kisch shouted so all could hear. "This fellow does not know Gaelic himself!"

Three policemen stepped forward to seize the journalist. Someone closer to the window shouted, "Bail's been denied. They're taking him into custody!"

Rowland made his way back to the reception and demanded to see Egon Kisch. He wasn't the only one. They were all told in no uncertain terms to get on their way and threatened with arrest if they resisted.

From the prison corridors in Police Headquarters, Egon Kisch roared about injustice and dirty tricks, the shame that it was for a peace delegate to be treated in this way.

"What do we do now?" Clyde asked.

"Delaney!" Rowland said. "We'll ask for Delaney."

"You'll do no such thing!" Colin Delaney appeared from behind a counter. He pulled them aside. "Are you trying to get me sacked?"

"Colin—"

"Sorry, Rowly, there's nothing I can do. The Immigration Act you know…"

"But—"

"You can't help him now… not here, anyway. Your best chance is to talk to lawyers."

They all blanched as Egon Kisch shouted for a lawyer and a doctor. Milton began to lose his temper.

"He's not being tortured," Delaney assured them. "I suspect he's just trying to make the sergeant's life miserable."

"Egon shouting is the least of his worries!" Milton threatened to storm the cells himself to take aid to the prisoner.

Rowland intervened before Delaney was forced to arrest the poet. "Perhaps we should call on Miss Jollie Smith—find out what she's doing to get Egon released, and see if there's anything more we can do—" He glanced at Milton. "Aside from a gaol break."

The offices of Christian Jollie Smith were in the Manchester Unity Building on Elizabeth Street. It was by now well beyond normal business hours, but Rowland expected the solicitor would be burning the midnight oil in preparation for Egon Kisch's day in court.

It was as they entered the building that they encountered Alcott, Smith and Brown. The three were standing by the corridor which led to Miss Jollie Smith's rooms, waiting.

Milton swore. He recognised Alcott of course, but also Smith. "That's the bloody peace officer from Parliament House," he said quietly.

Rowland stepped in front of Edna.

Henry Alcott unfolded his arms. "Rowly... fancy meeting you here, old boy. Are you taking your Commie mongrels for a walk?"

"I believe you gentlemen are wanted by the police," Rowland said coldly.

Alcott stared at him. "My god you look like Aubrey... even now, ten years older than he was..."

"What are you doing here?" Rowland asked suspiciously. Alcott seemed to be stalling.

A scream from down the corridor, and then a man's cry. "You won't defend Red rats anymore!"

"What the devil—" Rowland broke for the corridor.

Alcott leapt to grab him. Another scream. Rowland turned and swung. Then all the men threw themselves into the fray. Smith produced a knife. Milton parried a slash with his walking stick and then thrust it like a sword into the man's stomach. Smith doubled over but he did not release his weapon.

Alcott charged, slamming Rowland against the wall. For a moment he was winded as Alcott laid into him. Rowland could feel blood soaking through the fabric of his shirt, and it was that rather than any pain or debilitation that told him the stab wound had reopened. Clyde pulled Alcott off.

A door opened in the corridor and Christian Jollie Smith stumbled out. The lawyer was bleeding profusely from the head as she ran blindly along the hall.

Rowland regrouped, bolting into the corridor as he left Clyde and Milton to hold back the three men.

The solicitor collapsed outside another door, just as Lamb emerged into the corridor from her office. He held an iron pipe about three feet in length in both hands.

Rowland put himself between Lamb and his victim. "Drop the pipe, Mr. Lamb."

"Finish it!" Alcott bellowed as he tried to break free of Clyde.

Edna slipped past the men to reach the crumpled form of Jollie Smith. She banged frantically on the door of the dentist's offices at which the solicitor had fallen, shouting for help as blows were exchanged around her.

Lamb raised his pipe above his head and ran towards the two women, swinging wildly as Rowland blocked his way. A thud as the pipe made contact with Rowland's chest. Gasping, Rowland fell to his knees, but he grabbed Lamb as he did so, bringing his assailant down with him.

The door was opened by a man who was presumably the dentist, and between them he and Edna dragged and carried Jollie Smith into the relative refuge of his surgery.

"The police... we need the police!" Edna handed the semi-conscious solicitor into his care.

Rowland gripped Lamb's hand and slammed it against the ground, trying to force him to release the iron pipe. Someone kicked him in the back, dragged him off Lamb, and threw him into the wall. Dazed, Rowland tried to focus. Alcott.

"I won't miss this time." A knife.

Rowland drew back as Alcott thrust. The blade nicked his jacket but nothing more. He struck back before Alcott could recover, seizing Alcott's wrist and punching at the same time. The blow caught Alcott on the jaw, stunning him. Rowland followed with another blow and another. Alcott dropped the knife. Rowland seized him by the collar, light-headed now. "Damn you, Henry!"

"Rowly, behind you!" Clyde's voice.

Rowland turned quickly, with Alcott still in his grip.

Henry Alcott grunted as the knife meant for Rowland plunged into his spine. Lamb's eyes widened as he realised what he had done, and he stepped back. Smith and Brown tried to run but by now help had arrived and their way was barred.

Rowland did not release his grip on Alcott—holding him up as his limbs became loose and heavy. Alcott clutched Rowland's shoulder as the light faded from his eyes. "Don't leave me, Aubrey... help me."

Rowland tried, calling for help as he attempted desperately to stem the bleeding even as he bled himself. But Henry Alcott was dead.

36

MURDEROUS ATTACK ON WOMAN LAWYER IN HER OFFICE

Beaten With Iron Pipe

MISS JOLLIE SMITH IN DESPERATE STRUGGLE

ALLEGED ADMISSION BY MAN WHO IS CHARGED

VICTIM NOW IN HOSPITAL

SYDNEY, Friday

With severe wounds on the head, alleged to have been inflicted by a man armed with a piece of iron piping, Miss C. Jollie Smith, well-known City solicitor, was taken to Sydney Hospital this morning.

There she was immediately treated by several doctors for a nasty wound on the head, which necessitated several stitches. Later in the day a man was charged at the Central Court with having assaulted her with intent to do bodily harm, and was remanded.

Miss Jollie Smith's office was the scene of the sensational encounter. She said later that she feared for her life. "I was in my office preparing the affidavits in the Kisch case," she said. "Nobody else was in, but suddenly the door opened. A man rushed into the room and then dived at me across my desk…"

WEAPON SECURED

Constables arrived soon afterwards, and they took a man to the Central Police Station. A piece of water-pipe more than two feet long, which had the appearance of having been freshly sawn from a longer piece, was given to the constables. Miss Jollie Smith was taken by the Central Ambulance to Sydney Hospital where it was found necessary to shave part of her head to treat lacerations to the scalp. She was admitted for observation. "I think I'm lucky to be alive," she said. "My greatest disappointment is that I have had to miss the application to the Court in the Kisch case, which promised to be most interesting."

MAN CHARGED

Alleged to have admitted that he intended murder, Ernest Gustave Lamb, 51, accountant, was charged at the Central Police Court later in the day with having unlawfully assaulted Christian Jollie Smith, occasioning her actual bodily harm. Lamb was also charged with unlawful common assault…

The detective added that Lamb said: "I went there for the purpose of doing her in. I want to be committed for trial for this for murder." Detective Cartwright said Miss Smith was now in Sydney Hospital. Three stitches had been inserted in a wound in her head, but she had not been certified as being in a dangerous condition. Lamb was remanded to November 27.

The Newcastle Sun, 16 November 1934

It was never clear how exactly Wilfred Sinclair was alerted to the incident at the Manchester Unity Building. Perhaps he had been notified by the police, or some bystander, or, more likely, he'd had his own spies watching his brother. Rowland for his part had not known Wilfred was even in Sydney.

Christian Jollie Smith was taken immediately to the hospital, as the police attempted to ascertain what precisely had occurred in the corridor. Smith and Brown claimed to be passers-by set upon by Communist thugs of whom they claimed Lamb was one. Lamb confessed quite proudly that he had intended to kill Christian Jollie Smith, and wished to be arrested for that crime. With regards to Alcott, he would say nothing. Smith and Brown, on the other hand, claimed it was Rowland who had wielded the knife and delivered the fatal blow.

Of course Clyde, Milton and Edna provided a vastly different version of events. Shaken after watching a man die as he held him, Rowland was quiet. He, too, was taken to the hospital when it was discovered that not all the blood on his clothes belonged to Alcott. His friends were detained at the scene.

Wilfred Sinclair arrived at the Manchester Unity Building with New South Wales Police Commissioner Childs. It was difficult to tell which of them commanded greater authority. The scene was cleared soon after that. Smith, Brown and Lamb were taken into custody, Alcott to the City Morgue. Clyde, Edna and Milton gave their formal statements at Police Headquarters while Egon Kisch still bellowed for justice from his cell.

At the hospital, Rowland remained under guard as the wound, which it seemed had gradually been reopened by repeated impact, was given the appropriate attention.

He got dressed, though the doctors advised him against leaving and the police guard prevented him from doing so. He waited in the private room to which he'd been confined in a suit still splattered with Alcott's blood and his own. Wilfred Sinclair found him there. "How are you holding up, Rowly?"

Rowland looked up, surprised. He hadn't expected those to be Wilfred's first words. "I don't know. I just feel a bit… I don't know."

Wilfred nodded. "It's not easy to watch a man die."

Fleetingly, Rowland wondered how many men Wilfred had watched die. His brother had been a soldier. Perhaps this feeling was why Wilfred never talked of the war. "I didn't kill him, Wil. I didn't intend—"

"I know that." Wilfred sighed. "Not that anyone, most of all me, would have blamed you for defending yourself. I'm sorry it came to this. Henry was quite a nice chap before the war. He and Aubrey were great chums."

Rowland swallowed. "He thought I was Aubrey in the end."

"It might have given him some comfort. You do look like Aubrey, or what he would have looked like if he'd lived to be your age."

They sat in silence for a while, both dwelling on the brother they'd lost, the absence they still felt keenly.

"The matron tells me that you're insisting on going home as soon as the police are finished with you."

"Yes. I wish they'd hurry up." Rowland glanced down at his blood-stained clothes. "I'd really like to change."

"Mr. Ley came to see me in Melbourne," Wilfred said suddenly.

"Why?"

"On behalf of his client."

"Jemima?"

"No. The lady's husband, Mr. Oswald Roche."

"What?" Rowland knew this wouldn't be good.

"He informed me that Roche intends to sue you for seducing his wife and consequently destroying his marriage."

For a moment Rowland was speechless. "And Jemima?"

"She has apparently lodged proceedings for divorce, naming you, which of course substantiates his case."

Rowland cursed. His part in this had been so neatly engineered. "So why did Ley come to you and not me?"

"I believe he was hoping for a substantial out of court settlement. He assumed, quite correctly, that I would be more concerned about your reputation than you might."

Rowland groaned. Jemima seemed to wreak havoc without ever meaning to... or perhaps she was as complicit in this as she had been in everything else. "Did you pay him?" he asked wearily.

Wilfred took off his spectacles and met his brother's eye. "No. We spoke frankly. In the end, Mr. Ley decided to return to England quite urgently. He embarked the day before yesterday. Oswald Roche may decide to press his claims through another solicitor, but Mr. Ley is no longer acting for either him or Jemima Roche nee Fairweather."

"Ley's gone?"

"Unless, of course, he chose to leap from the ship while it was in port... yes, he's gone."

Rowland rubbed his face. "Look, Wil, this business with Egon, I'm sorry—"

"I don't want to talk about it, Rowly. Take your friends and go home. I'll do what I can to make sure your part in this latest mess does not appear in the papers."

"You don't have to—"

"I do. You're a Sinclair, Rowly. Whatever you choose to do, I will not have you disgrace us publicly again."

"Egon—" Rowland began wearily. He couldn't just leave his friend in prison.

"He's where he belongs, Rowly."

"When Germany wanted to put me in prison, Egon got me out of there, Wil. He's injured. I've been in those cells... they are no place for an injured man. He should be in a hospital."

Wilfred used his handkerchief to polish his spectacles. He replaced them before he spoke. "Perhaps."

The courtroom was crowded for the bail hearing, with all the benches taken and people standing, pressed shoulder to shoulder at the back. Rowland squeezed in beside his companions after relaying a last minute message to the accused from his barrister. "This is a bail hearing—make it clear that you are unlikely to escape."

Having been suddenly transferred from prison to hospital the night before, Egon Kisch was carried into the court in his pyjamas and set down in the prison dock. In moments, he collapsed.

To gasps of horror and cries of "shame", the injured journalist was then placed on the floor in front of the bench. He was pale and did not seem lucid. His lip trembled and he suppressed a groan from time to time.

"What the hell did they do to him in the hospital?" Clyde muttered. "He was in better shape when he left the prison."

Piddington, K.C., a barrister of the most distinguished and ancient kind, began his oration, outlining that his client had been illegally denied entry in Fremantle, and again in Melbourne where he was attacked and forcibly taken on board a ship, and then when the High Court released him in Sydney, he was kidnapped again and a murderous attack made on his lawyer.

All this while the accused lay in fevered agony on the floor.

The prosecution argued that the only question was whether the accused had passed the dictation test.

Mr. Piddington claimed the test was illegal, demanded an adjournment, and that his client be released on bail.

Immediately the prosecution rose in protest. "The accused is a dangerous agitator and his audacious leap from the liner only demonstrates the great risk of his escaping."

The accused whimpered weakly.

"What?" The judge, a practical jurist by the name of May, interrupted. "You can't tell me that a man with a broken leg is going to run away!" He set the bail at £100 and adjourned the proceedings for a week.

Now, finally free, Egon Kisch jumped up from what had appeared his death bed and hobbled like a resurrected messiah to the door. For a moment onlookers gaped at the miracle and then laughter broke out, followed closely by cheers.

And so Egon Kisch was unleashed upon the innocent citizens of the Commonwealth, but first he was required to return to the Sydney Hospital to be formally discharged. There he spoke with the four young people who had fought so hard to bring him onto Australian soil.

"Thank you, comrades and Mr. Sinclair, who is not a comrade but nevertheless a friend." Egon shook their hands and kissed Edna's. "I know what you have risked for me and I am humbly grateful."

"How are you, Herr Kisch?" Edna asked, glancing at his elevated and plastered leg.

Egon smiled. "My English is broken, my leg is broken, but my heart is not. It is full of the friendship shown to me, and buoyed by the fact that I will fulfil the task entrusted me by the anti-Fascists of Europe. I will speak to the people of Australia." He shrugged. "They can arrest me again after that. I will have told my story, spoken the words Mr. Menzies believes so dangerous."

"Well we're glad you're here," Edna said. "And when you're not rousing the masses, you must come to *Woodlands*."

"I will come, Miss Higgins, I will leap from a dozen ships to do so!"

"Or I can send the car," Rowland offered.

Clyde laughed. "We'll be at the Domain tomorrow to hear you speak."

"How is Miss Jollie Smith? Have you heard?" Egon asked.

"I saw her," Rowland replied. "She is on the mend. Mr. Piddington expects her back to prepare your case against the dictation test tomorrow."

"And the man who attacked her?"

"He is in prison."

Egon sighed. "Perhaps we will meet there, if the dictation test prevails."

All too soon, other visitors demanded their time with the great man, and Rowland and his companions made their farewells. They returned to *Woodlands House* from which they had all been mostly absent for months. There they found Elisabeth Sinclair waiting for them behind a selection of the day's papers from which she was taking notes and making cuttings.

"It seems the girl from Shanghai is alive and well," she informed them, as she cut through a picture of Egon Kisch to save the article on the other side of the page. One of Edna's cats had settled atop the stack of papers, and protested as Elisabeth pulled another publication from the pile.

"What girl from Shanghai, Mrs. Sinclair?" Clyde asked.

"The one they thought was that poor girl in pyjamas," Elisabeth replied. "Good gracious, Aubrey, do you and your friends not follow current events?"

Rowland glanced at her cuttings. "I see. I take it they're no closer to identifying her?"

"No. I suppose they've been busy dealing with that fellow from the ship." Elisabeth Sinclair gathered her notes. "I must change for dinner." She smoothed down her son's lapel, frowning as she noticed a small spot of yellow paint. "You might consider doing the same, Aubrey. You're not in Tourist anymore!"

"I too have been concerned about slipping standards," Milton added gravely, his dark eyes glinting.

"If only Aubrey had your sense of style, Mr. Isaacs." Elisabeth gazed admiringly at the poet's pristine if eccentric attire.

"It's unfair to compare… Mrs. Sinclair." The poet's smile grew with the realisation of each accidental rhyme. "I'm sure he does his best."

"Oh God!" Clyde groaned.

"It's his at least," Rowland muttered.

"More's the pity."

With a typically theatrical show of offence, Milton called them philistines, offered Elisabeth his arm, and escorted Rowland's mother to her private wing.

Edna pulled out the remaining newspapers from under her cat and read out the articles on Kisch. "Egon has made quite the entrance."

Rowland removed his jacket, hanging it on an easel before loosening his tie and rolling up his sleeves in a way that might have driven Elisabeth Sinclair to despair had she seen it. He set a new canvas on the easel and squeezed sepia pigment onto his palette. God, how he loved the smell of oils and turpentine, the promise of a blank canvas.

"Sit for me, Ed," he asked. "Please."

"Now?" she said, surprised. "I believe your mother wants us *dressed* for dinner." Rarely did Rowland paint her as anything but a nude.

He laughed. "Just as you are."

Edna obliged, making herself comfortable in the yellow leather armchair in which she often modelled for Rowland, and curling her legs up onto the ample seat. She rested her head in a crooked elbow.

"Look at me, Ed." Rowland was already shadowing her form on the canvas with broad, loose strokes and dilute colour.

She raised her eyes and fixed them on his face, smiling gently as she watched the intensity with which he worked, applying paint with such vigour that it occasionally seemed the canvas might buckle.

Clyde settled back on the couch, and Lenin joined him, resting his long, one-eared head on his old friend's chest. Shortly after Milton returned, Mary Brown brought Colin Delaney to the door of Rowland's studio. She announced the detective with a pointed reminder that dinner would be served in an hour.

"I won't be long." Delaney glanced at the servant apologetically.

"Be as long as you like," Rowland grinned as he observed the ease with which his housekeeper made a detective sergeant cower. "Why don't you join us for dinner?"

"Don't mind if I do," Delaney said tentatively.

Mary Brown's sigh was more the kind of exhalation one would expect from a charging bull, but she said nothing, nodding curtly and returning to her duties. To her mind, Rowland's propensity to entertain policemen at the house would only lead to idle speculation as to why the constabulary needed to call on *Woodlands* so regularly. But the young master seemed to have no idea or concern for how things should be done. Mary shook her head. If Mr. Wilfred Sinclair was not relying on her to keep an eye on his brother she would have found a more respectable situation years ago.

"I've just heard unofficially from Canberra," Delaney began.

"So Alcott and his mates were responsible for the murder of Jim Kelly?" Milton handed the detective a glass of gin.

"They've accrued quite a few charges between them." Delaney took a seat as he explained. "It appears they were all members of some group called the Commonwealth Legion... comprised of several old boys of the Fascist Legion, the Riverina Movement, the White Guard and various veterans' leagues. They've been targeting Communists. There have been a number of reported assaults. Jim Kelly's was the first murder." Delaney glanced at Rowland. "Lamb claims Kelly was 'tried and sentenced by the Legion'."

"Sentenced to death?"

Delaney nodded. "Their man, Smith, and the peace officer assigned to the security detail around Parliament House are, as you suspected, one and the same. It appears the Legion had identified Kelly as an operative and, after attempting to undermine him, they executed the poor bloke. When Milt arrived on the scene, Smith had to act quickly."

Rowland changed his brush. "So he handcuffed Milt and went into Parliament House purportedly to telephone for help, but primarily to dispose of the murder weapon in the Lamson tube."

Delaney agreed. "Perhaps he intended to retrieve it before Lyons returned to find it."

"You're lucky they didn't just kill you too," Clyde said to Milton.

"They tried to rectify that omission with a Ford Tudor," the poet replied tersely. "But you're right. I wonder why they didn't."

Delaney shrugged. "Possibly there were other people around by then, or Smith panicked or it just didn't occur to him."

Edna spoke without disturbing her pose. "And the gentlemen in Queanbeyan?"

Rowland recalled the disgruntled husbands of Queanbeyan. "They may well have *wanted* to kill Kelly, but I don't think they were involved."

"Major Jones has looked into Sunshine Studios," Delaney said. "Fellow called Banks confessed to selling photographs of certain clients to a man with a distinct scar on his face."

"Alcott?"

"Possibly. He certainly fits the description."

"He used those photographs to turn Kelly's comrades against him," Milton said disgustedly. It seemed a low trick, but then these were murderers not gentlemen.

"So the Communist badges they pinned on their victims were to identify them as Communist?" Clyde asked.

"They wanted the 'executions' to act as a deterrent to others who might work for the Party, to expose Communists in our midst."

"Did they attack Rowly too?" Edna asked.

"According to Lamb and Smith, Alcott had a special interest in you, Rowly." Delaney patted Lenin who it seemed had become bored of Clyde and was seeking attention elsewhere. "Apparently, the Commonwealth Legion had a spy in this anti-war group that brought out Kisch. They had always intended to stop him landing but when Alcott learned that you were involved, he thought it an opportunity to teach you a lesson too."

"A lesson?"

"You had a very lethal enemy in Alcott, Rowly."

"But now Mr. Alcott is dead, so Rowly has nothing to worry about," Edna said more hopefully than confidently.

Delaney frowned. "We don't know how large the Commonwealth Legion is, Miss Higgins. We might have carved the heart out of it, we might only have severed a limb."

"Every man has enemies, Ed," Rowland said quietly, inspecting the soft image already coming to life on his canvas. "To be honest, I'm quite proud of which men consider me theirs."

Epilogue

KISCH ENGLISH

All shades of Left-wing opinion, from pale pink to the deeper vermilion, were represented at the dinner given to Herr Egon Kisch by the Writers' League in Melbourne. Interest, in the main, was centred on discovering some of the benefits, alleged or actual, to be derived from affiliation with the Writers' International to which, according to Herr Kisch, every literary man of European repute belongs. The only literary men of any importance in Europe, he said, held Left-wing or Socialist views (says the "Age"). There were few, if any, writers of international fame who were not members of the Writers' International. Ludwig Rehn and several German Left-wing authors were in prison. Hans Falada was the only Nazi author of any repute, and even the Nazis looked down on him since they were more interested in military than literary matters. Australian authors were unknown in Europe, or, if they enjoyed any repute, they were estimated as British writers. Herr Kisch displayed a lively sense of humour in his attitude towards the amount of "nursing" he has had from the Commonwealth authorities. He apologised for the occasionally halting phrases of his speech, asking the audience not to discriminate too closely between "Kisch English and King's English." Two of his books, "Secret China" and "No Admittance," are to be translated into English and published by a London house. The latter title, he declared, had nothing to do with Australia.

Newcastle Morning Herald and
Miners' Advocate, 6 March 1935

On 19 December, 1934, the full bench of the High Court of Australia ruled that the dictation test used to exclude Egon Kisch from Australia was invalid because, among other things, the constable who administered the test did not have himself a sufficient knowledge of Gaelic. A second declaration under the Immigration Restriction Act overcame the technical difficulty the court found with the first and Egon Kisch was convicted by the Central Sydney Police Court of being a prohibited immigrant and sentenced to three months with hard labour. This was again appealed to the High Court which released Kisch on bail pending a hearing of the full bench.

During this legal to and fro, Kisch travelled the country addressing rallies and crowds in Queensland, New South Wales and Victoria, spreading his message against Fascism and the excesses of Adolf Hitler and his Nazi Government.

In desperation to rid themselves of the "Raging Reporter" the Commonwealth Government offered to remit Kisch's sentence, abandon legal proceedings, and pay all the Czechoslovak's legal costs if he would leave by 11 March, 1935. Having achieved an audience and notoriety far greater than the Movement Against War and Fascism ever hoped, he agreed.

The Honourable Member for Wentworth failed to arrange a Canberra reception for the international peace delegate, despite repeated requests from his constituents at *Woodlands House*.

The Immigration Restriction Act (which became known as the White Australia Policy) was not dismantled until 1973.

John Thomas Ley returned to England with Mrs. Brook. In 1947 he was sentenced to death for the torture and murder of John McCain Mudie whom he'd believed to be having an affair with Mrs. Brook. The case was widely reported as "The Chalk Pit Murder". Before he could hang, Ley was declared insane and sent to Broadmoor Asylum for the Criminally Insane, where he eventually died.

Jemima Fairweather Roche was granted a divorce from Oswald Roche. Rowland Sinclair was named as co-respondent. After the death of her grandmother, Jemima sold the Fairweather property to Wilfred Sinclair before settling permanently in the United States.

Bertram Middleton never did finish his novel but, with practice, his backhand became quite excellent.

The identity of the "Pyjama Girl" continued to be a mystery, until 1944 when Antonio Agostini, a waiter, identified her as his wife Linda and confessed to her murder. While it is almost certain that Agostini did murder his wife, there are still doubts over whether she was in fact the "Pyjama Girl".

Despite repeated invitations to join the Australian Communist Party, Rowland Sinclair remained, at best or worst, a fellow traveller. Even so, he continued to speak what some called the truth and others considered a dangerous language.

Acknowledgments

A writer rarely acts on her own. There are many parties in the literary conspiracy behind the production of a book. For this, the eighth Rowland Sinclair mystery, the usual suspects line up once again. The fact that this is not their first offence only makes me more grateful.

My husband, Michael, who has aided and abetted me at every stage. My boys, Edmund and Atticus, who are my motive for everything. My old friend, Leith Henry, with whom I consult for more than just the racy bits.

My dad, who is still driving the getaway car. My sister, Devini, who harbours me whenever I'm in the area. My mother, who taught me to read and in doing so started me on this path. My personal aviator, David Tennant, who not only found me a plane but told me how to fly it.

Fellow writer, Dr. Kathryn Fox, who advised me on how and where to stab a man without actually killing him. The incomparable Carmel Shute, who became my informant on Egon Kisch's time in Melbourne.

All my warm, witty and dangerous cohorts at Sisters in Crime.

Steven Mair, who proofs my manuscripts into shape.

Sarah Kynaston and Lesley Bocquet, who listen to me ramble about unfolding plots, help me come up with absurdly elaborate cakes for each launch, and ensure I stop writing occasionally to go out to lunch.

My extraordinary agent and friend, Jo Butler, and the Cameron Creswell Agency, who are accessories before, during and after the fact.

The talented, vibrant, generous team at Oldcastle Books, who have given me the means and opportunity to share my work with readers.

Everybody at the Museum of Australian Democracy at Old Parliament House, where I spent a month as the Eminent Writer in Residence, wandering the halls and chambers interrogating the staff about where in the House one could most efficiently murder a man and dispose of a weapon. There were rather a lot of possibilities... Parliament it seems is an excellent venue for more than just political assassinations.

The ACT Writers' Centre and Arts ACT for their support of the Eminent Writers' Program which not only gave me access to the Museum of Australian Democracy but, for the first time in my writing career, afforded me a month to do little else but write.

The greater community of reviewers, bloggers and readers whose support of my work has allowed me to be a serial offender.

Thank you all for your time, your attention and your enthusiasm.

I am so very grateful.

If you enjoyed

A Dangerous Language

then look out for the next book in the
Rowland Sinclair series, *All The Tears In China*

Sign up to The Crime & Mystery Club's newsletter and get
the eBook of *All The Tears In China* for FREE.

bit.ly/AllTheTearsInChina

1

THE WOMAN'S WORLD
CONDUCTED BY WINIFRED MOORE

———————◆———————

DEAR READERS OF MINE
Though eavesdropping as a habit is not regarded with favour
in the best society, it is an amusing and sometimes instructive
occupation when the matters overheard are of a general and not
a personal nature. Indeed, if one's sense of hearing is acute it
is almost impossible not to collect a few items of other people's
business when going about the city even if they are not sought
deliberately. As the poet might have said: "A little eavesdropping
now and then is relished by the wisest men…"

Courier Mail, 31 May 1934

Rowland Sinclair's Chrysler Airflow was prone to attract
attention, both admiring and aghast in equal measure, and so
the presence of three men loitering curiously by the motorcar was
not particularly unusual. The automobile's revolutionary design
and all-metal body, not to mention its yellow paintwork, made it
distinctive amongst the black Austins and Ford Tudors also parked
in Druitt Lane.

Rowland handed his seven-year-old nephew the key to the
Airflow's door. "Let yourself in, Ernie, while I have a word with
these gentlemen."

Rowland had become accustomed to explaining his automobile

to inquisitive strangers. He was, himself, still enamoured enough with the vehicle not to find the interest tedious. Still, on this occasion, he was in a hurry, and the men in question had placed themselves in the way of the car. They'd probably want him to show them the engine.

Ernest Sinclair ran directly to the driver's side door with the key clutched tightly in his fist while Rowland strode over to the men leaning on the Airflow's bonnet.

"Afternoon, gentlemen."

"Flash car. She yours?"

"She is."

The man who'd asked glanced at his companions. "You Sinclair?"

At the mention of his name, Rowland tensed instinctively. Apparently this reaction was reply enough. They fell upon him, fists leading. In the face of the onslaught, Rowland gave no quarter and responded in kind. The situation was not one with which he was unfamiliar and he knew to keep the three men in front of him—if one was to grab and hold him from behind, the scenario would become grim indeed. His assailants, too, were clearly not novices in the dubious arts of street fighting. They forced him away from the car, raining blow after blow and using their number to bypass his defences. Eventually Rowland went down.

The surface of Druitt Lane was warm and hard against his face. He used it to steady the world, to focus on fighting back. Rowland wanted to shout at Ernest to run, but he was not sure if that would simply alert what might be a band of kidnappers to the boy's location.

He was almost relieved when one of the men—he could not see which—called him a "Commie-loving traitor". This was about him, not Ernest. Whatever their purpose, it was probably not child abduction. The jagged impact of a boot against his ribs drove the breath from his lungs. And then another.

"Oi! What the hell's going on here?"

From the ground, Rowland knew only that it was a voice he'd not heard before. In the moments that followed, he could almost hear the indecision, and then the pounding feet of men in flight.

"Are you all right, mate?" A concerned hand on his shoulder.

Rowland pushed himself gingerly off the road. "Yes, I think so."

"Mongrels! Bloody mongrels! Did they rob yer?"

Rowland shook his head slowly.

The Samaritan—a large man with a strong and steady grip—helped him stand. "They were giving you one hell of a kicking, you sure you're—"

Rowland's head began to clear. "Dammit! Ernie!"

"I beg yer pardon, mate?"

"Ernie, my nephew. He was..." Rowland stepped unsteadily towards the Airflow, panicked now. He couldn't see the boy. "Ernie!"

A tousled head rose hesitantly above the dash, blue eyes wide.

Rowland stopped to breathe. He opened the front passenger door. "Ernie, thank God!"

Ernest was pale and obviously shaken. "I wanted to help, Uncle Rowly, but you told me to stay in the car."

"I'm glad you did, mate." Rowland leaned against the doorframe, still trying to get his breath.

"You're bleeding, Uncle Rowly." Ernest remained in the protection of the Airflow's cabin.

"It's just a scratch, Ernie. I'll be all right."

"Who were those men?"

"To be perfectly honest, I'm not really sure."

"Why were they cross with you?"

To that, Rowland did not respond. He could guess why, but there was no point frightening Ernest. "We should get home to *Woodlands*."

"Are you up to driving that contraption, mate?" The man who'd stopped the attack regarded first the Airflow then Rowland Sinclair with equal scepticism, before drawing back sharply. "Hold your horses there a minute..." He rummaged inside his jacket to extract a newspaper.

Rowland sighed. He really didn't want to get into another fight, but at least there was only one man this time.

The man held the front page beside Rowland's face. "That's you!" he said. "That's you with that fella, Keesch."

Rowland glanced back at Ernest in the car. Egon Kisch was regarded as either a peace advocate, or a dangerous Communist subversive. The three men who'd just tried to pound Rowland into the ground were indisputably of the latter opinion. Still, Rowland had never been a man to deny his friends. "Yes, that's me."

"Well, whaddaya know, from the front page! The wife will never believe it."

Rowland relaxed. He put out his hand and introduced himself, relieved that the gentleman seemed more starstruck than offended by the picture. "I appreciate your assistance, sir."

"Barry Love," he said, shaking Rowland's hand solemnly. "Always pleased to help a gentleman. You'd best be on your way lest those jokers come back. There's some folk pretty worked up over your mate Keesch."

"It would seem so."

Rowland farewelled Love with more thanks and slipped behind the steering wheel, wincing as he settled.

Ernest watched him intently.

"I'm sorry you had to see that, Ernie. But I'm fine, you know."

"You were on the ground."

"Yes, that was a little undignified—but I was about to get up."

"Pater said that half of Sydney wants to kill you."

Rowland smiled faintly. Wilfred hated being called "Pater" but Ernest was rather enthusiastic about learning Latin. "He told you that?"

"He told Dr. Maguire. I was leavesdropping."

"I believe the term is *eavesdropping*, Ernie."

"Even if we were in the garden?"

"Even then."

"Oh."

"And eavesdropping is not generally the done thing, old boy, not if you're a gentleman," Rowland added, keen to distract Ernest from the subject of who might want to kill his uncle.

"You're not going to tell Pater, are you?"

"No, I won't tell your father. But perhaps you should try to do less of it anyway."

"What if they're talking about me?"

"Especially if they're talking about you."

"What if I was there first and they walk in talking afterwards?"

"Well, you should leave or let them know you're there."

"Pater says I shouldn't interrupt."

By the time young Ernest Sinclair had thoroughly defined the parameters of eavesdropping, the Airflow had turned into the long drive of *Woodlands House* and pulled up at perhaps the most grand and stately home in Woollahra, which was not a suburb lacking in magnificent abodes. Ernest jumped from the car to greet the misshapen, one-eared greyhound that leapt down the entrance stairs to greet them.

"Sit, Lenin, sit, sit, sit!" Ernest shouted. The greyhound licked his face but otherwise ignored him.

Rowland climbed out of the motorcar and called his dog to heel. He was only slightly more successful than his nephew. The emergence of two men from the house did little to abate the hound's excitement.

Milton Isaacs threw open his arms and declared, "I am sir Oracle, and when I ope my lips, let no dog bark."

Lenin barked.

"Clearly Len has no respect for Shakespeare." Rowland reflexively attributed the words. A self-proclaimed poet, Milton seemed to consider that repurposing the verse of the great bards with passion was creative effort enough. To Rowland's knowledge, his friend had only ever composed one original line—more akin to a nursery rhyme than verse—though that was not something that bothered any of them unduly.

"Lay down, Len!" Clyde Watson Jones' attempt to silence the hound was more effective if less elegant. Raised in the country, Clyde was as direct and practical as Milton was theatrical. Years on the wallaby track, scavenging for work and survival, had infused a necessary pragmatism into his otherwise romantic soul. Lenin settled beside Rowland's feet, eyeing them all resentfully.

Clyde turned to Rowland, his arms folded across his chest. "What's happened? You look like you've gone a couple of rounds."

Rowland glanced uneasily at his nephew who was, as usual, listening intently. "Ernie, why don't you be a good chap and take Len into the kitchen? I'm certain Mary was saving a ham bone for him."

"Yeah, go on, mate," Clyde added. "She's been baking those little jam cakes."

Any reluctance to leave thus overcome by jam cakes, Ernest set off into the house with Lenin in tow.

"So?" Milton asked as they watched boy and dog disappear.

"Three chaps grabbed me as I was getting into the car. They must have been waiting."

"Ernie?"

"He was already in the car. I don't think they realised he was there."

"So they just gave you a kicking?"

"Yes," Rowland admitted ruefully.

"Do I need to ask why?"

"The gentlemen objected to my association with Egon Kisch, I believe."

"God, if Egon knew—"

"There would be nothing he could do, so telling him would be pointless," Rowland said firmly.

"You're going to have one hell of a shiner," Milton observed.

"I suppose I should clean myself up. I promised Ernie we'd—"

"Hello!" Milton interrupted as a racing-green Rolls-Royce Continental came through the gates and negotiated the sweeping drive. "Isn't that your brother's motor?"

© Edmund Blenkins

A reformed lawyer, Sulari Gentill is the author of the *Rowland Sinclair Mysteries*, ten historical crime novels (thus far) chronicling the life and adventures of her 1930s Australian gentleman artist; the *Hero Trilogy*, based on the myths and epics of the ancient world; and a standalone mystery called *After She Wrote Him*, for which she won the 2018 Ned Kelly Award. She lives with her husband, Michael, and their boys, Edmund and Atticus, on a small farm in the foothills of the Snowy Mountains in Australia, where she grows French Black Truffles and writes.

Sulari has been shortlisted for the Commonwealth Writers' Prize – Best First Book, won the 2012 Davitt Award for Crime Fiction, been shortlisted for the 2013 and 2015 Davitt Award, the 2015 Ned Kelly Award, the 2015 and 2016 Australian Book Industry Award for Best Adult Book, the NSW Genre Fiction Award, commended in the FAW Jim Hamilton Award and offered a Varuna Fellowship. She was the inaugural Eminent Writer in Residence at the Museum of Australian Democracy, and toured the US in 2019 as an ambassador of Australian Crime Fiction. *The Woman In The Library*, her latest novel, will be released in June 2022.